RACE
AGAINST
TIME

RACE
AGAINST
TIME

GILLIAN RISKO

atmosphere press

"If you put your mind to it, you can accomplish anything."

– George McFly

CHAPTER 1

Toy

With a sense of relief, Toy closed her notebook, signaling the end of a long day of studying. She knew she had done everything to ensure she got a good grade on the ACT so she could get a scholarship and go to college.

Toy gazed at the pink notebook. Memories flooded her mind. The countless hours she had spent poring over its pages. The words "Toy Fawn" written in cursive in the corner almost faded away. She traced a finger along the cover, feeling the indentations and grooves. While her peers were enjoying their winter break, she dedicated herself to relentless studying. With a sigh, she placed her notebook inside her pink backpack.

The sound of voices to her left brought Toy out of her thoughts. She turned and saw Julia and Brodie talking. Toy wasn't particularly close to Brodie or Julia. They were more Goldie's friends, but they often hung out together at school.

"Yeah, I plan on attending college in California when I graduate."

"No shit? Me too."

Toy left the library and ran to the bus stop to wait. It took no longer than five minutes for the next KAT to pull up. The shiny white bus with its many advertisements caught onlookers' eyes, the door plastered with the two most known brands around, the bottom one being Prismatic, a hair dye for the people who were born with non-colored hair, and the other a restaurant, Twirllee's, a mom-and-pop restaurant with games and jungle gyms for kids—and let's not forget the food; it's to die for.

Toy stepped onto the bus as soon as the door swung open. Immediately, the warm scent of the vehicle enveloped her senses. A combination of body odor and exhaust.

"Where you going?" the driver asked.

Toy gave him her home address. With a smile, he closed the door, and she settled into a seat behind him. The ride home was about ten minutes. Toy gazed out of the window, watching the passing buildings and trees.

Toy's mind wandered back to the hair dye ad as the bus drove down the street. How different would the world be if human DNA didn't mutate? What, 640 years ago? It was 2010 and genealogists still didn't know why this happened or why it caused vibrant hair and eye colors. Who knows what else that change did? What would the world look like if it didn't happen? Like in an alternate universe where Obama wouldn't have his signature azure hair. In that world, would his hair be black or brown? Or perhaps he might even be blond! Would there even be a United States of America? Would it still exist like it does today? If Toy's hair wasn't this vibrant shade of yellow—or canary, like it said on her ID—what color would it be? Would it be a classic blonde or something else?

With a gentle tap of the KAT driver's hand on Toy's knee, she emerged from her thoughts. "Here's your stop, ma'am," the driver said.

Toy paid the driver and stepped off the bus. Today was the first day of the year 2010. The festive Christmas decorations were still everywhere on the house. Because of Toy's mother's cancer, she couldn't take down the decorations herself.

She had been telling Toy to take care of it, but she had been putting it off. These decorations were the sole source of color within the home besides their hair.

Toy unlocked the door and walked in, met with the sight of her mother making her way through the living room with a suitcase.

"Hey, Mom," Toy greeted as she entered the kitchen, a short distance away from where Emma stood. She settled onto the cushion of the spinning stool.

Emma, Toy's mother, sat on this stool for hours. As soon as the need for another cushion arose, she went out and bought one. It was a dingy gray, like most items in the house. All the walls were a cream color except for Toy's bedroom. The landlord had painted the whole room except the brick wall an ugly olive green, which very much darkened the entire room, much as she had tried to decorate with pink and white.

The living room had the same color scheme, with all the furniture in various shades of gray. The kitchen followed suit with a gray or black palette, from the cupboards to the kitchen appliances, yet a touch of warmth shone through the oak chairs and stool, which stood out.

"I'm off to Columbus," Emma explained as she set her suitcase by the door, not even stopping her flow to say hello to her daughter.

"Again?" Toy whined.

"Toy Aria Fawn, you are seventeen years old. You can handle me leaving the house for two weeks. Now, I expect you to text me at least once daily since I will be stuck in the hospital."

Toy's mother, physically, was clearly an older version of Toy, yet their views on life were completely different. Emma was a workaholic; she believed in approaching every task with the utmost dedication, while Toy was a more carefree and spontaneous person.

"I will."

"You better, or I'm taking your phone when I come back.

And I don't want you going over to that boy's house while I'm gone," Emma said as Toy opened the fridge.

"Mom, I've told you before that I don't like being home alone."

The fridge was almost empty, and the cupboards were too. It had been weeks since they last went grocery shopping.

"Mama always says that if I ever need to, I can stay over at their place. They have plenty of food to eat, Mom, actual meals."

"I told you not to call his mother that; if you need to address her, it's Mrs. Sallow, it's more mature."

"Sorry..."

As Emma went outside, Toy trailed behind her, unnoticed. Emma paid little attention to Toy as she got inside her rusty car and drove off. Toy waited ten minutes before going to her room to pack her suitcase for the next two weeks. On her way out, she remembered to grab her backpack since school started again Monday. She walked down the street. Bonnie's house was three streets down on Willow Road, which was close to both the school and Twirllee's. When Toy made it to Bonnie's house, she saw the Christmas decorations were down and the sidewalk cleared of snow.

Toy knocked before she went in. She felt the stark contrast between the warm air of the living room and the cold winter air outside. It took a moment for her nose to adjust to the dry, cozy atmosphere, and breathing almost felt painful at first.

"Mama?" Toy called out as she took off her shoes and coat. "Mom's out of town. Can I stay here for a couple of weeks?"

Bonnie's mother, Mia, emerged from the chaotic kitchen. The style of the house was a stark contrast to Emma's taste. Not only that, but Mia's personality was also completely different from Emma's. Her viridescent hair shone brightly, glasses perched on the edge of her caramel-colored nose, and she wore her work shirt for Twirllee's.

"Hola, Toy!" she started, giving Toy a tight hug before she

put on her coat and grabbed her keys. "*Por supuesto, cariño,* you can stay over! Is your mother in the hospital again?"

"Yeah, for two weeks."

"Well, Bonnie is in his room working on something, Goldie's *estudiando* in his, and Drake is at work. *Tengo que irme.* They need *ayuda* work, but Bonnie will help you *acomodarat* in."

"Thanks, Mama!"

"*Por supuesto,* now there is some *enmoladas sobrantes* in the fridge if you kids get *hambrienta.* I'll be home at midnight."

"Okay! Bye, Mama!"

"*Adiós cariño.*"

Mia bid Toy farewell with a gentle wave as Toy made her way to Bonnie's room. The door emitted a faint creak as it opened.

It was a simple bedroom. Cream paint and posters covered the walls. The furniture was crafted from a reddish wood. Between his bed and the one Toy "slept" in during her visits was a blue and white rug. Dressers sat at the foot of each bed and a desk on the other side of the room by the closet.

"Bonnie, I'm home," Toy joked.

Since 2008, Bonnie had been Toy's boyfriend. At nineteen, Bonnie knew he wanted a career in music, while Toy had set her sights on becoming a preschool teacher after graduating. They had always been each other's biggest supporters, encouraging and motivating one another. Looking toward the future, they even had plans to move into a house together once Toy graduated.

Toy dropped her suitcase and backpack by her dresser before she reached for the hair tie on her wrist and secured her hair back into a neat ponytail.

Bonnie was on his bed, sipping a cup of coffee. It struck Toy as odd since it was already five in the evening. He placed the cup on the bedside table before he returned his attention to whatever task he was doing. His broad caramel-colored shoulders obstructed Toy's view. His complexion was lighter than Mia's, while his vibrant amethyst hair was from his father. His captivating magenta eyes were the same as his mother's.

"Hey Bonnie...Bonnie Sallow," Toy called out, noticing how he brushed his hair aside with his hand. His headphones were on, connected to his black MP3, which was playing the song "Slave & Master" by The Banana Band. As the song ended, "Circus of Psychos." by The Banana Band started playing. It was no surprise; The Banana Band was his all-time favorite rock band. Startled, he jumped a little when Toy placed her pale hand on his shoulder.

"Oh! Sorry, *niña*, I didn't see you there," he exclaimed as he smiled at her and took off his headphones. "How are you tonight?"

"I'm all right, but I'm not sure you can say the same. You look like you haven't slept in days; you should go to bed, baby," Toy answered as her hands worked at the knots in his shoulders.

"Should that insult me?" he asked as he shifted his body toward Toy, and she seized the chance to settle herself on his lap.

"No, I love that face, but you look exhausted. Is something bothering you?"

"No, no, nothing's bothering me. I've been working on something with my guitar, that's all," he told Toy as he motioned to his father's red electric guitar.

"Oh, do you have something big coming up?" Toy asked as she played with his fluffy hair; it smelled of his New Spice shampoo.

"Yeah, I'm trying something different."

"Really? I hope it works out."

Toy shifted away from him, giving him the space to work. She grabbed the book she had been reading from her backpack. They sat side by side—simply being in each other's presence was enough.

CHAPTER 2

Toy

The sound of Bonnie's ringtone pierced the air. It was the iconic song "Created for Lovin' You" by The Banana Band. Toy tapped Bonnie's shoulder, and he removed his headphones. Their eyes met, and Toy responded with a sweet smile before she buried her face in the pages of her book. Bonnie let out a sigh, placed his guitar on the bed, and reached for his phone. As he picked it up, Toy glimpsed the contact photo, spying fiery cardinal hair that seemed all too familiar.

"Hey, man," they heard Forrest grumble once Bonnie answered. "Is Toy there? I need to talk to her."

Toy couldn't help but wonder what Forrest wanted. She didn't like him. She only knew him because he was dating one of her closest friends, Mable.

"Hey, Forrest... What's up?" Toy asked.

"Have you seen Mable? We were supposed to hang out two hours ago, and she won't reply to my texts."

"I haven't seen her, but I can message her," Toy said as she put her book down and grabbed her phone from her pocket.

"That would be great," Forrest grumbled before hanging up.

Bonnie threw the phone aside and moved his guitar back to his lap.

"Did you know Julia and Brodie are going to California when they graduate?" Toy started.

"Nope, but that's pretty cool. That will be like stepping onto a different planet after growing up in Ohio." He plucked a cord before tuning it.

"Yeah, but it's going to be so weird not having them around. Or when fall comes, and I have to go to college and not the Career Center. Part of me wants everything to stay the same."

Bonnie let out a sigh and shifted his gaze toward Toy. She felt his hand gently rest on her thigh.

"Our high school friends aren't always going to be around, but that's life, Toy. They all have their own lives they must go through." Bonnie spoke with a sort of mocking tone. "No one can change fate."

Toy found his typical sense of humor enjoyable, but she couldn't help but feel uneasy about what he had said. With enough effort, anything could change, since nothing in life was permanent.

The pair sat in silence for a moment until Bonnie finally broke the silence by saying, "*Te amo.*" Spanish for *I love you.*

"I love you too."

He gave her a quick peck on the lips before he turned back to his work.

Toy's stomach growled as she looked toward the door. "Hey, I'm getting pretty hungry; wanna get something to eat?" she asked Bonnie.

"Twirllee's?"

"You read my mind. I'm gonna ask Goldie if he wants to come with us."

"All right, I'll be in the living room waiting."

With a burst of energy, Toy left the room and made her way to Goldie and Drake's room. She knocked on the door before she called out, "Hey, Goldie, it's Toy!"

"What's up?"

Goldie and Drake's room was the same as Bonnie's. It had only a few distinguishing features, such as posters on the walls and gray sheets. Goldie sat at the desk. His canary bangs covered one of his brown eyes. He had already changed into his sleepwear, a white T-shirt and flannel sweatpants.

"What are you working on?" Toy asked him, and he looked up, the freckles on his pale face on display.

Goldie was not related to Bonnie and his family. Drake had found Goldie outside of Twirllee's in 2006 and they became friends. It turned out that Goldie and his brother had run away. Bonnie had been hesitant about the idea of Goldie and his brother Owen moving in, but he grew fond of them. Mama always expressed her joy at seeing the house filled with love and laughter.

Bonnie and Drake used to share a room, while Owen and Goldie shared another. Things changed when Bonnie and Toy first met. Around that time, Owen disappeared and Goldie was uncomfortable sleeping alone in their shared room, so Drake switched rooms, leaving an extra bed in Bonnie's room.

"Studying for my college classes," Goldie said to Toy. "Why? What's up?"

His dream was to be a doctor, a dream he'd had for as long as he could remember. At eighteen, he was already the top student in his class.

"Bonnie and I were heading to Twirllee's for dinner and were wondering if you wanted to come with us."

"Nah, I'll be fine; I'll eat the leftover *enmoladas* from last night."

"Are you sure?"

"Yeah, you guys go without me. Have a good time."

"We'll be home later."

"See ya."

After Toy closed the door behind her, she walked down the hall. True to his word, Bonnie waited for her in the living room.

"Goldie coming?" Bonnie asked as Toy put her shoes on.

"No, he says he's gonna eat leftovers."

Before Bonnie opened the door, Toy put on her coat and grabbed Bonnie's hand. As they strolled down the road toward Twirllee's, Toy squeezed his hand and looked up at him.

"I love you." She smiled.

He smiled back before he leaned closer and planted a tender kiss on her lips. "*Yo también te quiero.*"

They made it to Twirllee's indigo and salmon-colored sign with the fox in the chef getup looking down at them.

What did a fox have to do with Italian food, anyway?

Bonnie kindly opened the door, and they walked inside. The smell of freshly cooked food and the sounds of children playing in the playroom filled the air. It made Toy's stomach growl in anticipation.

"Hey, Toy," Joanna started. As her voice reached their ears, they instinctively shifted their gaze toward her. Her eyes, a mesmerizing shade of blue, crinkled as she greeted Toy and Bonnie with a warm smile. "I wasn't expecting to see you today."

"Yeah, we're hungry, and Twirllee's sounded good."

"Well, lucky for you, we have an empty table for two."

"Sweet," Bonnie said as Jo grabbed two menus.

Jo led them to their usual booth in the other room, and as soon as they sat down, she took their drink order. Bonnie opted for a refreshing pop, while Toy chose a glass of water. Jo walked off to retrieve their drinks, giving them some time to look over the menu and decide on dinner.

Bonnie settled on an SM Twirllee's Stromboli with pepperoni, sausage, black olives, and mild peppers. Toy decided on an XSM pizza with black olives and a biscuit on the side. The biscuits were Toy's favorite. Ten minutes later, Jo returned to Toy and Bonnie's table to take their order, and before long, their food arrived.

As Jo wiped her hands on her apron, Toy reached for the

first piece of her pizza. It was amazing, like always.

"How's the money for law school going, Jo?" Toy asked.

"Good!"

"Hey Jo, where's Mama and Drake at?" Bonnie asked.

"Your mother is working in a different section and your brother is on sides today."

"Ah, who's managing today?"

"Dean. You wanna say hi?"

"Nah, I'll see everyone tomorrow when I come in for my shift."

Jo left and the pair ate their food in silence. Toy wondered what to do when they got home. She could study more but she felt like that's all she did anymore. She could spend some quality time with Bonnie by playing a game or watching a movie together. That sounded nice.

Laughter caught Toy's attention. She turned her head and noticed Fredrick and Brendan, two boys from their school, enjoying their meal at a booth across the room. Sensing someone's gaze, they looked over. Brendan appeared frightened while Fredrick flashed Toy and Bonnie a warm smile. Fredrick then pulled Brendan to his feet and dragged him over.

"Hey, man," Bonnie chirped as they stopped before them.

"Hey, guys!" Fredrick exclaimed.

Fredrick was one of Toy's close friends, the only black kid her age around town. Back when Toy was living in Pittsburgh, most of her friends were black. Fredrick and his family were amazing, even after what happened. Toy had met Brendan through Drake. He had curly hair like Fredrick, although not as tightly coiled.

Brendan had dual-colored hair. Most people with dual-colored hair had a primary color and streaks of a second color, but Brendan's hair was a fascinating blend of two distinct colors. It wasn't like Mable's hair, which was white with streaks of fuchsia, but rather started azure at the top and melted into a warm brown shade toward the bottom. Many people judged it like they did non-colored hair. It made Brendan feel self-conscious.

Bonnie and Fredrick engaged in conversation. Brendan's face, adorned with pale freckles, remained flushed. His green eyes shifted back and forth between the blue of Fredrick's eyes and the magenta of Bonnie's. Joanna walked over, her laughter filling the air as she took in the sight of their animated discussion.

"If you want, you can all sit in the same booth; both tables are in my section."

As they shared a collective smile, Toy and Bonnie's eyes met before Fredrick dashed back to his table. With Jo's help, he came back with both his and Brendan's meals and drinks. Fredrick settled down next to Bonnie, engaging in an ongoing conversation. Brendan joined Toy on her side and went back to his burger.

"Hey, Toy, can you help me with something real quick?" Brendan asked.

Toy finished chewing the food in her mouth and shifted her attention to him. "Yeah, what's up?"

"I need help with a floral arrangement. Fredrick says what I have planned won't work."

"Is this for your lab at school?"

"Yeah."

"Do you have photos?"

He took out his phone; his wallpaper was a photo of him and Fredrick at Christmas. It made Toy smile while she waited for him to find the photo of his arrangement idea. When he pulled it up, Toy gasped—it was a delightful composition of vibrant spring flowers. Toy loved the daffodils in it, as they held a special place in her heart. Those flowers had been a frequent gift from her father to both her and her mother. A cherished reminder of his love before he left.

"Fredrick doesn't know what he is talking about; that's beautiful."

"See, Fredrick!" Brendan exclaimed. "I told you it would work."

"Sorry, there is a reason I want to be a gym teacher and not a florist like you."

After they all shared a hearty laugh, they continued to eat their meals and soon finished. When it came time to settle the bill, Toy insisted on paying for her food, but Bonnie adamantly refused to let her do so. With their meals paid for, they all left the restaurant together, still in high spirits and exchanging jokes. Before parting ways with Jo, they left her a twenty-dollar tip.

The group walked home; the boys followed Bonnie and Toy since Fredrick's house was on the same street as Bonnie's. They reached Fredrick's place, and Toy's phone went off, interrupting their goodbyes. While the boys continued their conversation, Toy took out her phone to see that it was Mable calling.

"Hello!" she chirped. The sounds of shouting and objects being thrown were all she could hear, the noise so deafening that even the boys heard it, completely taken aback by the commotion.

"Who is it?" Bonnie asked.

"It's Mable, but she's not talking."

"Mable?" Brendan said into the phone as the rest of them listened.

"Can't you tell me where you're going for once in your damn life?!" Forrest yelled as he slammed something in the background, making everyone jump. "Oh wait, you couldn't, because you were out being a slut."

Forrest's words left everyone in shock. They exchanged glances with one another. While they had heard Mable speak about her and Forrest's frequent arguments, this was the first time they heard one for themselves.

"You're not my dad; I don't have to tell you what I'm doing every five minutes!" Mable yelled back. "And for your information, I was out with my family!"

The sound of her voice gave it away. She was on the verge of crying. Toy could picture tears welling up in her bright primrose eyes, her fair complexion turning red and blotchy. They heard a door slam shut, and the phone fell silent except for the soft whimpers that escaped Mable.

"Mable?"

"Yeah, I'm here, Toy. I'm here," Mable answered, her voice shaking.

"Are you okay? Where are you?"

"I'll be fine; I know how to handle him, Toy. I'm on my way back home. I'll text you when I get home."

"Okay, I love you."

"I love you too."

As soon as Toy finished speaking, Mable ended the call, leaving her stunned. The group exchanged concerned glances, unsure what to do now.

"That was kinda a buzzkill..." Fredrick mumbled as he shuffled closer to Brendan, trying to stay warm.

"Fred!" Brendan exclaimed.

"What, Bon? It's the truth."

"Do you think Mabel's okay?" Toy said, interrupting their bickering.

She glanced at Bonnie; he extended his hand toward her. The question remained unanswered still by the time they arrived at the house around 8:45. They walked in to find Drake and Goldie playing a game of *Stranded Dead* in the living room. As soon as they noticed Toy and Bonnie, they made room for them on the couch. The boys switched to the game circle, which allowed for everyone to play.

"No, Green bean, stop!" Goldie exclaimed as he watched Drake mess with the memory card.

Toy found it adorable how he referred to his best friend by that nickname. On the day they first met, Goldie had been talking to Cherry. He couldn't recall Drake's name, even though it was on the tip of his tongue. To remember, he pointed to his head and said, "Green bean." Drake found out and began calling Goldie "Sunshine" in return because of his canary hair.

"If the memory card isn't working, you must blow it!" Goldie snatched the card from Drake's hand. The room fell into an eerie silence as Goldie brought the card to his lips and blew into it. He froze and turned his gaze toward Drake, who wore a smirk on his face.

Goldie gave Drake a forceful shove after he uttered the word "Harder." The unexpected action caused everyone around them to burst into laughter. Drake threw his head back in laughter, revealing his resemblance to his mother. He had the same viridescent hair and captivating magenta eyes. His skin tone was paler, like Bonnie's.

After getting everything up and running, they gathered around to play some *Peter Party*. The excitement reached new heights as they earned moons and played mini-games. Their gaming marathon continued until Mia returned home around 12:30. As soon as she laid eyes on the group, she promptly told them to get ready for bed, reminding them they had school starting back up Monday. It didn't matter that Bonnie didn't have school or that they were all in their late teens. Mia declared that staying up until two in the morning wasn't an option. Honestly, Toy couldn't complain; she was exhausted.

As they all settled into their individual beds, Mia inspected each room to ensure they had indeed retired for the night and weren't studying or wasting time on their phones. Once she completed her rounds and Toy heard the faint sound of the door closing, she slipped out of her bed and into Bonnie's. He emitted a peaceful sigh as he embraced her. Soon enough, he was asleep, but there was one thing that prevented Toy from following suit.

Mable never texted her back...

CHAPTER 3

Toy

Mia banged on the door, jolting Bonnie and Toy awake. With a sense of urgency, she shouted, "Breakfast, *monos*, let's go!"

As Toy regained her senses, her first instinct was to reach for her phone, hoping for a message from Mable. Meanwhile, Bonnie rolled onto his back and stretched, taking his time to wake up.

No texts...

Toy sat up on the edge of the bed, throwing on her socks. Bonnie shuffled over to her side, wrapping his arms around her waist and kissing her neck.

"Bonnie..." Toy sighed, leaning into his touch. "We have to get up; Mama will come banging on the door again if we're late."

"I know... I know..."

With a swift motion, he got out of bed and slipped on his slippers. They both left the room, Bonnie turning to go to the bathroom while Toy went to the dining room. The scent of breakfast wafted through the air.

"Ah, *¡buenos días, cariño!*"

"Morning..."

"*¿Bonnie se ha levantado?*"

Toy stopped for a second, only understanding "Bonnie."

"Bonnie's in the bathroom," she said, and Mia nodded.

"Sit! Sit!"

Toy sat beside Mama and glanced around the table. Her eyes landed on the variety of food before them. Her gaze skated over the milk and orange juice pitchers, but the breakfast puzzled her. Among the dishes were sunny-side-up eggs accompanied by what appeared to be salsa.

"It looks good, Mama," she told Mia, making her smile. "What's it called?"

"Huevos Rancheros," Bonnie answered as he walked into the colorful dining room and sat beside Toy with a kiss.

"*Buenos días, Bonnie, ¿sabes si los otros dos están despiertos?*" Mia asked.

Toy just stared at Bonnie, clueless.

"*Sé que Goldie lo es, estaba esperando un turno en el baño cuando salí, Drake no lo he visto,*" Bonnie said to Mia before he turned to Toy. "She's asking about Drake and Goldie."

"Ah...what's this 'Huevos Rancheros' again?"

"*¡Monos!*" Mia yelled, interrupting right when Bonnie was about to answer Toy.

"Huevos Rancheros is a traditional Mexican breakfast dish with egg, salsa, and tortillas," Bonnie whispered into Toy's ear.

The sound of doors opening and footsteps echoed through the hallway. Moments later, Goldie and Drake walked in and made their way to their seats.

One chair left empty at the other end of the table was where Owen used to sit.

"*Buenos días, Mamá,*" the boys said in unison.

"*Buenos días, monos.*"

Before they ate, they said prayer, a tradition everyone followed but Goldie—he didn't believe in God—then everyone served themselves. They filled their plates with delicious food and poured drinks into their cups.

As they ate, Toy couldn't help but glance up at the clock

and notice it was already 9:28.

"*Muy bien, monos.* Drake and I are leaving for work at ten," Mia started as she wiped her mouth.

"When will you be home?" Goldie asked as Drake passed him the orange juice. It had no pulp, like they all liked it.

"I won't be home until eleven *esta noche*, but Drake should be here around four."

"Yeah, if Dakota doesn't hold me hostage..."

"Dakota doesn't hold you hostage; they can keep you later if they need you to stay later. You're not scheduled to get off at four. That's just the time you normally get off," Bonnie explained.

"I know..."

"Bonnie, are you working today too?" Toy asked him after she swallowed the food in her mouth.

"Yeah, at four until whenever they let me leave."

"Goldie?"

"Nope," Goldie mumbled through the food in his mouth.

"So it's just gonna be Goldie and I for a few?"

"Yes."

"I would appreciate it if you guys help with the laundry tonight," Mia interrupted.

"We will."

They kept eating until Mia looked up at the clock to see that it was 9:40.

"Drake and I have to get going. Be good today."

"We will."

"Mama! Mama!" Bonnie interrupted, stopping Mama from clearing off the table as Drake ran into the other room. "We can clean up from breakfast; it's fine."

"All right then, Drake, let's go!"

"Coming, Mama!"

Drake rushed out of his room, ready for the day, with his backpack in his hand. He put on his blue zip-up hoodie over his white T-shirt to combat the chilly weather. Without wasting a moment, he and Mia slipped on their shoes and grabbed their coats. The two left, leaving three teenagers inside to enjoy a few hours of solitude.

The boys cleared the table while Toy took a quick moment to send a "Good morning" text to both Emma and Mable. She only got a reply from Emma. While Toy was on her phone, Bonnie and Goldie had already put away the leftovers. With that and the dishes done, they went to work to clean up the bedrooms.

Bonnie and Toy worked together to gather the clothes that were on the floor and tossed them into the hall. Goldie waited in the hall to catch the clothes and put them in the laundry chute in the bathroom.

The last stop was Toy and Bonnie's room. Toy continued to throw clothes out of the room when Bonnie grabbed her, pulling her close. In a surprising move, he shut the door and locked it.

"Guys?!" Goldie's voice interrupted the moment as he called out to them.

Before Toy could respond, Bonnie kissed her neck, causing her to laugh.

Goldie's annoyance was clear in his tone as he exclaimed, "Seriously, guys?!"

"Yeah, man!" Bonnie laughed.

"Ugh. I guess I'll start the first load."

"Yeah, you do that."

With a swift movement, Bonnie spun Toy, causing her back to collide with the door.

"Poor Goldie, that was mean." Toy giggled.

"He'll get over it." With a burst of laughter, Bonnie tugged her closer and passionately kissed her. "We have a Mama-free home; we might as well make the most of it.

After spending some time in the bedroom, Toy settled on the couch and watched *Silver's Anatomy*. They both enjoyed the show, and since Toy was a few episodes behind, it was the perfect opportunity to catch up. Bonnie made his way up the basement stairs. Hearing him coming, Goldie turned up the volume to drown him out. Bonnie entered the room with a basket of clothes and placed it on the end table to sort through them.

"This episode is amazing!" Toy exclaimed.

Goldie's lips curled into a smirk. "Oh, wait until you discover the true identity of the mysterious Jane Doe," he said, his gaze fixed on Toy.

Toy's eyes widened. "Hey!" she yelled. "Don't spoil it!"

"Sorry! Sorry!" Goldie blurted out.

With a swift motion, Toy hurled a soft pillow toward his head. He lost his balance and tumbled off the couch, but instead of getting upset, he laughed. After a moment, he regained his composure and stood up, ready to continue.

"Pillow war?" he asked with a grin.

Clutching the pillow, Toy nodded with unwavering determination. Little did she know what awaited her. Goldie's battle cry pierced the air as he charged toward Toy. Bonnie watched as Goldie snatched one of the folded towels and lunged at Toy.

"Hey! My towel!" Bonnie yelled.

Toy raised the pillow to shield herself. Goldie seemed to know all the spots to hit. Before Toy knew it, she flipped onto her back, both hands raised in surrender.

"I'm sorry for challenging you!" Toy shouted.

Goldie dropped the towel, and with a sigh, Bonnie stooped down and picked it up.

"How did you learn such skills?"

Goldie grinned. "I grew up with Owen. He's a monster when it comes to pillow fights." He sat back down on the couch and pulled out his phone.

"Whatcha doin'?" Toy asked him as she looked over his shoulder.

"Texting Mama," Goldie answered with a sigh. "She wants us to go grocery shopping. Who wants to come with me?"

"Me!" Toy yelled as she jumped off the couch and bumped into Bonnie. "Oops, sorry, Bonnie."

"No worries, *niña*," he told her. He leaned in and gently pressed his lips against her forehead, leaving a tender kiss, then walked away and grabbed his keys from the bowl nearby. "You guys ready?"

With sudden energy, Toy dashed out of the house, exclaiming, "Shotgun!" at the top of her lungs.

Bonnie couldn't help but chuckle as Goldie shuffled toward the back seat.

"Again…" he groaned.

After they climbed into the car, they pulled out and drove to the store. It took about thirteen minutes to reach the store and find a parking spot. They couldn't park right by the entrance, but they found a pretty close spot. Everyone piled out and walked toward the entrance.

"Mama sent me the list," Bonnie said. "So let's grab the stuff and go."

Goldie grabbed a shopping cart and ran before jumping on it. The cart glided into the bustling shopping area.

"Hey!" Bonnie cried. "Don't hog the cart; I wanna ride too!" He ran after Goldie as Toy laughed.

"Boys," Toy said with a laugh. She ran after the boys, earning glances from nearby adults.

Once Toy caught up with the boys, they tossed various things into the cart. Toy worked on the fruits and vegetables before she helped the boys find the odds and ends.

"Gross!" Toy gagged as she tossed a tin of sardines in the cart.

She looked over the list, then at the cart. Sardines, avocados, apples, jalapenos, plum tomatoes, tomatillos, onion, garlic, cilantro, spinach, limes, cucumber, rice, blueberries, raspberries, strawberries, milk, chicken breast, both flour and corn tortillas, habanero peppers, and eggs.

Goldie's eyes widened. "Shit, I need Honey Nut Cheerios!"

he exclaimed before he ran a few aisles down.

Bonnie and Toy laughed.

"Is this all we need?" she asked, as they waited for Goldie.

Bonnie gave a slight nod. Toy's eyes shifted upward to the shelf above Bonnie. There it was—a bottle of sriracha sauce, its vibrant red color catching her attention.

"Don't we need more of that?" Toy asked. "I'm pretty sure I finished it this morning."

He turned around, saw the bottle, and groaned. "Oh yeah!"

Toy jumped, trying to reach the bottle. "Boost me up."

"I can get it."

"No, I want to!"

Bonnie laughed and grabbed her around the waist. "You ready?" he asked.

"Yeah!"

As Toy's feet lifted off the ground, she looked at Bonnie in awe. She still, after all these years, couldn't believe how easily he could lift her up. She grabbed the bottle and motioned for Bonnie to put her down. He ignored her and continued to hold her around the waist.

"Hey!" Toy yelled at Bonnie. "Let me down, baby!"

"No." He sounded like a little kid. "You're huggable."

Toy laughed. "I'll hug you if you let me down!"

Bonnie carefully lowered her to the ground. With a laugh, Toy embraced him and rested her head on his chest. The rhythmic thumping of his heart and the soft sound of his breath filled her ears. A smile spread across her face, knowing deep down that this was her place and nothing could change that.

CHAPTER 4

Toy

The clock was nearing five, signaling the end of the day. After they returned from the store, they sat in front of the TV, occasionally getting up to attend to the laundry. Bonnie left for work at four, and Drake was still not home.

Goldie and Toy were engrossed in a game of *Roddle* on the Ybox 280, taking turns whenever one of them lost or won. It had been Goldie's turn for the past ten minutes, but he kept pausing the game to check his phone.

"Goldie!" Toy grumbled as he looked down at his phone again, his canary bangs covering one of his brown eyes. "Stop texting your boyfriend and play your turn!"

His head shot up, his freckled face red. "Don't call him that; Drake is not my boyfriend."

"Uh huh…"

"He's having a rough day at work; one of his coworkers is being a big asshole today."

"Let me guess…the one he calls 'shrimp'?"

"That's the one."

Soon the controller passed between them again, but again, it got stuck on Goldie's turn. Toy sighed as she checked her phone. Bonnie texted her about "shrimp." She ignored the message and relaxed on the couch.

"I should go check on the load in the dryer," Goldie started, breaking the silence.

"Here, I'll help."

With a nod, Goldie rolled his shoulders before they walked toward the basement. Toy opened the door, and they walked down the stairs. Toy couldn't help but think of the message Bonnie had sent. She wondered if things were getting better for both him and Drake at work.

Goldie headed to the dryer, emptying the clothes into the basket. He grabbed a single towel and sniffed it for good measure. Together, they walked over to the folding table. On the floor was a pile of clean blankets.

"Great, who did that?" Goldie groaned as he pushed his bangs out of his face again. "Some of these are Drake's. Give me a second, and I'll sort them."

"Why did you clean Drake's sheets?"

"He asked me since he's working today."

Toy watched as Goldie reached for the top blanket when a sound drifted through the air. A groan.

Toy's heart skipped a beat as Goldie pulled back the blanket to reveal a head adorned with tangled canary locks that looked just like his. The sound of blood rushing through Toy's veins drowned out any other noise, leaving her in disbelief. Could it be...

"Owen," Goldie gasped. He pulled on Owen's shoulder, trying to get his brother's attention. But he noticed the change in Owen's expression and the glossiness in his gray eyes. He stopped, allowing the man to remain on his side. Toy placed her hand on Owen's face and felt the heat of a fever and the rough texture of his dry skin.

Toy couldn't help but wonder what had happened to him. Why was he here? They were down here just an hour ago, and he hadn't been there. It had been two years since anyone had seen him. Toy couldn't imagine how Goldie must feel seeing his older brother. Was he injured? Did someone hurt him?

Owen had a deep cut on his forehead that extended to his ear, blending into his hairline. The dried blood around the wound formed twisted smears, like he had tried to wipe it away. Goldie carefully moved the blanket, allowing him to see more of his brother's body. Toy's teeth gritted as she noticed the rope marks on Owen's wrists, the irritated skin showing signs of friction.

Goldie lifted the edge of his brother's soiled T-shirt and allowed his hand to glide over the warm skin. Owen's eyes widened as a shudder ran down his entire body.

"Ribs seem okay, no breaks I can feel, collarbone's intact, but..." Goldie stopped, feeling raised flesh.

As he pulled the shirt down, they caught sight of furious purple bruises, the borders gradually turning the color of mustard. Owen's back and chest were covered in welts from what seemed to be whipping. Goldie's chest heaved with forceful and enraged breath.

Laundry could wait. They needed to get Owen to a hospital.

"Here, Owen." Goldie patted Owen's cheek as Toy handed him a water bottle from the fridge. "Wake up, man. You need to drink."

Toy dipped a washcloth into a different bottle and dribbled a few drops of water onto Owen's dry lips. Owen's reaction was swift as he started flailing about and shook his head to avoid their touch.

"No, no, c-can't..." Owen mumbled.

Goldie grabbed hold of Owen's chin. "You need to drink."

"Owen, it's okay; we're here to help," Toy told him, placing the damp washcloth on his forehead. She prayed the cool washcloth helped with his fever.

"No!" Owen bolted upward. He got as far as lifting his shoulders off the floor before crashing back down into Goldie's waiting palm.

"Easy. Owen, come on, wake up." Toy sprinkled more water over his lips, hoping to bring him around.

Owen forcefully twisted his entire body and curled up. His injured hands instinctively shielded his face, as if trying to hide from the pain. "I can't, I can't. I have to save Goldie. Please don't do this. Kieran, please!" Huge, stuttering sobs shook his solid frame. "Don't want it, don't want it, don't want it."

This was getting them nowhere.

"Owen! Wake up right now and drink this goddamn water!" Goldie funneled every nuance of anger into his voice that he could muster. "Not a request."

Owen's sudden stillness was palpable as he swiftly brought his hands down to his chin, his gaze fixated on Goldie. He looked like a little kid playing peek-a-boo.

"Awake now?" Toy went for a smile to reassure him but wasn't sure it worked. She probably had worry creases permanently burrowed into her forehead.

"Fevers did a number on Owen when we were little. We need to get this fever down," Goldie interrupted.

"Goldie?" Owen let himself flop onto his back, then squeezed his eyes tight at the flash of pain. "Why are you here?"

Goldie slid his hand beneath Owen's shoulders to lift him. "You're in the basement of Mama's house."

Owen's head shook. "You're not Goldie. That's not water. It's a trick...go away, Neira. Go tell Kieran this little trick isn't working."

"I'm not..." Goldie frowned at Owen. What was happening in that freaky brain?

"If it's not water, then what—what has this Kieran been giving you?" Toy asked Owen.

Owen's eyes opened and his gaze latched onto hers. "Drugs, so he can have a better grip on me. They want to try something new, a sickness. But I didn't, I didn't."

Exhaustion seeped into Toy's very being as she stared at his fatigued face.

"Owen, you don't have to say that," Goldie sighed. "It's not your fault that he forced you to."

Owen's forehead creased, his brows lowering as he looked from Toy to Goldie. "But I didn't. He's not forcing. He wants..." His chin trembled. "W-wants me to give in, so I no longer fight him. That's why..." He stopped and lifted his slouched shoulders in a tiny shrug.

"That's why the beatings," Toy finished for him.

"I didn't drink it." Owen's head shifted in Goldie's hand. "I didn't drink it. I didn't. Not when Silver tried to force it down my throat."

"Silver?" Goldie and Toy asked in unison. She looked over at Goldie. There were tears in his chocolate-brown eyes.

"Not when either of them... Oh God." Owen pulled his hands back over his face as a long shudder rippled through his weak muscles.

"Hey, hey, it's okay, Owen. It's okay." Goldie gently cradled Owen's head in his lap, feeling a sense of relief as Owen allowed him to do so. "Toy, I need you to run upstairs into the bathroom and grab the first aid kit. It's in the second drawer under the sink," Goldie instructed her.

In a rush, Toy got up from the ground, sprinted up the stairs, and into the bathroom. Her mind focused on finding the second drawer, repeating the words in her head. She ripped open the second drawer and hastily retrieved the first aid kit.

Without bothering to close the drawer, she ran toward the basement, stopping to grab her phone on the way. She attempted to call 911, only to discover that the phone had lost service.

What the hell was going on?

Frustrated, she put her phone in her pocket before she dashed down the basement stairs.

"Goldie?" she heard Owen mumble.

"Yeah?"

"I didn't drink it."

"Okay."

"I wish you were here so you would know that."

"Owen..."

"Well, go on, answer your brother. I'm dying to hear what you're going to say," Toy heard a man say.

The muscles in her face tensed up, causing it to feel tight and rigid. She found herself unable to move. After a moment, she mustered up the courage to take slow steps down the stairs. Trying to remain as quiet as possible, she reached the bottom, leaned over, and peeked around the corner of the wall. She spotted two men standing a few feet from Owen and Goldie.

"Oh, come on! Answer the dying man!"

She watched Goldie shift Owen off his lap, preparing to stand guard.

"Kieran..." Owen whimpered.

"Awww." Kieran cocked one hip out, rocking on the heel of his boot. "Not happy to see me?"

He appeared ordinary at first glance, with his short, dark brown hair and gray eyes. But as Toy watched him from her hiding spot, an overwhelming sense of fear washed over her. Confusion and panic gripped her.

Goldie stood to face him, adrenaline coursing beneath his skin. "I'm happy to see you. 'Cause this time, the cops are going to catch you."

Kieran just looked at the ceiling. "Again? That's getting old. I try to kidnap you; you call the cops. Yadda yadda. Same ol'. Besides, I already have another meat suit picked out upstairs. He has stunning green hair. It's like one-stop shopping, though I'd like to stay with Owen for a while. He's comfy." Kieran tilted his head and directed his gaze toward Owen.

Goldie attempted to move himself between Owen and Kieran.

"Enough of this," Kieran barked as he moved closer. "Silver wants me to move onto the next phase."

"Stay away from him." Goldie shoved him away before he swung out at the other man.

"Hmm, sorry."

With a grin, the second man dragged Goldie up the rough cinderblock wall. Goldie couldn't breathe; his feet dangled close to Owen's head. Kieran chuckled and helped Owen stand up.

Fear paralyzed Toy as she longed both to escape and protect the boys from the men. The haunting question lingered: what would these men do if they found her? Would they do to her what happened with Sky? Would they take her away, never to be seen again? If anything, she felt, could be trusted, it was one thing.

She did not want to get caught.

CHAPTER 5

Toy

Owen's eyes struggled to focus on Kieran. Kieran reached into his pocket and pulled out a vial containing a murky brown liquid. He pushed the vial beneath Owen's nose.

"Drink," Kieran growled.

Panic surged through Toy's body as her heart lost its rhythm. Owen's expression hardened, his lips pressed tightly together, and he shook his head.

"Just do it." Kieran leaned in closer, his voice barely above a whisper. "It only takes a little."

"Nuh." Shivering, Owen turned his face away.

Kieran straightened. "Fine, then."

He held out his hand, and the man pinning Goldie against the wall pulled an object from his pocket. With a smirk, he handed it to Kieran. It was a flexible wire measuring two feet long, with a sizable chunk of metal at the end that appeared sharp. Without hesitation, he swung the metal object at Goldie, hitting him in the head.

When Goldie raised his head, Toy watched a small stream of blood flow from his scalp, down his forehead, then down the side of his nose, across his closed lips, and finally drip off his chin. Kieran broke the silence by asking Goldie if he liked his "Freak-be-good stick."

Owen couldn't help but recoil in fear as soon as he saw it. His hands instinctively balled up into tight fists. He raised his head, trying to be brave, but his trembling body gave away his genuine emotions. With each appearance of the wire, a mixture of anxiety overwhelmed him. His chest heaved, and his breathing became rapid and irregular.

"Oh." Kieran moved the wire toward Owen's face. "Did you think this was for you?" He mocked a frown. "No, I'll be using it on your brother over there. Unless, of course, you'd want to take a little sip of this. Not much, just a little sip. Save your brother a wealth of hurt."

Toy's nostrils widened in anger and frustration. She realized this was their cunning plan all along. They brought him to the house, fully aware that Goldie would find him.

Owen's voice cut through the tension, his words dripping with defiance. "Go ahead."

Go ahead? No one expected that.

Owen smiled. "That's not my Goldie. My brother's not even here."

A wide smile spread across Toy's face, and Goldie couldn't help but join in.

"Oh, really?" Kieran lunged, whipping the wire out.

Surprise took Goldie as the blow landed on his side. He let out a yelp, but he composed himself, bracing for the next strike that crashed down on his chest. Kieran turned toward Owen, positioning himself so that Owen could see every strike. Owen's gaze met Toy's. She could see a sense of defeat overwhelming his eyes as he shifted his attention back to Goldie.

Kieran had lost all composure. "Still think that's not your brother? That he's not real?"

The wire lashed out once more, causing Goldie to tense his muscles and clench his teeth in pain. The agony was clear on his face, but he remained silent, enduring each blow. His eyes sought his older brother's gaze. When their eyes met, Goldie shook his head, conveying, *"Stay strong; I can handle this."* Little did he know that this seemingly insignificant gesture would have dire consequences. Toy could see the resolve drain from Owen's face. He knew Goldie was really there, and he was taking a hell of a beating for him...

Owen's eyes filled with shock and tears. Deep inside, Toy wished for Owen not to do anything that would reveal he knew. She begged him to continue pretending and not let Kieran know.

But when the wire lifted again, Owen's voice squeaked out, hollow and defeated: "Stop."

With the wire still raised, Kieran glanced over his shoulder at Owen. "Did I hear you right?"

Tears streamed down Owen's cheeks. "Just stop. Please stop."

Kieran turned and pulled out the vial again. "You know what to do to make it stop."

"Owen..." Goldie rasped.

Owen's chest was heaving. His eyes darted between the upheld vial and Goldie. "I can't. I can't. I have to prove to Goldie that I won't. I won't. I have to prove it. I gotta save my Goldie."

"Owen."

Owen's gaze shot to Goldie, wretched, barely holding it together.

"Drink it."

Toy shivered as Owen's trembling intensified, causing her to bring her hand to her mouth to stifle her gasp. His voice quivered as he struggled to form coherent words. "Nuh... Can't. Gotta... Gotta prove to you."

"Already have, Owen. Just do what they want so they don't kill you."

The room fell silent as the men shifted their gazes between Owen and Goldie. Kieran's eyebrows furrowed as he brought the vial toward Owen's lips. Owen's body trembled as he instinctively turned his head away. His focus seemed scattered, as if he couldn't grasp his surroundings. The rapid pace of Owen's breaths only added to the growing tension in the room. His once pale complexion was now flushed an unsettling hue.

The choices were too overwhelming and distorted. Toy saw him withdraw from the situation, unable to handle the size of the decision. Suddenly, his body became rigid. His head jerked backward, and the veins in his neck became prominent. Then, he gasped for air. His legs gave way and his bound arms began to flail in a seizure-like motion. Surprised, the man holding Goldie against the wall lost his grip, and Goldie fell to the floor.

Goldie was across the room, shoving at Kieran in a second. "Get off him! Don't restrain him. He's having a seizure!"

Kieran dropped Owen from his grasp, allowing him to fall into the waiting arms of Goldie. Goldie lowered Owen to the floor as the seizure ran its course.

Amid the chaos, Toy faintly heard Kieran instructing the other man to step back. Toy and Goldie were so absorbed in the moment, they hardly noticed when Kieran and the other man vanished, leaving them alone to witness the final tremors subsiding in Owen's body.

"Owen? Goldie?" Toy cried out as she shuffled over. "I'm so sorry; I wanted to stop them. I did."

Goldie ignored her as he lifted his brother's eyelids. He looked for any sign that the seizure hadn't done too big of a number on him.

Toy gasped for air. The recent events kept replaying in her mind. The basement seemed cramped, suffocating her further. The pain that Owen and Goldie had endured was all her fault; she just stood there, frozen. Her heart raced, threatening to burst out of her chest, while her hands shook.

Am I about to die? Did this event set off a colossal heart attack that would kill me in a few short minutes? I don't want to die...

"Toy!" Goldie shouted. "Calm down. You're going to make yourself have a panic attack, and I need you right now."

It was already too late for Toy and she collapsed to her knees as she attempted to regulate her breathing.

"Toy, listen to me. We are okay. They are gone. I need you now; we must wake Owen and get help."

Goldie tried to soothe Toy's anxiety while also helping his brother. Toy slowly regained her composure, and Goldie could focus on his brother. He examined his eyes and tapped his cheek. "Just a small sign, Owen, please!" Goldie pleaded.

Owen pushed Goldie away with both hands, and a wave of relief washed over them.

"All right, okay. God, Owen, you scared the crap out of me."

"Why?" Owen slurred, his eyes still closed. "What'd I do?"

The question startled them.

"Ah, you...you had a seizure," Goldie told him as he pushed his hair out of his face.

Toy grabbed Owen's hands. She noticed how loosely his fingers hung.

Owen's eyes fluttered open, surrounded by noticeable dark circles. "Seizure?"

"Yeah."

"Fever-induced seizure probably...you're okay now."

"Do you remember anything?" Toy asked him.

Regret filled Toy as she realized her mistake by asking that question. Owen's forehead immediately displayed his displeasure, deep furrows forming half-circles, and his eyebrows came together at a sharp angle.

"Did I...? Goldie, I didn't, did I? Did I drink it?"

"No, no. That grand mal had perfect timing. Took you out right before you made that choice."

"Grand mal?"

"Yeah."

"Must have been pretty bad."

"Um, Owen. They will not stop," Goldie murmurs.

"I'm trying so hard, Goldie. I won't let you down. If I drink it, he will have full control of me, and I'll hurt you. I'll hurt your friends…" Owen buried his face in his hands. "If I don't drink it, they're going to hurt you anyway. I don't know what to do. I can't let you down, and I can't let them hurt you."

Owen's body trembled once more. Goldie could feel the shudders. He knew this was breaking Owen.

"Owen. Owen. Just stop. Hey, stop," Toy interrupted.

But Owen wasn't listening to them anymore. He just rocked back and forth.

Goldie pulled Owen's hands away and held his brother's face between his palms. "Look at me. We'll figure this out. You trust me. I promise we will get through this, just like we did with Father."

Owen went quiet, looked up at Goldie, then Toy, and nodded.

"Okay, good. First things first. You need to get some water in you."

Owen stiffened again.

"It's just water. Promise."

"You're here, right?"

Toy patted Owen's shoulder. "Yeah, we're here. I'll be right back."

"Where—where are you going?" Owen asked Toy as she stood up to get the water bottle.

"Water's across the room, Owen. Hopefully it didn't get knocked over."

"Yeah, okay."

Toy scooped up some blankets and the water before she returned to Goldie and Owen. Kneeling over him, Toy shook his shoulders. "Hey, hey. Owen."

"Unnnn." The eyelids lifted. "Goldie."

Goldie coaxed Owen's head up. "Here, drink."

"Don't want it."

"Not starting that again. It's water, Owen. Only water."

"Sure?"

"Promise. Drink."

Toy raised the bottle to Owen's mouth, and he took a small sip at first, then another, and another. Then his grip tightened around the bottle as he swallowed the water as if it was the most valuable thing he had ever tasted.

"That's good. That's good."

Drained of energy, Owen slumped back in exhaustion. Toy rolled up a blanket and placed it beneath Owen's head. Owen looked up at them before drifting back to sleep. Goldie and Toy sat by his side while Goldie held Owen's hand.

Toy could tell Goldie was in pain. Each time he took a deep breath, it made a raspy sound. Toy felt Owen jerk, and she looked down to see him wide-eyed before he shot up.

"Owen?" Goldie murmured.

"Hey, little brother," he replied.

"What are you doing? Lay back down," Goldie told him as he tried to push him back down.

"And if I don't? What would you do about it, little brother? Kill me?" Owen challenged.

"Owen, what has gotten into you?" Toy demanded.

"Kill me! I dare you! I know you don't have the guts to do it, little brother! You never had the guts to stand up to Father!" Owen exploded.

"Owen, stop! You're going to hurt yourself!"

"Owen? Oh, Toy... It's Kieran."

"How..."

"After all I had done, it didn't cross your mind that I didn't sneak some into the bottle when you two weren't looking?"

With a laugh, Kieran kicked Toy away. Her head collided with the folding table; the side of her head pounded right above her ear. The pain was excruciating, and she could feel blood drip from the wound. She struggled to keep her eyes open; she watched Kieran hit Goldie with a pipe that was on the floor.

"Nighty night, fag." Kieran laughed at Goldie before he

made his way over to Toy. Her heart clenched in fear. "Come here. Silver wants to see you..."

Toy spat in his face before he grabbed her. He growled and punched her. The world spun before it went dark and Toy went limp in Kieran's arms.

CHAPTER 6

Owen

Despite being aware of the cold air and the coarse support pole in the basement, Owen remained numb.

Kieran secured Goldie and Toy to a support pole while Owen struggled to regain control over his body. When he did, agonizing pain coursed through his veins. The intensity of the pain was so excruciating that it forced Owen to the ground. Why didn't they consider the possibility of Kieran poisoning the bottle?

Owen grappled with the pain. He could feel Kieran claw at his mind and the relentless plague pulse through his body. He tried to get up and reach his brother, but the pain persisted, leaving him unable to walk.

When Kieran regained control and pushed Owen back, the pain subsided, yet fear consumed Owen. He was determined to prevent Goldie from the same fate as him or Sky.

This is all my fault, Owen thought as he felt Kieran straighten out his body with unnatural ease. *If I had just been stronger.*

"You won't be able to do that again; I promise you that," Kieran hissed. "God, you're such a pain in my ass!"

"Leave them alone! Why are you doing this to them?! They did nothing! I drank it; you don't have to hurt them!"

Owen shouted, but only Kieran could hear him.

"Shut up!"

"Get out of my head, Kieran!"

Kieran turned his head, and the reflection in the mirror sent a wave of nausea through Owen. He wished he could throw up. The sight of darkened veins weaving from his face down his chest to his heart terrified him.

"You know why I'm doing this, Owen? This is your punishment. All you had to do was give in, and everything would have been fine, but no, you had to let all those subjects out of their cells. We lost years of research that night at OASIS due to you."

"They were kids..."

"No, they are monsters! And now you are too...this is your damnation. Just like your father would have wanted for your damned soul. This is the punishment Silver deems you deserve."

"Don't hurt them; please leave Goldie out of this! Just take me! Kill me! I'll do anything!"

Owen could feel the plague growing within him. It spread through his bloodstream, the darkened veins becoming increasingly prominent. The affliction had traveled from his face to the tips of his fingers in a matter of minutes.

What is happening to me? Owen cried as Kieran took the shirt off his body. He did a slow 360 in the broken mirror to show Owen exactly how far the plague had gone.

"You like what the Bajulatorius Maledictio is doing to your body, Owen?"

The darkness had not only spread to the tips of his fingers—it had traveled further, past the waistband of his jeans. The blackness appeared to have developed a love for the skin over his heart, pulsing in sync with its beat. Owen's attention was drawn to a gasp as Kieran reached for the shirt he had discarded, and turned to see Goldie awake. He had seen the whole little display.

"Someone finally woke up. Like the new ink?" Kieran asked as he did another spin. "This was in the vial. What made him weak enough to take control?"

Goldie's face was drenched in tears as he watched the webs of plague crawl up and down his brother's torso.

"Look who I have, little brother," Kieran said as he motioned to another bound body—Drake. "This is only the tip of the iceberg. Since yesterday, I have been kidnapping your friends. This is all your brother's fault; all he had to do was listen, and no one would have gotten hurt. Now, you all get to be a part of his damnation."

"Untie him, you asshole! He has nothing to do with this!" Goldie yelled.

"He?"

Kieran seized Drake's hair and raised his head. Drake's left eye was bruised and swollen. A cut marred his light caramel skin just above his eyebrow. Drake tried to fight back using techniques Goldie taught him, which Goldie had learned from Josiah.

"You mean Drake?"

"Let him and everyone else go!"

"I never understood why you cared for this boy so much."

"Owen knows exactly why!"

Owen knew exactly why. But he hoped Kieran would come to a different realization. They couldn't allow Kieran or Silver to gain any more leverage.

"Whatever."

Kieran let go of Drake's hair. His head fell back into its original position. The sound of the front door opening and footsteps filled the air, causing fear to permeate the space. Goldie and Owen felt helpless. They knew they couldn't do anything to stop Kieran.

Kieran emitted a low chuckle, a deep rumble that thundered from Owen's chest. "There goes the dinner bell again. I'll be back soon, baby brother..." Kieran popped Owen's neck before he made his way to the basement stairs. "It looks like our three hours of fun is coming to an end. By the time you see me again, you and your friends should be onto phase two. See you soon, Goldie."

"Get back here and fight me!" Goldie yelled as he continued to struggle against the ropes around his wrists. He pulled and pulled, breaking the skin and making himself bleed.

"Yeah, no," Kieran answered as he shut the door to the basement.

The stairs groaned under his weight with every step. When he reached the top, Owen found the house to look the same as it did two years ago. Owen longed to feel the familiar texture of the worn-out carpet beneath his feet. Or catch a whiff of the tantalizing aroma of Mama's tamales. Most of all, Owen yearned to look at the woman who had embraced Goldie and him as if they were her own children. Who cared for them more than their father ever did.

They were not their father's, but hers. She was more of a parent to them than their father ever was. Despite how much he wanted Mama to be here, Owen found solace because she wasn't there to witness his downfall to the Maledictio.

As Kieran entered the living room, he saw Bonnie exit the kitchen. He called out to the rest of his family. Bonnie glanced up and saw Kieran's smiling face. Owen shouted for Bonnie to run, but Kieran just laughed.

"Owen?!" Bonnie exclaimed. "What are you doing here? Where have you been? What happened to you?"

"The same thing I'm going to do to you," Kieran snarled.

"Owen? What do you mean? Where are the others?"

With a laugh, Kieran pulled out a knife and walked toward Bonnie. Bonnie knocked the weapon out of Kieran's grasp. Kieran effortlessly regained his composure. He body-slammed Bonnie with a chuckle and before Bonnie knew what happened, he was in a chokehold. He struggled against Kieran, throwing feeble punches as his face turned a shade of blue.

Bonnie's strength waned, but Kieran maintained his grip. Kieran relished the sadistic pleasure as he watched Bonnie's terror-stricken expression.

Owen imagined sinking his teeth into his tongue. That feeling of sharp pain that surges through your body. However, it failed to divert his attention. The Maledictio and Kieran's actions had trapped him in a never-ending cycle of pain.

Unexpectedly, the situation took a turn for the better. Owen experienced a profound lack of emotion, as if he was disconnected from the world around him.

Owen stood outside of his body. He watched as Kieran controlled another man, someone other than himself. He watched as this person, with a body covered in black web-like patterns, inflicted pain upon his family. Kieran's laughter echoed in the air, a harsh and raspy sound that used to belong to Owen but now held no meaning to him. Kieran let go of Bonnie, and Owen watched as Bonnie's body slumped to the floor.

Owen found himself back in his body, regaining a small amount of control that Kieran had granted him. This allowed Owen to experience the pain inflicted on his body by the Maledictio. Owen's fingers twitched, and he realized cold sweat had trickled down his face. An ache pulsed throughout his body.

"This was too easy," Kieran laughed.

The pain was unbearable for Owen; it overwhelmed him completely. He let go of the limited control Kieran had granted him and retreated to the depths of his mind.

"Please stop..." Owen cried.

"Oh, Owen, we just started having fun!" Kieran cackled. "This is just the beginning!"

CHAPTER 7

Goldie

When Goldie came to, he wasn't aware of the fact he was tied up. He only felt his head pounding with pain. He tried to reach the wound on the back of his skull, and only then did he realize he was tied to the support beam in the basement. The zip ties dug into his wrists. Every little movement made his head pound harder. He soon realized that was the least of his worries once he heard Kieran speaking with Owen's voice and saw Toy and Drake tied to a different beam.

Goldie continued to fight against his restraints until the pounding in his skull was unbearable and blood was dripping from his wrists. He stilled, closing his eyes and taking a deep, stuttering breath.

Why is Kieran doing this? Is it because Owen and the others stopped him from kidnapping me back in 2008?

He tried to relax to stop the pain, pressing his head into the cool metal behind him. The cold surface eased the pain a bit. He pried his eyes open. He huffed out a breath in frustration. He slowly worked his jaw, trying to think of a way out. Even if he screamed for help, he knew no one would hear him. He yanked at his restraints again; they still wouldn't budge.

He stretched out as far as he could, trying to kick either Toy or Drake awake.

"I'm screwed," Goldie muttered, tears threatening to fall. He blinked them away. He would not cry; he could escape this, but how?

The door creaking open from above his head interrupted his train of thought. He jerked his head up, trying to see who was walking down the stairs, but he couldn't.

"Who's there?" Goldie called out. "I need help! Please!" He looked toward the bottom of the staircase to see Zenith—a man Goldie had not seen since he was nine. The man who taught him to control his powers and how to hide them.

"Zenith! Thank God!" he said. "A man that tried to kidnap me in 2008, his name is Kieran. He's back! He gained control of my brother; we thought it was water!" Goldie fretted as Zenith pulled out a knife and cut him free of his binds.

"I know. Stop him; I've got your back," he replied as he helped Goldie to his feet.

Goldie swayed as he regained his balance, his head pounding. "How? If I hurt him, it will hurt Owen, too."

"That's a risk you will have to take. He will not leave your brother unless Silver tells him to, or if he feels his life is in danger."

Goldie left Zenith with Toy and Drake as he ran up the basement stairs into the living room. Then he saw him...

All he could do was stare in horror at the black web of veins that pulsed on Owen's now-broad, terrifying frame. It took all Goldie could muster to run over and push him away from Bonnie.

"What the hell was that?" Kieran asked, his voice low in frustration.

"We need to talk."

"About what?" Kieran demanded, raising his voice.

Goldie also raised his voice. "About everything. Why are you here? What's the big deal about Owen and making our life hell?"

"Oh, Goldie, come on, you can have a Q&A with Silver at OASIS after I finish this," Kieran interrupted. "I don't have time for this!"

"Last time I saw Owen, he said it was too dangerous for him to be around me; now out of the blue, he shows up with you on his tail. Now something big is going on, and I wanna know what!" Goldie yelled.

"It's none of your business; now get back in line!" Kieran growled.

"No!"

"I said get back in line, or I'll do it for you."

"Yeah, and I said no!" Goldie retorted. "You sound like my father!"

Kieran grabbed the front of Goldie's shirt and pulled him toward him. "Well, guess what, punk? I'm the boss now, so unless you want to be beaten like your father used to do, I suggest you fuck off!" Kieran's voice was still low.

"That was the reason Owen and I left," Goldie muttered, pulling himself from Kieran's grasp and turning away.

"What did you say?" Kieran asked.

"You heard me!" Goldie shouted, turning back around to face him. "I don't understand why you care!"

Kieran stalked after him. "Yeah, you left! Your father needed you in his life! You walked away, Goldie! You walked away! What about Madely? Huh? Yeah, your sweet baby sister, what about her?"

"Owen and I ran, but my father closed that door, not me! He was just pissed off he couldn't control us anymore!" Goldie yelled. "I hated him more than I have ever hated anyone! He was an obsessive bastard! I was a child! I didn't deserve what he put on me!"

Kieran lost it. He swung his fist out, connecting with the side of Goldie's face. Goldie spun around, his legs unable to hold him. He dropped like lead to the floor, hitting his head against the side of the end table.

Kieran advanced on Goldie, anger radiating from him. Then he stopped dead in his tracks. He dropped to the floor. He turned to look at Goldie, who was struggling to get back on his feet. There was a look in his eyes that Goldie knew so well from years of seeing it growing up. Fear and pain...

Owen...

Goldie could tell Owen's protective-big-brother mode had kicked into overdrive. He tried to reach out to Goldie, but crumbled to the ground. Whatever was pulsing beneath his skin seemed to pulse faster. It was clear it caused him pain.

Goldie reached out toward his older brother, not caring that his face was a mess. Goldie's anger returned when he saw the look on Owen's face; he could tell he was fighting to keep control. The two locked eyes. Goldie knew Owen could see the hurt and anger in his eyes; he almost looked scared. He knew there was nothing he could do; he didn't even know what Owen was infected with.

Goldie finally moved once he saw Kieran regain control. Goldie threw the next punch. He knew he could send him to the floor like Kieran did to him. Josiah taught him that. Kieran moved slowly and deliberately. Goldie's once-pale face was painted red with anger. Kieran felt plenty of anger himself and rewarded Goldie with a punch, swift and brutal and in the exact spot that should draw the curtain closed.

The force of his fist sent Goldie staggering back, but he didn't go down this time. He tried to shake off the punch like he would a playful shove from a child. Kieran saw this and didn't intend to give him a chance to do much else. He was business-like in his attack and knew what he was doing, where he needed to strike, just like Josiah used to fight.

He was going for the knockout.

Raw fury would always win in an otherwise evenly matched fight. Goldie just needed one small window. But Goldie was done as soon as his forehead splintered into the mirror on the closet door. He could be as hard-headed as he wanted to be, but in a fight, there was no coming back from that. The guys that win aren't the ones picking glass out of their faces later. But he still tried. He grabbed Kieran's jacket and pushed them away from the broken mirror.

Kieran didn't need to put much energy behind the kick that sent Goldie flying and left him gasping on the floor. He tried to draw in a breath to clear the spots in his vision when Kieran's shadow fell over him.

Goldie was dealing with some pretty severe tunnel vision when Kieran reached down. For a brief oxygen-starved moment, Goldie thought Owen might be back in control and looking to help him up. But before he knew what happened, Kieran's hands locked around his throat, squeezing. Even through the gray haze of hypoxia, Goldie knew it didn't mean "I'm going to kill you." It meant "You need to know that I can." He knew because Kieran released him right before he completely lost consciousness. Goldie was forced to watch in horror as Kieran pulled out a knife. Kieran grabbed Goldie, stopping him from moving, and sliced into the skin on his stomach. Kieran laughed as he squeezed the blood from his wounds into Goldie's.

Infecting him...

Goldie could hear the bass of his brother's voice booming above him more than he could interpret the actual words he was saying. He clung to the familiarity and used it as a reference point when he felt the drowsy tug backward. The room grayed out around the edges of his vision, oxygen coming in thin and painful. Not enough to keep the encroaching blackness at bay. Enough breath left for one thought...

Goldie tried to get up but failed. He rolled onto his side and sat up on an elbow, and was struggling further upright when a nuclear explosion went off behind his eyes. He forgot how vital breathing was while attempting to move around with more than one cracked rib, a concussion, and a stab wound.

"Oh Goldie, you're so naïve...now you must suffer for it!"

Kieran laughed. "Well, I have to go; Silver wants me to report back, but don't worry, I'll be back... I always come back..."

Goldie looked into the eyes that had once been his brother's one last time before his vision went out like a light.

CHAPTER 8

Bonnie

When Bonnie regained consciousness, he found himself in an unfamiliar room. A flickering bulb hanging overhead provided dim lighting. His body felt sore, a lingering reminder of the intense body slam he had endured from Owen. Going off the colors of his bruises, it felt like the incident had occurred days ago. What day was it? Where exactly was he?

The room was damp and chilly, what one would expect in a typical deserted structure. The room appeared in shambles, but that wasn't what grabbed his attention. It was the fact that he wasn't alone; scattered across the room were his friends. Julia, Brodie, Mable, Forrest, Kurt, Joanna, Brendan, Fredrick, and Goldie were all here.

In the opposite corner, Toy lay alone, battered and bruised, her clothes barely clinging to her body.

"Toy!" His body and voice trembled. He shuffled toward Toy, his eyes welled up with tears. With a trembling hand, he reached out to her. "Oh, my god! Toy, wake up!" He sobbed as he shook her with both hands and Toy's eyelids fluttered open.

"B-Bonnie? W-where are we?" she asked as Bonnie removed his shirt and helped Toy put it on, offering her some modesty and protection. "Where's Goldie? Owen?"

"Who did this to you, Toy?" he asked as Toy tried to stand up, but he forced her to keep seated.

"It was Kieran, he... W-where are we?" she asked again.

"I don't know. Who is this Kieran?" Bonnie continued as he moved some of her canary hair out of her eyes.

"I'm going to rest," Toy said, ignoring Bonnie's question.

Toy shut her eyes and drifted back into a peaceful slumber. Bonnie scanned the room, his gaze fixated on their friends, who were also fast asleep. The best way to help Toy was to wake the others. Bonnie rose to his feet and attempted to awaken Joanna, Kurt, Mable, Brodie, Goldie, Forrest, and Eric. To Bonnie's bewilderment, none of them stirred, no matter how hard he tried.

Julia, Brendan, and Fredrick all awoke feeling sore but alive. They noticed Drake was missing and wondered where he could be. Before Bonnie could panic about his missing brother, a sharp pain pounded in his head.

"God! My head," Bonnie yelped as he grabbed his head.

"Bonnie, are you okay?" he heard Fredrick ask as he jumped over and steadied him. Before Bonnie could respond, he collapsed into his arms. "Bonnie! Brendan, Julia, get over here and help me get him to the ground!"

Fredrick laid Bonnie on the ground, and the world seemed to fade away.

After some time, his vision came back, but this time, he found himself curled up on his side, feeling like shit. He felt sore and groggy, as if he had drunk six or seven energy drinks to stay awake all night for school and crashed. It was not a nice feeling.

Bonnie rubbed his eyes and rolled onto his back. His blankets pressed into his skin like coarse pavement. He ran his hands across his face and peered through the small spaces between his fingers.

The thought *Where am I now?* echoed in Bonnie's mind like

a repetitive melody. He stared at the towering trees above him as they swayed in the breeze. These trees had an eerie appearance, resembling those seen in scary films with their gnarled branches illuminated by the golden and orange hues of the setting sun.

Did I fall asleep outside? That can't be right. It's way too cold for that...

Despite the protest of his aching back and the shooting pains in his limbs, he mustered all his strength to sit up. His surroundings became clear: he found himself in a deserted parking lot with one car parked on the side.

The old asylum-type building stood tall. Its brick-faced exterior stretched over the parking lot. Its appearance was average for buildings of its kind, giving off an air of age and familiarity. As he glanced at it, it took him a moment to recognize where he was—the old Summerhill Sanatorium on Legacy Ridge, positioned between Howard and Mount Vernon. Eerie tales from his childhood had always surrounded this place. The unsolved attack on a police officer two years ago didn't help. It was believed that more than cobwebs and debris lingered within its dark confines. People claimed to still hear the screams of the tormented souls who died within its walls.

A few feet away, another boy lay unconscious, his face pressed into the hard pavement. Bonnie mustered all his strength and dragged himself to the motionless man, the rough edges of the pavement piercing his palms and scraping against his knees. The pain was sharp and intense, making him flinch and confirming that this was not a dream. The surrounding colors seemed almost surreal. The chilly air bit at his skin and a metallic taste lingered in his mouth as he reached the man. Every sensation felt so vivid and tangible, leaving him with no doubt he was awake.

"Hey." Bonnie started shaking the stranger. "Hey, man. Come on, don't be dead. Please?" He reached out and grasped his shoulder, giving him another vigorous shake. "Come on, come on..." Bonnie muttered, brows furrowed. "I'm not going anywhere until you wake up."

The man groaned and rolled onto his back. He opened his eyes; he struggled to focus and blinked several times until his gaze met Bonnie's. The atmosphere was tense and awkward. Suddenly, Bonnie recognized the man as Goldie, the kid who lived in his home for almost four years. Why did it take him so long to figure it out? Almost like something was wrong with this familiar face.

"Um, hello?" Goldie wrinkled his nose. "Why are you in my room?"

"Uh...yeah." Bonnie swallowed. "Hey there. You wouldn't know anything about this, would you? Like... How did we get here?" he asked as he motioned to the sanatorium and parking lot.

"You know, I don't know. I remember fighting my brother but not much else." Goldie frowned and shook his head in disagreement, his gaze fixated on the building ahead of them. "We're in your head."

"Are you crazy?! Wait, are you dead?! Wait, am I dead?" Bonnie panicked.

"No, I'm not, and neither are you. Somehow, I survived what Owen did to me. You know you can't wake up some of our friends."

"I could only wake Julia, Toy, Brendan, and Fredrick."

"The rest are infected with a plague by Owen. The only way to wake them is to remind their spirits that they are not this plague. Allowing them to heal from it."

"How do we do that?"

"You need to touch the spirit's head, which will have you enter their memories. You will need to find a child version of the spirit. Then you will do whatever it takes to remind them who they are. You will only be able to do it once, then someone else will. I will tell whoever has the power who has it next once they have used it. After you save all your friends, you will retrieve me out of your mind. Then I...I will end my brother..."

"Can't we leave and get help?"

"No! If anyone in your group leaves the premises, then the spirits will be trapped there forever, and your friends will die."

"Oh..."

"Remember that this is all Owen's fault..."

Bonnie rose to his feet at a sluggish pace. His limbs creaked and cracked with every movement, and an uneasy sensation washed over him. As Goldie stood up, an unexpected heaviness descended upon Bonnie's shoulder. It made him want to retreat, but he composed himself. A nagging thought persisted in Bonnie's mind, telling him something was wrong.

"Hey, come on. I know what you're thinking: whatever happened that landed us here... There is no way it's anyone's fault but Owen's," Goldie said firmly as he squeezed Bonnie's shoulder. Bonnie's T-shirt felt hot as Goldie's fingers pressed against the thin fabric.

Bonnie pulled away, creating a space between himself and Goldie. He could feel the lingering warmth on his skin.

"Let's get *you* out of here. We can take that car and figure out what to do from the road. Sounds good?"

"Sure, why not?" Bonnie's shoulders lifted in a nonchalant gesture. He instinctively folded his arms across his chest. His mind was in turmoil, refusing to settle.

Goldie couldn't help but let out a soft chuckle as they walked toward the car. A playful smile danced on his lips. They reached the car, and Goldie settled into the driver's seat, Bonnie in the passenger seat, seeking shelter from the biting winter breeze outside. The cold seemed to get worse as they sat there. Bonnie's focus shifted to the car itself. The owner's meticulous care and attention to detail were clear in the car's immaculate interior.

Goldie struggled with the keys as Bonnie explored the glove box. A stack of papers caught Bonnie's attention. The car was registered to a Micha Vázquez. This discovery only fueled Bonnie's curiosity. He dug deeper into the papers. Among them, he found a photograph of the car's owner. He bore a striking resemblance to Bonnie's mother, with caramel-colored skin. However, the man in the picture had a head of black curls instead of the familiar viridescent hair. To top it off, the man was wearing a kippah—a traditional Jewish head covering, which piqued Bonnie's interest even further.

Goldie discovered a set of keys and tried them in the ignition. No response. No flickering lights or any sign of life from the engine. The vehicle seemed to be completely dead. Bonnie couldn't help but feel a shiver run down his spine.

"You have got to be kidding me," Goldie deadpanned.

He tried the key again, then a second time, and even a fourth time, but to no avail. He banged his head against the steering wheel with enough force to trigger the car horn.

"Okay… We'll come up with a Plan B." Bonnie attempted to inject a sense of optimism into his voice. He returned to the parking lot, now blanketed in falling snow.

"Does sobbing count?" a gloomy voice echoed behind Bonnie.

"Um, we can call that Plan C." As Bonnie rummaged through the back seat, he stumbled upon a coat. *It may be snug, but it's better than wearing just a T-shirt in early January.*

"What's Plan B?"

"Seeing if that guard station over there has something we can use to get help."

"All right, good. Plan B is the guard station, and Plan C will be to sob pathetically. I'm going to hold you to that," Goldie said as he made his way to the front of the car. "Now, let's see what we have here," he muttered as he popped the hood.

Bonnie tried to suppress his overwhelming sense of hopelessness. He jogged to the guard station. He hoped to find a telephone or even a cell phone inside, but it was empty, to his dismay. He peeked inside and saw a desk, but the door was locked. Bonnie clung to the possibility that a cell phone might be in the drawer.

"Hmm. I should be able to improvise," Bonnie mumbled under his breath. "What about—ah, perfect!"

Bonnie spotted a rock the size of a fist hidden in the dirt. He snatched the rock and with all his might threw it toward the station's window. He heard the loud thud of a car hood slamming shut immediately followed by the sound of breaking glass. A sudden outburst of curses erupted from the direction of the car that left Bonnie with little doubt about what happened.

"Sorry!" Bonnie called out.

"Yeah, okay," Goldie groaned. "But, um... So that you know? A small warning next time wouldn't go unappreciated."

"Heard!"

Bonnie cleared away the scattered glass of the station window before he reached his hand in and turned the lock.

"Any luck, by the way?"

"Uh... Not really," Goldie admitted. "I'm not as good with cars as I hoped. But from what I can tell, the battery is shot to hell." He poked his head around the vehicle. "How about you? Anything?"

"Well, there isn't a lot in the guard station. There was no cell phone, and someone cut the wire for the landline on the desk. That doesn't fill me with confidence. All the computer monitors are dead, too."

"Shit..."

"Hang on," Bonnie told him, opening a small drawer on the desk. Moments later, Bonnie emerged from the guard station and joined Goldie outside. With a swift motion, he passed him a flashlight.

"Just this and a few batteries."

Goldie smacked the flashlight into his open palm.

"Hey, it's better than nothing," Bonnie said, trying to stay cheerful.

"I'm thinking that we should try walking." Goldie glanced over his shoulder toward the road. "If we stay on the road, we should make it into town to find help."

A gentle wind rustled through the trees. The branches creaked and a flurry of snow danced across the deserted parking lot. Bonnie couldn't help but let out a nervous chuckle, breaking the silence.

"Heh, heh...ah." Bonnie rubbed the back of his neck. "You first?"

"Hey, I'd rather take the creepy walk than meet up with a crazy man in the asylum. Any damn day of the week." Goldie snorted. "Come on, I'll protect you. Don't worry so much. Not yet, anyway."

"Yeah, thanks." Bonnie grinned. "It's been a long time since I've been near any woods. I'm probably going to need it. Even if we are just... Walking down this deserted road into town. There could be wild animals lurking in the shadows.

"What? Like... Bears. Or rabid possums or something."

"How about rabid possum bears?" Bonnie smirked.

"That's impossible. Do not even start with that now. That is just... That is so not funny."

"It's a little funny."

"No, no. It isn't. Now that I think about it, are there even bears in Ohio?"

"I don't think so."

Bonnie tried to estimate how long they had been walking. It was nice until he turned around and stopped. Not only did he stop walking, but he also stopped speaking. Bonnie even suspected that his heart stopped beating as his face lost all its color.

As soon as Goldie noticed the change in Bonnie's mood, his smile faded away, replaced by a look of concern. "What? What's wrong? Do I want to know?" He followed Bonnie's unblinking gaze and... "Oh... Fuck," he said quietly.

"Yeah, that." Bonnie gulped.

It turned out they had gone nowhere. They had gone in circles, made no progress. Despite the feeling that time had passed, the sun stubbornly stayed fixed on the horizon.

The atmosphere remained calm and peaceful. The soothing orange glow enveloped everything. The Summerhill Sanatorium loomed ominously in the distance, its bold red bricks standing out starkly against the sky. The building appeared as if it was on fire.

Bonnie released a tired exhale and rubbed his hands over his face. Looking down at his own form, he noticed he was disappearing. The unfolding sight scared him more than you can imagine.

"Goldie?!"

Goldie shifted his eyes away from the sanatorium and to Bonnie, his expression filled with sheer panic. Bonnie's entire body experienced an intense sensation, as if flames consumed it.

"Bonnie? What's happening?"

"I don't know!"

As he tumbled to the ground, his sight became hazy and indistinct. He caught the faint sound of Goldie's voice calling out his name, echoing through the air before he slipped away.

CHAPTER 9

Bonnie

"Bonnie... Bonnie, wake up," is what Bonnie heard when he finally came to. He opened his eyes, and Brendan helped him sit up. His friends surrounded him. It was clear on their dirt-covered faces they were terrified.

"What's wrong with Toy?" Julia asked Bonnie the first chance she got.

"She needs help and a change of clothes, Julia," Bonnie huffed.

"Oh..."

"Fredrick, come with me," Bonnie decided.

"Okay," Fredrick said as he brushed dirt off his brown skin and pushed back some of his tight, curly brown hair.

After Bonnie snatched the flashlight from the table, Fredrick trailed behind him. It was the same type of flashlight he had stumbled upon during his time with Goldie. Wherever that place was, it felt real. He approached the doors and tried to open them.

"Locked." Bonnie sighed. "There has to be another way out." He clicked on the flashlight; its beam shined around the room.

"You said you have extra batteries for this thing, right?"

Brendan asked. His eyes tracked Fredrick as he walked around the room.

Bonnie nodded and patted one of his pockets. "Only three, and it takes two. Why? We should be all set, shouldn't we?"

"I don't know," Brendan said. "I mean, I hope so," he added when Bonnie noticed his pale expression.

"Okay." Bonnie swallowed. "We try to find more batteries, then."

"Yeah, that might be a good idea."

Before he approached one of the metal grates, Bonnie took a deep breath. The group went quiet. With the flashlight in hand, he directed the beam toward the floor. His gaze couldn't help but wander to the sleeping figures scattered around the room. Each displayed faint black veins creeping across their faces, a disturbing sight that sent shivers down everyone's spines.

The unsettling atmosphere made everyone feel like they were being watched. Bonnie turned his attention to Fredrick and Brendan, who were engaged in an intense conversation, their foreheads almost touching.

"Fredrick," Bonnie interrupted, grabbing his attention. Fredrick looked over before he looked back at Brendan, trying his best to give him a reassuring smile.

"We'll be okay, Bon."

Fredrick walked over to Bonnie. Bonnie handed Fredrick the flashlight. He pulled off the grate and crawled in first. He took the light from Fredrick so he could follow. They made it to the other side and stretched their limbs.

"You aren't afraid of heights, are you?" Bonnie asked.

The building's side was adorned with platforms. Rickety ladders ascended toward a single open window, which emitted a sickly yellowish light.

"I'll be giving the matter serious thought after this," Fredrick told him.

Bonnie chuckled under his breath. A spark of warmth stole

away a fraction of the icy panic creeping through his veins. He didn't blame him; Bonnie was a little scared, too. He looked over the railing below. He could see the same parking lot he saw in his dream. The only difference was the car wasn't there.

They were really trapped at the Summerhill Sanatorium...

Despite being comfortable with heights, Bonnie's heart was in his throat. He and Fredrick climbed the thin wooden planks and swaying metal beams. As they reached the window, something caught Bonnie's attention.

His quick reflexes saved the day as he steadied Fredrick, who almost lost his balance because of his sudden turn. Bonnie's years of dealing with Drake's clumsiness made it easy to react without even thinking.

Bonnie reached out to grab the paper about to fly away. Fredrick's heart skipped a beat, and he sighed in relief. "Christ..." Fredrick huffed, leaning back against the side of the pane. "I thought I was gonna fall or something!"

"Sorry." A prickle of guilt stabbed Bonnie's chest. "I just didn't want to miss this... Whatever it is." He showed Fredrick the worn scrap of paper, and he frowned.

Fredrick leaned close, shining the flashlight onto the rushed black print. "I'm gonna go with... No." He sighed. "This isn't helpful at all. And is that blood?" He jabbed his pinkie finger at a smear of something dark and not quite reddish across the top. "That looks like blood."

Bonnie would have answered him, but he was still distracted by what the note said—and not in a good way.

It was all about twins named Nate and Ann. After the first paragraph, they were referred to as T-R13s3A and T-R13s3B. It seemed they had these weird powers that allowed them to manipulate dirt, sand, rock, or other minerals. There was mention of a large metal container that a man named Silver would place in a dark room. He would seize the twins by their hair and submerge their heads underwater. The next paragraph introduced the use of stun guns and air deprivation, where

Silver would secure the twins' hands and feet with zip ties and place a plastic bag over their heads.

There was a sentence scribbled in red pen in the corner at the bottom of the page. *"This is Owen's fault."*

"Fuck," Bonnie choked out, his entire body numb and cold. "What the hell is this?"

"I think whoever...or whatever brought us here is the same one who did that to the little boy and that little girl. They're trying to fuck with us. We can't let them screw with our heads, Bonnie. Which I know is going to be much easier said than done..." Fredrick blew out a heavy breath, blue eyes pleading with Bonnie.

"Owen is the reason we're here. He attacked us at home, and this note says it right here." Bonnie sighed as he handed the note to Fredrick; he was not ready to tell people what Goldie had said. No one in their right mind would believe him.

Bonnie watched Fredrick's face as he put all his energy into staying calm. Wasn't it only fair that Bonnie did the same?

"Jesus..." Fredrick muttered, and Bonnie attempted a weak smile when he looked up at him.

Fredrick climbed through the window, Bonnie right on his heels. They landed in what appeared to be a lounge room with overturned furniture seconds before the light above their heads burned out with a pop of sparks.

Bonnie could feel Fredrick flinch beside him as he moved the beam of the flashlight through the gloom. They adjusted little by little to the oppressive silence. There was a blanket of shadows, with some pockets so dark they seemed to swallow up the flashlight beam like a black hole. The odor wasn't too unpleasant. It was stale and musty, like a basement that hadn't aired out in decades. They ventured further and the air irritated the back of their throats, a thick and sour-sweet essence hidden beneath layers of dust. It was like garbage left to bake under the scorching sun, emitting a putrid stench. The presence of something decayed and lifeless was undeniable. Adding to the unsettling atmosphere, they saw dried blood puddles scattered across the floor.

"Christ," Fredrick muttered. "I thought this kind of stuff was intense enough through a damn TV screen, but seeing all of this right in front of me..." He exhaled a shaky breath. "I guess I'm still waiting to wake up, you know?"

"Well... It could always be worse, man," Bonnie said, attempting to reassure him before he took the plunge and walked deeper into the room.

Fredrick choked on a laugh somewhere behind him as Bonnie missed a few stairs near a closed door. Pale, watery light filtered through the cracks.

"I'm pretty sure that it's the stench of blood and decay in here making me dizzy. Really hope this door's unlocked." Bonnie waved Fredrick over and tried not to think about what might wait for them on the other side. He clicked off the flashlight as they pushed the door open. Bonnie looked left. Fredrick looked right. And then they both look at each other. "Good?" Bonnie whispered.

"We're good," Fredrick whispered back.

A broken mess of shelves and filing cabinets blocked one side. Bonnie and Fredrick exchanged worried glances as they walked. Fredrick's brows furrowed.

"What's wrong?" Bonnie asked, trying to sound calm.

"I was thinking about Owen," Fredrick said, his voice trembling. "I can't believe he would do something like this."

"Like what?" Bonnie asked, his voice low.

Fredrick hesitated for a moment before finally speaking. "Hurt us, you know? Bring us here," he explained. "What I can't understand is why? He used to be such a chill dude."

"We don't know what happened while he was gone. What we know is this wouldn't be happening if it weren't for Owen."

The duo exchanged a concerned look before they stepped into the vacant doorway ahead of them. As they entered, they found themselves in what appeared to be another living room-like space filled with wooden chairs and bookshelves. The tall windows were adorned with moth-eaten curtains. Suddenly, an ear-piercing scream echoed through the air, causing Bonnie to instinctively recoil.

The dreadful sound reverberated through Bonnie's ears, causing him to flinch. He instinctively raised his hands to protect his ears, unaware that he dropped to one knee. The scream subsided after a few seconds. Bonnie remained frozen in place until he felt a firm hand on his shoulder. Startled, he flinched once more, his heart pounding in his chest.

"Are you okay?" Fredrick frowned. He looked pale and worried. "It's me, Bonnie."

Bonnie struggled to get to his feet, a little too shaken up to be embarrassed by his reaction. "You heard that, right?" Bonnie glanced toward the open door before his gaze caught on the corner. In the only dark part of the room was a spirit, his body covered with black veins that shimmered on his ghostly frame.

"What...the...fuck...is that?" Fredrick exclaimed.

Bonnie had to agree with that sentiment. What the hell was going on?

He moved the flashlight beam to the ghost to get a better look. As the light pierced through the ghost, it transformed into a mesmerizing display of burning embers. The pair stood frozen in disbelief, their eyes wide with shock as they processed the unimaginable sight.

They exited through the second entrance without uttering a single word. Fredrick and Bonnie found themselves left with no choice but to take a left turn down the corridor. The floor was littered with stained papers, but neither paid attention to them.

They made their way forward and came across a bent filing cabinet that only partially blocked their path. Fredrick attempted to squeeze past it, making an exaggerated expression.

"How people in video games make this look so easy, I'll never know," he grunted, pushing through with Bonnie following along behind.

The space they squeezed into was cramped and uncomfortable. Peeking around the corner, they saw a storage room and scanned the space, searching for any valuable items.

Fredrick pulled open the drawers of a nearby desk, and his face lit up with joy when he found more batteries. Bonnie gave him a high-five, and Fredrick's happiness was clear before they moved onto some boxes.

"There's some clothing, all too big for Toy, and there are no medical supplies; we're running out of time." Fredrick sighed as he moved another box to the side after handing Bonnie a shirt.

Bonnie was in the middle of a conversation with Julia on the phone. He was updating her about their situation. He tried to reassure her they were doing everything they could when he lost the signal.

"Hello? Julia? Can you hear me?" Bonnie said, his voice echoing in the empty room.

Bonnie walked around the room, hoping to find a spot with better reception. He tried dialing Julia's number but only got the same message: "No service."

As he walked, Bonnie's thoughts raced. What if they couldn't get out of the sanatorium? What if they were trapped there forever? What if something happened, and he couldn't even call for help?

"What did she say?"

"There's another room we can check, but we will have to go farther," Bonnie explained as he put his phone back in his pocket, a paperweight more than anything else now.

"Then let's go."

They sneaked down the hallway. Bonnie heard a clang behind him, but when he turned, he saw nothing.

"Come on, let's go," he muttered.

Bonnie and Fredrick made their way through the halls. Their flashlight cast eerie shadows on the peeling walls. The air was thick with dust and the musty smell of decay.

"Keep your eyes peeled for anything," Bonnie whispered to Fredrick.

Fredrick nodded, scanning the shelves and cabinets as they walked. "This place gives me the creeps," he muttered.

"I know, but we have to keep looking. We need to find something to help Toy."

They continued down the hallway, their footsteps echoing off the walls. Suddenly, they heard a loud creaking noise coming from one of the nearby rooms.

"Did you hear that?" Fredrick asked, his grip on the flashlight tightening.

Bonnie nodded, his heart racing. "Let's check it out," he said, trying to sound brave.

They approached the door, the flashlight trained on the handle. They pushed it open and found another old storage room filled with dusty boxes and rusted medical equipment.

"Jackpot," Bonnie whispered, a smile spreading across his face. They quickly searched the boxes after shutting the door. They pulled out bandages, antiseptics, and other supplies they hoped would be useful. As they worked, they heard strange noises coming from the other side of the door.

"Did you hear that?" Fredrick asked, his eyes darting around the room.

Bonnie nodded, his heart pounding in his chest. "We need to hurry," he said as he shoved the supplies into a backpack.

Bonnie's phone buzzed. He pulled his phone from his pocket and saw Drake was calling him. A surge of concern washed over Bonnie as he answered the call on speakerphone. Tentatively, he addressed his brother, his heart sinking when he heard Drake's weak voice on the other end. They heard someone pound on the door. Drake pleaded for Bonnie to let him in. Without hesitation, Bonnie pocketed his phone and rushed to the door. He unlocked it, and it swung it open, only to reveal Owen instead of Drake.

"Howdy!"

Bonnie's eyes widened as he slammed the door in Owen's face. Panicked, he locked the door while Owen banged on it. The laughter emanating from Bonnie's phone transformed from Drake's voice to Owen's and then to a voice neither Bonnie nor Frederick recognized before the phone lost service again. Bonnie looked around the small room for a way out. His eyes caught on another grate. Bonnie handed the backpack to Fredrick and ran to the grate. The banging on the door continued as he grabbed the loose grate and ripped it off.

"Get in," Bonnie said as he grabbed the bag from Fredrick's hands.

Fredrick got on his hands and knees. He fought to crawl into the vent, but his broad body made it difficult. Once Fredrick got in, Bonnie followed, putting the vent back in place, and Owen busted the door down.

"Come out, come out, wherever you are," they heard him say before he laughed. "I know you're in here..."

They moved away from the metal grate and crawled through the dimly lit ventilation shaft. The vent creaked as they crawled through.

After a moment or two inside the vent, the floor beneath them gave way, causing them to plummet to the level below. Fredrick landed on his side while Bonnie ended up on top of him. Both of them gasped for air, but it was Fredrick who quickly regained his composure and rose to his feet. Extending a helping hand, he assisted Bonnie in standing. Bonnie regained his balance. He leaned against the adjacent wall to steady himself.

"Are you okay?" Fredrick asked as he put his hand on his shoulder.

"Yeah, I'm okay; let's just find our way back before Owen finds us."

CHAPTER 10

Bonnie

"I forgot to ask before; are you claustrophobic, Fredrick? This vent is tiny."

"Never thought about it, but...I hope not."

"Me neither—or me too? Ah, whatever. We'll get used to doing things like this, so...fuck it. Guard this with your life," Bonnie told him, his low voice as he offered him the backpack. "I will venture into the dark and terrifying vent first. Watch my back, and...make sure nothing bites off my ankles. Please?"

Fredrick snorted and gave Bonnie a two-fingered salute as he held the backpack close to his heart. "Yes, sir!"

"Get in line, private!" Bonnie joked back, louder than he meant to. The metal of the vent sort of magnified his yelp as he scrambled to climb up. "Fuck, I'm sorry. I'll be quiet now." Bonnie looked back to see Fredrick gripping the backpack tightly. His head jerked around, looking at the blood splattered everywhere. "Fredrick," Bonnie whispered, making Fredrick's chin jerk up. "I'll take the backpack, and it will be pretty slow-going in here, just to let you know. Movies and video games always make this shit seem fun and simple and, guess what?"

"It's not?" Fredrick said dryly, passing up the backpack.

"Not even a bit," Bonnie grumbled. "Hell, I'm a strong guy, but not Superman. Which might come as a shock, but it's true."

Bonnie heard Fredrick grip the edge of the vent. And holy shit, they were going to have some tremendous upper body strength after this horrible adventure.

"And you could have fooled me, buddy," Fredrick grunted as he kicked out his legs to get some leverage. "About the Superman thing, at least. Goddammit..."

"Aw, now you're trying to make me blush," Bonnie said sarcastically. There was a clink of metal on metal as he set down the backpack and flashlight. Then he grabbed Fredrick's hands, helping him up.

It seemed to take a few painful hours before Fredrick clawed the rest of the way up. When he did, to neither's surprise, there was no room in the stupid vent to move right. They ended up smashed against the ceiling with about a foot of space between their faces.

"Hello there," Fredrick whispered.

"Cozy, huh?" Bonnie whispered back with a grin.

"It's in my top ten favorite vacation spots," Fredrick muttered, attempting to slink back a foot or three and banging his elbow into the wall, which looked like it hurt. A lot.

Bonnie chuckled under his breath and shook his head. "Come on." He picked up the flashlight and supplies before he turned around, only to realize the vent was caked with blood.

Fredrick and Bonnie inched forward. Their labored breathing and the occasional blood drip from the ceiling broke the eerie silence. The darkness enveloped them even with the flashlight, making it impossible to see more than a few inches ahead. They relied solely on their sense of touch, feeling the cold, sticky blood residue on their fingertips as they navigated the treacherous path. The vent seemed to stretch on endlessly, amplifying their anxiety and making them question if they would ever escape this nightmarish maze.

With each passing moment, Fredrick and Bonnie grew

weary, their muscles aching from the constant strain of crawling through the blood-soaked vent. The metallic taste of fear lingered in their mouths as they fought to suppress the rising panic. They could finally see the light at the end of the tunnel, only a few more yards before it dropped out again. At least there was a fair amount of light ahead. Bonnie had to shut the flashlight off because it was already flickering, the first of many ominous signs to come since they'd barely used the stupid thing. Well...the less they used it, the better.

They climbed down from the open grate with much less difficulty and landed in an oddly lit hall. Most of the wall in front of them consisted of tall, frosted windows. It seemed they overlooked a lobby—from what Bonnie could tell, anyway. He glanced down but backed away as Fredrick tried another door. They never knew who else might see them, and the longer they could avoid detection, the better.

Bonnie stepped up behind Fredrick when he peered through the gap between the frames, squinting into the murky darkness. The smell that drifted out was just...awful. It was a cloying, rotten stench so thick that it made them dizzy. Worse than the vent of blood they had crawled through. Breathing through their mouths barely helped.

"Ugh." Bonnie grimaced as he covered his nose and aimed the spluttering beam across dozens of strewn books and busted shelves. "I think we're going to need some batteries soon," he explained as he pushed the door open.

Before he could react, something dropped from the ceiling, causing Fredrick to leap into the air. As he came crashing down, he elbowed Bonnie in the stomach.

"Oof!" Bonnie wheezed, his arm wrapped around his gut and an image of a mutilated corpse with no head burned across his retinas.

"Oh, shit. Are you okay?" Fredrick latched onto Bonnie's arm with a vise-like grip, his eyes blown huge. "I didn't even... fucking dead body, falling from the ceiling..." He shook his head, trying to catch his breath. "I'm sorry, Bonnie."

"Uh, yeah. It's okay. I'm okay." Bonnie winced, already feeling the aching soreness of a nasty bruise beginning to form. "Just a ruptured pancreas. Nothing important or anything."

Fredrick's smile faded into a weak expression. Bonnie reached into his pocket, retrieved two batteries, and replaced the flashlight's dead ones. As they walked into the eerie "corpse room," Fredrick leaned too close for comfort. The room was filled with an abundance of lifeless bodies like the one that nearly crushed them. Another figure, also decapitated, hung upside down in front of a grimy window, its head missing. A dark pool of liquid shimmered beneath its severed neck while a tangle of intestines oozed out from a wide gash in its stomach.

Bonnie and Fredrick stumbled closer to the lifeless body, an experience that would forever be etched in their memories. The sight was shocking and unsettling, as they had never encountered such a gruesome scene before. The next lifeless figure lay on the ground, surrounded by an eerie silence that seemed to amplify their racing heartbeats. The air was heavy with a mix of fear and curiosity as they approached the scene, their minds racing with questions about what could have led to such a tragic end. The discovery marked a turning point in their lives, forever changing their perception of the world and leaving an indelible mark on their innocence.

An overwhelming wave of nausea washed over them. The sight was so shocking and disturbing that their stomachs churned, forcing them to expel the contents of their stomachs in a reflexive response. The gruesome scene before them was enough to make even the strongest of stomachs turn, leaving Bonnie and Fredrick feeling a mix of horror, disgust, and sympathy for the unfortunate souls who had met such a tragic fate.

"I can't..." Bonnie croaked.

"Was this Owen's doing?" Fredrick whimpered.

"I...I don't know."

They rounded the corner, hearing the sound of rocks falling against the floor, and Bonnie shined the flashlight toward another dark shape—one stuck through with a long, rusted pipe by the next window. They were expecting a third dead body, but it was so much worse because this one was still alive, and he was just a kid, younger than the others were.

With short cardinal-red hair, drooping eyes, and boyish features pinched with exhausted agony, one thing that popped out about the boy besides the pipe going through him was his tattoo: *T-R13s3A*. Wasn't he a little too young to have one? The rocks lifted off the ground before they dropped again; it reminded Bonnie of a heartbeat.

The kid looked barely twelve.

A wave of fear washed over Bonnie and Fredrick, and they froze in place. Fredrick's sudden flinch startled Bonnie, and they both turned their gaze upward in mute horror. Their hearts sank as they witnessed the child's desperate battle to stay awake.

"He killed us," the boy gasped. "Owen, he killed...Ann and Negan..." Down his face, a diluted combination of blood and tears dripped, staining his shredded clothing and forming dark droplets as they mingled with the blackish puddle beneath his feet. "He caught Ann. Stole her from me," he whispered, coughing and choking and spraying crimson across his lips. "We were almost out; we almost got away from Silver. You can't fight him... You...can only hide. Get to the...room, out the window, and don't let him..."

Bonnie and Fredrick watched the boy's body convulse. Amidst this unsettling display, his bloodshot eyes regained clarity and fixated on Bonnie with a disturbing sense of desperation lurking within their depths.

"Don't let them...take him from you, too," he breathed. "Get the fuck out of here."

The boy convulsed one final time on the metal pipe, and then went completely still. The stones that had been striking the surrounding floor crashed down for the last time. His eyes rolled upward, and an eerie silence engulfed everything.

Bonnie was left speechless, unable to find the right words to say. Even Fredrick was at a loss for words. In this unimaginable situation, what on earth were they supposed to say?

Bonnie couldn't even fathom the horrors that this young boy and his friends must have endured. As Bonnie gazed at the lifeless body, his eyes welled up with tears, his heart heavy with sorrow. The sight of the other two dead bodies they had encountered along the way only intensified his emotions.

"Shit. I'm so... I am so, so sorry," Bonnie muttered. He lowered his gaze and then swore again before he looked over at Fredrick.

We will not end up like these kids.
We will not end up like these kids.
We will not end up like these kids.

Bonnie repeated the words in his head until he felt sick, and not just in his stomach. It might not make sense, but the whole ordeal was making his brain feel sick as well. He didn't know how else to describe it. He just felt sick.

"Okay." Fredrick nodded. "Okay, we can handle this." He wrung his hands together, and they turned away from the poor, helpless kid impaled on a spike.

They side-stepped more blood and made their way toward the closed door. Bonnie hesitated when he reached the doorway and pinned Fredrick with his stare.

"What?" Fredrick frowned, shifting from foot to foot.

Bonnie bent his head next to his. "Stay close, okay?" he whispered. "We don't want to get split up here—no matter what."

"No matter what," Fredrick echoed.

Bonnie's bracing hand pressed into Fredrick's back, nails digging through his shirt as they stepped into the yellowish glow of a hall. They still saw nothing through the frosted windows. Bonnie's mind was still struggling to catch up with that last moment with the dying boy...

They crept around a few corners and tried to keep their heads down. Bonnie motioned to a pocket of debris cluttering the brightest part of the hallway. A small gap between shelves might just be wide enough for them to slip through. "You go first, and I'll follow..."

"Okay."

Bonnie and Fredrick maneuvered through a narrow crevice, their bodies contorting and squeezing tightly to fit into the confined space. The walls seemed to close in on them, creating an intense feeling of claustrophobia.

Owen suddenly emerged, his hands tearing at their clothes, the force of his grip so powerful that Bonnie and Fredrick were ripped out of the space.

"It's okay, little pig, just come here," a throaty voice growled, sounding nothing like Owen. They barely had time to react before a hand grabbed Fredrick by the neck.

In an instant, the flow of time came to a halt, leaving Bonnie in a state of suspended animation. Panic and adrenaline surged through his body, causing a tumultuous mix of sensations. Fredrick's desperate expression and pleading eyes urged Bonnie to flee, but there was an unwavering determination within him to stand by Fredrick's side, even in the face of danger. In that fleeting moment, Bonnie could not comprehend the inexplicable force that compelled him to stay. And then, to his astonishment, Owen Goddamn Miller lifted Fredrick from the ground.

Bonnie dropped the backpack and launched himself at Owen. Then Bonnie swung the flashlight like a sledgehammer at Owen's body. Bonnie wished he could say that it worked. Or that it did something—anything at all to help with their predicament.

It did not.

There was a horrible shriek of breaking glass and a rush of stale air as Fredrick was tossed through one of the hall windows.

As soon as he dropped out of sight, Bonnie didn't know—couldn't explain—what happened next because his line of sight fogged over with a blurry film of burning red and tears. All he knew was that he was screaming Fredrick's name when something clamped around his own throat, and then the world was tipping end over end, and he was falling.

"Good pig, good little pig..."

As Bonnie touched down, the echoes of his screams still filled the air. His vision faded into darkness. When he regained consciousness, he found himself sprawled on a frigid tile floor, bathed in the eerie glow of pale white lights, the shattered glass surrounding him a grim reminder that this nightmare was all too real.

He finally spotted Fredrick lying a few feet away, his broad chest rising and falling with an easy, reassuring rhythm.

"Fredrick?" Bonnie croaked out. Something caught in his throat and buzzed through his veins. He was just so damn happy to see Fredrick that nothing else mattered at the moment. "Hey, buddy," Bonnie rasped, crawling over as Fredrick stirred, "it's time to wake up."

"What?" Fredrick mumbled. "Bonnie?" He reached out toward Bonnie's voice and his fingers latched onto his arm.

"Yep, alive and kicking," Bonnie assured him. "Um, maybe not the kicking part..."

Fredrick's skin was hot and very solid against Bonnie's, sweaty and peppered with tiny cuts and scratches from their award-winning tumble from the second floor. They held on to each other as Fredrick sat up, then pulled apart as he rubbed his hands up and down his sweaty face.

They stayed there on the floor for a few silent moments amidst the glass and the blood. The two or three other headless bodies scattered around the lobby didn't bother them.

"Fuck," Fredrick finally huffed.

"That sums it up," Bonnie agreed.

Fredrick swore again and shook his head. "I can't believe you went after that asshole with a flashlight. Do you have a death wish or something?" His low voice was thick and scratchy with emotion. "Man. Don't you remember what that kid told us? About running and not fighting? We are no match for him, Bonnie. You could have..."

Bonnie raised an eyebrow at him. "What? Been tossed through a window? Are you honestly going to get mad at me for wanting to save your life?"

Fredrick's shoulders slumped as he let out a deep sigh. "No, no. I can't be mad..." He ran his hand through his hair in frustration, his intense gaze locked onto Bonnie's eyes. "I have no idea right now—except I'm incredibly confused." He furrowed his brow. "I wasn't sure if you were thrown down with me. I had this thought that perhaps Owen had taken you somewhere. And then I started doubting my sanity..." He took a moment to compose himself. "Damn it all."

At least it wasn't just Bonnie worrying and fearing for his sanity, and hearing Fredrick admit as much helped. God, it helped more than Bonnie could say. "It...it was the same for me," he muttered, feeling awkward and exposed beneath Fredrick's avid stare. "But we're okay, right? We're okay, and that's all that matters."

"And we're not crazy."

"Well, we're still trapped here. It's a little crazy."

Fredrick snorted with laughter, and Bonnie grinned back. If Bonnie could still make him laugh at a time like this, then there might be hope.

Bonnie clambered to his feet and pulled a groaning Fredrick up. He spied the intact flashlight by the main desk; it seemed to lift Fredrick's spirits. They even cheered after discovering that it still worked.

Bonnie, feeling a mix of nervousness and anticipation, glanced behind him for what felt like the hundredth or even thousandth time. Their anxiety grew as they made their way back to the backpack, hoping to stumble upon something valuable along the way.

Bonnie's skin was tight and crawling underneath his clothes as he swept the beam from corner to corner, trying to concentrate and not imagine Owen busting down the door and slamming their skulls together.

They found a door at the end of a hall, pulled the board out, and opened it to see the rest of their group.

CHAPTER 11

Toy

"Toy, please wake up," Toy heard Julia say. She opened her eyes and found Julia standing before her, her petite hands clutching a mirror.

With a tender smile, Julia informed Toy what Bonnie and Fredrick had done to help. Before Julia tidied up the room, she handed Toy the mirror. Toy gazed into the mirror to see a bandage wrapped around her head. It was concealing the spot where she was struck on the right side of her temple, just at her hairline.

She moved the mirror to see that her hair was braided just like Julia's, a beautiful French braid, ensuring the bandage would remain secure. Upon closer inspection, she saw a slight trace of blood staining the bandage. Julia walked over once again, this time offering a change of clothes, and Toy glanced down to see her clothes were torn and tattered. The only thing covering her body was Bonnie's T-shirt.

Toy changed into the clothes, her eyes catching on the deep bruises on the inside of her thighs. Where did those come from? She stood up and walked out of the room. In the other room, Bonnie and Brendan were playing checkers. The place was a dump, but it seemed they had cleaned up a little and boarded up a safe area.

"How are you so good at this?!" Brendan groaned as he put his head down on the table.

Toy heard Bonnie laugh as he moved the final piece he needed to win. "I honestly don't know," Bonnie answered with a chuckle.

Toy watched as Fredrick bent down to Brendan's level and whispered into his ear as he rubbed his back. Whatever he said made Brendan squeak. Fredrick chuckled and stood back up.

"Hey, guys," Toy started.

"Toy! You're okay!" Bonnie beamed as he ran over and hugged her.

"The others in that room. Why are they still asleep?"

"They're spirits now and are being brainwashed to work on Owen's side... I know how to get them back."

"How?" the others asked as Toy shook her head.

"It's not Owen; it's a man named Kieran," Toy interrupted.

"I've seen it with my own eyes. Owen tried to kill Fredrick and me."

"Kieran is controlling Owen! Goldie knows this, too! Kieran poisoned Owen, and now he's weak enough for him to control him."

"Toy, that's insane!"

"That's insane? What about saving spirits? This isn't that *Unnatural* show!"

"Goldie is the one who told me how to save our friends. They are our ticket out of here. We save them, Goldie will kill his brother, and we will get out of here."

"Goldie told you? How?"

"When I passed out."

This is crazy, Toy thought.

"How do we save our friends?" she asked, deciding to play the game.

"First, touch the spirit's head. You will enter their memories. You must find a child's version of the spirit in their memories and remind them who they are. The spirit will be on our side. We can bring Goldie back after we have all the spirits, and he will defeat his brother."

"Oh, wow... Okay, um... I'm going back to the security booth," Brendan interrupted.

After a few minutes had passed, Toy turned to Bonnie and expressed her intention to lend a helping hand to Brendan.

Bonnie responded with a concerned tone. "Be careful, *niña.*"

"Don't worry, I'll be careful. He's down the hall."

Toy walked away from Bonnie and approached the security booth where Brendan was stationed. Curious about his activities, Toy asked what he was doing once she entered. Brendan explained he was attempting to fix the computers so that they could monitor Owen's activities, but it was proving challenging. Determined to help, Toy moved the desk chair aside and kneeled beside him.

"Do you know what you're doing?"

"No clue, but I have to at least try."

Before leaving to talk to Bonnie, Toy bid Brendan farewell. He reciprocated the goodbye with a nod, and she made her way back to Bonnie.

This is crazy; this all has to be a dream! A few days ago, I was worried about ACT and friends moving away. Now I'm supposed to believe my friends have been turned into spirits? I was with Goldie when Kieran took control of Owen; I know what happened. Why would Goldie even think killing his brother would be the way to go? But this isn't something Bonnie would just make up...

"Bonnie?" Toy yelled.

Gosh, where is he? Is he outside? Toy walked over to the window to see him sitting on the roof, watching the snowfall. She walked over to him and put her hand on his shoulders. "Bonnie?" Toy started. "Bonnie?"

His eyes widened, and he shook his head. "Oh, sorry, *niña.* I was lost in my thoughts."

She sat down next to him and rubbed his back. "It's okay, Bonnie."

Bonnie looked up at the snow falling from the clouds, then back at Toy. "The sky looks beautiful tonight." He smiled.

Toy looked up at the snow, then at him.

"*Te amo, niña.*"

"I love you too," Toy cooed as he walked her back into the warmth of the building.

Toy put her hands on his face and pulled him close. Bonnie looked into her eyes as her hands moved down to his chest.

"When we were getting things to help you, Owen attacked Fredrick and I...I was so scared I couldn't make it back in time to help you."

"But you did, and that's all that matters."

His soft lips met hers, and she melted into the kiss. She felt his weight shift into her body, his hand caressing her face. His body was warm against hers. She felt him nuzzle her neck, kissing it softly, causing her to shiver.

A mysterious sound that echoed through the room startled them. With their curiosity piqued, they stopped what they were doing and turned their heads toward the noise. As they approached the sound, their hearts raced with anticipation. To their surprise, they found Julia. Her unexpected arrival brought relief to them but also a sense of dread as they saw the spooked look on her face.

"We found one of the spirits of our friends!" Julia explained. "It's true! What you said was true!"

"Come on, Toy, we need to go help!" Bonnie decided. He made to run off, but stopped. "Wait!" he yelled. "What if it's a trick? It could be Owen."

"How could it be Owen? This is all crazy!" Toy yelled.

"Earlier, I got a call on my phone from Drake when we were out looking for things, and I answered it. He said he was hurt and needed to be let in; I unlocked the door for it to be Owen."

"If you are going on this witch hunt, so am I."

"Fine, let's go, but you must stay close."

"Deal."

"I'm coming with you!" Julia interrupted.

"We need you to stay here and watch everyone."

Toy's courage dissipated once they passed the designated safe area like ice cubes under the scorching summer sun. As Toy bumped into a towering stack of boxes, Bonnie almost jumped through the roof.

"Sorry," Toy whispered. "I'm just...um..."

"I know," he replied, and he sounded a little shaky, a little embarrassed. "Me, too." He waited for her when he reached the doorway behind the boxes. It led into a filing room and then back into the hall. "Brendan said to head for the infirmary..."

Toy watched as Bonnie ran a hand through his amethyst hair, letting out a soft sigh. She couldn't help but wish there was more she could say in this situation, but deep down, she couldn't help but question if there was anything at all that either of them could say to make things easier.

Toy explored the filing room. She found a loose battery tucked away in a hidden corner. Moving to the next hall, Toy noticed the flickering bulbs casting an eerie glow. They came across what appeared to be a spirit slumped unconscious in a wheelchair, his transparent body covered in dark veins, giving off an unsettling vibe.

The realization hit her like a ton of bricks. Could what Bonnie told them actually be true? Toy's mind raced with thoughts as she tried to process the implications of this encounter. The idea that spirits could roam around was both terrifying and intriguing at the same time. Toy couldn't help but wonder what other secrets this place held.

Bonnie's warning broke through Toy's thoughts, his voice a whisper as he leaned close to her ear. He cautioned about the possibility of the spirit reaching out and grabbing one of them. The gravity of the situation sank in, and Toy felt a shiver run down her spine.

"Okay, that's...not great." The words stumbled out of her mouth as she leaned against the wall, her attention captivated by the grayish, sunken face. "Could we be preemptive about it? Like, wheel him to the stairs and push him down?"

Bonnie gave a near-silent chuckle, his breath ghosting across Toy's face. "Not so much, but I like how you think, *niña*. We don't want to call any...attention."

There were days when Toy regretted asking if "*niña*" meant "love" in Spanish. It actually meant "little girl." Bonnie found it amusing, and now it was his nickname for Toy. Despite Toy's initial reservations, she grew to love it when he called her that.

Her face contorted with a scowl as she felt the warmth of a blush spreading across her neck. Slowly, they moved closer to the wheelchair. Toy tried to disregard the shiver that ran through her entire body when Bonnie leaned in again.

"Don't look so worried, *niña*. We'll be okay."

"Me—worry? No way, Bonnie. I'm as cool, calm, and collected as they come..."

In the next room, three spirits lingered, all trapped in a state of either excessive medicated stupor or profound emotional wounds that prevented them from seeing Toy and Bonnie. The sole light source in the lounge room came from a television. It cast a dim light that revealed blood splatters. The zombie-like spirits were clearly drawn to its distraction as it emitted a hushed static sound, the group sitting in the shadows, staring at the screen.

It was...well, it was sort of sad. Sure, this was still a place for the insane. But the ambiance was exhausting; it felt like a thick smog that suffocated Toy and crushed her spirit.

As they navigated through the debris and broken furniture, they stumbled upon another entrance barricaded with wooden planks. Without hesitation, they crouched and made their way through it. As soon as they entered the next room, their flashlight illuminated a computer screen in the far corner. They approached it and found a motionless figure slumped in a chair.

"Is that..." Toy frowned.

"What? Another...one of the kids I told you about?" Bonnie drew out the last word in resignation, his voice brushed with a lick of icy anger. "Yeah, it looks like it. Another damn helpless kid."

The girl was fresh out of her teenage years with dark azure hair, gray eyes, and sun-kissed skin. Her head tilted back, barely hanging onto her neck, revealing a tangled mess of swollen red-purple veins. The front of her body was completely covered in dried blood. She must have been there for days, judging by the putrid odor.

It was mind-boggling. Toy couldn't even find the right words to describe how messed up the situation was. Everything about it was terrible. Bonnie gave her a few minutes to empty her stomach in the room's corner.

A solitary piece of paper was attached to the girl's shirt, and she clutched an old key in her hand. Bonnie took the key while Toy removed the stained paper with a disgusted look. It was one of the notes Bonnie mentioned before.

"Come on, don't bother with that." Bonnie touched the back of her arm. "We shouldn't play his games by reading those things."

"I was just...oh." Toy swallowed. "It's...um, information. On the kid."

Toy read the meaningless words, her stomach heavy as a rock.

Hey, there! I'm A-298, and I'm part of the Alfresco Project. I'm in my second year of experiments since he took me. I was doing well by allowing Silver to learn more about my special ability: pathfinding. Until, of course, I tried to escape; now look at me.

Below that note, there was another in different handwriting.

*Good going, subjects! You've found another note. Doesn't A-298
seem like a lovely little girl? So vibrant, so full of promise. All she
had to do was be good; she would have made her dead parents so
happy. Do you make your parents happy?*
What happened to your parents?

It was a deceitful, foolish ploy designed to assess and
manipulate them. There was no way this Silver knew what
Bonnie and Toy had gone through. There was no way he knew
about Toy's irresponsible father and ailing mother.

But Toy couldn't dwell on that now. She mustn't let herself dwell on it.

She can't...

CHAPTER 12

Toy

A thin layer of tears blurred Toy's vision. Her own trembling surprised her. She only realized it when Bonnie placed his larger, stronger hand over hers. The intensity of Toy's trembling was so great that it shook both of them, and her breath caught in her chest.

"Toy... *Niña*, hey..." he whispered. "Hey, you can't believe anything these notes say, understand? They're nothing but lies, a bunch of goddamn lies made to chip away at us until we...until we fucking crack."

His hands glided up to her shoulders, and he embraced her, pulling her closer to him. His face, filled with a mix of emotions, came within a breath's distance from Toy's. She blinked to glimpse his features, determined not to let her tears obstruct her view.

"The sole purpose of these notes is to fuck with our heads," he told her, and his voice was an impossible octave of darkness and comfort in this absolute insanity. "That's it. That's all there is to it, Toy. Whatever is going on here...it's not real."

And then he took the note from her fingers and shredded it.

Toy knew the situation and knew she shouldn't allow it to

affect her, but unfortunately it had gotten to her. It was frustrating because those last two inquiries of the sinister note had already become ingrained in her mind. She couldn't seem to shake them off. The image of her mother's current predicament kept replaying in her head on a loop, and it was driving her insane.

Had it been that long?

Had it been...over two years?

"I didn't think...I mean, I'm sorry. I know, and I'm sorry."

Bonnie's touch caused Toy to recoil. She rubbed her face and took a deep breath to compose herself. She tried to ignore the fleeting glimpse of pain that crossed his face.

"Christ, you don't need to be sorry. It's...are you okay?" He frowned. His hands hung by his sides, the movement betraying his unease and uncertainty as he grappled with confusion, trying to figure out how to navigate the situation.

Toy watched the worry on his face, his nervousness. Despite his clear distress, he refrained from attempting to confront her. This brought forth a mix of emotions within Toy: a profound sense of relief and yet also deep disappointment. The conflicting feelings swirled within, leaving her torn between avoiding an uncomfortable encounter and longing for a renewed connection.

"Oh, yeah. I'm fine," Toy lied, plastering on a blank smile and dying a little on the inside. "I won't read anymore. So, um. We probably should..."

Toy pivoted and made her way to the corridor. She slipped back into the lounge room where the spirit patients sat before Bonnie could catch up with her. It was a sneaky move, leaving her feeling guilty, but she couldn't bring herself to discuss personal matters in this place. It didn't feel right, as if the asylum would somehow seize control if she vocalized her thoughts and emotions.

To Toy's relief, Bonnie proved to be an exceptional team player. Despite believing she didn't deserve it, he respected her need for space and refrained from pressing the subject further. They both attempted to ignore the subtle tension that had settled between them.

They made their way back into the hallway where the spirit patient in the wheelchair still sat. The spirit lashed out when Toy tried to pass. Bonnie's reflexes came to her rescue as he aimed a beam of light from the flashlight, causing the patient to vanish like fading embers in the wind. Toy turned to Bonnie, taken aback by his quick thinking and effectiveness.

"Are you okay?!" he fretted.

"Where did it go?" Toy gasped.

"I don't know..."

They didn't stick around to find out. Instead, they bolted together, moving at a reckless and synchronized speed. They sprinted through the crowded filing room, maneuvered around the desks in the computer room, and finally stumbled into the main lobby. Gasping for breath, Toy clutched her sides and, for some inexplicable reason, they grinned at each other like complete idiots.

Toy couldn't quite explain it, her heart pounding like a thunderstorm in her ears, yet, despite everything, she couldn't wipe this silly grin off her face. It spread as if it had a mind of its own.

"What the heck is our problem?" Toy snorted.

Bonnie shook his head, a bubble of laughter audible in his throat. "Man, I don't even know. I just...fuck! Watching something like this from the safety of our home in the form of a movie does not compare to real life. Which is a given, yeah, yeah. I know," he added. He rolled his eyes as Toy snickered at him. "Come on! Cut me some slack, would ya?" He gave her a playful push.

Of course, Toy pushed him back with a smirk. "Hey, Bonnie. I didn't say anything."

"You didn't have to," he huffed. "It was all in the look on

your face: the *I can't believe I'm trapped in an asylum with someone this stupid* look. Don't bother denying it, either. I know what I saw."

"You don't. Because I was making the *I'm so glad I'm trapped in an insane asylum with the love of my life who can still make me laugh* look," Toy corrected.

Bonnie's surprise was clear in how he blinked at Toy, a radiant smile stretching across his face. It was a smile Toy loved so much, and its warmth melted away some of the dark clouds looming, though not all of them. Regardless, Toy couldn't help but feel grateful for the brief relief.

Bonnie and Toy navigated through the lobby and ventured into another hallway. This hallway had many rooms branching off from both sides. They decided to explore the first few rooms, only to find a grim sight of blood, batteries, and lifeless bodies. Unfortunately, there was no sign of their friends.

However, their luck changed when they stumbled upon the infirmary a few doors down on the left. Bonnie twirled the key he had taken from the unfortunate wheelchair girl before sliding it into the lock. With a creak, the heavy metal door swung open, revealing a room filled with about a dozen beds lining one wall. On the opposite side, there was a computer that caught their attention as well as two standing lockers at the end of the room, their hinges rusted from years of neglect.

A doctor slumped behind the door, very dead.

"So, where is Jo?" Toy asked, leaning on the back of the desk chair as Bonnie sat down. "Why do I feel that something is about to go wrong?"

"Because, *niña*...something is about to go wrong."

After reading the sticky note on the terminal, Bonnie typed in a few words before a video feed popped up.

"What are you doing?"

"Look, there's Jo, and there's Owen."

Over on the adjacent screen, he pointed to Owen as he stepped into the frame.

"It's a security system!"

"We might want to get into those lockers quickly because—"

Toy's heart pounded inside her chest as the room was engulfed in complete darkness. The darkness was intense, almost unimaginable, so dark they couldn't see their own hands in front of their faces. Bonnie seized Toy, making her gasp.

"Can't risk the flashlight," he hissed. "Come on, we have to hide!"

"Where?!"

Toy's head spun as he twirled her around, disorienting her completely. The sound of squeaky hinges reached her ears, and she stumbled into a cramped space that felt like the walls of a coffin closing in on her. In a matter of seconds, Toy managed to flatten herself against the back of the locker, narrowly avoiding being hit by the door just as emergency lights flickered on above.

She saw Bonnie attempting to offer her a reassuring look through the grates before he disappeared into the other locker. As soon as he vanished, the door rattled in its frame, echoing the pounding of Toy's heart in her ears.

The situation was beyond comprehension. It was insane to think Kieran wouldn't check these lockers. They were trapped, and the impending doom became clear.

Kieran's frustration boiled over, and he unleashed a growl as he broke down the door. The sound reverberated through the confined space.

"You were here, weren't you, pig?" Kieran rumbled. "I'll find you. I'll find you and that Protector..."

Toy's hands instinctively covered her mouth as she tried to suppress any sound. Her eyes widened in fear as she inched away from the grates on the locker door. She watched as their friends' spirits entered the room, the sight sending a chill down her spine.

It suddenly dawned on her that this was not some twisted nightmare, but a horrifying reality. She felt paralyzed as she wondered how much Kieran and the spirits could actually see. Did the faint red light seep through the grates in the locker door? If he examined closer, would he see them?

As Toy focused her gaze on Kieran, she noticed dark veins spreading across Owen's body, a disturbing sight that wasn't there before. A closer look at their friends revealed that they, too bore these eerie black veins, connecting them in an unsettling way.

Kieran and the spirits moved through the room, every step filled with hesitation. Relief washed over Toy, almost making her dizzy, when Kieran finally retreated into the darkness with the spirits following close behind. Even when they were gone, she didn't dare to move.

Bonnie and Toy must have had the same idea because they stayed hidden for a while. Each passing second felt like an eternity in the heavy and stagnant air. Toy's heart was filled with nervous energy, pounding against her chest.

After what felt like either five minutes or twenty years, Toy pushed the door open. She flinched at the groaning sound of the hinges, but neither Kieran nor the spirits came running back.

Toy released a huge sigh of relief, almost laughing as she did. She wiped the sweat off her forehead with the back of her hand while the other locker rattled.

"Are you alive in there, baby?" Toy asked.

"I don't know," Bonnie gasped, almost falling into Toy to get out. "Holy shit." He shook his head, his hair a ruffled mess. "I might be a little more claustrophobic than I first thought."

Toy grabbed his arm to steady him, frowning. "So...vents are okay, but lockers are problematic? We can try to avoid them in the future if it's that bad."

"No, no. We don't need to do that." He attempted to smooth his hair down while Toy took the flashlight. "It's fine. I'll be fine. I need a minute...to breathe, and not have an aneurysm."

"Yeah, sure. No problem."

Toy watched him, worried, but she didn't question it further. How could she? They were barely surviving as it was. They needed to have faith in themselves and in each other. If he claimed he was okay, she had to trust him.

Toy offered a reassuring pat on his back as she approached the entrance. She crouched and glanced beyond the shattered doorframe, first to the left and then to the right.

Kieran was nowhere to be found, which left Toy uncertain about her emotions. Should she feel relieved or more worried? She turned on the flashlight and scanned the area, only to discover Jo standing in the middle of the hallway, frozen like a deer caught in headlights between the blinking light cutting the shadows and the flashlight beam.

"Look! It's Jo!" Toy gasped, making Bonnie bolt after her.

The lights flickered, and the hallway went frigid once Jo saw Bonnie coming for her.

"I have to catch her!" Bonnie yelled.

He leaped onto Jo, pressing his hand against her temple. With a resounding thump, they both collapsed onto the ground. Toy's heart sank, and she cried for Bonnie as she rushed to him. Grasping his shoulders, she shook him with all her strength, desperate for him to come to.

Her vision blurred with tears, a mixture of confusion and anguish overwhelming her. The scream trapped in her throat felt like a sharp shard of metal. When Bonnie finally opened his eyes, a wave of relief, almost tangible in intensity, washed over Toy.

"Bonnie? Bonnie, oh my gosh, are you okay?"

"Y-yeah," he replied as Toy helped him sit up.

"Did you do it?"

They looked over to Jo to see her open her eyes. The blackened veins on her form faded before she did, too.

CHAPTER 13

Goldie

Goldie regained consciousness only to find he was no longer in the comfort of his own home or the sterile environment of a hospital. Instead, he found himself in a familiar library, yet he couldn't quite place how he recognized it. Goldie looked down at his body to discover that the wound inflicted by Kieran had vanished. All that was left was eerie black veins that seemed to sprout from where the cut should have been.

Was this some surreal dream? Had he slipped into a coma? But the vividness of his surroundings contradicted such notions. The texture of the wooden table beneath his trembling hands, the scent of aged books in the air—it felt real.

Goldie's father, Gabriel Philip, turned the corner and approached the table. The blood drained from Goldie's face as he questioned how his father could be there. How was he even here himself? Why wasn't Gabriel reacting with shock or disbelief? Instead, Gabriel took a seat, running his pale hand through his cropped canary hair, engrossed in the file he had retrieved from the car.

Goldie couldn't help but wonder what kind of purgatory he had stumbled into, forced to relive haunting memories and confront his father after all these years.

Goldie recalled it was a Monday afternoon. To keep Goldie occupied, Gabriel forced him to go to the library after school. He handed him some picture books while he gathered files and prepared for a lengthy afternoon.

"Father..." Goldie let out a squeak, but his father didn't respond. Goldie was surprised by how high-pitched his voice sounded. Or how Gabriel seemed to loom over him, even though they were both sitting. "Daddy," Goldie said, louder this time.

"What is it, Goldie?" Gabriel sighed.

Goldie positioned his picture book at the center of the table, as he had done years before. "I told you; I'm getting another book. The ones you picked for me are for babies..."

Goldie leaped off his chair and approached Gabriel. He peered over his shoulder to see what he was reading. "That boy's sick, isn't he?" Goldie whispered. "He's got the demon I have, right?"

Gabriel enveloped Goldie in his arms. It was a rare display of affection from Gabriel. Around this time, Goldie had discovered his extraordinary ability to teleport anywhere he wanted. While Goldie considered it a special talent, Gabriel saw it as a malevolent force, referring to it as a "demon." As the years went by, his cruelty toward Owen and Goldie intensified as he tried to rid his youngest son of this "demon." Gradually, Goldie distanced himself from using his powers as if he had lost connection with the source that granted them to him.

The yearning to use his teleportation ability still lingered beneath his skin. An incessant itch that could not be relieved. Goldie was uncertain if he could even still wield the power... The mere thought of escaping this nightmarish *inferno* of chaos and despair compelled him to use it. Instead, he leaned against his father, his stomach writhing in agony right where the blackened veins were.

It didn't like the idea of Goldie leaving.

"Yeah, but I'm working on getting you better. God will

help us; we must continue with the treatment at church."

Who was that more of a comfort to? Despite trying to treat it like a typical case of the common cold, Gabriel was drowning in the same information over and over, getting nowhere close to finding anything that would help.

Goldie nodded and slipped out of Gabriel's embrace once the pain in his stomach subsided. "I'm gonna go look for a new book."

Gabriel resumed his personal investigation. Unfortunately, he couldn't find any helpful information to assist Goldie. Neither he nor the reverend had discovered anything new. Goldie observed from afar as Gabriel reviewed the file again, his finger pausing on the victim's name.

"Father? Can we go back now?" Goldie asked.

Gabriel grunted a low, "No, still working here, son."

"That's not even stuff from here. I wanna go back to Owen..."

"He wouldn't want you stuffed up in your room, Goldie. And besides, don't you have...some...homework or something for school?"

Goldie frowned, a look that was becoming all too common for him. "I'm six, Father. In first grade. I don't have home-work."

"Pick one of those Dr. Zeuss books you like," Gabriel sighed, attempting to placate him.

Goldie could tell he was trying, but he was making it so hard. Owen understood because the brothers shared the bond of knowing the truth—them against the world.

But Goldie's relationship with Gabriel was a different matter. Gabriel was trying too hard to protect him. Gabriel's eyes darkened as Goldie turned away, disappearing into the maze of shelves.

Goldie returned and let out a deep sigh, hoping to catch his father's attention. When Gabriel didn't react, he tried again, this time louder.

"What do you want, Goldie?" Gabriel asked, rubbing the bridge of his nose.

"I want to go home. I've been at school all day."

Gabriel drew a few calming breaths before replying, "Goldie, we've already been over this..."

Goldie huffed and grumbled, "It's not like you care about us anyway..."

"What was that?"

Goldie closed his mouth and scowled at his father. His cheeks turned crimson, and his brows furrowed with youthful anger.

"What did you mean by that, Goldie Joel Philip?"

"You're never home," Goldie hissed venomously, careful not to raise his voice and draw the attention of the librarians. "Even after I became sick, you've been gone, and when you are here...you beat us for every little mess-up! Don't you even think about us?"

Gabriel's eyes flashed in anger. "You know I care about you and your brother."

Goldie stood up, fingers clutching at the book he found. "Then why are we here, Father?!"

"I'm not having this discussion with you."

Goldie and Gabriel sat in tense silence, engrossed in their respective readings for another thirty minutes. Goldie's anger was palpable, while Gabriel's frustration mounted as he encountered more and more unhelpful clues. Gabriel's patience wore thin, and he started organizing the papers into a file folder, leaving Goldie to simmer in his thoughts.

"Pack up your stuff, son," he ordered.

Goldie threw his things into his backpack and shrugged it onto his shoulder. "I need to check this book out," he mumbled.

"Don't take that long," Gabriel said, not giving him an inch of room to protest otherwise. He placed his hand on Goldie's back and guided him toward the front. From there, he watched Goldie check out the book and stuff it into his backpack.

"Goldie, we'll go back to Owen right after a small errand," he said, trying to sound as calm as possible.

"Where are we going?" Goldie asked, not bothering to hide the hurt lining his voice.

Gabriel tensed. "Just going for a walk. Clear our heads a bit."

Without waiting for Goldie's response, Gabriel motioned for him to follow and led him to the back seat of his beat-up Chevy. He took his place behind the wheel, not expecting a reaction from Goldie, anyway. Adjusting the rearview mirror, Gabriel stole glances at Goldie, who was engrossed in his book. It was when they pulled into the driveway of their southern family home that Goldie looked up. The anger that had consumed him earlier seemed to have subsided during the drive. As they walked down the trail, Gabriel was lost in his thoughts, unaware of Goldie's presence. Goldie, on the other hand, moved with a sense of urgency, as if Owen was leading the way and he had to catch up.

"Son!" Gabriel called out, studying the ice that had collected on the path.

Goldie turned around and looked blankly at Gabriel. He tilted his head and whispered a quiet, "Father?" once he saw the beginning of a *fire* in his father's eyes.

The excruciating pain that caused him to collapse in agony again struck Goldie. Black veins snaking across his stomach seemed to pulsate with each wave of pain, leaving Goldie writhing in discomfort, his mind racing with questions, searching for answers. They were the same black veins Owen had brandished after Kieran tricked him into drinking the liquid in the basement. The black veins were like a haunting enigma.

When the pain passed, he pulled himself to his feet to find his father leaning against the bridge's railing, looking out at the water below, unbothered by what had just happened, as if it hadn't happened at all.

"I'm scared Owen is gonna get a demon like me," Goldie rasped, his voice nearly gone from screaming moments before.

Gabriel sighed and looked over the edge of the bridge; the water was calm. Gabriel grabbed Goldie's tiny hand.

"He won't. Come on, son. Time to go..."

CHAPTER 14

Toy

Toy and Bonnie sat there, a moment of reflection washing over them. A gentle touch on Toy's shoulder startled her. "Sorry," she gasped, holding the flashlight up for him. "So everything looks okay. But, since we have no power, does that mean we have to flip a few circuit breakers somewhere?"

Bonnie accepted the light. "You guessed it—our life will be so much harder without it." He nodded. He still looked wired, but he sounded calmer and more in control. "I mean, it might be a generator, not circuit breakers, I'm not sure."

"That stuff is usually in basements, aren't they?"

"I think, yeah."

They shared uneasy looks, but they didn't have a choice. They decided they must push forward and stay alive. If that meant exploring the basement of a former mental institution and hoping for the best, then so be it. Well, at the very least, Toy hoped they wouldn't meet their demise. She'd been praying for that a lot today...

"Sorry I didn't believe you about the spirits, it was just so crazy," Toy mumbled.

"I understand; something in life like this changes, and people aren't too keen to believe it."

"Who has the power now?"

"Goldie said he would let the person know."

In the main lobby, there was a staircase located to their right. Taking a deep breath, Toy looked at Bonnie, who shrugged in response. Without exchanging words, they descended the stairs together.

The air became cooler. It's not just cooler but also damp, sticky and unpleasant with mildew. The reason for this became clear when they turned the corner and saw a broken pipe hanging from the ceiling, spraying brownish and foul-smelling water onto the cement floor.

"Thirsty?" Toy joked as they reached the bottom step.

"Hell yeah..." Bonnie grimaced. "I'm definitely thirsty enough to drink anything we come across in this place." He paused, his brows furrowing. "What is safe in an old asylum? The doctors might have put hallucinogens in the water tanks or something. How do we know?"

Toy snorted. "That is an astute observation, Bonnie. I'm impressed."

"As you should be, *niña*. I'm an impressive guy." He puffed out his chest and flashed her a big, smug smile.

Toy nudged him. She couldn't help but roll her eyes and let out a chuckle. Her laughter turned into groans of disgust as they walked through the water. Her high-tops soaked through within minutes, and her socks soon followed. Toy had no clue how they could maintain their stealth now. Her shoes were going to squeak for hours...

They spotted a gap between the walls and a jumble of crumbling stones. They squeezed through with some difficulty. Toy ended up scratching her arm, nothing serious. Bonnie caught his T-shirt on the bricks, tearing the hem, eliciting an annoyed moan.

"Goddammit!" He looked down with a huge sigh. "Okay, never mind. I'm good. I'm okay. It's just my shirt and not my... eye or anything important. I guess. No reason to get upset..."

"It's all right to mourn your shirt, you know," Toy told him as she attempted to blot some of the blood from the cut on her forearm. "This is a judge-free zone. Ah, mostly. I promise nothing if you say or do something foolish, honey."

He considered that and then nodded. "Fair enough, and the same goes for you."

Toy shook her head, unable to suppress a smile as they continued. It was difficult to remain silent while wading through the water, but they did their best. They came across the generator room, but things were never as straightforward as they seemed—and why should they be? They needed to activate the gas pumps and the main breaker to restart the generator. They strained their eyes to examine the control panel. The flashlight flickered and died.

"So, how many batteries does that leave us with?" Bonnie asked, a trace of nervousness in his voice. He fumbled with the top of the flashlight, and it took him a few extra moments to screw it back on. Toy checked and double-checked her pockets.

"Uh, one. I think. Hang on."

As Toy was about to double-check, she heard a sound. Footsteps? She wasn't sure, but she turned her head and felt a sudden, intense pain shoot up her neck from how fast she turned.

"What's wrong?" Bonnie whispered, immediately shining the light behind them.

"I don't...know." A strange chill wrapped around her spine. "I thought that..."

The next thing that filtered through the white-hot haze inside Toy's head was: *Holy crap, what just hit me?* It was tight and solid, definitely a body. It sent her tumbling back into the ankle-deep water with a strangled cry. A dizzying fog of pain and fright stabbed at the corners of her brain, but the match-strikes of adrenaline against her veins overwhelmed all else.

Bonnie screamed Toy's name. The glare from the flashlight bounced every which way. And it revealed...a girl? It was just a girl, about Toy's age, her eyes huge and filled with tears and a crazed, desperate expression on her face. And she was trying to smash Toy's skull in with a freaking brick.

"Hey, hey!" Toy yelped, struggling to shove her away. "What are you doing?"

Toy overpowered her, as the girl was much smaller, not to mention a little crazy. Toy struggled for control, and the girl's head went under the water. She fought not because she couldn't breathe under the water but because she wanted to get up and kill Toy.

"Come on, Chyseleia—finish her!" an unknown voice demanded as Toy ripped the brick from the girl's hands. Toy pinned her flat to the floor near the generator, the only dry ground in this place. "We have to stop them before they kill more of us!"

The girl resisted, flailing and thrashing beneath Toy, crying for a boy named Ordovic. Toy's attempts to reason with her were futile, like talking to a wall. Toy couldn't divert her attention to the nearby fistfight because she was focused on restraining the girl with all her strength. Chyseleia bit a chunk of skin from Toy's arm, and everything became a blur of anger and pain. Toy recalled her screams for Ordovic. Then there was something heavy in her hands and a disturbing silence as something wet and warm splashed onto Toy's face.

"Toy?"

Toy recognized that voice—didn't she? Yes, it belonged to Bonnie. She turned her head to the right and spotted him kneeling. He was holding a boy—Ordovic—in a firm headlock while he struggled and squirmed to get to Chyseleia.

"Toy?" Bonnie said again.

The question was a rough scratch from his throat, and Toy didn't know if he could see her...but the other kid could. When his eyes found Toy's and then dropped to the body next to her, he let out this gut-wrenching howl that drove into Toy's brain like a spray of nails.

I can't believe it. No, no. Oh my goodness, what have I done? What have I just done? Oh my goodness, I've taken a life. A young girl who could have had a future just like me. I feel sick; I could have prevented this. Why? Why? Why did I end her life? I'm a murderer now; I can never return to my previous life.

Overwhelmed with fear, Toy grappled with the reality of taking someone's life for the first time. Panic coursed through her veins, causing her heart to race and her hands to tremble. The weight of her actions pressed on her mind. It left her questioning her morality and the consequences of her choices as she heard Bonnie calling out.

"Toy!"

"I'm...I'm here, Bonnie," Toy choked out. "I'm here."

The brick slipped from her grasp and crashed onto the ground, creating a loud splash. Toy was frozen, unable to react or do anything. She sat in the water. The darkness contrasted with the faint glow of the fallen flashlight, illuminating the scene before her. The girl was lying in front of her, her body battered and covered in blood. It was a devastating sight, and Toy was numb for a moment until a grunt of pain broke the silence, followed by a muffled shriek.

Her attention was drawn to a figure launching toward her—Ordovic or someone else, it didn't matter. His knuckles were adorned with long claws and he barreled toward her, a hurtling two-hundred-pound mass of anger and despair. Instinctively, Toy scrambled backward, her limbs trembling with fear. Bonnie lunged for his legs, attempting to bring him down. Toy's high-tops connected with his face in a stroke of luck, causing a few teeth to fly out between his lips. Blood spilled, staining the water. Bonnie cursed as he received an elbow to the gut, but he didn't give up.

Toy found the brick again, and together, Bonnie and Toy fought back. The kid, despite being a complete wreck, continued to fight. He sunk his teeth into Bonnie's arm and clawed at him. Bonnie tightened his grip around his neck, and Toy swung the brick with all her might, striking his pitiful face. The impact was so forceful that her arms went numb. Her chest felt like it was about to burst, and tears of pain and frustration blurred her vision. At that moment, she was completely detached, unable to feel anything.

"Hey, hey," someone rasped with a gentle brush of fingers. "You can let go, Toy. Please, let go."

Toy dropped the brick and slumped against the wall. A strange, salty, and wet sensation filled her mouth. She stared at the motionless bodies of the children and the sight of their blood staining her skin and clothes. Overwhelmed, she bent over and threw up again. It felt unreal, like a nightmare. She couldn't believe this was happening; it just couldn't be real.

Toy didn't intend for any of this to happen. She struggled to regain her composure, dizziness and violent tremors consuming her. Bonnie came to her aid, comforting her with gentle strokes on her back and helping her stand upright.

"I killed them..."

"I know, I'm sorry."

At that moment, Toy realized something inside her had finally snapped because she couldn't push him away.

Bonnie wrapped his arms around Toy, trembling like she was. His eye was bruised, his lip swollen, and pink drops stained his shirt collar. Tears clung to his lashes and marked his face. Without a word, he rested his head against Toy's, and she held him closer, squeezing her eyes shut.

The fight was so loud. If there was anyone or anything else nearby, they would surely be coming to investigate. They needed to leave and find a hiding spot. They had to go...

Toy's legs wouldn't support her even if she tried to stand, let alone run. Plus, she didn't want to leave Bonnie's embrace. She didn't want to think about what she did—or think at all. Bonnie was warm, safe, and right here, the only thing Toy had to hold onto in this terrible place.

After only a few minutes of them clinging to each other

in the cold, dark crawl space, they heard noises. It sounded heavy, like something slamming into a wall or door. Toy had to bite her lip to keep from whimpering as Bonnie and her struggled to get to their feet. She was so exhausted that even the slightest movements hurt, especially the wound on her head from Kieran, but she pushed through. Bonnie remembered to grab the flashlight as they made their way to the set of stairs behind the generator, tripping and stumbling into each other along the way.

The room was dim, with musty shadows, scattered electronic equipment, and damaged shelves. Bonnie struck a switch on the nearest machine, causing the pump to tremble and come to life. One less thing they needed to worry about.

A new concern arose as Bonnie guided Toy to a hiding spot amidst loose stones and debris. A peculiar sensation surged through her limbs. It was like the feeling of a leg falling asleep, originating from the tips of her toes and the edges of her fingers, and...she wanted to sleep...

"Bonnie?" she whispered, her voice catching.

They hid in a corner, barely noticeable from the entrance, but still able to see most of the room in the dim light.

"What? Is something wrong?" He ripped his bloodshot gaze from the door, and Toy silently looked down at their linked hands. He followed her line of sight...and his face dimmed with confusion.

"Yeah, you could say that," Toy muttered.

"*Niña?*" He swallowed. "What's wrong?"

Toy shook her head and drew in a stuttering breath. She barely had the mental strength to string sentences together by this point. She couldn't come up with answers even if she was paid to. She was just...

She was so tired...

"I'm sorry," Toy managed, and a film of tears blurred across her eyes.

"What?" he whispered.

The door to the room rattled, but there was nowhere else for them to go. They were trapped, and the options were grim—either they got caught, or Toy fainted. She couldn't decide which outcome was more terrifying. She shut her eyes and pressed her face into Bonnie's neck.

CHAPTER 15

Toy

"¿*Niña*? Are you okay?"

Bonnie's voice echoed in Toy's ears, making her open her eyes. She was no longer in the dark basement but standing in Mama's living room.

Bonnie looked at her with a puzzled expression and a slight tilt of his head. "Toy? You zoned out there." He looked worried. "Is something wrong?"

What about everything? The mere recollection of their recent encounter made her stomach churn.

"Um, I've gotta..." She moved past him.

The sensation of suffocation overwhelmed her, leaving her gasping for air. Disoriented, she navigated through the house, trying to reach the bathroom.

With a sudden realization, frustration took hold of her. She swung open the bathroom door and lunged toward the sink. Toy's eyes stung, and her throat felt raw. Cold sweat formed on her forehead, trickling down her spine like frozen droplets. Toy remained hunched over the sink, gripping its cool surface as if her life depended on it. A solitary sob escaped her lips as she leaned her throbbing head against the smooth mirror.

How did I end up at home? What is happening to me?

She felt like her sanity was slipping away. The reality of the situation felt so surreal and terrifying. It felt wrong to be in this place, and the fear was overwhelming.

She trembled as she splashed water on her face, trying to steady her shaking hands. Toy glanced at the mirror hanging above the faucet, and what she saw sent shivers down her spine. Dark, swollen circles beneath her vacant eyes. Dirt-smudged cheeks. Dried blood staining her clothes, and pale scars on her arms, along with faint bruises around her neck. The longer she stared, the more distorted and haunting her reflection became.

With a sudden jolt, she turned away from the mirror and slumped against the wall. The room was quiet, the lighting softer, and the shadows more pronounced. Toy couldn't help but wonder if she should stay locked away in this small room. It felt like a sanctuary, a place where she could hide forever.

No more encounters with disturbed individuals.

No more encounters with the tormented spirits that haunted that asylum.

Just pure silence.

Confused and curious, she squinted and gazed out the window. Snow was falling. It hadn't ceased for the past two months. Wanting to change out of her dirty clothes, she called out to Bonnie for a fresh set of clothes before stepping into the shower. Moments later, she heard the door open, and Bonnie dropped off the clothes. Stepping out of the shower, she dried herself off and got dressed.

She wiped away the mist on the mirror above the sink, preparing to brush her hair. Letting out a yelp, she instinctively ducked and covered her head, avoiding a colossal punch from Kieran. Instead of knocking her out with a single blow, his massive hand collided with the mirror. It shattered it into countless shards. The broken glass scattered in all directions, piercing Toy's exposed skin as she fell to the ground.

She didn't have a moment to process the sheer absurdity of this situation before he called her "Protector." In a panic, she crawled through his legs, her heart pounding with fear and adrenaline. Toy stumbled through the doorway. Kieran's thick fingers grabbed at her hoodie but missed. Without thinking, she sprinted down the hall, relying on her instincts.

She was alone in the house with Kieran. Where on earth could she hide to escape from this guy? Every step he took behind her sounded like he was breaking through the floor, and she was at a loss for where to go. Desperation set in as she tried the back door, only to discover it was locked from the outside. The windows were covered with heavy bars, leaving her trapped.

She made her way to the basement with no other options, aware that it could be a trap. She opened a nearby door, causing it to slam against the wall, before she opened the basement door and shut it behind her quietly. The noise might throw off Kieran and buy her time to find a hiding spot. The basement was a chaotic mess of cluttered shelves and broken furniture.

She lost her balance on the last step as she took in the sight before her. This wasn't the house's basement anymore; she was somehow back in the asylum. The clean clothes she had put on had turned back into the old, disgusting stuff she was wearing before. Her eyelids felt heavy, like she just woke up.

"Oh, no. Oh, no!" Toy croaked. "Okay, gotta hide. Um..."

Her heart pounded in her chest. Without a second thought, she chose a random direction and sprinted as fast as her legs could carry her. Crumbling stone walls seemed to materialize out of nowhere, forcing her to change course to avoid colliding with them.

Her hasty movements led her to an unexpected obstacle. She plunged into more icy water that reached up to her ankles, causing a shiver to run down her spine. She must be close to the generator room. She needed to find Bonnie.

The sharp sensations of pain intensified in her stomach. She slowed down and took a moment to catch her breath. The absence of Kieran's pursuit was a slight relief. Still, she couldn't let her guard down completely. She cautiously entered a room with a broken door, its hinges barely holding on, and scanned the shadows for any signs of immediate danger.

It appeared safe for now, but wait...was that an electrical box? Amidst the excitement, a wave of concern washed over her. How was she going to find Bonnie in this labyrinthine place?

She rushed to find a secluded and dimly lit spot and took another moment to sit down and gather her thoughts, which were spinning out of control. She found a small area of darkness across from the electrical box that had a good vantage point of the entrance. Leaning against the damp and chilly stone, she placed her trembling hands over her face.

Okay, calm down.

I'm fine.

No one is chasing me.

Pull yourself together...

As her heart rate returned to normal, she noticed a faint sound coming from the hallway. It sounded as if someone was attempting to move through the water, trying to remain undetected. Then someone poked their head through the doorway.

A muttered "It's about time!" was all it took for Toy to jump to her feet, relief crashing over her so hard it almost knocked her down again.

"Bonnie?" Toy whispered as she stepped into the light.

He spun around, eyes wide. "Toy? Oh, man... What are you doing here?"

He moved closer with a single step, his expression radiating an indescribable warmth. The encouragement in his eyes was more than enough for Toy. They met halfway. His strong arms enveloped her, and she instinctively wrapped her arms around his neck.

They didn't exchange any words, but it didn't matter. An unspoken understanding between them transcended the need for verbal communication.

They leaned away from each other. Despite their challenges, Bonnie's face still lit up with a broad smile, even with a bruise and a scabbed lip.

"So... Come here often?" he joked.

"Oh, God." Toy snorted, knocking her forehead into his shoulder.

"I'm flattered, but... Nah. Bonnie is fine. You don't have to call me God."

She found herself unable to control her laughter. The situation seemed absurd to her. Everything they were going through was so ridiculous.

Bonnie squeezed Toy's shoulders, a short burst of laughter escaping from his chest, and they finally let go of each other.

"That was so lame," Toy huffed at him.

"But it still made you laugh." He winked. "So, what are you doing here? I left you in the safe space we found right before you passed out."

"I went looking for you."

With a quick sidestep, he bypassed her and reached for the handle next to the breaker box. "I found the other gas pump before coming here." He beamed. "The generator should be all set. We have to turn it on."

Everything felt surreal, almost like a dream. They made their way back to the generator room, moving through the corridors as if they'd been doing it all their lives, even though it had only been a few hours. Amidst the tension, they still found moments to converse and share a few feeble attempts at humor.

They entered the generator room, and a strange sensation of complete detachment from their surroundings engulfed Toy. The presence of Chyseleia and Ordovic's broken and lifeless bodies were visible in the lit shadow. What caught Toy's attention, though, were the notes pinned to their chests. Her breath froze in her lungs, and emptiness, guilt, mockery, and shame flooded her mind.

"It... It was them or us, Toy," Bonnie said from her left, his voice low and heavy. "They didn't give us a choice."

"Whether or not we had to, this still bites," Toy forced out through clenched teeth, balled hands shaking down by her sides.

Toy knew they were mere pawns in this place, like Ordovic and Chyseleia were.

"Come on," Bonnie muttered. "We should keep moving."

He restarted the generator and Toy held the flashlight and inserted the last two batteries she had. Without saying a word, Toy handed it over to Bonnie as the generator made wheezing and sputtering sounds. They chose not to discuss Ordovic and Chyseleia or the notes, and as they left, they didn't cast a glance back.

"I had a dream while I was passed out; I was back in the house. It felt wrong, like it wasn't home anymore."

"I'm sorry. Like you said, it was a dream, and your fear now translates into your dream."

As they ascended the staircase toward the main lobby, they detoured to a security booth to look for a map back to the others. With no clear reason or prompting, Bonnie spoke.

"I've used my guitar as an escape for as long as I can remember," he began.

With a puzzled expression, Toy glanced at him but refrained from interrupting.

He proceeded after taking a quick, unsteady breath. "My dad got me into it when I was young. Three or four. We would play together on his guitar for hours. It wasn't until he got me my first guitar that I started playing things on my own." He nudged a loose tile on the ground. "But still...I would always go back to him while he played his guitar. It never ceased to amaze me."

As he shrugged, a gentle mist shrouded his eyes while the vivid scenes unfolded within his mind, evoking a mix of wonder and profound sadness. It stirred a deep ache within Toy. She longed for the days when life was different. She knew those moments could never be relived again.

"80s rock 'n' roll was his favorite."

Toy smiled again without even realizing it.

"We lived in a pretty small house then, so the radio was hooked up in his and Mama's bedroom, and I...I can remember hours, days, and even whole weekends of laying on the bed next to him as he taught me about the music he loved." He drew in another shaky breath.

"After we switched houses, though, those times became few. We moved a lot when I was little. We had little money, so Dad had to get a second job. He and Mama began fighting about what was happening with Drake. Mama said Drake was born at twenty-eight weeks and had to stay at the hospital. He had a lot of problems when we were little. But they got bad when he was two and I was three, which made us move because my parents spent their money helping Drake.

"I started playing my guitar with my headphones plugged into the radio to drown out the crying from my parents and the screaming from Drake. When I wasn't playing my guitar to distract myself, I wrote songs to play to Drake. I tried so many...so many strange ones. Sometimes, the crying would stop for a few weeks, and Drake would get better. Sometimes, my parents almost seemed content with their life. I was too young to realize how miserable they were. But the music always helped.

"When we finally moved into the house that my mama's still in today, I was about four. Things were looking up for once. Dad could quit his second job. Drake no longer had to take medicine, and we were back to playing guitar together on the weekends..." His tongue caught against his teeth. "I can't..." He stopped, taking another breath. "I can't remember when it happened after that. I was in second grade. But everything started going downhill again," he whispered, blinking back the stabbing in his eyes. "We were in the car one day, and..."

Without realizing it, he kicked one of the computer towers as they passed by.

"Drake dropped his toy, and I couldn't reach it. Dad unbuckled and reached back to grab it; only for a minute did he take his eyes away from the road... That's all it took... He was hurt, but Drake and I only had a few bumps and bruises. Mama... She got the phone call the next day. We had come home from the hospital. Drake and I were fine to go home, but Dad had to stay. I was trying to finish a drawing for Dad when I heard the front door slam and her crying downstairs." He swallowed. "No matter how long, no matter how many years have passed...I can still remember those two days clearer than any other. And I know that I always will.

"Dad was dead," he choked out. "He had...passed away that morning an hour after we left," he sobbed. "I have never said it out loud before, and I just... It's been fourteen fucking years, and the words do not exist in my brain. It feels like walking on glass. There were no signs. There were no warnings. Or there were. I was too young to see them. Maybe... Maybe I was too scared to...

"I stopped playing my guitar for almost two years," he croaked. "I couldn't do it. I couldn't even look at my guitar without feeling sick. My mama was out looking for jobs, and I helped out more with Drake...I didn't know what to do. I was...I was scared, I didn't want to lose my mama too. So I started playing my guitar again. I had to. I had to do something to get my head away from how fucking awful everything had become, and the radio was turned on again; things got better."

He rubbed at his watering eyes again as he led the way into the security room. "I was lost and angry and miserable, and I was so fucking done with everything. I had no idea what I was doing with myself. I still don't." He grinned bitterly. "I still blame myself for what happened and always will. But... Hey, know what happens next?"

Since he started speaking, Toy had yet to utter a single word. She was focused on watching him, giving him the utmost attention she had ever given anyone, her brows furrowed, her mouth closed, her eyes reflecting both sorrow and empathy to where Bonnie almost broke down in tears right then and there.

"What happens next?" Toy asked him.

"I met you." He forced out a laugh because he had to. Because he would splinter apart if he didn't. "I'm not good with this stuff, if you can't tell. And I don't want to freak you out any more by saying something crazy, but I...I want you to know how thankful I am for meeting you." He shoved his hands into his pockets, blushing. "It's not the same, and it won't ever be the same with what I had with my dad... But it still helps. When I was saving Jo, I was reminded of all of it... I had to relive all of it and I wanted you to know that, too. So... There," he huffed. "That's my sob story."

He looked like he wanted to punch a hole in the wall; Toy's heart went out to him. Her gaze filled with compassion and an overwhelming sense of sorrow. His gaze shifted to her, and a sudden surge of fear filled his eyes.

"Are you all right?" Toy asked.

"Get down!" he shouted, making a wild grab for her arm.

With only a moment to process the terror etched on his face, a sharp object pierced Toy's neck, causing the security booth to blend and vanish. The next thing she knew, her vison was clear, and she was unsure how much time had passed. She felt disoriented. There was no physical pain. She gathered her bearings; she was in a cell, a realization that did not bring her any joy as she struggled to stand up.

She touched the side of her neck, discovering a peculiar, raised bump coated with a small amount of dried blood. Approaching the closed metal door, she ignored the unsettling message scrawled in blood on the wall that read, "*Rest in pieces.*" Peering through the dim glass, she refrained from calling out or making any noise, fearing other people may be nearby.

A shadow passed the small window, causing her to recoil. After a moment, the shadow reappeared, and she breathed a sigh of relief upon recognizing a familiar pair of eyes. The door swung open, revealing Bonnie on the other side. Although he wore a somber smile, there was a hint of something else lurking in his eyes.

Oh, that's right. When they were together, he bared his heart and soul to her...

"Bonnie," Toy began, and a hot wash of guilt spilled down his back.

"No, no. Look. Don't even... Don't bother, okay?" He shook his head as she joined him out in the cell block. "You don't have to say anything about what I told you before. I had to get it off my chest. It's... It's not important in the grand scheme of things, anyway. Like, weren't we drugged and tossed into a cell?"

Toy frowned at him. "Not important? You can't say that. You can't tell me all of those...those private, meaningful things, and then say that they aren't important. Everything that you have to say is important, okay? We don't have to talk about it, but...I want you to know that I understand."

Raising her hand, she paused before placing it on his upper arm.

"I know what it's like to lose someone like that. I know what it's like to lose one of the staples that...that keeps the threads of your life together." She tried for a pained smile. "I understand, Bonnie," Toy repeated. "And you're not alone."

A strained expression crossed his face as if his happiness was trapped within him. The situation left him at a loss for words, unsure how to react.

They locked eyes, and a brief silence hung between them. It was as if an intangible change had occurred, altering the dynamics of their connection. Toy struggled to pinpoint what caused this shift, let alone predict what would change. All she could figure out was that there was a noticeable difference in the way his hand clasped hers.

"*God te amo, niña.*"

"I love you too."

"We're almost back to the others... Oh! Look out up ahead; there are some naked teens, and they would not take what I gave them to cover themselves," he told her.

The sudden shift in conversation caught her off guard, and she knew she must have been making the weirdest face. But, despite the unexpected change, Toy couldn't deny that she appreciated having a new topic to occupy her thoughts.

"Excuse me?" she asked. "Naked teens?"

"Yeah, come on." Bonnie nodded. He gave her shoulder a long, lingering squeeze before he dropped his arm.

"Well..." Toy paused. "At least we won't get bored."

"Bored? Here? Come on, Toy. The fun never ends here."

The corners of her lips twitched upward. "I believe it, baby. Lead the way."

CHAPTER 16

Julia

As soon as Julia heard her walkie-talkie crackle, she immediately got up from her seat and grabbed it. "I'm here; what's up?" she asked.

Fredrick's urgent voice came through the walkie-talkie. "Come to the security booth; Brendan is saving Forrest! But the other spirits are coming!" he exclaimed.

Without wasting a single moment, Julia responded, "I'm on my way!" She put the walkie-talkie in her pocket and dashed toward the security booth.

Upon reaching the booth, Julia found Fredrick and Brendan, who had already delved into Forrest's memories. Despite their efforts, the atmosphere remained cold.

"Look! The other spirits are coming; we must get Brendan before the spirits do," Julia gasped, but as she did, Brendan woke up and looked around, confused.

"Brendan!" Fredrick and Julia yelled.

"Brendan, get over here now! The other spirits are behind you!" Fredrick yelled.

"I-I'm coming!" Brendan said as he ran to them.

"God, Bon, are you okay?" Fredrick gasped as he grabbed Brendan and pulled him into a quick hug.

"I'm fine; Forrest's saved," Brendan answered.

As the group gathered around, their attention was drawn to the darkened veins that covered Forrest's figure. They watched in awe as the veins vanished, causing his form to fade into nothingness.

"Let's go!" Julia blurted out.

As the other spirits drew nearer, Julia's heart shattered as she saw her remaining friends still under Owen's influence. She turned and urged the boys to move forward, leading them back to the safety of their designated area.

"Brendan, what the hell?! You can't just go find a spirit! You almost got yourself killed!" Julia yelled. "With Bonnie and Toy M.I.A. we can't be putting ourselves at risk!"

"Sorry, I saw Forrest and—"

"No! We don't go without mentioning it to the others."

"Fine... Julia, you have the power now," Brendan muttered.

Brendan started to walk away, with Fredrick following behind, while Julia sighed. She couldn't help but wish that Bonnie and Toy would return soon. Yet, as they were about to continue, someone knocking on the door stopped everyone.

"Someone's here," Brendan said.

"Brendan, don't—it could be Owen," Julia added.

He opened the door before she could finish what she was saying.

"It's a giant wooden box."

Brendan opened the box as everyone gathered around, revealing Drake inside, to their relief. Thankfully, he wasn't injured like Toy was.

"Guys, Drake is in the box!" Brendan exclaimed.

"Julia, you helped Toy. Can you help Drake?" Fredrick asked.

"Yes," Julia answered.

Fredrick and Brendan helped pull Drake from the box and carefully placed him on the ground. Fredrick then offered Julia one of the few remaining unopened water bottles. Julia poured water onto Drake's neck and chest to clean away the dirt and examine him for any injuries.

Drake regained consciousness. He opened his eyes and instinctively shielded them from the blinking red light, trying to adjust to his surroundings.

"Hey, Drake. There you are. How are you feeling?" Julia asked as Brendan and Fredrick helped Drake sit up before the two of them left and went back to the security booth.

"Okay, I guess. Is everyone else okay?"

"The best we can be with our situation. Where were you?"

"I don't remember. I remember having breakfast before Mama and I had to go to work. Then, seeing Owen when I got back, I followed him, and that's all I remember. Where are we?"

"An abandoned asylum with a built-in maze of hallways, as Fredrick put it," Julia replied. "The Summerhill Sanatorium."

Julia's response elicited a disdainful snort from Drake, showing his clear disapproval or disbelief at what she had just said.

"Sorry, I shouldn't have laughed; it sounds ridiculous."

"I don't blame you; it is ridiculous." Julia sighed. "Do you want to see the security booth? Brendan and Fredrick are in there."

"Sure."

Julia reached out and clasped Drake's hands, lending him a helping hand to get back on his feet. As he stumbled slightly, he leaned into her for support, but swiftly regained his stability. Together, they exited the room and navigated through a labyrinth of hallways until they arrived at the security booth.

"Hey guys, Drake wanted to see the security booth."

"Hey, um, where's Goldie?" Drake asked.

"Oh, he'll come back when we have saved the spirits of our friends," Julia answered.

"Okay, but where is he?"

"You will not believe me, but Goldie is in Bonnie's head,

so he wouldn't die."

"That's such bullshit. Wait! He was dying?"

"Yeah, it's hard to believe. I know."

"Where's Bonnie and Toy?"

"They went to save Jo and have been M.I.A. It's too dangerous to look for them, and we have no cell service, so neither can answer their phones. Which is why we are using walkie-talkies."

"Oh... So, umm, Brendan, what are you doing?" Drake asked.

"Watching Owen so no more of us need to go into Bonnie's head to survive. Also looking for Toy and Bonnie," Brendan answered, making Drake give him a dirty look. "What?"

"That's not funny, not at all," Drake grumbled.

Then Fredrick walked into the room. "Oh, hey, what are you doing here?" he asked as he blushed, and Julia gave him a confused look.

"I'm just showing Drake around," Julia answered as she wondered what was up with Fredrick. "Hey, Drake, do you want to go outside?"

"Yeah."

Drake and Julia exited the security booth, leaving behind the strange and unexpected atmosphere that had enveloped it. They stepped outside, venturing into the open air.

Once again, the walkie-talkie crackled. Julia swiftly retrieved it from her pocket and pressed it against her ear, ready to listen to the incoming message.

"Hey Brendan, I'm still here with Drake; what's wrong?" Julia questioned.

"Mable is on camera; she's in the room near the end of the safe zone. If you hurry, we might catch her," he answered.

"Okay. We're coming."

CHAPTER 17

Goldie

Owen's senses picked up on Goldie's presence as soon as he stepped foot into the house. It was as if Owen had a sixth sense for detecting trouble when it came to his family. This memory was one of many that Goldie dreaded reliving in this torturous state of purgatory.

"Goldie?" Owen's voice echoed through the living room as he called out, searching for his little brother. "Are you here?"

With a sigh, Owen dropped his book bag onto its designated spot on the closet floor. It had become a routine for Goldie and Owen to stow away their school bags there, not caring to hang them up.

The tranquility was disrupted when Goldie heard Gabriel emit a low growl from the sofa.

"Goldie is in the bathroom."

Gabriel was unaware that Goldie was watching his every move through the cracked door, filled with fear. Gabriel closed the book he had been reading and glanced at his oldest son. Despite being only thirteen years old, Owen was already quite tall.

"Your brother messed up today, and I told him to stay put.

I'm not sure I could control myself if I saw him right now," Gabriel remarked.

Owen's gaze shifted to the partially closed bathroom door, and he sighed. He could see the redness and tears on Goldie's face.

"So, what did he do this time?" Owen asked.

"He went and told his teachers about the church and his treatment and then showed off his demon." He paused and let out a heavy sigh through his nose. "Child Protective Services was here for about two hours. Thank God I got home last night. If I hadn't, you and Goldie..." He paused once more, but he rested his head in his hands this time. "Owen, I don't know what I'd do if I lost you boys."

Owen sighed. "Father, look, I know he... I know we're not... Father, I know he didn't mean for that to happen; he's a stupid kid like all kids are his age."

Gabriel interrupted, shaking his head. "No, son, this is way more than being a stupid kid. I mean, mind my language, stupid he fucking is, but this is more than that. Your brother damn near got both of you boys taken away."

Gabriel rose to his feet, his eyes filled with unwavering resolve. With a deliberate motion, he loosened his belt from its loops, producing a grating sound that made both boys flinch.

"Father, come on. Don't whip him. Just..."

Goldie's eyes followed Owen as he positioned himself before Gabriel, who was already on his way to the bathroom.

"He's looking for attention."

"He's about to get some more of it, then, isn't he?"

"More of it?" Owen cocked his head, unsure what Gabriel was implying.

Gabriel gestured toward the coffee table. He watched as his son turned his gaze in that direction. A look of horror appeared on the boy's face. A board with three spikes lay on the coffee table, and Owen quickly comprehended the situation. Goldie's tears were not because of fear of being disciplined, but because the mere thought of enduring another punishment on top of the ones he had already received was overwhelming for him.

"Father, you can't beat him twice."

Gabriel's sharp tongue cut Owen off. "No, I better see Goldie's ass on the table in ten." He said this loudly so Goldie would hear him.

Goldie feigned surprise as he caught Gabriel's words and cried louder. Gabriel had already warned him about receiving another punishment, but Goldie did not know when it would happen. Now that he knew, fear consumed him completely.

All Goldie wanted to do was get out of this purgatory...

"Father, please... Can't you let him off this one time?" Owen begged.

"This one time?" Gabriel repeated. "I have let him off way more than I should. If nothing else I've done will get through to him, I will ensure that this does; at this rate, he is going to hell."

"If you want to get through to him, then beat me."

Gabriel's laughter reverberated through the air, relishing in the "joke," yet his amusement dissipated as he noticed Owen's unresponsive demeanor. Peering into Owen's eyes, the solemn expression that adorned the young boy's face took Gabriel aback.

"Well... You're serious, aren't you?"

"As a heart attack, Father."

Proud, all-knowing Gabriel Philip was reduced to confusion at that moment. "Owen, why would you suggest something like that?"

"Because I know that if you gave Goldie a whoopin' for something I did wrong, I wouldn't do it again. I'd be one of God's angels after that." Owen paused, closing his eyes for a moment.

"You're right, son."

Owen's change in behavior was clear to Gabriel, and he agreed that the best way to reach Goldie was by disciplining

Owen. Goldie didn't want to witness this, but he couldn't tear his gaze away from the scene unfolding before him, his wide chocolate eyes fixated on the events. Owen didn't object when Gabriel took his coat and guided him to the dining room table. The touch of Gabriel's hand on his shoulder surprised Owen, and the sound of the belt hitting the table made him turn to face Gabriel.

"I'm so proud of you, son," he whispered. Goldie almost missed it. "You are a child of God, my son."

"Thanks, Father." Owen's voice was soft. "Enough with the baby stuff, huh?" He chuckled. "So, uh... How are we gonna do this, Father? I bend over, and you, uh, hit my thigh or something to make it sound all big and scary?"

"No way, son." Gabriel gave a small, apologetic smile. "I will not go easy on you. This will be the same whipping I intended to give to your brother. The kid has to learn the consequences of his actions, even if he doesn't physically feel them."

But after a moment of self-pity, a determined, toothy grin spread across Owen's face as he spoke. "Bring it on, Father." He held his arms open in a grand gesture of submission.

"Goldie, please come out here," Gabriel bellowed.

"Just wake up! Fucking wake up!" Goldie shouted, but neither Owen nor Gabriel reacted.

"Father, does Owen have to be here?" Goldie couldn't keep his voice from breaking.

"Yes, as a matter of fact, son, he does." Gabriel gave Goldie a no-nonsense look, squared his shoulders, and picked the belt up off the table. "Owen, strip down and lay down on the table. I want two pillows underneath your hips. Make sure you're, uh... Make sure your balls are covered. While you position yourself, I'm going to talk to Goldie."

Goldie's eyes widened in disbelief as Owen followed Gabriel's instructions. He placed two pillows on the table before unbuttoning his jeans and removing his shirt. The initial shock quickly faded, and Goldie couldn't help but vocalize his disapproval.

"What the fuck are you doing? Owen, stop!"

"First off, Goldie, I'd better not hear another cuss word out of your mouth today. I can add some extra licks with the paddle if you'd like. I don't think Owen would appreciate that too much. Son?"

"Goldie, man. It'd be great if you kept your mouth shut, okay?"

"Father, please, I'm sorry for telling Miss Justineau, but I didn't mean for anything to happen. Honest! I just...I wasn't thinking. She was so nice and just asking me questions and... Father, please, I didn't think." Goldie could feel the tears prickling in his eyes. He gripped the hem of his red flannel shirt. "Owen did nothing wrong, Father. It was all me. I'm sorry." Goldie's voice was soft and broken. "Punish me instead, please!"

Owen had already removed his clothes and neatly stacked them next to the table. He positioned himself comfortably on the pillows, placing his head on his forearms.

"Goldie, I know your brother did nothing wrong. This is to ensure that nobody jeopardizes our family or church again. Owen offered to take your punishment."

Goldie yelled angrily, "Well, I don't want him to take it!" The tears spilled over now, and he wiped his face on his sleeve. "Please, Father, you can't..."

Goldie glanced toward Owen, who was lying completely unclothed on the table. He immediately averted his gaze, hoping to preserve his brother's dignity if possible. Witnessing his brother, who was usually confident and fearless, in such an exposed state made Goldie feel uncomfortable.

"Sorry, son, but you don't get a choice here. Think about this: if I hadn't come home last night, what would have happened when the people from CPS came today?"

"I-I don't know."

This was a lie, of course.

Gabriel knew it was a lie, and Goldie was evading. He was determined to make a point with this one. Owen had given himself up as the scapegoat.

Gabriel picked up the belt and brought it down sharply on Owen's bare backside in a swift motion.

Owen bucked into the pillow, barely stifling a cry in his arm. It might not have been so bad if he'd been expecting it.

"Geez, Father," he panted. "Give a guy some warning next time?"

"Sorry, son. No, I can't do that. You offered to take your brother's punishment. And that means his real punishment."

"Yes, Father."

Owen buried his head in his arms again, bracing himself for the impending blow. Uncertain of Gabriel's intentions, he knew that whatever was about to happen was solely for the sake of Goldie. At that moment, he reminded himself to hold on to this knowledge as Gabriel lifted the belt again. And just as the belt was about to strike, Goldie's voice echoed through the air, piercing the tension-filled atmosphere.

"Stop it! Please! Owen did nothing!"

The veins on Goldie's stomach appeared to throb with pleasure as his fear and anger continued to intensify. The sound of the belt striking made Goldie flinch, and tears streamed down his face. It pained Goldie to see his brother being punished for something he had done.

"Goldie, any foul word that comes out of your mouth will add five licks with the paddle at the end of your punishment. Any extra punishment that you may rack up here will be given to your brother. The second rule is that you will remain silent unless asked a question. Now, that means crying; real men don't cry, son. If you protest or try to interfere, Owen will get five extra. Owen will get another five if you look away, cover your eyes, or anything else. And if you are asked a question, for the love of our lord, son, answer me. 'I don't know' is not an answer. There are five extra if you lie to me or refuse to answer." Gabriel paused, giving Goldie a hard look. "Do you understand?"

Goldie nodded wordlessly. He felt like he couldn't breathe.

"All right, now that we have the rules out of the way, back to the question. What would have happened had I not come home last night, Goldie?"

Goldie spoke with a deep, steadying breath. "Owen and I would have been taken away. They—they would have taken us away and maybe even separated us. And you would have gone to jail. With you in jail, unable to help me continue my treatment, my demon would gain full control." Goldie looked down at the ground, not even bothering to stop the tears. "I'm so sorry, Father."

"All right, son, I want you to stand up by the head of the table." He gestured with his hand, and Goldie obeyed.

"Father?" Goldie's voice was quiet. He felt a surge of fear as he worried about the potential consequences of speaking. He knew deep down that he was indeed breaking the rule, and the thought of Gabriel possibly increasing his punishment only added to his anxiety.

Gabriel reached down to pick up his belt. "Yes, son?"

"I know...I know you didn't ask me a question, but..." Goldie stumbled over the words, unsure of how to say what he wanted to.

"Come on, Goldie, spit it out. And look at my eyes when you're talking to me." Gabriel's voice was gruff, unkind.

Goldie snapped his eyes to meet Gabriel's. "Father, please add no more licks..." His voice shook as he spoke. "But can I hold Owen's hand? Please? This is all my fault, and it's so unfair to him... Please let me help him."

Gabriel mulled over the question for a moment. Goldie had broken a rule, which should earn added punishment, but the heart behind the request was clearly in a good place. He couldn't deny that.

He was so much like his mother, it scared Gabriel.

"I won't add any extra licks for that, son. And it is very good of you to offer to comfort your brother. It's okay with me, but ask Owen to ensure that's what he wants."

When Goldie nervously repeated the request, Owen smiled. He held his left hand out but kept the right one underneath his chest. Goldie took Owen's left hand in both of his, squeezing softly.

"I'm sorry, Owen." Goldie met Owen's eyes to ensure his brother knew how much this meant.

"No sweat, Goldilocks." Owen smirked, unable to resist teasing Goldie momentarily, trying to get him to laugh. "You know I can't stand seeing my poor little bro get his ass whooped. Besides, I've had the belt before. You haven't."

CHAPTER 18

Goldie

Gabriel's heart fluttered as he processed what Owen had said. The burning sensation that the belt inflicted was something Goldie had never experienced. Gabriel knew it would be difficult for him to comprehend the pain Owen was enduring.

"Goldie, with me." He snatched the belt and strode over to the couch.

While Goldie didn't understand, he didn't protest.

Owen whipped his head around, pushing his body off the table. "Father, what the hell? You said that I could take his punishment."

"You will, Owen. This isn't punishment. I will give Goldie ten licks with the belt so he knows how it feels." Gabriel propped one foot up on the couch and tugged his wrist. "Over my knee, son."

Gabriel gripped the belt in his hand while Goldie positioned himself over Gabriel's knee. Gabriel wasted no time disciplining him. He tore off Goldie's shirt and pulled down his sweatpants and underwear. He snapped the belt down on the middle of Goldie's back without hesitation.

Owen heard the belt meet Goldie's flesh, and he cringed. He wanted to save him from the pain. Goldie winced in agony as the belt struck his back, feeling as though it had cut a deep gash across his skin. The pain was unbearable, and he couldn't help but let out a cry that echoed through the room. The lashes continued to rain down on him, each more intense than the previous. Goldie whimpered and wriggled, attempting to escape the torment. A harsh lash landed on his lower thigh, causing him to go limp, his body draped over Gabriel's knee.

Gabriel laid down the final two lashes under the under curve of Goldie's backside. He dropped the belt before righting his clothes and plucking his son off his knee.

"F-Father," Goldie choked out, "please—please don't do that to O—to Owen. Please."

"Son, stand at the head of the table next to Owen."

With a whimper, Goldie moved over to the head of the table and took Owen's hand once more, tears still spilling from his eyes. "Owen, I am so, so sorry."

Owen flashed another reassuring smile toward him, but he remained silent this time. He maintained steady eye contact with Goldie for a prolonged moment before lowering his head again and shutting his eyes.

The absence of words lingered in the air, followed by the piercing sound of the belt slicing through the atmosphere and striking Owen's back. Despite the pain, Owen suppressed any vocal response. His grip on Goldie's hand tightened as he tried to remind himself of the reasons that led him to this moment.

"I'm sorry, Owen," Goldie whispered each time the belt connected with Owen's flesh.

After seven lashes, Gabriel paused. He snapped his fingers to get Goldie's attention. "Goldie, he knows you're sorry. Remember the rules, son."

The warning was gentle. Again, Goldie cried out. "I'm sorry, please, Father, don't... I didn't mean to speak; I'm sorry!"

Goldie's breath hitched and became shallow. He put one hand on Owen's soft hair, trying to calm himself. This was too much for Goldie. He had caused Owen's pain.

"I'm so sorry, Father."

"I will not add extra for that, okay? But Goldie," Gabriel made sure that his son was paying attention. He met Goldie's eyes before continuing, "mind your tongue. Your tongue got all of us in this situation." He paused and gestured to Owen, lying limp over the pillows. "This whole thing is to remind you to mind your tongue."

Goldie swallowed hard and nodded. "Yes, Father."

Gabriel's conviction was unwavering. He believed that Goldie's inability to keep quiet was the root cause of their current predicament.

Goldie closed his eyes but refocused. If Owen dared to endure the punishment on behalf of him, then Goldie was determined to be just as brave. He wanted to make Owen proud.

Gabriel understood Owen could adapt to any situation, whereas Goldie was more delicate. Goldie grappled with his emotions and required more support than Owen had. Gabriel speculated that this might be because of Goldie growing up without a mother, unlike Owen, who had a few years with their mother, Alessia.

With methodical precision, Gabriel administered each stroke of the belt. He followed a consistent pattern, starting from the top of Owen's back and working his way down, stopping above the backs of Owen's knees. Gabriel timed himself, watching for any signs of distress from his sons. He knew his boys well and understood their individual needs during times of punishment. Yet, this case was different. Gabriel recognized that, for this to work, Owen needed to shed tears. Gabriel would continue disciplining Owen until he heard sniffles; it was crucial for Goldie's sake.

Owen proved to be a challenging puzzle to solve, but he understood it would all end once he surrendered to his punishment. He knew that shedding a few tears wouldn't work. He recognized Goldie needed to witness his older brother, whom he admired, completely shattered.

After five minutes and countless strokes, Owen still refused to break. He wasn't giving in at all. Damn stubborn Philip pride.

"Goldie," Gabriel said, looking at Goldie again, "go get me a washcloth and a small bowl of cold water."

Goldie's silence persisted as the punishment continued without further tears. He believed he had shed every tear he had within him. Despite Owen's tight grip on his hand, Goldie remained resolute, determined to match his brother's strength. The pain inflicted upon Owen by the whipping outweighed Goldie's own discomfort. Although his body still stung from the lashes and chastisement, it was the torment in his mind that plagued Goldie the most.

Goldie's attention was diverted when Gabriel's voice broke the silence. He had been so engrossed in Owen's suffering that he had forgotten about Gabriel's presence. Upon hearing the command, Goldie snapped his head up and hastened to comply.

Grateful for the temporary respite, Goldie went to the bathroom, his mind set on finding a washcloth.

Oblivious to the stack of washcloths placed on the shelf next to the shower, his thoughts consumed him. He only wanted to awaken from his current state, locate Owen, and protect Drake. These thoughts stirred up a fresh wave of tears, overwhelming him.

Goldie's piercing screams of "Wake up" echoed through the room, reverberating off the walls as if he were pleading for someone to respond. With each cry, his voice grew more desperate, filled with a sense of urgency that seemed to consume him. The sheer intensity of his screams was enough to send shivers down anyone's spine, as if he was pouring every ounce of his being into those words.

After a short while, Goldie found a washcloth and brought the water bowl to Gabriel. Gabriel accepted the cloth from Goldie but requested him to hold on to the bowl. Looking into Goldie's eyes, he could sense a mixture of curiosity and fear.

Goldie did not understand what was about to unfold.

Goldie stood by, observing as Gabriel submerged the washcloth into the bowl. He then squeezed out the excess water before wrapping the cloth around his hand again. Gabriel took the cloth with his other hand and coated the strap with the cold water, ensuring every inch was soaked. Once satisfied, he dipped the cloth into the water again, refraining from wringing it out. Holding it above Owen's upper back, he squeezed the cloth, letting the water trickle down.

The cold water caused Owen to yelp. "Oh, fuck!" He had kept quiet until that moment. The shock of the water was startling. "Father, what are you doing?"

A deep sense of terror overwhelmed him, causing his heart to tighten. The sheer intensity of fear in Owen's voice took Goldie aback.

"Owen, do you trust me?" Gabriel stilled his hand, but kept the cloth over Owen's back.

"Y-yes, Father," he replied in a shaky voice.

"How about you, Goldie? Do you trust me?"

"Yes, Father. Of course." Goldie didn't need to think about the answer; he knew what Gabriel wanted to hear.

"Good."

Owen was taken aback when the belt struck his shoulders once more. The unexpectedness of the blow caused him to emit a sound that he would have been embarrassed by had he known it came from his own mouth. In response to the pain, his body instinctively tensed, and he jerked upward. "Father, please!" he yelped, trying to push himself up off the table.

Owen couldn't hold back the tears as the first lick landed on his shoulders. The pain was unbearable, even for him. Desperate for relief, he turned to Gabriel, locking eyes with him and begging for mercy. Gabriel pressed on Owen's left shoulder, forcing him to lay face-down on the table again. Without hesitation, he brought the belt down on Owen's upper back, causing another wave of agony to surge through his body.

Gabriel knew that the combination of water on Owen's back and the belt would amplify the pain tenfold.

After three strikes of the belt on his shoulders, Owen was sobbing. When he felt Owen reaching out for him, Goldie dropped the bowl and knelt beside his brother. He hushed Owen, attempting to provide comfort by rubbing his thumb on Owen's hand.

"Owen, it's okay. You're okay. I'm sorry, Owen." Goldie's voice was soft; he thought nobody could hear him.

Owen's shoulders were subjected to two more forceful strokes before Gabriel finally ceased his actions. He dropped the belt onto the table as he made his way to the opposite end, near Goldie. In a display of approval, Gabriel squeezed Owen's bicep and ran his hand through his hair. A moment of silence followed as Gabriel observed both boys, assessing the situation.

Owen remained motionless on the table, unashamed of his vulnerable state as Gabriel's gaze lingered upon him. Despite his loud cries, Owen had regained composure and attempted to calm himself after a few minutes, yet the burning sensation from the belt's impact on his shoulders persisted even after Gabriel had ceased his actions. The pain was so intense that Owen refrained from speaking or making any movements.

Goldie continued to make quiet, gentle noises to comfort his brother. "Owen, I'm so sorry." He clasped Owen's hand, providing a reassuring touch to let him know he was by his side.

Gabriel released his grip and approached the compact kitchen, deciding he would not help the boys clean up from the punishment.

CHAPTER 19

Toy

Bonnie's description of the naked teenagers was accurate but not comprehensive. Not only were they completely naked, but they were not human. These peculiar beings shared a single body, two heads attached to a large, deformed body, the skin a grotesque shade of puke-green. A secure metal gate separated Toy and Bonnie from them as the monsters discussed how they would divide and devour them. Toy and Bonnie had no intention of sticking around for a conversation. They descended the stairs and ventured into the unpleasant-smelling area.

There were a handful of spirits here. They didn't acknowledge Bonnie and Toy's presence at all. As Bonnie and Toy continued, they came across a shocking sight: a lifeless body impaled on the stone wall. It was a teenager, another boy their age, with burned flesh and empty eye sockets. Attached to his chest was a note. Bonnie glanced at it and shook his head before he led Toy to an unlocked cell at the end of the row.

"There's a hole in the wall that we can fit through."

Toy squeezed through the narrow gap between the stones. She couldn't help but wince when her shoes made a loud thud on the pipes hidden behind the cell. The atmosphere in this cramped space was hot and dense. She was already struggling to catch her breath, and Bonnie slid in beside her, adding to the tightness of the surroundings.

Before Bonnie gripped the edge of the upper floor, he handed Toy the flashlight. With determination, he lifted himself up enough to clear his head over the cement. His grip on the edge was short-lived as he let go upon glimpsing something above.

In a split second, Toy decided—she dropped the flashlight and extended her arms, ready to catch him. The thought of both of them crashing to the ground was terrifying. Bonnie regained his balance by grabbing onto the pipes. Toy remained steady, refusing to leave his side. He tipped back into her with a pained grunt, his landing nearly snapping Toy's arms off at the elbows.

"Oh, hey," Bonnie gasped, turning his head. "You caught me." He was surprised, blinking at her as he straightened.

"Well, you know, catching heroes in certain distress..." A slight grimace appeared on her face. The discomfort was no more intense than the other sensations coursing through her body. "...is one of my many talents, my friend."

Toy reached for the flashlight and looked at Bonnie. She wondered if whatever he saw up there was as terrible as it seemed. She squinted to look at him better. He ran his hand over the back of his neck and avoided eye contact. Then she noticed a crimson blush creeping up his neck, causing his face to darken.

Was Bonnie actually blushing? What on earth? This made even less sense.

Toy shook her head, convinced that her eyes must be deceiving her. Her comment was meant to be a joke, so why would it elicit such a reaction from him?

"Anyway, yeah." He roughly cleared his throat. "Thanks for not letting me crack my skull open. I had this idea that something was up there, but it still surprised me when I saw them."

"Uh...them?" Toy's frown deepened. "Is that a non-violent them, or should we look for a new way to go before they serve us with baked beans and a nice beer? Because most of the rooms here are locked."

He glanced toward the hole in the ceiling again and shrugged. "As far as I know, we should be okay. There are three or four pretty spaced-out spirits up there, but I'm pretty confident they will leave us alone." He chuckled. "Nice reference, there."

A raspy giggle echoed from the floor above, the unsettling sound followed by the harsh sound of a hand striking flesh and then a muffled sob. Although Toy could feel the warmth from the nearby piping system, a sudden chill ran through her body as the faint, swirling steam surrounded her. Her grip on the flashlight tightened, and she could feel her hand becoming moist with sweat.

"Let's not drag our heels and make friends with the locals, okay?" Toy gulped. "I never thought that I'd say this...but can we go somewhere else in the asylum, please?"

"That sounds like a brilliant idea," Bonnie agreed. "We were due to come up with one."

Navigating through the spirits proved to be a challenge. They aimed to avoid attracting any more attention to them. Their priority was to distance themselves from the two individuals who were engaged in a disturbing blood ritual on a lifeless body. Bonnie and Toy escaped through a rugged opening and proceeded along a lit corridor. They traversed a narrow ledge alongside where the floor had completely collapsed. The experience was physically and mentally exhausting. Toy was so preoccupied with checking behind her she almost overlooked a sign on the far wall, stained with a drying red substance.

"'*God always provides away*,'" Bonnie read. "Follow the blood... That's great..." He nodded at a weird-looking hall to their left with grated steel floors and bright yellow lights.

"Into the decontamination chamber we go, *niña*. The blood trails, I hope, will lead us to the exit."

Toy glanced at the bloodied words and then looked at the sealed room. "Yeah... That's the part that has me worried, baby."

"I'm always worried about this place," he admitted with a touch of sarcasm that did little to hide the concern lurking underneath his tone.

"Likewise," Toy muttered.

As they stepped inside, the chamber sealed shut, enclosing them within its walls. A chemical was released into the air, only to be sucked back out before the doors unlocked. The entire process happened in seconds, leaving them bewildered by its strangeness. Toy couldn't help but worry that whatever they inhaled might have been harmful to their survival. In this asylum, nothing seemed to be as it appeared.

The air was silent as they ascended at least two flights of stairs on the other side. Toy discovered a fortunate find amidst the debris they passed—a pair of batteries. It was a stroke of luck, a rare occurrence in this place.

Upon reaching the top of the stairs, their eyes met a solitary figure standing beside a bucket. Dread filled Toy's mind as she realized what the bucket's contents might be. She hoped that it was thick red paint that the man was smearing across the wall, yet a lifeless teen in the room with them shattered any hope Toy had left. It was blood...

This situation keeps getting worse.

The painting man muttered, "Down the hole," while scratching his nails into the peeling plaster covered in blood. His message pointed to yet another hole in the floor.

Bonnie and Toy approached the scene, intrigued by the cryptic message. The corridors in this area were illuminated, sparing them the need to waste their limited supply of batteries for the flashlight.

"See anything?" Bonnie asked, brows furrowed.

Toy took a knee and squinted deeper into the oily yellow gloom. "More blood. What a surprise. And...the locked door to another decontamination chamber, but that's it."

"Okay. Down the hole, then."

He knelt beside her and jumped down. Without a moment's hesitation, Toy followed suit. The impact reverberated through their ankles, causing a sharp, stinging pain to surge through their bodies. Suppressing an uncomfortable grimace, Toy gathered herself and stood upright once more. Bonnie had already positioned himself at the corner, peering into what appeared to be a holding area. Curiosity piqued, Toy joined him at the entrance. While most of the lit cells within the cramped space were unoccupied, one was inhabited.

Nestled in the darkest corner, it wasn't a spirit who cowered there. Instead, it was another kid, huddled with their legs pulled to their chest, swaying back and forth. Their shredded clothes and torn nails, along with bloodied sores, covered their scalp and face.

"Ah, fuck," Bonnie muttered. "Hey...kid?" he called out. "Hey, are you all right? Do you want some help?"

Leaning against Bonnie's arm, Toy bit her lip.

The boy didn't acknowledge their presence. He continued to rock back and forth, lost in his own world. Toy wondered how long he had been trapped in this place. Was he a glimpse into the bleak future that awaited them if they didn't find a way out?

Bonnie approached the boy in the cell, and Toy followed, keeping a few steps away. While Bonnie engaged with the boy through the solid steel bars, Toy took a moment to search through the computer desk. Amongst the papers and clutter, she found a battery.

"Toy."

She slipped the battery into her pocket and moved closer to Bonnie. She looked and saw yet another one of those intriguing tattoos on the child's right wrist: *O-R11s14.*

"Has he said anything?" Toy asked, not wanting to get too close to the cell. "There weren't any keys on the desk. I don't know how we'd be able to spring him from this."

Bonnie shook his head, his handsome features creased with aching sympathy. "Not yet. We could—"

"No. No, no, no, no."

The two of them shared a concerned look before redirecting their attention to the child. His rocking motion had stopped, and now his vacant, lifeless eyes were fixed upon them. It was as if he was looking at them, or right through them.

"No, no, no. Can't get out. Can't let me out," he said, and his voice was a rasp of sandpaper grinding against his throat. "Have to stay to keep her safe. Have to stay, have to stay... Keep her safe. Please, please...keep her safe." Dark tears leaked from one of his infected eyes as his pointed ears twitched.

"Keep who safe?" Bonnie wondered. "What happened?"

The kid whimpered. "Ki'ki. Ki'ki... They took her from me. I held her...and she was gone. We were so close. We were so close!" The sound that escaped his lungs was a tight, gasping sob. A desperate cry that resonated with pure hopelessness.

The sound sent shivers down Toy's spine, so unlike anything she had ever heard before. It surpassed the rabid shrieks that echoed in this eerie place; surpassed the mournful cries of the spirits that haunted these halls. The sound was something else...a raw and broken expression of despair, a haunting reminder of a life devoid of hope or purpose.

Toy stood there, unable to tear her attention away from the heart-wrenching scene. She felt a deep sense of dread wash over her. The grip of Bonnie's hand was firm and sweaty, a physical manifestation of the fear that coursed through both of them.

"They told me they could save her," the boy continued as he rocked again. "That they could bring her back, but... I couldn't... Be with her. Couldn't see her anymore. They told me… I had to stay," he whispered. "I have to stay here to keep her safe, Ki'ki. And I will, I always will… Ki'ki…"

The silence descended and remained unbroken until Bonnie and Toy moved away from the holding area.

"God…" Bonnie broke the depressing silence. He rubbed at his bloodshot eyes but still didn't let go of her hand. "Who's saying if those assholes kept their word? His girlfriend might still be dead, and he promised to stay trapped in this hell for nothing."

As they approached the doorway, a bright red EXIT sign loomed above, emitting an unsettling buzzing sound.

"Maybe they did succeed, in a way. Maybe they reached the end, but she still died," Toy said. "And maybe he was given a choice: be free without her…or stay here while she went back instead."

Bonnie fixed his gaze on Toy, and his face took on a sudden intensity that made it difficult to decipher his emotions. His expression hardened. "Stop it," he growled.

Toy gave him a disapproving look, attempting to free her hand. To continue, they had to navigate around a misaligned table obstructing the way. It was impossible to climb over it while they were still holding hands.

"Stop what?"

Toy found herself in a state of confusion as his grip on her tightened, prompting her to look down.

"Whatever you're thinking about…just stop it. We're both getting out of this, okay? We're both going to get out, and we're both going to go home," he said, and tugged Toy away from the table and right back into his personal space, his hand leaving hers only to wrap around her upper arm.

Toy's heart jumped, and her pulse tripped through her veins as his magenta eyes held her immobile. They were standing a little too close together, and his hand was scorching against her skin, and Toy had never seen him look so serious before…

"No one is staying behind, you hear me?" His low voice hummed with perfect clarity down her spine, and Toy felt a rush of heat spill across her face.

"What if something happens?" Toy mumbled. Something would happen, she knew it. Despite trying to avoid envisioning the worst possible outcomes, Toy couldn't resist. Although she was optimistic, they had to prepare themselves for any situation.

"Nothing is going to fucking happen!" he whispered, as if stricken by the mere thought. He stuck the flashlight into his back pocket and shook her. "Look, if something does—which it won't—and they give you a choice...you have to promise me you will leave. No matter what, *niña*. You promise me you will leave this nightmare behind." His eyes filled with darkness and intensity, overwhelmed by emotions.

"No." Toy shook her head and stepped back. She didn't even realize she was shivering until his hands were no longer on her shoulders. "You can't. You can't ask me to promise you something that stupid because I won't do it."

He opened his mouth, his growing frustration clear as he tried to approach Toy again. But she took another step toward the table, shaking her head even faster.

"No! Bonnie. If they give me some screwed-up option to save your life for mine, don't you think I'd take it? I wouldn't even hesitate!"

"And you think I wouldn't?" he snapped. "You think I wouldn't do the same fucking thing if our positions were reversed? I wouldn't let anyone give their life for mine, especially not someone that—" He cut himself off with a curse, raking his hands through his hair.

"You know what?" Toy leaned against the table and crossed her arms. A tired sigh buckled her posture as her pulse slowed to a normal pace. "We are actually arguing about which one of us gets to die for the other... We have no idea if what happened to that kid and his partner is going to happen to us."

Bonnie's gaze fixed on her, he approached and sat beside her on the outskirts of the scattered wreckage. They remained in that desolate, blood-stained corridor for what felt like an eternity, enveloped in silence. The dim, lifeless yellow lights cast a somber atmosphere around their weary bodies.

"I'm sorry," he said finally, his voice worn thin.

"Yeah. I am, too," Toy whispered. She hesitated after she dropped her arms, then reached out and fit her hand over his.

He nodded, his gaze falling to their linked hands. "We'll be all right, *niña*. We're... We're going to get through this, and we're going to be fine."

"I know." Toy gave him a small smile when he looked down at her again. "We'll be fine."

He smiled back, and it hurt to see how sad and dark the expression on his face was.

CHAPTER 20

Toy

Trying to readjust their routine felt awkward, but Bonnie and Toy found their rhythm. They communicated more through actions than words: a quick smile, a comforting touch on his arm, a guiding hand on her waist. After being in the asylum for so long, they both had concerns about being trapped there.

The corridor led to more locked rooms and another security booth, both guarded by roaming spirits they knew would chase them if they were not careful. The first spirit was occupied by trying to attack another teen, so they avoided him, but the second spirit was more intelligent and observant. Bonnie and Toy had to hide in lockers and wait for him to leave before they could enter the next security booth.

Bonnie pressed a large red button among the various dials and switches on the counter as Toy watched the monitors. Oversized red buttons bring trouble, but this one opened the decontamination chamber in the hallway.

The eerie messages instructed them to follow the trail of blood, so they retraced their steps through the chamber. As they entered a new hallway, a drawn red arrow pointed deeper into the darkness, which was not exactly reassuring. Unfortunately, they had no other options.

It was hard to ignore the unsettling presence of the naked monster-twin thing, resembling an ogre that almost slipped Toy's mind. When they turned the corner, they were met with a dead end, and there they were. They watched Toy and Bonnie from behind a locked metal gate, discussing who would have Bonnie's liver and tongue, while the other seems fixated on Toy's eyes and fingers.

"This is... I don't know. Is this flattering?" Toy nudged Bonnie in the side as they took cover in the shadows next to a headless guard lost in an ocean of his own thick, crimson blood. "I feel like I should thank them before I tell them to screw off or something."

He snorted, flashing her a pearly white smirk. "No, *niña*. It's not flattering. Someone wants to gouge your eyeballs and serve them in a delicate mushroom sauce. That's one of those bad things that we talked about."

Rolling her eyes, Toy hit him on the arm. "All right, wise guy. What's our next move? We can't turn back; hopefully, that gate will remain locked forever."

Bonnie, always the gentleman, responded by tickling her. "As a matter of fact, I think we can shimmy along the edge of the windows and climb up behind the naked teens," he said, his voice mockingly bright. "Don't say that we do nothing fun now."

For a moment, Toy wanted to lean closer. She missed kissing him, holding him, not being afraid that one simple moment of love would be their downfall. Their heads were almost touching as she spoke and all she would need to do is lean a little closer...but Toy knew she shouldn't think like this in this place. She glanced behind her, embarrassed, as she took a deep breath. They couldn't afford any distractions, especially not this one. It would only make things more complicated because of emotions. Emotions always ruin everything. Gosh, she sounded like her mother...

"Shimmying. Windows," Toy repeated, mimicking his

exaggerated cheer. "Avoiding the dinner menu. Yep, sounds like our kind of thing, baby. Let's go."

They proceed forward, navigating the narrow ledge beside the gate. It was not as terrifying as they expected, yet Toy couldn't help but think of other activities that would be more enjoyable, considering one wrong step could lead to a fatal fall. She made the mistake of glancing downward. Lesson learned: never look down. They climbed through another open window on the opposite side. There were no signs of the naked thing's whereabouts. They found more locked rooms, computers, a battery, and even more bloodstains. As Toy was about to follow a second arrow painted on the wall, Bonnie pulled on her arm.

"Wait, there's a locked door around that corner," he told her.

"How do you know?"

"The heavy lock at the top of the door is present, which means it's locked." He paused, making a weird face.

"I bet we must go through this busted decontamination chamber and find a key."

"Damn. These are stupid; why can't the same key work for all of them?!"

"Your nice, enjoyable company may work on it," Toy deadpanned. "So, why haven't I left you behind?"

"Because I'm smart, strong, and handsome...and you'd miss me too much?" He counted the reasons on his fingers and scrunched up his nose. "Hey, wait a minute. You think my company is enjoyable?" He shot her a sly smile. "Well, that might be one of the sweetest things you've ever said to me, niña."

Toy passed him and entered the room ahead, shaking her head and trying to ignore the slight redness of her face. She hoped he didn't notice. "Savor the moment, and let's continue, okay?"

"Oh, I'm definitely savoring it," he murmured behind her,

making her giggle, and she was glad he couldn't hear the sudden thwack of her heart punching into her ribs.

They found themselves on a quiet, dimly lit pathway to a second cell block. Only a few spirits wandered around, and Toy peered through the fence links that kept them from falling onto the floor below. Bonnie moved to the opposite side of the pathway, twenty feet away from Toy, and paused next to a lifeless body leaning against the wall. He appeared to know what he was doing, so Toy stayed back and waited.

Toy covered her mouth in shock, her eyes widening with fear. Kieran was below them. Not only that, but he was dragging someone by their hair. The remaining spirits scattered into the corners as he halted beneath the lights. It was as if they were also afraid of him.

Kieran muttered something unintelligible and then threw his victim onto the floor in front of him. It was difficult to discern, but... Oh. Oh no—this one was a girl. Toy's fingers tightened over her mouth as all the warmth drained from her body.

The girl was dirty, and her shirt was missing, blue and black bruises covering her skin. She got to her knees, crying out for someone named Negan, blood dripping from her chin. Kieran watched her feeble attempt to escape, a laugh rumbling from his chest. He allowed her to crawl almost to safety.

Toy watched as the girl reached out to one spirit, uttering the name "Negan." She extended her hand, brushing her fingers through, and a scream escaped her as blackened veins crawled up her arm. Kieran grabbed her ankle and dragged her back into the center of the room, where everyone could witness her death.

Was that the consequence of touching the spirits without the "power"? Toy was oblivious to Bonnie's hesitation and urgency to leave. All she heard was the sound of a head being violently torn off its body and a deafening silence that followed.

Kieran threw the twisted skull at the metal fencing,

exactly where Toy was moments ago. She couldn't believe he spotted them. Holding Bonnie's hand, they sprinted out of the cell block, not understanding what was happening but feeling disoriented as the scene around them spun. The walls trembled in a small room, another security booth, and red lights flashed. The piercing alarm forced Toy to cover her ears. She had no idea what was happening, but her eyes searched for any movement, causing her head to ache.

Inside the decontamination chamber, Kieran found himself trapped, unable to escape. Owen's once-vibrant gray eyes now appeared dark and black as sinister darkness engulfed his irises, spreading from the outer edges toward the center. With immense force, Kieran's body collided with the dividing glass, causing it to crack. The sound of the impact startled Toy, causing her to flinch and seek refuge among the nearby shelves instinctively. A wave of panic, reminiscent of a metallic taste, overwhelmed her.

Kieran entered the room with a mischievous laugh, his hands raised. As he did so, the ground beneath them trembled, accompanied by a piercing screech that filled the air. Amid this chaos, something broke open in the adjacent room, and a horde of spirits rushed in, flooding the chamber.

"Oh, no. Oh, no!" Toy squeaked.

"Toy!" someone yelled, sounding partly shocked and partly terrified out of their mind. "Holy shit—turn around! Turn the fuck around and get up here!"

Bonnie.

Without conscious thought, Toy's eyes fixated on the open vent beneath the flickering lights and the desk behind her. Bonnie leaned as far as possible without risking falling out, stretching his arms and reaching out for hers.

"My hero."

As an explosion rocked the room, Toy sprinted to the desk, debris flying everywhere. The force of the blast sent sparks flying, singeing her clothes and causing a sharp, stinging sensation. Toy pushed through the pain, focusing on reaching the desk and the safety it provided within the circle of the flashing light. She noticed Bonnie's desperate eyes, the deep gash on his brow, and his sweaty, trembling fingers as they gripped her wrists. In those terrifying moments, Toy had never felt such intense fear in her entire life, kicking her feet and struggling to climb up as the world crumbled around them.

The fear of death consumed Toy, and she could feel the rivers of perspiration streaming down her face. Bonnie, too, was drenched in sweat, his face covered in shiny droplets mixed with blood from his wound. He cursed and screamed at Kieran, who was close behind Toy.

Bonnie saved her, pulling her into the vent at the very last second. He had always been a joker, claiming he wasn't Superman, but in that moment, it was clear that only someone with superhuman strength could have performed such a feat.

"Come on!" he urged.

They both squeezed through the cramped area, colliding with the ceiling. Meanwhile, Kieran's furious cries echoed below as he punched the metal above him. The intensity of his outburst caused their surroundings to creak, groan, and screech. The vent beneath Toy and Bonnie's hands and knees wobbled, giving the impression that the entire world was on the verge of collapsing. At that moment, Toy couldn't help but hope that this wouldn't mark the end of everything.

"Crap, crap, crap!" Toy cursed, wincing when she slipped and tumbled into Bonnie.

"Oof!"

The impact of his body against the wall reverberated through the vent. Toy's nails dug into the fabric of his shirt as they avoided colliding with the corner. Exhausted and overwhelmed, they collapsed onto the ground. The weight of the following silence echoed in her mind like the incessant tolling of church bells. They must have moved away from the security room. Otherwise, Kieran would still be trying to reach them.

Toy's heart pounded in her throat with a rapid and erratic

beat. The sound of a pained groan escaped from Bonnie. He shifted his position until he was on his back, bearing the weight of Toy's body on top of him, her face nestled against his chest.

"Are you...okay?" he whispered.

Toy felt his arms wrap around her, solid and secure, his racing heart a thunderstorm against her ear.

"Yeah, thanks," she mumbled, not wanting to leave the safety of his embrace—and not caring that she was clinging to him. "Are you okay?"

"Mmph," he grunted. "That vent grate fell open right on my head. I think it cut somewhere above my eye... Haven't had the chance to check how bad it is." He lifted a palm and pressed it against his brow, grimacing when he glimpsed the redness on his flesh. "Nothing seems broken, though."

"Head injuries bleed a lot, but it looks pretty shallow." Toy propped her chin on his chest to see him better. She ripped the hem of his shirt and tied it around his head, like Julia had done for her. "There."

"Twinning!" He gave a short laugh, trying to make her smile.

"Um... Do we still have the flashlight? Our life will be much harder without light. One brush, and it's all over..."

"I tossed it up here first. It must have rolled that way." He pointed to the hole about four feet from them, then exhaled a vast, wavering breath. "Fuck, Toy... He ran his hands over his face to rub at his eyes. "That was so...and I thought that..."

His deep magenta eyes met Toy's. There was a noticeable shift in the atmosphere between them at that moment as if unanticipated, tingling energy filled the air, creating a sense of unease within her but also bringing about a certain level of comfort.

"I thought that was it," Bonnie rasped. "I had no idea you fell, and when I looked down again and saw you there with that monster..."

Toy's spine shuddered as a surge of electricity coursed through it. The sensation was so intense that she almost leaped out of her body. His hand rested on her lower back, radiating nervousness and a mysterious blend of emotions Toy couldn't describe. It felt like an explosion of unexplainable feelings rushing through her veins, leaving her both exhilarated and bewildered.

"I have never been so scared," he admitted.

"Me neither," Toy whispered, her face burning underneath his unblinking eyes.

And she still was.

She was so scared.

They untangled their sore and achy limbs and made their way to the end of the vent before descending through the hole and landing on the hard cement floor.

Bonnie grabbed the flashlight while Toy glanced behind him, feeling uneasy and restless. It was as if the entire world was tilted, throwing off her balance.

They didn't have time to exchange words because the door closest to them cracked in its frame. From the other side, they could hear Kieran calling Bonnie a pig and referring to Toy as a...Protector?

"You ready for round two, Bonnie?" She flashed him a strained, lopsided smile.

Toy had had enough. She had become an expert at compartmentalizing her already-chaotic life. If it weren't for her ability to do so, she wouldn't have been able to endure all the challenges that had come her way. With her mother's current situation and the ongoing chaos, Toy's dry sense of humor was her only solace, helping her maintain her sanity and composure. Everything else was locked away in little corners, waiting to be dealt with later, far into the future.

With his broad grin and a bruise above his eye, Bonnie looked unfairly attractive, with a streak of bright red blood on his face. Toy had never seen anyone who exuded such irresistible charm before. It was frustrating and captivating at the same time.

"You go, I go, *niña*," he promised.

Kieran kicked the door off its hinges, creating a loud noise that echoed through the hallway. At that moment, Bonnie and Toy joined hands and sprinted down the corridor, their hearts pounding with adrenaline.

CHAPTER 21

Goldie

Gabriel received an unexpected phone call that disrupted the tranquility of their home. Goldie saw the world through Owen's eyes while also being aware of his younger self, who was known as Goldie Philip rather than Goldie Miller. This duality confused Goldie, as even though it was his younger self, he felt that referring to him as "Goldie" didn't quite fit anymore. Instead, he believed Philip was a more suitable name for this version of himself. Goldie wasn't a Philip anymore, but this younger Goldie still was...

The piercing sound of the phone's ring pulled Owen from his slumber. But Philip, still half-asleep, mumbled and instinctively moved closer to Owen for comfort. Owen lifted his head and gazed at Gabriel, who spoke into the phone and rose from the bed in response to the call. With urgency, Gabriel made his way to the living room, leaving Owen and Philip behind.

"Yes, yes, of course, I'm interested. Hang on a second."

As Gabriel and Owen exchanged a brief glance, the bedroom door closed, leaving Owen unable to decipher Gabriel's words. Owen then resumed his position on the bed, gazing at the ceiling, yet a feeling of unease crept in.

Owen sensed that something was not quite right.

Throughout their lives, Goldie had possessed an uncanny ability to expect when things were about to go awry, relying on his intuition, which had never failed him. This sixth sense had saved Goldie's and Owen's lives, and his instincts urged him to flee, to take Philip and Owen and escape from this place as soon as possible.

Owen's muscles were tense, his body rigid like a board, straining his ears to catch any sounds from the living room. It proved to be futile, as all he could hear was the muffled voice of their abusive father. The intensity left Goldie wondering why he didn't remember this.

After an hour had passed, Gabriel emerged from the living room carrying his go bag and clutching his Bible. He avoided making eye contact with Owen as he spoke, casting an air of tension and uncertainty upon the room.

"I'll be back in a few days. Don't go anywhere."

Owen untangled himself from Philip and explored the room. He searched the nightstand, discovered his Bible, and flipped through its pages. Then he tossed it back in the drawer.

Owen locked the door and moved a chair across the room to prop it beneath the handle. He took the time to check if all the windows were locked. He wanted to ensure that no entry points were left vulnerable. Once satisfied with the security measures, he shifted his attention to the kitchen. Owen inspected the food supplies, noticing some bread had become stale. He also found some meat and cheese and a few soda cans in the refrigerator.

Goldie's gaze shifted back to his younger self, who was still asleep. In Owen's absence, he sprawled across the bed, his long and slender limbs occupying as much space as possible. Faint snoring sounds escaped his open mouth, drool staining the pillow.

Owen's thoughts suddenly came through the memory.

Christ, the kid'll be ten soon. It's like one day he was a toddler. Small and clinging to my hand as we crossed the street, and the next he was turning ten. Teachers keep saying how gifted he was. Every single time, Father went tense, and his eyes went wild. But I didn't have the heart to tell Goldie to knock it off and pretend to be normal.

It was weird for Goldie to hear his brother's thoughts, almost like they were his own.

Both Owen and Philip had school, but Gabriel's sudden departure made Owen anxious and uneasy. Owen was not comfortable letting Philip out of his sight until Gabriel returned. As a result, when Philip finally got out of bed, it was already half past ten. Owen was busy preparing sandwiches by microwaving bologna.

"Where's Father?" Philip asked almost immediately.

Owen glanced over and almost winced at Philip's face, drawn tight with worry.

It's only been a few months since Goldie got thrown into the world of the church and realized what Father and I have been doing his whole life. The different ways Father has been trying to get rid of this demon nearly killed Goldie a couple of months ago. But I would like to forget that ever happened; it hurts to remember.

What...Goldie nearly died? Gabriel, his own father, almost took his life when he was nine years old! It was hard to fathom. Goldie's only memory of being badly hurt at that age was when Gabriel discovered him injured on the roadside. But now, doubts arise. Could it be possible that Gabriel fabricated the whole incident? Did he inflict such a brutal beating that Goldie's mind repressed the truth?

"He went to help at the church. I promise he'll be back; it's got nothing to do with you."

After a brief pause, Philip gazed at Owen, squinting as he pondered the situation. Owen was known for his honesty, especially with Goldie, but he omitted specific essential facts.

After a moment of contemplation, Philip gave a curt nod and grabbed a set of clothes from the dresser. "I'm gonna shower."

"Go for it—you reek."

After being confined for two days, Philip was growing restless. Unlike Philip, Owen handled the situation better. Philip was sulky, spending most of his time scowling at the television or giving Owen glares. Every time they spoke, Philip would snap at Owen, his voice filled with excessive teenage angst for a nine-year-old, accompanied by sarcastic remarks he had learned from Owen at a young age. Philip possessed a sharp tongue, capable of delivering quick and biting comments, which he wielded like an expert weapon.

Owen ordered pizza as a peace offering. He then asked Philip if he preferred it delivered or if they should go to the restaurant to eat. The mere thought of leaving their cramped, unpleasant home caused Philip's eyes to light up, and he skipped toward the door.

The outing was a success. Philip breathed in some fresh air, and the physical activity helped ease the tension between him and Owen. Although Owen had to spend ten dollars, he considered it worthwhile.

They returned to their house, their steps slow and their stomachs full. Owen wrapped his arm around Philip's shoulders, and Philip leaned into him, gazing up at Owen with a smile that had been absent for the past few days. It was the smile that made Owen feel invincible, like he could conquer anything.

As they turned the corner, Owen sensed Philip's surprise and mixed emotions through the gasp that escaped his lips. Owen followed Philip's gaze and immediately spotted the truck. A frown formed on his face, and his stomach sank. He realized Gabriel was home, and whatever Owen had been dreading all this time was no longer impending.

It was here.

Owen took the lead and entered the house, smiling at Gabriel. Gabriel was upset and furious, and Owen forced himself to step aside and allow Goldie to enter the room.

"Where've you been?" Gabriel demanded. He didn't look

at Philip, but kept his eyes focused on Owen.

"We went out for pizza." Owen shrugged as if it was that easy. It wasn't; he knew it wasn't, but Owen was good at playing pretend.

Gabriel studied him for a moment before he turned away. "Get packed. We're leaving."

Philip acted on autopilot, gathering a selection of clothes, a few books, and his trusty hairbrush. In contrast, Owen stood frozen in place, his eyes fixed on Gabriel with disbelief and astonishment.

Although it may seem insignificant, ordering pizza went against Gabriel's rules. Owen had defied a direct order, breaking the rules, which included not leaving the house when Gabriel was absent. Yet what troubled Owen the most was Gabriel's clear lack of concern.

When Owen took Philip outside, he put him in danger. Gabriel should have been angry, shouting, lecturing, and calling Owen irresponsible and reckless, but he didn't, leaving Owen confused about how to handle the situation.

"Owen." Gabriel's voice was hard as steel and sharp like a dagger. It cut through Owen's thoughts and the haze of confusion building in him. "Get to it."

Owen started moving, but he couldn't shake the building dread.

The car was filled with tension as they embarked on a long drive. The absence of music only amplified the uncomfortable silence and grated on Owen's nerves.

Gabriel was wholly absorbed in the task of driving, gripping the steering wheel with white knuckles. Owen sat beside him, on edge and anticipating something. Meanwhile, poor Philip was in the back seat, feeling helpless, confused, and distressed, with a pinched expression.

"Father." Philip's barely audible voice was filled with guilt, yet it contrasted with the silence and disrupted the tranquility.

Owen turned to Philip, but the only sign that Gabriel

heard him was his grip tightening on the steering wheel.

Philip licked his lips, his eyes shifting between the back of Gabriel's head and Owen's. "Father, I have to pee."

Gabriel pressed harder on the accelerator, and Philip looked pained.

Owen bit his lip and cleared his throat. "Hey, um. Father? Could we stop? I have to pee too."

Gabriel glanced at him, then his eyes flickered to the rear-view mirror to meet Philip's gaze. "Almost there, Owen. Wait."

Owen's awareness of time and distance became overwhelming as he gazed out the window, fixating on mile markers. As they reached mile forty, Philip showed discomfort, causing Owen to clench his fists. At sixty, Philip's pain intensified, with his eyes shut and his fingers gripping his pants. By ninety, the smell of urine filled the air, and Philip appeared humiliated. Owen stopped counting, realizing that Gabriel only intended to stop once they reached their destination.

Overwhelmed with anger, fear, and confusion, Owen stared out the window. After three more hours, Gabriel finally stopped before a church. It cast a shadow with its impressive steeple as the sun set. Owen and Goldie had always hated churches, angels, and God.

It must be a meeting, Owen decided. *Churches usually mean church...stuff; it could be as simple as that.*

Gabriel exited the vehicle and headed toward the trunk while Owen ignored it. He got out, pushing the seat forward and helping Philip get out. Philip appeared unsteady on his legs, with a wet and tear-streaked face. His clothes were drenched and unpleasant, but Owen didn't react. He put his arm around Philip's shoulders, intending to guide him inside. Gabriel appeared and grabbed Philip's arm, pulling him away from Owen.

"You stay here, Owen." Gabriel's voice was firm, void of emotion.

Owen's heart raced as he watched Gabriel push Philip into

the church. The heavy doors slammed shut, leaving Owen with a glimpse of Philip's pale and frightened face. Restless, Owen paced back and forth, kicking up dust. He bit his lower lip, tasting the metallic tang of blood. After what felt like an eternity, Owen circled the church and peered through a distorted stained-glass window. He struggled to make out the figures of Gabriel and Philip, with Gabriel's imposing presence overshadowing Philip's smaller form.

Owen wasted no time and started moving, circling the church. Toward the rear, he discovered a cellar door and lifted the heavy wooden door from the ground. He then descended the steps into a musty cellar, where the air was thick with dust.

Owen stifled a cough by covering his mouth with his shoulder. He made a makeshift mask by pulling his jacket sleeve over his hand to filter the air he breathed. The darkness in the cellar made it challenging to see, with only a faint glow coming from the open door behind Owen and the sun setting. As he explored the basement, Owen felt the walls until he came across a ladder, which gave him hope that there might be an entrance to the church. He climbed the ladder and opened the trapdoor above him, peering into the church.

Gabriel paced back and forth while Philip lay motionless on the ground. Nearby was a water basin, likely used for baptisms, and an altar with a heavy Bible and a towering cross. Gabriel grabbed Philip again. As he dragged Philip to the cellar, Owen closed the trapdoor and hid against the wall. The door above was torn away, revealing Gabriel's angry face before Philip was thrown through the opening, landing on the floor with a muffled cry.

"Stay there," Gabriel said, his voice low. His eyes remained on Philip, taking in the trembling of his limbs. "If you run, I'll make you regret it."

Gabriel closed the door, causing the remaining light to disappear.

Owen immediately embraced Philip. "Shush," Owen told him, and Philip immediately stilled. "It's okay."

"Owen," he croaked. "Owen, Father... He's—"

"I know, Goldie. I know."

Owen's mind raced, searching for a solution. He considered whisking Philip away through the alternate exit, up the stairs, and into the Chevy. They could escape, leaving Gabriel and this fucked-up situation behind. Yet uncertainty loomed. Where would they go? How could they ensure their safety if they were alone?

"We're going to get out of here, Goldie," Owen told Philip. "Okay?"

Philip looked up at Owen, eyes wide and trusting. He nodded, slow and hesitant, and whispered, "Okay."

Then came a menacing voice. "You aren't going anywhere, son..."

CHAPTER 22

Goldie

Owen's eyes widened in horror as he spun around to find Gabriel in the doorway. Gabriel's presence was overwhelming and intimidating. Philip, in Owen's arms, whimpered and clung to him. Gabriel walked forward and separated the brothers, both of them crying out as he took Philip and carried him through the cellar. Owen tried to follow, but the door slammed shut above him, refusing to open. He tried the trapdoor to find it locked as well. He heard Philip screaming for him, but the sound stopped. Through a crack in the trapdoor, Owen saw Gabriel taking out a syringe and preparing to inject Philip. Philip tried to resist and escape Gabriel's grip but was held down as Gabriel injected him with the needle.

Within seconds, the effects became clear as Philip slipped into unconsciousness. Owen found himself on his hands and knees, expelling the meager contents of his stomach due to a combination of exhaustion, fear, and helplessness. Overwhelmed by these emotions, he collapsed onto his side, completely drained.

After some time had passed, Owen woke up. His throat and nose stung from the acidic remnants of his stomach. His eyes itched from unnoticed tears, and he tasted salt. With great effort, he rose to his feet, using one hand to wipe away the evidence of his distress from his face.

A sudden realization dawned upon Owen—Gabriel intended to hurt Philip, and Owen was the sole person capable of saving him. Owen found himself at a moral crossroads, faced with an unfair decision. But honesty had been scarce in Owen's life, and he understood that there was no decision to be made.

Owen had always relied on Gabriel as his source of strength. This fearless warrior fought against the malevolent demons that threatened the church community, including vulnerable individuals like Goldie and Mother. Gabriel's presence ensured that no other family had to endure the same hardships and torments. Owen, compelled by blind loyalty, followed his father's lead and placed unwavering faith in him.

Yet, despite all that Gabriel was to Owen, Goldie held an even more significant place in his heart. Goldie was Owen's sanctuary, the beacon of light in his otherwise dark and gloomy world. Goldie embodied innocence, something that Owen himself lost at a very young age. Goldie was the reason for Owen's existence.

Goldie meant everything to Owen. He would confront any adversary, even if it meant standing up against Gabriel Philip himself. Owen understood that this was a battle he could not afford to lose. At that moment, he felt a surge of confidence, standing tall and empowered.

The silence was shattered by a piercing scream, a sound that Owen was all too familiar with from years of nightmares and abuse. The chilling cry sent shivers down Owen's spine, and he realized what had woken him up.

Gabriel had started.

Owen found himself paralyzed with fear, unable to move as he listened to the agonizing screams of his baby brother. Gabriel was adept at manipulating and exploiting people under the guise of helping them, all in the name of his faith. The victims would reach a breaking point, their cries of pain echoing in his ears. Owen's knowledge and skills in this twisted art had been passed down to him from his father. But he knew he still had yet to learn everything. While torture could lead to death, Owen understood, if executed skillfully, it could inflict far worse.

The power of pain was not to be underestimated. It could drive a person to the brink of insanity, shattering them in ways they never thought possible. Philip, Owen's brother, was a vulnerable and broken child.

Owen's frustration boiled over as he snarled at the thought of being trapped in the cellar any longer. In a fit of anger, he twisted his body and slammed his fist into the unyielding stone wall. The force of the impact split the skin on his knuckles. Despite his desperate roar of anger and fear, it did little to ease his emotions or free him from his confinement.

Owen hung his head in the darkness, battling the overwhelming urge to collapse onto the floor. However, a glimmer of determination flickered within him amidst his despair. He knew he was not helpless; he'd been trained since childhood to be prepared for any situation, much like a Boy Scout. Owen's confidence in his abilities surged as he recalled his past successes in evading Gabriel's watchful eye to spend time with a girl. With a resolute hand outstretched before him, Owen navigated to the other side of the cellar, feeling the cold stone beneath his fingers.

After a moment, his hand found the wooden bars and the rough rope that held the ladder together. Without hesitation, he climbed. As he reached the top, he realized something heavy obstructed the trapdoor. Undeterred, Owen pushed himself higher, using his shoulder to exert pressure against the door. The awkward angle strained his neck, but he persevered, determined to find the leverage he needed.

The trapdoor creaked open, causing a deafening noise that reverberated through the room. A sudden burst of blinding light engulfed Owen, causing him to squint and shield his eyes. Hanging from a sturdy wooden beam above him was a massive chandelier adorned with lit candles that emitted a bright light. It caused Owen's eyes to sting and tear up.

The intensity of the light overwhelmed Goldie, who experienced a sharp wave of pain as Owen fixated on the fiery glow emanating from the chandelier. Although Owen's body showed no signs of discomfort, Goldie's mind screamed in agony.

Determined to escape, Owen pushed himself against the door again, and this time, it gave way, allowing him to struggle out of the cellar. Still blinking to clear his vision, Owen looked upward, only to evade Gabriel's foot aimed at his head. Their scuffle was brief. Despite his youth and training, Owen was disoriented by the blinding light, yet still landed two solid punches before Gabriel overpowered him. The sound of metal clicking against metal filled the air, and as Gabriel's weight shifted off him, Owen attempted to roll away, only to discover that he was handcuffed to the church's altar.

"Son of a bitch!" Owen spat.

Gabriel shook his head, a look of sadness in his eyes. Owen remained indifferent to the situation, even as Philip, who was a few feet away, cried. Owen felt helpless, unable to bring an end to Philip's tears.

"You don't get it, do you, son? It's not him; it's not Goldie. It's never been Goldie," Gabriel explained. "It should have occurred to me."

As Gabriel moved away from Owen, Owen's attention was immediately drawn to Philip. Gabriel had secured Philip to a chair, using thick ropes to bind his shoulders, wrists, knees, and ankles. It was clear to Owen that Philip had endured a great deal of physical torture already. Blood stained Philip's face, dripping from his nose and mouth. A deep and unpleasant cut stretched across one of Philip's palms. The extent of his injuries became even more clear as Owen noticed the discolored bruises marring Philip's skin. Philip must have put up a fierce fight.

"I should have seen it sooner."

Gabriel was speaking, but Owen found it challenging to pay attention to him instead of Philip.

"That he wasn't my son."

Owen watched Philip flinch as if he had been hit. Tears glistened on Philip's face.

"Don't you see, son? It's the demon. He killed your mother and overtook your brother. He stole Goldie away from us. But we'll get him back, son. Even if Goldie's body has to die, it'll be better than him being possessed by that monster."

Owen's trembling caused the handcuffs around his wrists to make a rattling sound. The mention of the situation made Philip's breathing hitch. Owen wished he could reassure him and promise that everything would be all right.

Gabriel turned away from Owen and focused his attention on Philip. He picked up his Bible from the ground and flipped through its pages, holding it in one hand. With his other hand, he poured water from a canteen over Philip's head, wetting his hair and allowing it to trickle down his face.

Gabriel furrowed his brow and chanted in Latin. Reverend Smith once explained to Owen that exorcisms were like prayers, meant to end evil. Owen felt completely helpless, unable to move, and could only watch as Gabriel made preparations to harm and potentially kill Philip. The exorcism was lengthy, and Gabriel was drenched in sweat by the end. Philip's cries and whimpers ceased, and he slumped in the chair, unaffected by the words and water that Gabriel had used on him. Philip stared at the floor.

Disregarding his Bible, Gabriel freed Philip from the ropes, yanking him up to his feet by his arm. "I will expel you from my son, you son of a bitch, even if I must destroy his body to give him that peace!" Gabriel roared.

Owen struggled against the metal cuff, causing his wrist to split and bleed. Gabriel pulled Philip through the long church aisle, passing rows of wooden pews. With a strong kick, Gabriel opened the church door. Owen tugged at the metal, searching the room for something useful. He saw Gabriel's bag a few feet away, filled with books and forgotten. Owen stretched his leg and caught the bag's strap, feeling relieved. Although the key wasn't inside, he found Gabriel's church journal. Using a paperclip from its pages, Owen unlocked the cuff.

Weapons were nowhere to be found, leaving Owen desperate. His eyes darted around, searching for anything. His gaze landed on the statue of Jesus positioned on the altar. Without hesitation, he snatched it up, feeling the weight of it in his hands. Determined, Owen set off in pursuit of Gabriel.

Owen circled the church; his eyes scanned the surroundings for any sign of Gabriel. The sound of water reached his ears, accompanied by splashing and Gabriel's grunts. As he turned the corner, Owen's eyes locked onto the dark figure of Gabriel, standing knee-deep in a man-made creek. Philip was in his grasp, submerged under the water, a rosary wrapped around Gabriel's wrist as he uttered Latin words. Owen swung the heavy statue, striking Gabriel on the head.

The impact was immediate, causing Gabriel to collapse to the ground. Owen wasted no time; he removed Gabriel's weight from Philip's body. Although the blow wasn't fatal, Owen knew it would save them precious time. He helped Philip, who was coughing and struggling to catch his breath, out of the water. Owen's eyes scanned Gabriel's motionless form. Noticing that Gabriel's jacket was missing, he realized that the keys to the truck must be in one of its pockets.

"Come on, Goldie," Owen said, supporting his weight as they climbed from the bank and back toward the church. Owen sat Philip down on a pew and started searching for Gabriel's jacket.

"Hurry," Philip croaked, voice broken.

Owen glanced over, saw the bruises forming on Philip's throat, and felt red rage like he'd never known before. "Let me find the keys, Goldie," Owen said, turning away.

He finally found the jacket, snatched it up, and turned, immediately going still.

Gabriel stood at the door of the church, a gun leveled straight at Owen. "Can't let you do it, Owen. That monster killed your mother. You remember her, don't you, son?"

Owen's stomach clenched with tension. He recalled the events. In fact, there were moments when he believed his memory surpassed Gabriel's. While Gabriel, intoxicated by Jack Smith and Jim Rice, narrated tales of a stunning woman who was his everything—his flawless wife and their picture-perfect marriage—Owen knew the truth. It wasn't a fairy tale; Owen remembered the relentless shouting matches and endless fights that would stretch into the late hours of the night. He couldn't forget how Gabriel's reliance on alcohol had begun long before their mother's passing.

"Father. Father, it's—it's not the demon, okay? It's Goldie. Our Goldie."

Gabriel shook his head. "I'm sorry he's gotten to you, Owen. I'm so sorry, son."

The sound of a gunshot reverberated through the air and Owen felt an intense surge of pain in his shoulder. In response, he collapsed to the ground, struggling to catch his breath. As he fell, he knocked over a table adorned with flickering candles, adding to the moment's chaos. Meanwhile, Philip's voice became deafening, filled with an undeniable power as he unleashed a furious scream that echoed through the room.

An excruciating agony that felt like being set ablaze by searing flames consumed Goldie's mind. The fiery sensation overwhelmed every fiber of his being, leaving him in a state of unbearable suffering.

"No!" Philip screamed.

The temperature in the room skyrocketed, causing the pews to burst into flames. Goldie's heart raced with fear as he sensed the intense heat from the fire and the pain from Owen's gunshot wound. The fear intensified as the fire spread.

In seconds, they found themselves outside the church, away from the danger. Owen struggled to stand up, noticing Philip on the church stairs. This sight gave Owen a moment of hesitation, but he pushed past it, ignoring the sharp pain in his shoulder as he lifted Philip.

Alongside the fear coursing through Goldie's veins, there was also a burning anger. He couldn't help but feel enraged that, years ago, he used his powers to save his father from this burning building—the same powers his father beat him for, called him a demon for.

Gabriel scanned his surroundings, catching Owen's attention as he turned around. Owen paused, unsure of what to do, but the urgency in Philip's grip on his shirt prompted him to speak.

"Father! We have to go! You don't have to do this to Goldie; Reverend Smith can help him! You know that," Owen yelled. "Do you think a demon would save our lives? No! This is Goldie! Our Goldie!"

Owen dashed toward the back seat of the truck, retrieving the keys from Gabriel's jacket with one hand while the other embraced Philip's slender waist. Meanwhile, Gabriel settled into the driver's seat.

The car roared to life, emitting a soothing purr that was as recognizable as Gabriel's voice or Owen's infectious laughter. As the flames engulfed the church, Gabriel shifted the truck into drive, causing a solitary tear to trickle down Owen's cheek as Philip buried his face against Owen's neck.

It was as if his head was engulfed in flames, tormenting him. Goldie longed for a respite from this fiery torment, hoping for tranquility and peace as the church and the fire faded from view.

CHAPTER 23

Goldie

Goldie had endured unimaginable hardships, that much was certain. However, the current situation felt like a close second. The anger within him was palpable as he opened his eyes to the dim glow of a nearby lamp, struggling to focus on the blurry surroundings. His head throbbed painfully, and his blood seemed to flow sluggishly through his veins as if transformed into thick tar.

Goldie found himself utterly alone in this desolate place, unsure whether the solitude brought comfort or heightened his fear. Every movement was a struggle, as if heavy sand weighed down his limbs. Despite his immense effort, he compelled himself to rise from the bed. Only then, when he stood and uncovered the sheets, did he discover a sturdy leather strap tightly fastened to his right ankle, connected to a long chain. Desperation consumed him as he sank to the ground and desperately pulled at the unyielding material, realizing with panic that it refused to give way.

Goldie approached the window, and, drawing back the worn-out curtains, he gently ran his fingers along the glass before he slammed both fists against it. Surprisingly, the glass didn't feel delicate or show any signs of damage when his fists collided with it repeatedly; it remained solid and unyielding. Feeling dizzy, Goldie turned to sit on the edge of the windowsill, willing his vision to stabilize and his weak legs to support him. At this moment, he finally took notice of the bedroom he found himself in. The wallpaper and floor shared the same worn-out appearance as the drapes. The room lacked any decorative pictures or additional furniture except for the small nightstand by the bed and a small table with two chairs. However, what caught Goldie's attention were the restraints fixed on the floor and ceiling on the opposite wall, designed for wrists and ankles, proudly displayed. As he glanced back at the bed he had just crawled out of, he quickly realized that it, too, had restraints attached to its four posts; the sheets reminded him of those from his childhood.

Panic overtook him, resulting in sweat pouring down his face. The room seemed to close in on him, leaving him nowhere to go. He felt trapped, like a caged animal, unable to control his actions. He sat on the bed to calm himself, hoping that the overwhelming sensations would subside. He reassured himself that this situation couldn't be that difficult to endure. Goldie anticipated spending a few hours in this predicament before Owen or Drake would discover his absence and begin searching for him. He convinced himself that he could wait it out. Glancing at his watch, he noticed it was already 10 a.m. Calculating that he would likely be free by 3 p.m., he tried to remain patient. However, suddenly, sitting on the bed became nearly impossible for Goldie. Restlessness and agitation consumed him, animating him with an urgent need to move.

The feeling of suffocation intensified within him despite the slow rotation of the ceiling fan allowing cool air to seep into the room. Goldie's long legs paced back and forth, devouring the limited space in just a few strides, which only heightened his frustration.

"It's only a matter of hours," Goldie reassured himself,

urging relaxation to take hold.

To distract his racing mind, Goldie scoured his thoughts for an activity to occupy his time. If only he had a couple of books, like the ones Mama had given him during his struggles with anger, he could find solace in the pages. *The Mortal Plague* series by Kathleen Aiken came to mind; it was the same series Mama had bought for him. However, to his dismay, there were no books in the room. Frustrated, he attempted to recite some of his and Drake's favorite songs, but confusion set in, causing him to lose his place midway through. He tried to start over, but his focus slipped away even quicker than before.

Panic consumed Goldie once again. Beads of sweat formed on his forehead and trickled down his neck while shivers coursed through his body as the fan continued twirling. A nagging feeling gnawed at his mind, signaling that something was amiss. Struggling to see the time on his watch, Goldie grew uncertain of how much time had passed. Surely, Owen or Drake would find him, right?

"Owen!" he yelled, his hands trembling uncontrollably.

Despite his efforts to stop the shaking, the tremors gradually spread from his hands to his arms and eventually reached his torso. The intensity of the tremors made Goldie panic.

"Drake!" he screamed, unsure if anyone could hear him.

As the earthquake-like sensation continued to travel through his body, Goldie realized his legs were also trembling. Worried that he might collapse, he quickly sat down on the bed to ensure he wouldn't fall. Goldie's gaze fell upon a water pitcher on a table halfway across the room.

Uncertain about his walking ability, Goldie dropped to his knees and crawled toward the table. His mouth was parched, and the need for a drink was overwhelming. He eagerly gulped down the water, but to his dismay, his thirst remained unquenched even after the pitcher was empty.

Slowly, Goldie made his way back to the bed, his body still trembling and his restlessness growing. Taking deep breaths became increasingly difficult, leaving him agitated and unable to find relief. The brightness of the sunlight streaming through the window was so intense that Goldie had to close his eyes as the small shaft of light caused discomfort and pain.

This experience was unlike any memory Goldie had encountered in purgatory. It felt completely new and unfamiliar to him. Despite his efforts to stay focused and keep his mind occupied, a familiar voice suddenly took Goldie aback.

"Why, Freckles?"

As Goldie attempted to rise and survey his surroundings, a wave of nausea washed over him, not solely because of the abrupt motion but also because of the flood of memories triggered by that voice.

"Josiah?" Goldie asked, unable to believe he was there. "Josiah, what are you doing here?"

Goldie knew Josiah was far from here. Despite this, Goldie understood that in purgatory, anything was possible, and one could experience unimaginable suffering.

Josiah stood before him, looking as handsome as ever. He had aged significantly since the last time Goldie had seen him.

"Why, Freckles?"

"Why what?" Goldie answered.

"I loved you, Goldie. I loved you more than I could ever tell you. Why did you let me go? Why have you done this to yourself?"

Goldie cried, "Josh, you have no idea. You don't know what I've been through or what I've had to face."

"Of course I do, Freckles. I've been watching over you. I've always been here with you."

"No."

"Yes, Goldie. I've seen everything that's happened. I saw what your father was doing, what was happening with Owen, and how well your life was going before Owen showed up; I was waiting for you to come to me, and Madely..."

"I wanted to find you, Josiah, and take you and Madely

with us, I swear. I just...didn't have a chance."

Josiah smiled. "I know. And it's okay, I understand. But I don't understand why you've done what you've done."

"I've done what I've needed to do. For Drake. For you. For Owen. Can't you understand?"

Josiah approached Goldie, enveloping him in his embrace, and Goldie instantly melted into the comforting warmth.

"This has gone too far, Goldie. It was never supposed to go like this."

"I need...I need..."

"I know, Goldie. But you can't. I need to leave now, Freckles, but please know that this isn't your fight. Listen—really listen to what's being said."

"It's not Owen's fight! He can't do this alone!"

"You need to give in to it..."

After Josiah disappeared, Goldie laid back down, attempting to comprehend the bewildering events that had just unfolded. Goldie shut his eyes again, only to be overcome by a new wave of tremors coursing through his body.

As Goldie's eyes remained shut, an unsettling sensation began to creep up his arms. It felt like something was crawling on his skin, causing him to instinctively raise his arms to ward off the invisible intruders, intensifying the already-present tremors.

Despite Goldie's best efforts to concentrate and clear his mind, the sensation refused to dissipate. The invisible presence continued to crawl on his arms.

"Goldie."

He would know that voice anywhere. As if the tremors weren't enough. He shivered.

"Is this how I raised you? Is this what I taught you?"

"Father, wait. I can..."

"You can explain? You can explain to me why you let your brother go, why you're not living with your real family. You're living with a fag—why, you're practically a full-blown demon!" Gabriel yelled.

"Stop it," Goldie told Gabriel. "Don't call Drake that."

"No, son. When did my flesh and blood start trusting a fag?"

"Stop it; he's just a friend."

"You sure as hell don't act like it. You act like you trust him more than you trust Owen."

"Owen understands."

"Owen shouldn't have to understand! You let him down. You let us down!"

"Don't!" Goldie screamed. "Don't say that to me! I did everything I could!" Tears poured down his face. "I did..." Then the tears overtook Goldie, making him unable to speak.

"I always knew you were the weak one, Goldie." Goldie sobbed as Gabriel berated him. "I'm disgusted with you. You should have died with your mother."

"You don't mean that. Tell me you don't mean that."

"I wish I could. You deserve everything that happens to you." With that, Gabriel vanished, leaving Goldie distraught.

Goldie found it challenging to forget the words that Gabriel had spoken to him. Deep down, he had always suspected that Gabriel thought that about him, but now those words echoed incessantly in his mind, tormenting him.

Just when Goldie least expected it, the one person he had hoped would not appear suddenly stood silently beside him.

"Why did you do this to yourself? Right. Escaping Father? That's the big excuse. But why? Revenge? Revenge for what? Beating us? Did you notice we're alive and kickin'? So what's the point?" Owen asked.

"How about living a life we were always scared to live?"

"Not going to happen for you, man. So you got any other fantastic excuses?" Owen paused and walked around the bed. "I know why you are really friends with that fag, man."

"Please, just leave me alone."

"Makes you feel strong. Invincible. Prince Charming protecting the distraught princess."

"No. You're wrong, Owen."

"It's more than that, isn't it? It's because your whole life, you've felt...different. Am I right?"

"Stop," Goldie pleaded.

"I hit a little close to home, huh? Not different because you were some lonely kid or because of your power?"

"Stop it," Goldie commanded.

"Because you're a monster."

"Shut up! Just shut the fuck up!"

"You were always a monster. And you only feel right when you're sucking down more poison and more evil!" Owen leaned down. "Monster, man. Monster. I tried so hard to pretend that we were brothers. But you were one of the filthy things that Father taught us to hate. We're not even the same species. You're nothing to me."

"Don't say that to me. Don't you say that to me!"

"You should just let the Maledictio take control..."

Goldie shifted his gaze, only to find that Owen had disappeared, leaving him alone. As the trembling intensified, he couldn't determine whether it resulted from the unsettling information he had received from Josiah, Gabriel, or Owen.

"Here we go again."

Goldie peeled his eyes open at the sound of Owen's voice returning.

"You know, Father already tried this. It didn't work. If you recall, you gave up and returned to your demon."

Goldie closed his eyes again. "You're not him. You're not my Owen."

He laughed. "Nope. But I could be. After the way you treated him, he's gotta be pissed as hell."

Goldie maintained a stoic silence, refusing to utter a single word. Deep down, he felt no need to respond. There was no way that any of it could be true. Owen, his beloved brother, would never treat him in such a cruel manner. However, despite his doubts, Goldie couldn't shake off the nagging feeling that there might be some truth.

Slowly, he opened his eyes and turned toward Owen's voice. Standing before him was his brother, his face marred by bruises and blood, with dark veins crisscrossing his body like a sinister web. And the red marks on Owen's neck, remnants of a whip's merciless assault, served as a painful reminder of the brutality he had endured.

"You can't honestly think he'd still care about what happens to you after you did this to him. After you fucked up and got him beaten."

Goldie shook his head. "I didn't mean to. I was a little kid."

"I know… I know… It was the demon that you willingly submitted to. You left us and crawled back to that evil fag to suck down more of this evil, and this is what happened." Owen gestured to his neck.

"I know. I'm sorry. I'm so sorry."

"You think I'll accept that apology now? Father's been telling you for months, years even, not to trust your demon, but you chose it over me, your own family, and now, thanks to you, Kieran has me in his claws, put this plague in my blood."

"I didn't know—"

"Which is why you should have listened to me! But now it's too late, Goldie. Look at what our life has become, and it's all because of you. And here you are, dying and leaving me to clean up your mess."

"Stop it," Goldie whispered, holding back the tears. "Stop it."

Owen laughed as he approached Goldie.

"Stop it. Stop it," Goldie yelled again.

"Goldie, will you listen to me?" Owen yelled, his voice suddenly high-pitched like a child's. "The only way for you to get out of here is for you to—" Owen stopped as he watched Goldie close his eyes. "Goldie…"

CHAPTER 24

Toy

The desensitization process has peaked, causing a shift in Toy's perception. The relentless pursuit by spirits or Kieran, along with the fast-paced and chaotic nature of their situation, had made the scenes of death and violence less shocking. Discovering the bodies of other mutilated teenagers no longer evoked guilt within Toy. Instead, she found herself experiencing a mix of sadness and relief. It may seem terrible to think this way, and it bothered her somewhat, but Toy chose not to dwell on that aspect.

Her priority was to ensure Bonnie's and her survival until the very end. Feeling remorse for circumstances beyond their control would only drain her energy and burden her mind with unnecessary emotions amidst everything else they faced.

Once they navigated through the cell blocks and reached the showers, the sight of an excessive amount of blood pooling on the floor and splattered across the walls, forming the words "*Ernchester*" and "*Reis*," elicited no significant reaction from them.

Bonnie appeared to be experiencing a similar numbness. It was not immediately noticeable, but Toy saw it in how he responded or didn't respond to certain situations. They could engage in further discussions about the dark humor surrounding their environment and their present goals, all with no concerns, frustrations, or unnecessary arguments about sacrificing themselves for one another—assuming it even reached that point.

A large, gaping hole in the concrete marred the shower stalls, revealing a tangled mess of rusty pipes and damp, slippery stones. Curiosity getting the better of him, Bonnie directed the flashlight's beam into the murky abyss before cautiously sliding into it.

"Oh, that's..." He recoiled, automatically blocking his nose. "Okay...that's just disgusting..." He shuddered. "Hope you like the smell of raw sewage in the morning, Toy."

"Next to Twirllee's biscuits, it's my favorite smell."

As Toy approached him, a wave of disgust washed over her, the foul odor hitting her like a punch. It was hard to bear the putrid smell that filled the air, reminiscent of a septic truck that had accidentally released its contents under the pleasant rays of the summer sun.

"So, the sewers," Toy began casually, following the sharp beam of the flashlight ahead. "I believe that last blood note said something about drains...or draining, earlier. Are we walking into the poop flood of the century down here? I rarely make a habit out of exploring places like this."

Bonnie snorted his laughter. "Yeah, I'd prepare for the worst. And it's great we're stuck wearing the same clothes without washing them." He ducked beneath a set of thinner pipes and dropped another four feet into the gloom. "Owen will, without a doubt, be on patrol, though. That's the one thing that we really have to watch out for. He'll pop out of nowhere, and there is no easy way to be quiet with these stupid puddles around."

"Awesome. Gotta love a challenge," Toy huffed, clearing the pipes and climbing down after him. "Then what?"

"Uh, valve-things. We have to turn...two? And they drain

the water out of one of the tunnels that leads into the lobby."

"And that will get us back to the others?"

"Yes."

Toy descended into another slanted crevice. Unsettlingly damp air brushed against her skin upon landing beside Bonnie. The sensation was almost as repulsive as the time Toy fell into a heap of dismembered body parts. She was still in the process of removing the remnants from her shirt. And just a few minutes ago, she had discovered a fragment of a jawbone entangled in her shoelaces. To lighten the mood, Bonnie suggested they keep it as a morbid trophy to display on their bedroom wall. The comment was so absurd that it elicited a laugh, prompting Toy to toss the jawbone at him. Much to her surprise, he retaliated by throwing it back.

There they stood, the two of them, at the entrance of the asylum's sewers. A wall had been completely torn away as if someone had desperately clawed through the bricks with their bare hands. The sight was astonishing, and Toy wouldn't be shocked if someone had attempted such a feat.

Bonnie swiftly scanned the surroundings with the flashlight, illuminating every direction before switching it off again. Although they still had four batteries remaining, the intermittent patches of eerie light flickering from the ceiling bulbs should be enough. Toy hoped so, at least.

The tunnels amplified even the slightest sounds to an extreme degree, so they refrained from speaking. Instead, they stayed close together, their hands intertwined, and tried to move through the murky brown water as quietly as possible. Holding Bonnie's hand had become such a natural part of Toy's existence, as if her life depended on it, that she didn't even think about it anymore.

As they navigated through the maze-like corridors, they came across two sharp turns, only to be confronted with the sight of more lifeless bodies. To their dismay, they were forced to maneuver through a narrow passage by crawling on their hands and knees. The muddy water engulfed their fingers, leaving a grimy residue on their skin. The water temperature added to their discomfort, exacerbating the situation and leaving additional stains on Toy's dirtied jeans instead of cleaning them. Suppressing the urge to retch, Toy regained her footing with Bonnie's help, unintentionally almost toppling him over in haste to escape the claustrophobic passage.

"Sorry," Toy grumbled, cringing as she rubbed her palms raw against the thighs of her pants. "I seem to have lost my enthusiasm."

"Oh, don't worry about it." He sighed. The noise was dramatic while he tried to fix his amethyst hair. "On our next date, we'll go somewhere more romantic. Somewhere...less likely to turn into a battle for our sanity." A wide grin spread across his face, causing a rush of warmth to flush Toy's cheeks and a silly smile to tug at the corners of her mouth as she shook her head in disbelief. "Laser tag can be romantic, right?" Bonnie continued, rubbing thoughtfully at his chin. "We could improvise. Like laser tag on the beach? Or maybe with candles? That sounds fun and slightly dangerous..."

Wow, that is absolutely adorable, but there's really no need for him to do that. Toy was just about to express her gratitude, but suddenly, something strange zoomed past the other end of the tunnel. It appeared to be one of the spirits, but...could it be something else entirely?

Toy extended her arm to stop Bonnie, trying to glimpse the mysterious figure that disappeared into the shadows.

"Hey, I like the beach thing more than the candle, but I just saw..." She shook her head again as they hesitated underneath one of the light bulbs. "Well, there was something."

Bonnie followed her stare, his eyes narrowing. "Uh, at least we don't have to go that way. There's a gap between those wooden structures over there. The rooms with the valves should be on the other side."

A chilling sensation ran down Toy's neck as her frown

deepened, causing her to shiver. Reluctantly, she followed close behind, stepping into Bonnie's shadow. There was an undeniable presence lurking nearby, and she couldn't help but hope they wouldn't encounter it soon. It was eerie, just like how Kieran had transformed Owen's body into something otherworldly.

Past the wooden structure, it was almost unnaturally bright, raising suspicions in her mind. Then her gaze fell upon a faded map hanging on the wall to her left. Across from it, there was a ladder leading down into a flooded section, marked as the lower junction by a sign above it. It was peculiar to see helpful resources like maps and symbols in this place.

The more Toy thought about it, the more she was convinced that it was a trap. The combination of the unsettling presence and the overly illuminated surroundings raised red flags in her mind. It was a deliberate attempt to lure unsuspecting individuals to their death.

"That would be our destination; all we have to do is find the valves and unflood that tunnel." Bonnie pointed at the ladder on the map, and Toy nodded. "And the valve rooms are easy to find. The getting there and the getting back here will be the hard part."

Peering through narrowed eyes, Toy glanced over her shoulder, her gaze extending beyond the haphazardly placed crates. Once she confirmed they were the only ones present, they cautiously approached the map, examining its well-worn surface and the intricate paths marked with various colors.

"Um, that is a dead end." Toy frowned and pointed at their current location. "And, if this area is like a sealed-off circle-thing...it might be more prudent for you to head toward one valve and me toward the other and meet up at the ladder afterward. Hey, hey!" Toy raised her hands just as he opened his mouth, an annoyed look on his face. "I know, I know. Splitting up is bad and stupid for all reasons. I'm not arguing with you about that. Except..."

"Then what are you saying?" Bonnie interrupted, knocking the top of the flashlight gently against her arm. "We stick together no matter what—which means we don't lose sight of each other, Toy. Yeah, it might be easier or whatever to distract Owen if we aren't together, and maybe it might take us less time to reach the valves. But, no." He scowled. "We are not doing that. There is no way in hell I'm jeopardizing your safety for the sake of...of convenience."

"Okay." Toy grinned lopsidedly at him. "I'm sorry. I won't suggest it ever again."

"That's right, you won't. Don't even think about it."

"Understood, baby."

He huffed under his breath, though his eyes were hopelessly fond as he bumped her shoulder with his. "What am I going to do with you?"

Just as Toy was about to respond, she saw Kieran emerging from the end of the tunnel, abruptly interrupting the conversation. Bonnie, clearly frustrated, quickly pulled her to the left, guiding them around the curved and damp wall, ensuring they were no longer visible. The location where they were standing, with the map in hand, was positioned at a pivotal point resembling the heart of a four-way intersection.

"Down this tunnel across from us will lead us to both valve rooms?" Toy whispered, nails tangling in his shirt sleeve as she hurried along the shiny, wet stone. It was hard to remember what the map said with her heart punching at her ribs.

"Yeah, and we're off to a decent start," Bonnie said, his voice low and rushed.

"I'd rather not be caught and killed even once while we're doing this, though." Toy gulped. "You never know... It could happen."

The dark tunnels that branched out from the central section were utterly devoid of light, making it impossible for them to run. Walking quickly was their only option, as a fall could cause an ankle injury that would significantly impede their progress. It would make them vulnerable targets for Kieran, and Toy refused to let a mere sprained ankle cause their demise.

They navigated through the labyrinthine tunnels, stumbling occasionally because of the twists and turns, but it didn't significantly slow them down. The sound of colossal footsteps behind them reverberated off the walls, creating an eerie and thunderous effect. Perhaps Kieran was merely searching the perimeter, unaware of their presence.

The moment the flashlight beam shined on yet another wooden obstruction ahead, Bonnie swiftly picked up the pace, causing Toy's fingers to tighten around him as she peered behind them.

"Um, he found us," Toy croaked.

"It doesn't matter—just go through there!" Bonnie pushed Toy toward the tiny space between the boards, his face barely visible in the jumping glow of the flashlight. "He won't catch us if we hurry!"

Without wasting a moment, she shot herself through the narrow opening, wincing as the rough wooden fragments pierced her hands like sharp spikes and mercilessly scraped the delicate flesh beneath her nails. The surge of adrenaline partially numbed the pain. The damp warmth stung her wrists, and the exit seemed unattainable in this suffocating space where the air was scarce, making breathing nearly impossible.

Suddenly, Toy crashed onto the ground, her mind clouded with confusion as she desperately gulped down large quantities of oxygen, oblivious to the repugnant odor that surrounded her. Tiny bursts of blinding white light erupted at the corners of her vision, and as she cast a glance downward, she was confronted with a horrifying sight—her palms were torn to shreds, oozing blood that stained everything they touched.

Struggling to regain her balance, she got to her feet, her body trembling. She turned back to the gap. A chilling sensation ran down her back as though a bucket of icy water had been poured over her. Already halfway across the space, Bonnie desperately clawed at the wooden surface, his nails digging deep into the wood. Just a few feet away, Kieran stood at the entrance. It became painfully clear that Bonnie's chances were slim.

"Bonnie!" Toy screamed, diving toward him, arms reaching out.

The stinging sensation of acid filled Toy's eyes, while her lungs felt as if they were filled with shards of glass. Frustration mounted as her fingers futilely slipped and slid against Bonnie's while Kieran struggled to break in from the opposite side.

"You aren't going anywhere, little pig," he growled.

In a stroke of luck, Toy's hand unexpectedly grabbed a firm body part. A wrist? An arm? Toy wasn't sure, but instinctively held it tightly. She pulled Bonnie with all her might, causing him to emit a dreadful, anguished cry. The impact of that sound hit Toy like a sudden blow to the jaw. Kieran must have also grabbed hold of him.

"Goddammit!" Toy yelled, furious tears running down her face. "I'm not letting go, do you hear me? I'm not letting you go!"

Bonnie's intense, deep gaze locked with hers, filled with fear and pain. Without warning, Toy found herself forcefully thrown back onto the hard cement. The impact stole the air from her lungs, leaving her gasping for breath. Amid the chaos, she saw stars streaking across the darkness. The weight of nearly two hundred pounds crashed down on top of her.

Paralyzed by the weight on her chest, Toy struggled to move. Every fiber of her being screamed for her to get up, to find safety, and to help Bonnie escape. But her body refused to respond, leaving her trapped.

CHAPTER 25

Toy

Fresh screams echoed through the tunnels, reminding Toy of their imminent danger. Their survival thus far was likely because Kieran had shifted his attention to other victims who were more accessible.

"Bonnie?" Toy cleared her throat. "It's okay. I've got you. I've got you."

Toy closed her eyes and ran her fingers through his hair while he embraced her. Her fingers, stained with blood, traced a path up the back of his neck. His face remained buried against her collarbone and she could feel a gentle warmth seeping into her shirt as he attempted to stifle his tears. Toy was unable to hear his sobs, which made the situation even more heartbreaking. His entire body trembled with tension, yet an eerie silence surrounded them as if all sound had shattered.

"I'm...I'm sorry," he finally choked out and dragged himself onto his knees with the fading strength of an old man. He paused, wiped his face, and... "Oh, god." A faint whisper. "Holy shit... I want to go home..."

As his tone changed, Toy's eyes, filled with anxiety, shifted downward from the dark shadows, and she saw him kneeling beside her. The flashlight must have fallen nearby because its beam illuminated his face. With urgency, he tore off a piece of his T-shirt's hem and wrapped it around Toy's hands.

His face revealed a mixture of pain, disbelief, exhaustion, and sheer panic. The gravity of the situation weighed on both of them as they navigated through the sewers, returning to the main section near the map. The uncomfortable sensation of pins and needles returned to their tired limbs, a reminder of this ordeal's physical toll on them. They avoided any further attacks from Kieran. Still, the distant sounds of sobs and shouts from other teenagers echoed behind them.

Despite the heartbreaking cries of fellow captives, they chose to ignore them, focusing on their own survival. Each time they encountered such scenes, it became easier to detach themselves emotionally as self-preservation took precedence.

"Well...all right, then." Bonnie stared down into the once-flooded ladder tunnel. "I guess someone else got to the other valve?" He glanced over at Toy, brows furrowed. "We should go. Get as far as possible."

"I'm right behind you, Bonnie." Toy nodded, leaning against the stone wall next to him and bordering dead-on-her-feet levels of consciousness. "Better make it quick, though. I don't know how much climbing we can do with our wounded hands."

He snorted, a brief smile appearing on his face, though it was clear it took a lot of effort for him to do so. Whenever he glanced at Toy, she could see the worry etched on his face—the deep crease between his magenta eyes and the tension that tightened his lips. He wore his emotions plainly, unable to hide them even if he wanted to.

Toy found herself drawn to this aspect of him, the way he wore his heart on his sleeve. It was something she admired about him. In contrast, Toy struggled to understand her jumbled emotions, let alone feel for others, no matter how hard she tried. It was easy for him.

He pulled Toy closer swiftly and seamlessly, his large hand resting on the back of her neck. He leaned in, his lips brushing against hers, and she couldn't help but feel a rush of familiarity.

Toy's eyes widened, and her pulse seemed to stop as she stood there, her trembling limbs barely able to support her. Bonnie, too, appeared surprised by his own actions—or at least he tried to appear that way. They both knew that they shouldn't be engaging in kisses or intimacy, especially considering the danger they found themselves in.

They stood there, unable to do anything else, until they both jumped back as if each other's presence shocked them. It was the same intense feeling they had when they first kissed two years ago. The entire moment couldn't have lasted more than a few seconds. Toy's mind went blank, her mouth agape as she stared at him in disbelief. She knew she wasn't thinking, but she couldn't stop. Not even the possibility of Kieran showing up could deter her.

Before Bonnie could move out of her reach and climb up the ladder, her arms instinctively reached out toward him, and her fingers grasped the collar of his shirt. Toy didn't think he expected her to do this any more than she did, especially after they had agreed not to be affectionate. With her eyes shut tight, she wrapped her arms around his neck and tried to kiss him again. It was an awkward fit, their teeth clicking together, but Toy soon felt him tilt his head and his hands slide into her hair. As he kissed her back, everything fell into place, like it always did. His lips melded with hers, igniting a fiery heat and a surge of longing. Toy's movements were frantic and desperate in the lit shadows.

An intense and restless energy crackled between them as they tried to hold on tighter and press their bodies closer together. And when they were finally forced to break apart, they saw stars. The passion and desire they shared in that moment were undeniable, leaving them both breathless and craving more.

"*Te amo,*" he groaned before placing a kiss on her forehead, not caring about the grime.

"I love you too."

Once more, their lips met, reigniting the passionate flame of desire and longing. As they shared this intimate moment, laughter bubbled within them. Their embrace grew tighter, as if their lives depended on it, for the fear of losing even the slightest connection between them felt unbearable.

"Bonnie," Toy choked out once she pulled away. Her forehead bumped into his. "Bonnie, we have to..."

"I know, I know," he said, but he didn't let her go. "We have to keep going."

Toy was overwhelmed by adrenaline and captivated by his intense gaze as he grasped her hand. At that moment, a sharp pang in her chest and a trembling sensation in her heart clarified that she had fallen deeply in love with this boy. Despite her attempts to resist, there was no escaping the overwhelming feeling.

The realization hit her like a ton of bricks—*I want to spend the rest of my life with him.* As they both took off running, Toy couldn't help but think what terrible timing it was for this epiphany. Bonnie and Toy reached the bottom of the ladder and swiftly made their way up. The atmosphere felt different up here, brighter but colder. The air hung heavy and sweet, reminding them they were finally back in the lobby. They had to hurry back to the others before it was too late.

They cautiously returned to the designated safe zone. They couldn't help but feel a sense of unease. The once-bustling area now appeared eerily deserted, devoid of any signs of their friends. The empty halls and abandoned security booth stood as a stark reminder. The silence was deafening and broken only by the distant sound of their footsteps echoing through the desolate surroundings.

They stumbled upon the door to the room they had woken up in. They found it securely locked. Frustration washed over them. Bonnie and Toy exchanged glances, their expressions mirroring a mix of disappointment and confusion. They had come so far, only to be halted by...a door. The door stood before them, unmoving, as Bonnie jiggled the door handle.

He smirked at Toy, confusing her before he turned. The sound of Bonnie's foot colliding with the door reverberated through the corridor. The door, once a barrier, now lay open and defeated as Bonnie triumphantly stepped into the room. He turned to Toy to say something when someone from inside the room came at him.

As the man lunged forward, brandishing a pipe, Bonnie sidestepped his attack, avoiding any potential harm before grabbing the pipe's end. He took this moment to look at the man's face and gasped.

"Drake!" he yelled.

Drake's astonishment was palpable as he looked at them. The sight of Bonnie and Toy sent a jolt of surprise through his entire being, leaving him speechless.

"Bonnie!"

With a sense of urgency, he enveloped Bonnie in a warm embrace while Toy turned on the lights to see the rest of their friends in the room. They got up off the floor and gathered closely around them.

"Holy shit, Drake! When did you get here?"

"Yesterday. Where did you two go? The others said you were M.I.A."

"Fredrick and Brendan found Jo on the camera soon after they got it working; since I had the power, Toy and I went after her. Once we got there, we saved her. The power had gone out before, and we went to fix it; the next thing we knew, we were stuck in the maze that is this building."

"Yeah...it sucked."

"Wow...I'm glad you two are okay; we were scared something happened," Julia exclaimed.

"Why were you guys hiding in here?" Toy asked them.

"We heard someone coming and didn't know if you were friendly or not."

"Did you guys save any spirits when we were gone?" Bonnie asked.

"Yeah, we saved Forrest, Brodie, and Mable. But Julia pointed out something weird about each of their wrists," Drake explained as they all made their way to the security booth.

"What did she find?" Toy asked.

"Each of our friends that are or were once spirits now has a handful of numbers and letters inscribed on their right wrists. Brodie had *P-S19g20*, Forrest had *P-S27g20*, Jo had *P-S96g20*, Mable had *P-S71g20*, and Kurt had *P-S27g20*," Julia explained as she leaned up against the desk.

"The teens and kids we've run into here have similar tattoos. Do we have any idea why?" Bonnie asked.

"No idea," Brendan answered.

As the group talked, Toy watched as Drake pulled open the desk drawer. He snatched the first aid kit that hid inside before leaving the cramped security booth. Toy followed him, and halfway down the hall, he turned around, facing her with a frown.

"What's wrong, Drake?" Toy asked as she stepped closer.

"I just miss Goldie," he said with a sigh. "I'm...going to go try to patch him up."

"I know. We all miss him too, but he will be back."

Drake mustered up a fake smile for Toy before he walked into the room they had woken up in. Toy stood in the hall for a minute before she followed him, watching him quietly from the doorframe.

He knelt in front of Goldie, who was fast asleep. Drake had all the supplies to tend to Goldie's stomach wound. But deep down, he knew that even if he patched him up, Goldie wouldn't wake up. Drake was determined to help him; he had never helped someone like this before. He was more skilled with woodwork.

Drake removed the blood-stained shirt and tossed it aside. Gently running his hand over Goldie's abdomen, he noticed that there was no visible gash, contrary to what others had claimed. Instead, he observed dark veins spreading like a web from Goldie's stomach.

Toy could sense the unease coming over Drake. With a mix of panic and determination, Toy swiftly distanced herself from the door, her mind racing. She darted down the hallway and sought a room to conceal herself within. A couple of minutes later, Toy heard him.

"Toy, where are you? You need to come see this," Drake yelled down the hall.

"What is it? What happened?" Toy asked as she walked out of the room with a granola bar.

"It's Goldie."

Toy jogged to the room. "What's wrong?" she asked.

"It's his stomach; there's no evidence he was ever hurt, even though his shirt had a gash and wet blood on it," Drake said as he pointed at Goldie's body. "But he has black veins—the same black veins that the rest of our sleeping friends have on their bodies. But there's no reason he should be asleep; he could wake up. Why won't he wake up?"

"I don't know."

"While you're here, I need your help."

"With what?"

"I need your help with moving these boxes. I heard a noise behind them, and I want to check it out," Drake informed her. "I heard it right before I called out for you."

"Alrighty then."

Upon relocating the boxes, they discovered Eric's presence, calmly relaxing behind them. Startled by their presence, Eric hastily soared beyond their grasp. As a result, an eerie chill permeated the room, accompanied by flickering lights reminiscent of their unsettling encounter when stumbling upon Jo.

"Look! It's Eric!" Toy exclaimed. "Drake, do you know who has the power?"

"I do..."

"Can you catch him?" Toy asked.

"I can try," Drake admitted.

Despite their relentless efforts, Drake could not grab Eric as they pursued him.

"Hey Eric, come get us!" Toy yelled as a last resort.

Toy found herself trapped beneath a heavy box as Eric forcefully pushed it onto her. The impact caused her to collide with the ground, knocking her head sharply against the concrete. In an instant, her surroundings distorted, as if she was submerged underwater, with the world appearing hazy and the sounds muffled.

"Toy! Eric! *¡Déjala en paz! ¡Consíme en su lugar!*" Toy heard Drake panic as he flailed his hands in the air.

Eric distanced himself from Toy and swiftly pursued Drake. As Drake made contact with Eric's head, a sudden drowsiness overcame Toy, causing her eyelids to shut.

"Drake! Toy! Are you okay? Guys! Come quick! Eric attacked," Toy heard Julia yell.

"We're coming!"

Bonnie exerted his strength and lifted the box from atop of Toy, relieving the pressure and allowing her to breathe freely again. He pulled her closer, and she could feel the strength of his affection, a gesture that spoke volumes without the need for words. At that moment, she knew she was safe.

"Toy! Are you okay?" Bonnie asked as he pulled away.

"I'm...I'm fine. I only blacked out for a minute; Drake saved me after Eric pinned me down, and I hit my head," Toy answered as Bonnie helped her up.

"Where was Eric hiding?"

"He was hiding behind the boxes. Drake heard a noise. We moved the boxes to see what was making the noise. Then he attacked us." Glancing toward Drake, she observed his slumbering figure stir gently. "Look, he's waking up," she chirped.

"There you go," Bonnie started as he helped Drake sit up. "Hey, man."

"What happened?" Drake whimpered as he grabbed Bonnie's arms for balance.

"You saved Eric and me," Toy answered.

"I'm going to clean up the mess we made."

Bonnie watched as Drake slowly removed his hands from his arm. With a graceful motion, he rose to his feet, his tall figure casting a shadow over the room.

"Maybe you should rest," Bonnie interrupted.

"I'm fine... Toy, you have the power now."

CHAPTER 26

Goldie

Goldie sprinted away from the group, leaving Toy and Bonnie in his wake. With no clear destination in mind, he felt an overwhelming urge to escape. The image of his brother's life slipping away before his eyes haunted him. As he turned a corner, Goldie collided with an unsuspecting individual, causing him to draw his gun instinctively. However, his tense grip on the weapon quickly relaxed when he recognized Drake's familiar face. Drake embraced Goldie tightly, overwhelmed with relief, offering solace in their unexpected reunion.

"Goldie... Oh my God!" Drake acknowledged.

Goldie mirrored his actions and embraced him with an equal amount of strength. Suddenly, a loud boom echoed behind them, causing them to separate instinctively. Reacting quickly, Goldie stood up, firmly grasped Drake's hand, and swiftly led him in the opposite direction of the noise. As they hurriedly approached a nearby door, Goldie forcefully kicked it open and urgently pulled Drake inside. Once safely inside, Goldie swiftly closed the door and turned around, only to find Drake staring back at him. With concern, Goldie cautiously approached Drake and carefully examined his injuries. Drake had a noticeable cut under his eye, and his lip was both bruised and cut. Gently, Goldie ran his thumb over Drake's injured bottom lip, silently conveying his empathy and care.

"I'm so sorry," Goldie whispered, tears welling in his eyes.

Drake's gaze fixated on him as he gently wrapped his arms around Goldie's neck, their lips meeting in a slow and passionate kiss. The moment's intensity made Goldie feel as though this could last forever. As Drake eventually pulled away, Goldie remained in that spot, savoring the lingering sensation of their lips coming together.

"Sunshine, none of this is your fault. It's his," Drake explained, his hand in Goldie's hair.

With a wry smile, Goldie reached out and tightly held Drake's hand. Suddenly, a loud noise shook the room, causing them to release each other and move away quickly. It was clear that the door had been rattled, probably due to a nearby explosion, startling them both.

"Goldie, I don't think we're going to be safe here..." Drake trailed off.

Goldie was about to respond, but the door swung open abruptly before he could utter a word. To his surprise, it was none other than his father, Gabriel Philip, who barged into the room.

"My, my, Goldie! I did not know your faggot boyfriend had such a powerful demon in him!" Gabriel cackled as he shut the door behind him. Drake whimpered as he neared them. "It's God's will; he must die!" Gabriel snickered. He waltzed his way to Goldie and squished his cheeks.

Goldie pushed his father off of him. "You're not killing him. You're not even going to go near him!" he exclaimed.

Drake clutched Goldie's hand with a firmer grip, seeking solace and reassurance. Gabriel growled menacingly at Goldie, but his gaze shifted toward Drake. In an attempt to seize him, Gabriel extended his hand, causing Drake to retreat instinctively. However, Goldie swiftly positioned himself between them, obstructing Gabriel's path.

"I said you are not going near him," Goldie snarled.

Drake observed as Goldie swiftly drew his firearm and pointed it directly at Gabriel. The intense heat and anxiety caused beads of sweat to form on Goldie's forehead. Gabriel initially bared his teeth defiantly but quickly withdrew them when Goldie threw a punch, too frightened to use the gun.

In response, Gabriel growled and retrieved his gun, unleashing a barrage of curses in Goldie's direction. Drake sought refuge behind a cluster of scattered chairs, granting him a clear view and audible access to Gabriel's actions.

Gabriel's arrogant laughter reverberated while his canary beard fluttered wildly. His movements were graceful and calculated. Conversely, Goldie appeared clumsy and uncoordinated, his punches consistently missing their mark as he sweated profusely.

Goldie's hand trembled uncontrollably, his breath coming in short, rapid gasps. From the corner of his eye, he caught sight of Drake, his fingers tightly wrapped around his gun. Fear paralyzed Goldie, preventing him from launching an attack. However, Gabriel, quick-witted and observant, positioned himself strategically, ready to pounce in Drake's direction. Goldie sprang up from his hiding spot in a split second, his vision momentarily obscured as he searched for Gabriel and Drake. His eyes darted around the room until they finally settled on his father's frame, a glimmer of determination flickering in his gaze.

"Well, son, you still can't hit me. You're pathetic just like your—"

Goldie, letting out a furious curse, squeezed the trigger.

In a swift and graceful motion, Gabriel managed to evade the bullet, which now hurtled toward the chairs.

The same chairs shielding Drake from harm...

The room was filled with a piercing scream, followed by a chilling and sinister cackle. Goldie's hands trembled as he involuntarily dropped his weapon, his eyes fixated on the devastating outcome of his actions. Drake lay motionless in a pool of crimson. As Gabriel chuckled mockingly, he casually opened the door and left them alone.

Overwhelmed with shock and horror, Goldie felt his face drain of color. He frantically rushed toward Drake, stumbling over the scattered debris in his desperate attempt to reach him. Finally, Goldie collapsed on his knees beside his wounded friend, his heart heavy with guilt and remorse.

"No, no, no, no, no, no! Drake! Stay with me, Green bean, please," Goldie yelled, tears racing down his face.

Drake looked at Goldie, his mouth full of blood. "Goldie..."

Blood trickled from his mouth as he coughed, causing Goldie to flinch. Reacting quickly, he gently wiped away the crimson stain while applying pressure to Drake's wound, trying to stop the bleeding.

"Goldie, stop. There's nothing you can do," Drake gasped, tears tracking visible lines down his face.

Overwhelmed by fear and feeling utterly defenseless, Goldie's heart raced as he faced the harsh reality of his lover's impending demise. Tears streamed down his face uncontrollably as he sought solace.

"Goldie. I-I-I...I love you. You were my first and last love. I cannot—" Drake's violent coughs cut him off. "Goldie, I cannot love you enough." He smiled, his tears falling.

"This is my fault. I can't... I'm so sorry! This is all my fault. Drake, I love you so much." Goldie kissed his forehead and gripped his hand.

Drake coughed once more, his breathing becoming more uneven.

Goldie grasped his hand and squeezed it tight. "I will always love you, Drake Miller," he whispered.

"I will always love you, Goldie Miller."

And with his last breath, Drake fell silent.

Goldie widened his eyes, calling for Toy and Bonnie to get some help. "Damn it, Drake, why the hell—you...shit." Goldie tried to press on the wound harder. Trying desperately to keep Drake alive, he couldn't help but burst into tears. "No, no, no. Don't you dare die, no..." Goldie screamed as he saw Drake's hand fall from his. "Please, can't you stay? Please stay, don't go, please? Drake!" he sobbed.

CHAPTER 27

Toy

Toy and Bonnie watched as Drake tidied up the chaotic room. The sound of Drake's walkie-talkie interrupted the silence. Toy grabbed the device from the floor and pressed it against her ear.

"It's Toy, what's up?" Toy asked.

"Just who I was trying to reach! Toy, can you come to the security booth? I have something to show you," Fredrick answered.

"Okay, I'm on my way." Toy put the walkie back where it was on the floor before she turned to Bonnie. "I'll be right back, Bonnie; Fredrick wants to talk to me in the security booth."

"You can go," Toy heard Drake say. "We've got this."

With a nod, Toy hugged Bonnie and then jogged toward the security booth further down the hallway.

"So, what do you want to show me?" Toy asked as she hurried in.

"Come look," Fredrick said as he pointed to the computer.

Toy gazed at the computer screen to find Kurt seated in an unfamiliar room.

"Kurt!"

"Do you know who has the power? Maybe we can go get him."

"I do."

"Do you want to go get him? He's the last one we must save before Goldie returns, and we get to leave this place."

"Yes!" Toy exclaimed. "Let's get this over with!"

"All right, let's go."

They brought Julia into the security booth, ensuring she knew the situation. Toy turned on the flashlight she had taken from the desk drawer and searched for an escape route that wouldn't draw any unwanted attention from the others.

"You said you have extra batteries for this thing, right?" Fredrick asked.

Toy nodded and patted one of her pockets. "Only two left from earlier." He nodded before Toy noticed his expression." Don't worry." She swallowed. "We'll find more. They're everywhere in this place."

Fredrick and Toy peeked out of the security booth to see Bonnie and Drake exiting the room they woke up in. As quietly as they could, they maneuvered around Bonnie and Drake. Once they bypassed them, they entered the room. Toy approached the metal grate.

"This is how you guys left the first time?" Toy asked him.

"Yes, it leads to some scaffolding that we can use to get to the ground."

With a firm grip on the flashlight, Toy aimed its beam toward the floor, illuminating the path ahead. The eerie feeling of being watched lingered, causing an incessant twitching sensation at the back of her neck. It was undeniable that something or someone was watching them; truth be told, Toy had no desire to uncover who.

Not after what she had seen in this place.

Without hesitation, Toy handed the flashlight to Fredrick as she removed the grate and crawled into the darkness. Once inside, Toy retrieved the light from him. Finally reaching the other side, they took a moment to stretch their weary limbs, relieved to have made it through unscathed.

"You aren't afraid of heights, are you?" he asked Toy as she pointed the beam at the scaffolding.

The surrounding wind rocked the scaffolding, making them reach out for something to hold.

"A little, yeah. The wind is not helping..." Toy sighed.

"Same here; I already climbed this once, and it sucked."

A soft chuckle escaped Toy's lips, overwhelming fear coursing through her body. The descent down felt never-ending.

This. Sucked.

Finally, they reached the bottom, taking a minute to feel the solid ground beneath their feet. They sent a silent thank-you to anyone above who was still listening before they began their journey to the back of the asylum.

"Why are we going to the back? Won't Owen be there?" Toy asked.

"If Owen is waiting for us, he wouldn't expect us to come from the back," Fredrick answered.

"Why did we have to sneak out, exactly? The others could have helped us."

"They would have told us to wait 'til he was closer to the safe zone... That's what they did with Brodie. I want to get this over with, you know? I want to get Brendan out of this hell; he deserves so much more."

They reached the back door. Fredrick kindly held the door open for Toy. Stepping inside, they were taken aback by what awaited them.

"This side of the building looks like a fire happened. Gosh!" Toy exclaimed.

"Let's go," he responded. "Let's go get Kurt and get back."

"Okay."

They went over to the hallway door, and Toy grabbed the doorknob. "The door is locked," she murmured. "We need to find a key..."

"You know it can be open if someone in a security booth opens it," Fredrick explained. Toy watched as he picked up his walkie with a chuckle. "Julia, please open the hallway door on cam nine."

The sound of the door unlocking without a key reached Toy's ears, causing her to roll her eyes in annoyance. Bonnie and Toy would have had a much easier time if they could have gotten someone in the security booth to open the doors.

"Come on, Toy."

They entered the hallway and the door locked behind him, trapping them inside. With caution, they maneuvered around several corners, keeping a low profile. Fredrick pointed toward a debris cluster that cluttered the hallway's brightest section. There was a small, blood-covered opening between the shelves that they could squeeze through. Taking a shaky breath, Fredrick stepped aside, allowing Toy to go first. Without hesitation, Toy made her way through the narrow gap, only to feel a sharp wooden spike pierce her forearm, causing searing pain and a trickle of warm blood to run down her arm.

"Toy! Toy, what happened?"

"Look out. There's some wood here that will cut you," Toy told him as she made it to the end. Glancing down at her forearm, she noticed the blood from the cut, but what caught her attention was the black substance that seemed to be embedded in the wound, most likely from the wood. Toy removed the gauze from her head and repurposed it to wrap around her arm, providing much-needed protection for the injury.

Toy pulled down her flannel, acknowledging the unpleasantness of the situation, but realizing that the bleeding from her head had stopped. She prioritized tending to her arm. It wasn't like she saw any other suitable fabric in the vicinity.

Finally, Fredrick caught up, emerging from the gap, and joined her. "Is it bad?" he asked, pointing at her arm.

"It's deep, but I don't need stitches. Do you think there are many kids left?" Toy wondered aloud. "Or any?"

"It's...hard to say. We have to assume that there are and that we will come across them sooner rather than later. By this point, whoever is still hanging around has got to be more than a little desperate. Willing to do anything...everything, whatever, to get out of here for good." His voice was stern, unflinching.

They were not exempt from this unspoken reality, and Toy could discern it from the tension in Fredrick's stride and the glimmer of steel in his narrowed eyes. They made their way down a few flights of narrow stairs. Toy tried to conjure up something foolish or clever to say, just as Bonnie would do. A cold sensation enveloped her forearm, like she stuck it into the snow outside, and Toy could almost swear she could feel something growing beneath the surface of her skin.

When Fredrick wasn't looking, Toy rolled up her sleeve and lifted the gauze to examine her arm. A gasp escaped her lips, but she suppressed it. To her horror, she saw sinister black veins sprouting from the injury, mirroring the same eerie veins that had engulfed Owen and her friends' bodies. The same veins on the lifeless bodies and spirits scattered throughout this dreadful place.

Toy had seen firsthand the devastating effects of these black veins. They owned a lethal power that brought unimaginable pain. The gravity of the situation weighed on Toy, and she couldn't help but feel a sense of unease. It felt as if she was losing touch with reality, experiencing a disconnection that spiraled deeper with each passing moment. This feeling of detachment had plagued her since the chaos began, her mind operating on a different wavelength than the rest of her being. Toy struggled to synchronize her thoughts and emotions, leaving her overwhelmed by exhaustion and a profound, distant sadness that resonated in rhythm with her heartbeat.

Despite the overwhelming confusion and disorientation, one thing remained crystal-clear: an unwavering determination to protect her friends at any cost. This steadfast loyalty drove her, compelling her to follow them into the darkest depths of the unknown.

With a deep breath, Toy covered her arm, concealing the disturbing sight of the black veins, and turned her attention to finding Fredrick. In her haste, she collided with him, causing the walkie-talkie to slip from his grasp and shatter as it hit the ground.

"Oh gosh! Fredrick, I'm so sorry! I didn't mean to—"

"It's fine, we'll be okay."

They spotted a noticeable gap in the wall at the base of the staircase. With a sense of urgency, Fredrick directed the flashlight beam through the opening, allowing him to glimpse a relatively well-maintained security booth that appeared unoccupied. They squeezed through the wooden frames and found themselves in the new area.

This time, they didn't investigate the desks or cabinets. Neither of them had any interest in doing so. Personally, Toy couldn't care less. The throbbing pain in her head had already begun, and she had no idea how much time she had left. They couldn't afford to waste time exploring; their priority was finding Kurt.

Although they only had one battery remaining, they consciously decided not to go out of their way to search for more. It would be awesome if they stumbled upon any batteries in plain sight, but even if they didn't, they were confident that they would manage. After all, they'd done just fine so far, hadn't they?

Fredrick found a battery on top of a file cabinet and handed it to Toy with a small, crooked smile. "What would we do without Bob, huh?"

Toy stared at him. "Uh. Did you...name the flashlight?"

As they entered the adjacent security booth, Fredrick nonchalantly lifted his shoulders, a subtle blush appearing on his dark cheeks.

"I might have," he huffed. "Stop looking at me like that."

Toy's lips twitched involuntarily, and she instinctively shook her head to dismiss the sensation.

"It was either Bob or Wade..."

Toy strained to hear what Fredrick muttered, but she couldn't. As he shifted his eyes away from hers and looked at the interior windows to their right, his face turned a vibrant shade of crimson. Deciding not to make a big deal, Toy let it slide, not wanting to make him uncomfortable. Instead, she responded with laughter, causing him to punch her in the arm. Suddenly, a ringing sensation filled her ears.

"Oh, you'll get yours, Toy." His voice dropped to a whisper, accompanied by an uncanny sparkle in his bright blue eyes. "I don't know when or even where...but it will happen. Make no mistake about that."

As soon as Toy heard him, she knew it wasn't meant to be a threat, but to bring a smile to her face. They stopped near an entrance and, without thinking, Toy turned her head. A wave of unease washed over her.

"Um, wait." Toy swallowed. "Do you hear something?"

She fixed her gaze on the expansive room just beyond the security booth's entrance, but her attempts to concentrate were hindered by the trembling of her hands and the rapid beating of her heart. In her state of unease, Toy couldn't help but feel as though her tongue was about to suffocate her.

"Like what?" Fredrick eventually rasped.

Toy could sense it. Not only could she sense the blood in Fredrick's veins, or the nearby spirits, but Toy could sense his unsteadiness, mirroring her own attempt to suppress emotions.

"It was faint." Toy peered out into the yellow light, but the room was empty from what she could tell, and yet... At the end... "Maybe a voice?" She squinted at the scattered pockets of shadows by the far doors and another wall of interior windows. "Or—"

Toy's teeth felt the chill as the words froze upon them.

It was not just a voice that she heard, but melodious singing.

Fredrick cocked his head to listen and then let out a quiet groan. "Oh, no. Man, not this lunatic." He scrubbed a rough hand over his head. "No fucking way..."

Toy shot him a sharp look. "What? You know who it is?"

"Yep, sure do," he grumbled. "I figured that since we went around the building, we wouldn't just...randomly stumble across him. Goddammit," he cursed. "He better not have some...some messed up rat torture like he did to that one teen. You know, I'm still scared of what he did to him." A shudder coursed through him, and Toy was not sure if he was exaggerating.

"Uh...huh? This conversation just took a turn into the surreal—more so than usual, Fredrick. What the heck are you talking about?"

"His name is Victor," Fredrick muttered. "I don't remember his last name; some other teens here have called him the Rat Man. Obviously, because of the whole stupid medieval rat torture obsession that he had with that one boy..."

He guided Toy to an archway on the left side of the room, positioning her so that she faced it. He clicked on "Bob" to search the space, but fortunately, there was nothing. The sound of the singing became almost imperceptible, suggesting that the source was moving further away. This relieved Toy, allowing her to exhale and finally release the lingering feeling of unease.

"Okay, you're gonna have to start at the beginning...or something." Toy. "That sounds like it could almost be mildly entertaining. And entertainment would be good for us, Fredrick."

Toy could almost sense his eyes rolling in exasperation. A broad smile appeared on her face when he briefly looked back at her.

"Really, Toy? Now?" he huffed, sounding both overwhelmingly fond and incredibly exasperated as they edged around the corner and navigated down a scarcely lit hallway. "Escaping this place with our sanity and vital organs intact isn't enough entertainment for you?" He bumped Toy with his arm. "You can be so...so..."

"What? So...unbelievable?" Toy interrupted. "Yeah, I've been told." Her grin widened into a lopsided smile.

"Damn right," he grunted.

Despite Toy's efforts, she couldn't escape the overwhelming feeling of disappointment that pierced her like a sharp knife whenever she cautiously entered the unknown. The ground beneath Toy seemed to shift, causing her feet to lose their stability. In an instant, the earth rushed upward with astonishing speed.

CHAPTER 28

Toy

When Toy came to, she realized she was being carried. She instinctively glanced forward to see Fredrick walking ahead, which left her confused. She moved her head up to identify the person carrying her, only to discover that it was Bonnie.

"Bonnie? What are you doing here?" Toy whispered, her voice catching the boys' attention.

"I could ask you two the same thing, *niña*. What made you think sneaking out looking for Kurt was a good idea?" Bonnie asked.

"Fredrick found him on the camera, and it seemed easy."

"Easy? Toy, you know what is out there. Owen and all kinds of danger."

"How did you find out?"

"The shitty camera system went out, and Julia freaked. She came running, screaming about how you guys left and how she was supposed to keep watch. I told the others to stay in the safe room and followed you two, which was challenging. Brendan had his heels dug in about coming with, but I got him to stay to fix the computer."

"Did you bring a walkie?"

"No, there's only two—the one in the safe zone and the one that you two had. I didn't want to take the other in case you two tried to contact the safe zone. We survived without one before, and you two hadn't gotten far when Julia told us what you were doing."

Toy's brief moment of relief was abruptly interrupted by the familiar feeling of fear creeping back into her body, accompanied by the haunting sound of a singing voice.

"Rats invade, they come for me, oh no.
They crawl and gnaw, their hunger never sated
Rats invade, they come for me
Their sharp teeth, my skin they slowly break
As I scream and beg for mercy
The horror, the pain, the fear devours me
Rats eat me alive, eat me alive
I feel them, I hear them, they consume my flesh
I gave my all, my strength, my everything
But now the rats have won, I'm with them 'til the end
Their tiny eyes, their vicious scurrying
They feast upon me, their prey helpless and dying
Their tiny eyes, they watch me fade
In this nightmare, there's no escape
As I lay here, helpless and broken
The rats reign supreme, my fate is spoken
Rats eat me alive, eat me alive
I feel them, I hear them, they consume my flesh
I gave my all, my strength, my everything
But now the rats have won, I'm with them 'til the end
In this twisted dance of agony
I become the meal of their insanity
Rats eat me alive, eat me alive
I feel them, I hear them, they consume my flesh
I gave my all, my strength, my everything
But now the rats have won, I'm with them 'til the end..."

"You know...you never really told me what his deal was." Toy raised an eyebrow at Fredrick as Victor began the song all over again.

Fredrick let out a dramatic sigh as they cautiously approached some tables. The adjacent hall on the right was a dead-end, leaving them with no choice but to head toward the source of the voice.

How unsurprising.

"Okay. In short, he is obsessed with rats."

"No shit..." Bonnie interrupted.

"He sort of...uses rats to torture anyone he catches. On the camera, I saw... The kid was completely restrained and tied down. A rat was then placed on his stomach covered by a glass container. As the container was gradually heated, the rat began to look for a way out...through the kid's body." Fredrick's words caused them to cringe. "The rat took a few hours to escape once he was inside the kid. The kid...he just screamed in agony. I had to turn off the camera a couple times because of it, but every time I checked on him it was worse. I can still hear the screaming in my head... Let's pray that we never encounter him because he is truly disturbed."

"Yeah, all right." Toy grimaced. "That...wasn't as entertaining as I was hoping it would be."

"Not to mention, the terrifying mental images the explanation produced were not pleasant. Not. At. All," Bonnie added.

After a brief pause, they cautiously glanced through the narrow opening. As far as Toy could see, no one was on the opposite side. However, the melodic singing intensified with each passing moment, and the loud ringing in Toy's ears resurfaced with even greater intensity.

"We have to do it," Bonnie muttered and looked over at Fredrick, then down at Toy with a grim expression. "Quick and painless, just like... Like ripping off a band-aid."

"Sure, why not?" Fredrick mumbled.

As Fredrick maneuvered his way through the narrow opening, Toy inhaled deeply, seizing the opportunity. Bonnie released his grip on her, allowing her to swiftly scurry into the space before any objections could be raised.

"Rip off the band-aid and expose the raw, bleeding wound underneath," Toy mumbled.

"Have I mentioned how much I love your cheerful optimism?" Bonnie chuckled behind her.

"Yes. You did. I'm inspiring, huh?"

Whenever he laughed, Toy couldn't help but join in. His quiet giggles had this incredible ability to spread like wildfire, even in the most intense situations. They had an even greater effect in high-pressure moments.

Bonnie tuned on "Bob" to illuminate the corridors. was is about to pick up the pace when he shined the light from one end to the other, and it caught on something: a tall, broad-shouldered figure lounging near one of the distant doorways. A voice in Toy's head screamed danger, and Toy realized it was likely the doorway they needed to pass through.

Without hesitation, Fredrick and Toy dropped into clumsy crouches, and Bonnie turned off "Bob." Questions flooded Toy's mind—did the figure see them? Hear them? Were they still safe? Toy's eyes widened, and her heart pulsed in her throat. Toy stared intently at the spot where she last saw the figure, wondering how they would find a way around it. Were they already doomed?

Time seemed to slow as they held their breath, each second feeling agonizingly long. Bonnie's grip on Toy's upper arm offered some reassurance, but not enough to calm her racing thoughts. Suddenly, fingers wrapped tightly around Fredrick and Toy's throats, pulling them to their feet. A low, smooth voice purred in the darkness.

"Oh, is that you, Cibus?"

CHAPTER 29

Toy

The constant threat of being strangled by people had become incredibly annoying. Instead of succumbing to panic and fear, Toy's anger ignited like a rocket, bursting outward with the force of a carbonated bottle shaken too much. In a desperate attempt to free herself, she and Fredrick fought back ferociously, clawing and kicking at the assailant choking them.

Within moments, Bonnie joined the fray, swiftly striking the attacker's skull with a heavy thwack from Bob the flashlight. The man grunted in pain, his grip loosening just enough for them to escape. Toy gasped for air. It rushed back into her lungs, accompanied by an overwhelming surge of heat. The surrounding darkness spun, and Toy was momentarily blinded by the dancing white splotches that filled her vision.

"Don't you fucking touch them!" Bonnie growled.

"But Cibus, I'm doing this for the rats," Victor wheezed. "I have to get rid of the Carrier's Protector so I can feed my babies..."

Only then did Toy look at her attacker's face, and she wished she didn't.

Victor's physique bore the unmistakable signs of being ravaged and marred, as if it had endured a relentless feast by...

you guessed it—rats. No part of his body was unmarked; his face had to be the worst, marred by severe scars, revealing a lack of skin to such an extent that it appeared as if his bones were visible.

Despite feeling disoriented and unsteady, Toy maintained her composure and struck the side of his kneecap with the heel of her high-top. The impact caused him to emit a furious howl, and taking advantage of his distraction, Toy swiftly guided Fredrick and Bonnie down the hallway.

"Come on!" Frustration built within Toy as Bonnie continued to struggle, causing her to rasp out, "We need to go."

"He was fucking strangling you... That son of a bitch!"

Bonnie's frustration was clear as he struggled to articulate complete sentences. His anger manifested as spitting and cursing, creating a tense atmosphere as they navigated the hallway. Their primary goal was to evade Victor, all while ensuring their presence remained concealed. The urgency of the situation amplified as they sprinted around corners, a nerve-racking experience that left Toy disoriented and clueless about their location or how to reunite with the rest of the group. They focused on avoiding obstacles that would cause them to stumble or fall.

With a limp and disingenuous tone, Victor repeatedly called out for his beloved "babies."

"The rats know you didn't mean to hurt me!" he insisted. "It's the Carrier's Protector. She's poisoned your mind against us!"

Toy shook her head, unable to believe this jerk. Kieran had always been a source of fear for her, but this guy took it to a new level, sending shivers down her spine. The pain in her throat was a constant reminder, making it painful to swallow. Despite the throbbing headache, a glimmer of relief washed over Toy as they ran, diminishing the overwhelming sense of dread.

"I'm going to kill him," Bonnie grunted. "If I get the chance, I will."

Toy wondered whether she should feel flattered or concerned by that declaration. It was surprising to hear those words from him, especially considering how Bonnie had always been most affected by the challenges the other teenagers faced. However, there seemed to be a vindictive side to his personality that Toy never knew existed. It made her wonder if she knew him as well as she thought she did.

To avoid conflict or disagreement, Toy remained silent and refrained from expressing her thoughts. It was a challenging situation for her as she found herself at a loss for words and unsure how to respond.

They turned a corner, and the surroundings became brighter, prompting them to increase their pace.

Taking charge, Toy guided the boys through the doorway at the end of the hallway, passing beneath a hanging, headless body. Toy instinctively opted for a sharp left turn when faced with a choice. She saw the narrow gap between stacked shelves and tables in that direction.

"Hey, down here," Toy urged, giving Bonnie's hand and Fredrick's shoulder a squeeze. "We can hide behind that junk until the coast is clear."

Bonnie took a quick look back at Fredrick and Toy while smoothly maneuvering past the tables. "Okay, okay, but if he catches up to us again, that's it. I swear to God that will be it," he told Toy, eyes like darkened steel. "He isn't Owen, Toy. I can fucking take him."

Following Fredrick, a wave of discomfort washed over Toy, causing her stomach to churn. It was not her place to dictate what was morally correct or incorrect in this place.

"Okay," Toy finally sighed. "Okay."

It didn't seem likely that she would be able to alter his decision through conversation.

"But only if he catches up to us again. Corners us or something. And, well... We'll think of something."

Bonnie's gaze fixed on Toy, his expression transforming

from anger to surprise as a softness settled over his features. "We will?"

"Yes, you idiot." Toy gave him a gentle pat on the head. "You think that we would really let you do something so stupid alone? Come on..."

With a grin that stretched from ear to ear, he directed their attention toward the concealed room, which was camouflaged by various metal obstacles. The room appeared lit, making it unnecessary for Bob to be turned on. As they approached, they noticed that the left side of the wall was adorned with a row of bathtubs.

"Oh, what the hell is this?" Fredrick frowned. "No, wait. I've learned my lesson. Don't answer that, please."

Bonnie huffed a chuckle and shook his head. "Damn. And all this time, I thought you two actually liked my horrible stories."

"Well, yeah. I do. But I also like listening to you talk about... anything." Toy shrugged, a reddish flush burning her ears as she rested against the wall.

"Anything?" He raised a suggestive eyebrow. "In that case, how about—"

"No!" Toy's face warmed to a near-impossible degree. "No, no. Not that I don't appreciate the enthusiasm or anything. But, um. It's just not the best time for it, baby."

Toy turned away to glance back at the empty room, even though she could hear Bonnie whisper something to Fredrick about how he enjoyed seeing Toy blush, and Fredrick followed up with "You should see Brendan blush" before Toy tuned them out.

Whenever Toy got flustered, she became dumb and unable to speak right, making how she felt obvious. It was definitely not a great feeling. Luckily, Bonnie didn't continue down that embarrassing path of conversation.

As Toy surveyed the room again, a sense of dread washed over her. The feeling, along with the persistent headache and bouts of weakness, must have been symptoms of the infection taking over her body. The cold and frosty moonlight seeped through the barred windows behind the bathtubs, casting an eerie glow on the dirty white porcelain and the pools of red liquid shimmering on the tiles below them.

It was hard to imagine anything pleasant happening in this room. Unfortunately, a few bodies or body parts remained left behind, adding to the eerie atmosphere. Yet, as they stood there, a sudden trembling of the tables sent a wave of fear through Toy. Toy spun around, almost lost her balance, and bumped into the doorframe, her heart racing and her throat tightening.

And there he stood, towering over six feet and weighing over two hundred pounds. His seductive, snake-like smile sent shivers down her spine.

"Please, Cibus. Don't run from us," Victor crooned.

With his arms stretching through the narrow opening, which was too small for him to squeeze through, Toy pushed Fredrick and Bonnie into the room with the bathtubs. She did this just in time, bloodied fingers nearly grabbing hold of their clothes.

"I was told I could give you to the rats if I gave them the Carrier's Protector, did you know? Isn't that wonderful news?"

"Stop calling her that!" Bonnie snarled over Toy's shoulder. "You will not give her to anybody. Do you hear me?!"

Fredrick seized the opportunity to restrain Bonnie as Toy pushed him with intense, exasperated energy, preventing him from maneuvering around her.

"Go!" Toy yelled.

"He hasn't caught us yet; we must take advantage of that! Please, Bonnie, we have to go!" Fredrick yelled.

He may have seen the desperation reflected in their faces, or sensed it in Toy's frantic attempt to coax him into joining them in the room. Regardless of the reason, he uttered another curse directed at the man and allowed them to guide him through the room as they hastily traversed the unfamiliar space.

"I'm sorry," Toy heard him grunt. "He makes me so mad that I can't even think straight, *niña*."

"I know. Believe me, I know," Toy reassured him. "You don't have to apologize."

After a long ten minutes, they reached the far room, only to discover that it was, unsurprisingly, a dead end. Disappointingly, there was nothing of interest or value in the room. As they came to this realization, it became clear that there was no other option but to retrace their steps and go back the way they came. Yet, Toy was well aware of Bonnie's current state of volatility and how close he was to reaching his breaking point.

As Toy started to feel dizzy again, she collided with Bonnie, causing him to gasp in surprise. Toy quickly regained her balance and distanced herself from him without wasting time.

"I'm fine; we have to keep going."

As they approached the shelves once more, Victor's unsettling absence was both a relief and a cause for concern, as they needed to escape this area before he reappeared—or, worse, he may have already been waiting for them. The tension in the air was palpable, and the urgency to leave grew stronger with each passing moment.

Toy couldn't help but notice Bonnie's tight grip on Bob, his knuckles turning white with worry. Her concern deepened as she furrowed her brow and frowned at the back of his head. Despite their tendency to make sarcastic remarks, Fredrick and Toy understood the gravity of the situation and chose to remain silent, focusing on moving forward.

With a sense of urgency, they quickened their pace as they approached the doorway they entered just ten minutes ago. The sight of the headless body swinging from the ceiling served as a grim reminder of the danger they were in. Bonnie pointed to a faded red sign on the far wall to their left, a beacon of hope amidst the chaos, guiding them toward a possible escape route.

"Yeah, yeah—we're on the right path again!"

A familiar toothy smile lit up his face as he turned around to face Toy—the kind of smile that eased the tension in her chest, causing a few knots to unravel. Toy couldn't help but mirror his grin as his smile made her forget about the troubles surrounding them.

"Not surprised at all that you figured it out, baby." Toy beamed, clapping him on the arm.

"We have to make a point to finish this. Right at the end, when we're about to leave, we'll just... We'll torch everything, okay?" Fredrick interrupted. He retrieved his lighter and ignited it before stowing it away again. They couldn't help but stifle their laughter, finding humor in the situation.

Just as Toy was about to make a lighthearted comment, insinuating that they might not be roasting any marshmallows, an unexpected force collided with the side of her head.

Surprisingly, there was no pain, nor did she experience the typical swirling stars often depicted in cartoons. Instead, she was enveloped in a void of nothingness.

Toy

When Toy regained consciousness, she found herself disoriented in an upside-down world, her vision distorted by the sickening tilt. Confusion filled her bloodshot eyes as she focused on the back of a rumpled white dress shirt. The throbbing pain in her head intensified, and she could sense the dried blood clinging to her neck and one of her ears without even checking. An irritating itch accompanied the crusted lines of blood. The nauseating sensation overwhelmed her, making her feel like she might vomit. Yet, instead of succumbing to the urge, she reluctantly realized she was currently draped over someone's shoulder like a lifeless rag doll, a fact that profoundly unsettled her.

"What the—" With a scowl on her face, she tried to free herself from the grip of an arm that felt as heavy as fifty pounds of solid steel. "What the heck are you doing?" Toy demanded. "Where are you taking me?!"

With her fists wrapped in bandages, she forcefully punched her captor's back, simultaneously extending her legs and releasing a torrent of anger through spitting and cursing. The overwhelming rage engulfed her, intensifying her actions and fueling her determination.

"Let me go!"

"Protector, your noise is becoming unbearable," Victor growled, his tone utterly different from the gentle and innocent one he used when talking about his rats. As he tightened his grip around her waist, she instinctively pulled away, flinching in response. "Understand this; you will stay away from what belongs to my babies," he continued, his nails digging into her skin like shards of glass through her T-shirt. "Not that it matters, because where you're going...you won't be seeing anyone for a long time. That's what I've heard, at least." His tone was dismissive, showing no care or concern. "If you dare utter another word, I'll ensure your teeth are broken in by the time we get to Silver. Would you like that?"

Toy's hands tightened into fists, her tongue caught between her teeth as the agony coursed through her arm. The pounding in her head became almost unbearable. The deafening ringing made it challenging to focus. The overwhelming feeling of dread consumed her, forcing her to remind herself to take deep breaths and stay calm.

All right, fine. This guy clearly has the upper hand. His strength far surpassed her own, leaving her at a disadvantage. But what could she do in this situation? Toy winced, turning her head to distract herself from the searing heat and the throbbing sensation caused by the rush of blood in all the wrong places within her brain.

Toy knew she would faint again if she didn't get upright soon. And how much time had passed? She wondered what on earth Victor had done to Bonnie and Fredrick for her to end up in this state. This man desired her boyfriend and Fredrick to become rat feed, or something along those lines. But who knew? Maybe they were okay. Toy didn't know what "okay" entailed, and honestly, she didn't want to find out.

Struggling to see clearly, Toy strained her eyes to make out the shapes before her. The dimly lit hallway revealed only vague outlines and flickering lights reflecting off the bloodstains on the concrete floor. Suddenly, a realization hit her like a ton of bricks when she saw a figure silently trailing behind Victor. It was not Bonnie, but Fredrick, his finger, stained with blood, pressed against his lips, signaling Toy to stay quiet. To her horror, he clutched a menacing butcher knife in his other hand. Confusion and fear swirled in her mind as she tried to comprehend the situation. Where was Bonnie? Why was Fredrick alone? As Victor turned a corner, the lighting improved, allowing Toy to see more clearly.

Fredrick took his hand and spread his fingers. He lowered one finger, causing Toy's heart to skip in shock and disbelief as he lowered a second finger, followed by a third. The realization hit her like a ton of bricks, leaving her breathless and unable to comprehend what was happening. Soon, he had only one finger remaining, and without wasting a moment, he swiftly attacked. A heavy thud filled the air, accompanied by painful grunts.

Overwhelmed by the chaos unfolding before her, Toy was dropped to the ground. Her body ached and trembled. Fredrick launched himself at Victor with an intense fury. Confusion clouded her mind, and the hallway seemed to spin around her. She scrambled backward until she felt the cold touch of the wall against her back.

The sight that unfolded before Toy's eyes was both terrifying and mesmerizing. The two men engaged in a fierce struggle, their movements accompanied by vivid splashes of crimson. When Toy thought the chaos couldn't escalate further, a third figure entered the scene. There was no mistaking the anger etched on their face nor the deep, captivating magenta eyes that pierced through the chaos.

Bonnie.

Goodness gracious. Goodness gracious. The events unfolding before Toy were overwhelming; she could hardly comprehend the situation. Fredrick thrusted his knife into Victor, yet that despicable person was still standing? Despite the copious amount of blood pouring from his side, he remained on his feet and continued to throw punches. Hold on a second—how did he wrestle the blade away? Meanwhile, Bonnie, without hesitation, jumped into the fight, swinging Bob around as if possessed.

Three bodies entangled in a fierce struggle. A bone cracked under pressure. Suddenly, someone collapsed to the ground. In a final burst of violence, blood spurted out, accompanied by a cry of pain. As the deafening silence descended upon them, Toy swayed, horror coursing through her veins as she stood.

Bonnie was gasping for air, his breath coming out in choked sobs, sweat cascading down his face. With wild eyes, he turned to Toy and let Bob slip from his grasp, allowing it to clatter onto the ground. He wrapped her up in an almost aggressive embrace, as if trying to shield her from harm. Toy could hear him asking if she was all right; if Victor harmed her—yet all she could perceive was a strange buzzing sound in her ears as his voice faded in and out. While her arms remained locked around Bonnie, her gaze shifted beyond the lifeless body of Victor and landed upon Fredrick, who had endured a knife wound to his stomach to protect Toy.

"I'm...I'm okay," Toy mumbled, the answer instinctive. "I'm okay, Bonnie. He did nothing to me."

Toy struggled to break free from his grasp. Her body had taken on a will of its own. Despite her determined efforts to distance herself from him, he clung to her, refusing to let go.

"Bonnie. Please." Toy's tongue felt too heavy for her mouth. "I have to...I have to.."

She was unaware of the words coming out of her mouth, yet she could sense the desperation in her faltering voice. The taste of panic lingered on her tongue, sharp, metallic, and bitter, as Bonnie withdrew and stared at Toy with a sudden surge of alarm.

"What? What's wrong?" He gripped Toy's shoulders and held her out, his worried gaze scanning her from head to toe.

"Goddammit. Victor knocked us out with something after he got you; when I woke up, Fredrick and I didn't know where he took you. It wasn't hard to figure out where the fucker went, but it just... It took so fucking long, and I was so afraid he killed you..." He drew in a long, shuddering breath.

Toy pressed her hands onto his, feeling the warmth and strength she knew so well. Tears welled up in her eyes, but she fought the urge to cry out as she stared at Fredrick, her heart heavy with worry.

Without waiting for Bonnie to speak, Toy stepped away from the comforting heat of his presence, her legs trembling beneath her. She made her way to Fredrick, her steps unsteady. His complexion had turned a sickly shade of gray, his clothes soaked in blood and sweat. His fingers, once strong and capable, now clenched uselessly at the wound on his stomach. With a rush of emotions, Toy dropped to her knees beside him, her heart breaking at the sight of his contorted and pained expression. The whole scene reminded Toy of Cherry...

"Why?" Toy managed through gritted teeth. "Why would you do such a stupid thing?"

His eyes, a mesmerizing shade of deep blue, shimmered with emotion. A few glistening tears escaped as he gazed up at Toy, tracing a path down his cheeks.

"Maybe...it was stupid," he wheezed. "But I did it...because I could. Because...it was the right thing to do." Fredrick's hand tightened as the warm crimson liquid slipped through his fingers. Despite his weakened state, he managed a feeble chuckle, causing blood to trickle from his bottom lip. "That doesn't matter to me. None of that...none of that matters, you know? We can't let these assholes take what makes us...what makes us, us. We can't let them change us into another one of their experiments. We can't...we can't lose sight of what we're fighting for here." His speech faltered as he paused. "Surviving... It will mean nothing...if we forget how to be human."

His plain and direct words struck Toy with such force

that they pierced through her core, surpassing any weapon's sharpness. As a result, her shoulders slumped, her entire body crumbling under the weight of his words. Toy couldn't help but fold in on herself. Tears streamed down her face.

"It's okay," he whispered. "You...you aren't that far gone yet."

"How do you know?" Toy demanded. "How could you know that?"

A broad grin spread across his face, and he wrestled to extend his arm. Without hesitation, Toy grasped his hand; his palm felt damp and icy against hers. Toy clutched his fingers tightly, as if her sheer determination could somehow preserve his life. Toy could not bear to lose another person...

Please, dear God, spare me from any more losses...

"Because...you're here with me, aren't you? Like you were for my older sister..." He coughed. "You're sitting here, crying over a dead man. And that's something."

Her throat tightened hearing him mention Cherry. A sob threatened to escape while an intense pressure built up inside her chest like a volatile vat of acid ready to burst.

"When I was watching the cameras, I saw a girl killed early. First few hours you went missing," he murmured. "She was tall... Pretty. Like you. But... She was violent. So damn hateful. She never would have survived in this place with...with that much poison in her heart. You might...you might think you've done terrible things to get this far. But you aren't like her. And I'm... I don't regret it. Being stupid." He tried to smile again, and Toy could feel her ribs cutting into her heart at the sight. "I'm glad that I helped you." His breath stuttered, a spasm of pain spreading across his face. "I know...you'll be okay," he reassured her. "You and all our friends are going to be okay."

"Please don't die..."

As Fredrick's eyes drooped, Toy tapped his cheek until he opened them again, trying to get him to stay awake.

"Tell... Tell Bon that I love him... I love him so much... Tell my family I'm sorry..." Fredrick mumbled.

Bonnie and Toy didn't even try to hold back their sobs.

"Please," Toy choked out. "Please don't go."

She watched, studying every inch of Fredrick's face as the corner of his lips quivered. "Please tell Brendan I love him..."

"He already knows. He loves you so much, Fredrick!"

"Brendan... Brendan... Brend—"

And then his eyes slipped closed, and his fingers slid from Toy's. Toy pushed Fredrick's hands away and fought to keep pressure on his wound.

"Bonnie, help me!" Toy screamed.

"Toy..."

"Bonnie, we need—"

"Toy...he's gone..."

He's gone... Fredrick's gone... It's all my fault...

CHAPTER 31

Toy

Bonnie's gaze wandered around the room, avoiding direct contact with Fredrick's body. Curiosity got the better of Toy, and she rolled up her sleeve. A sharp cry escaped her lips as she discovered that the sinister black veins had spread to her shoulder.

"Toy, look..." Bonnie said, startling her and making her straighten out her flannel.

The deafening noise in her ears became unbearable. Toy glanced to the side and noticed a figure attempting to conceal itself from them. She couldn't help but wonder why this spirit seemed so fearful of them.

"It's Kurt!" Bonnie exclaimed.

With the last ounce of energy Toy possessed, she dragged herself to her feet and to Kurt. Her body felt weak, and all Toy desired was for the agony to stop.

I don't want to die...

Despite her weakened state, she approached Kurt, taking slow and deliberate steps so as not to startle him. "Don't be afraid. I'm not going to hurt you," she said as she got close enough to touch his head if he didn't move.

Startled, he recoiled as she placed her hand on his forehead. A wave of confusion washed over her as she found herself alone in an unfamiliar place.

The sight before her was chilling and unsettling; it resembled an abandoned psychiatric ward for children. The atmosphere was suffused with an eerie sadness that permeated every corner. It was difficult to fathom that parents would ever subject their children to such a place.

The heaviness in the air was palpable, like a thick smog that weighed on her lungs and shoulders. It felt as though the very essence of life was being drained from her heart, leaving behind a hollow emptiness. Time seemed to stretch on endlessly, and despite the silence, Toy strained her ears for any sign of life. Yet there was no sight or sound of another soul in this desolate place.

"Hello!" Toy yelled. "Is anyone here?"

She looked to her left to see a peculiar steel cell door with a small window covered in bars. Curiosity got the better of her, and she opened the door. To her surprise, a man with vibrant amethyst hair emerged from within. His complexion was a rich, dark brown, and his eyes were a captivating shade of gray.

"Hello, Toy," the figure hummed.

"Who are you? How do you know my name?" Toy asked.

"My name is Zenith Brooks; I'm here to warn you."

"Warn me of what?"

"A man is going to show up. He will, and he will take someone you care about. It could be years from now or tomorrow; I can't tell you when exactly, and you will not know he is about to strike 'til he already did."

Toy's body froze in disbelief as she stood there, completely taken aback. The thought of someone attempting to snatch something from her sent shivers down her spine. Questions raced through her mind, wondering who this person could be. The uncertainty of the situation left her feeling vulnerable and on edge.

"You have to play your cards right, Toy, or someone you care about will end up here..."

"I will."

Zenith vanished, leaving no evidence behind, and in his absence, a child version of Kurt appeared. Kurt had his dark brown hair neatly combed back, but his brown eyes were filled with fear. Kurt's body was covered in black veins. He wore a T-shirt adorned with a colorful cartoon character and a simple pair of blue jeans.

"Hey, I'm Toy; what's your name?" Toy asked the small boy. She needed to ensure she could remind him of his identity without causing him any more fear or distress.

"I'm Kurt," cried the small boy.

"What's wrong?"

"I'm lonely... I don't know where all my friends went; people keep showing up and taking us... I'm scared; I don't want to be next. Are you going to hurt me?"

"Don't be afraid—I promise I'm not going to hurt you. I'm here to help you."

To her surprise, he made his way to Toy and settled on her lap. "Will you protect me?"

"Yes," Toy answered.

The young child's face lit up with a radiant smile before he disappeared into the air as if he was never there.

CHAPTER 32

Goldie

It started at the Summerhill Sanatorium in Ohio; the chilling winter made breathing the dry air painful. Enjoying a delicious dish like Bisteces a la Mexicana sounded heavenly, yet the terror gripping Goldie's stomach was so intense that even the idea of food became nauseating.

Owen gripped Goldie's arm like an iron case, feeling the burning sensation in his lungs as if they were on fire. He struggled to keep his eyes open, blinking away the snow obstructing his vision. They ran with their lives at stake, leaving behind their friends in the chaos of a crumbling city.

The immense force caused the streets to tremble, with the concrete buckling under the pressure. As a result, buildings collapsed, and the horrifying screams of people being killed filled the air. The streets were stained with blood. The overwhelming stench of fear permeated the atmosphere, turning the air and sky acrid.

Goldie and Owen found a moment to catch their breath amidst the chaos. Owen's grip on Goldie's upper arm remained tight, as if holding on to life itself. From their vantage point, they could see the entire city. Even from this distance, Goldie saw the destructive fire and the restless spirits writhing in agony.

The situation in Mount Vernon, Ohio, was beyond fucked. The city was in complete disarray as more spirits emerged, causing the ground to rumble. The collapse of buildings added to the chaos, leaving destruction in their wake. Black helicopters hovered above the city, but Goldie doubted they could save anyone other than themselves, as there seemed to be no safe landing spot amidst the devastation.

Goldie stared at his brother, Owen, and noticed the exhaustion etched on his face, his eyes filled with a haunting emptiness. It all began with a simple cough, but Owen soon was plagued by a fever, chills, and a deep, relentless ache in his bones. Goldie dismissed it as just the flu and tried to ease his brother's pain and fever with a large bottle of generic Tylenol. But when his temperature soared past a hundred and four, even Owen had to admit defeat and allow Mia to take him to the hospital.

The medical professionals administered antibiotics and more vital pain medication. While they awaited the results of Owen's bloodwork, Goldie couldn't help but feel it wouldn't make much of a difference. They had hoped that Owen would recover despite being sick and in pain, yet the situation took a turn for the worse as nightmares plagued Owen's sleep and seizures wracked his body. Suddenly, Goldie was arguing with Mia, Bonnie's mother. She insisted they leave Owen at the hospital, but Goldie refused to entertain the thought of abandoning his brother to suffer alone.

Owen found himself in the center of the chaos as the ground beneath him trembled. Spirits materialized out of thin air, surrounding him from all directions. It was a surreal sight, with spirits of all shapes and sizes floating around him, their presence undeniable and all-consuming.

Feeling overwhelmed by the situation, Goldie turned his back on the city and inadvertently on his friends...his family. Among them was the woman he deeply admired, who had saved his life. Yet, she had also shattered the trust of her "adopted" son in a way that caught everyone off guard, leaving Goldie torn.

The urgency to escape the city and seek help for Owen grew stronger with each passing moment. The news filled with reports of the CDC offering treatment and shelter amidst the outbreak. Owen's condition was deteriorating, and their only hope now was reaching Atlanta, Georgia.

The spirits, relentless in their pursuit, multiplied rapidly, leaving destruction in their wake. Their dark, viscous essence stained everything they touched, leaving a trail of death and decay. These malevolent spirits appeared determined to eradicate all life in their path, their presence a constant threat to the survival of those trying to escape their clutches.

Goldie and Owen found themselves on a treacherous journey on foot in the vast expanse of Kentucky. A swarm of hellish spirits had thwarted their previous attempt to board a train; their malevolent presence had derailed it. The sight of abandoned cars was a grim reminder of the danger they faced.

The blood-stained remnants and decomposing bodies within these vehicles reminded Goldie of a different plague, the Ziragord virus from Zenith's world.

Despite the lack of communication from Mia, Bonnie, or Drake, Goldie found solace in the fact that Owen had been his caregiver since infancy. Now it was his turn to reciprocate. Yet, their journey was marred by frustration as the last two clinics they visited seemed more interested in exploiting Owen as a test subject. Goldie made his first of many mistakes in the biting cold of Kentucky.

The frequency of devoured cars increased, even on the less-traveled back roads that the brothers preferred. The streets became more congested, which made it difficult to navigate. The presence of more bodies and hiding spots made the spirits more dangerous.

Faced with a blocked road ahead, Goldie led them through

a nearby cornfield, hoping to find an abandoned farm where they could find supplies and spend the night. Unfortunately, their plans did not go as intended. Instead, they spent the night in a horrifying scene.

Walking through fields filled with dead cattle, they discovered that the farmer had slaughtered all his livestock and left their corpses to rot at the edges of his property. The ground was soaked with blood, which had mixed with the mud, creating a gruesome slush. Goldie wondered if they should have turned back as soon as they saw the carnage.

The problem of murderous hillbillies had never been a concern as he never expected it to become their problem. Hidden among the rustling cornstalks, Goldie and Owen could only watch in horrified silence as the farmer and his family hunted down and slaughtered a group of trespassers. Goldie tightened his grip on Owen's shoulder, silently urging him to move away as the old farmer carved into a young woman's flesh and reveled in his twisted amusement. With great caution, Goldie helped his brother climb through a high window in the barn, hushing him as he wondered about the fate of the people being chased outside. In his mind, it was a grim realization that it was better for them to suffer than for Goldie and Owen to meet the same fate.

As they reached the outskirts of the farm, Owen had another attack, causing him to stagger and experience excruciating pain that blurred his vision. Feeling a growing sense of helplessness, Goldie lifted his brother onto his back, hoping that the pain would subside soon. Sneaking through the murderous hillbilly farm was now an experience that Goldie never wanted to repeat. They would have escaped if it hadn't been for that treacherous woman who betrayed them in a desperate attempt to save her own life. It was unfortunate for her that the farmer gutted her before he and his deranged family turned their attention to Goldie and Owen.

Goldie sprinted into the dense undergrowth of the woods

with his brother on his back. As the daylight faded into dusk, the ground beneath their feet trembled, providing a glimmer of hope as Goldie lit a flare. The vengeful spirits would target the psychopathic hillbillies first, creating a chaotic distraction that would buy Goldie and Owen enough time to escape their clutches.

Upon their arrival at the hospital in Nashville, Tennessee, the alley that led to it was deplorable, filled with filth and dirt. Despite the hospital's reputation for maintaining a sterile environment, it seemed that they paid no attention to the condition of their backyard, which was quite disheartening.

Owen was admitted to the fifth floor as soon as the medical staff noticed the presence of black veins. A flurry of doctors and scientists immediately began conducting blood tests, asking questions, and running various diagnostic procedures. When Owen was being taken for scans, someone finally thought to inquire about the patient's family. Sensing an opportunity to avoid further questioning, Goldie, the only family member present, decided to disappear.

As Goldie stood in the alley, he placed a cigarette in his mouth, searching for his lighter with one hand while scrolling through his phone with the other. This was an old, dirty habit he had picked up from Josiah when he was thirteen. Although he had quit smoking by the time he met Mia and the others, the impending apocalypse made Goldie question his decision, thinking to himself, *What the hell? I'm going to die from something, anyway.*

Goldie contemplated whether to call Mia once again despite the nagging feeling of despair within him that told him she and the others were already dead. Lost in his thoughts, he was startled by the sound of a lighter being flicked open and the warm glow that illuminated the face of the man standing before him. Surprised by the sudden presence of someone sneaking up on him, Goldie accepted the fire, lit his cigarette, and expressed his gratitude as he took his first drag.

"Hello, Goldie."

Goldie initially believed that the person he encountered could have been a kind-hearted homeless guy. What puzzled him the most was the complete lack of response from the man when a gun was pointed at him.

"Why are you following us?"

"I'm not here to harm you; I'm here about your brother. I know he's sick; the doctors can't help him, but I can. I know his disease is linked to the flood of spirits on earth, and I know, despite your every effort, you doubt your ability to keep him safe. I'm willing to take him off your hands, use his body to try to stop this..."

Goldie refused to let the man finish and incapacitated the intruder by striking him with the butt of his gun. The chaos continued to escalate, with doctors in the hallway resorting to suicide as spirits flooded the area. Goldie wasted no time and grabbed Owen and escaped.

Huntsville, Alabama, had fallen into chaos, as shown by the blood-soaked sign several miles back. Two weeks prior, the city had been placed under martial law, transforming it into a quarantine zone. The military, police, and government personnel had established a strict regime resembling a communist rule. Yet, in such tense living conditions, there were bound to be individuals who rebelled against the oppressive authority.

Sneaking into the city had been daunting, but navigating through and escaping from it proved to be a bigger challenge than expected. It reminded him of the movie *Escape From New Jersey*.

In the past, his experience with stealth had been limited to evading drugstore clerks when he and Josiah were shoplifting or when he and Owen had fled from their father years ago. Once or twice he had to sneak past his exhausted stepmother, who would often be found asleep on the couch after a long workday. Despite his expertise, Goldie faced tight patrol shifts even in the abandoned districts of the city.

Goldie let out a cry of pain as the QZ guard slammed the butt of his rifle against his face. His head spun for a moment, and before he knew it, he found himself on the ground. The guard was determined to restrain him, attempting to put handcuffs on him while Owen watched nearby.

"Goldie! Please, get up! Get up!" Owen yelled as another attack washed over him.

The guard separated the two brothers, pulling one away from the other. As they were torn apart, Owen's eyes filled with tears, reflecting his fear and distress, which were further accentuated by the glow of the streetlights. At that moment, Goldie's vision blurred as if a crimson filter had been applied. Reacting instinctively, he retrieved a knife from his belt and drove it into the neck of the guard who was restraining him. Without a moment's hesitation, Goldie sprang to his feet and sprinted toward the guard who held his brother captive, propelled by a fierce determination that left no room for doubt or hesitation.

"Come on, someone probably heard us," Goldie whispered to Owen once the guard was dead.

Owen's safety was paramount to Goldie. Goldie was constantly amazed by the resilience of humanity, even in the face of sick individuals, terrifying quarantine zones, and nights filled with bloodshed. The depths of depravity that the human mind could reach and the atrocities they were capable of were even more horrifying than the malevolent spirits they encountered. While the spirits were driven solely by a desire to kill, their actions were somewhat predictable and manageable once one became accustomed to their patterns.

Humans were not...

CHAPTER 33

Toy

As Toy woke up from that weird place after saving Kurt, she was immediately hit by the overpowering odor of blood and sewage. The combination of these scents filled the air, making breathing difficult. Toy shifted her weight, feeling a dull, persistent ache spreading throughout her body. The hard concrete beneath her and the cold liquids seeping through her clothes only added to her discomfort.

She found herself unfazed by this unpleasant situation. The water surrounding her may have been contaminated, but it couldn't be worse than what was already coursing through her veins. Determined, Toy propped herself up into an unsteady sitting position, squinting against the eerie yellow light that flickered in the distance.

"Bonnie?" Toy whispered. "Where are you?"

The bubbling sound of the crimson water responded.

"Bonnie?"

Standing up, Toy took a moment to observe her surroundings, but a sense of mounting uneasiness washed over her. It was as if icy fingers constricted her heart, causing a bone-chilling coldness to seep through her entire body.

"Come on. Where are you?"

There was no way he would abandon her. Toy couldn't believe it, but she saw Bob a few yards away in the tunnel. The sight of the flashlight reminded her of Fredrick. Holding back her tears, Toy gazed at Bob. It was turned on, but its light was flickering.

"No," Toy choked out. "Not freaking possible."

Toy grabbed Bob as the light bulb flickered and died completely. To her dismay, Bonnie was nowhere to be found. Panic set in as Toy wondered if someone had taken him. Could it be Kieran? Or one of the subjects? And how on earth did Toy end up in the sewers of all places?

Overwhelmed by the situation, Toy instinctively covered her eyes with her hands, feeling the sting of frustration. Taking a deep breath, she tried to compose herself. Getting worked up wouldn't solve anything.

If Toy waited, maybe Bonnie would return. After all, he wouldn't disappear without a reason, right? But then again, there was Bob. It was doubtful that he would have left without taking Bob with him...

No, no, no!

Toy ran her fingers over her face, letting out an exasperated sigh. She was not dumb; she could handle things on her own. First, she would give it some time. She would wait a few minutes; if Bonnie didn't show up, she would start looking for him. Likely, he was somewhere nearby, and he would know where to go. He would probably be the one to find her.

All right. I'm fine. I can do this.

Toy's anxiety dissipated, a small glimmer of hope breaking through the gloomy clouds. It may have been a tiny flicker, but it was enough for now. Toy sat on the concrete, clutching her left arm against her chest while her right hand held onto Bob.

With her eyes widened, Toy observed the corners ahead while counting to one hundred under her breath, not just to distract herself from the loud bangs and creaks of the pipes but also to escape the eerie whispers of the blood flowing through the drains. Despite her efforts, she found no trace of Bonnie, and reluctantly, she had to admit she must keep going.

"Please, come and find me," Toy mumbled, popping two batteries into Bob as she stood up. "Or...I'll find you. I promise."

Toy's heart raced as she navigated the treacherous tunnels all by herself, knowing that the deadly substance flowing through her veins was slowly killing her. Fear consumed her, causing her to look over her shoulder, fearing the unknown lurking in the shadows ahead. Every little noise startled her, and the monotonous twists and turns of the tunnels only added to her confusion. Toy clung to the slimy walls, and feelings of discomfort intensified the already-sore state of her body.

The sense of dread that used to come and go had become a constant burden, weighing her down with no relief in sight. Could anyone truly comprehend the terror of being trapped in these sewers alone? It was enough to drive anyone to the brink of madness.

Toy experienced an overwhelming surge of fear every few minutes, especially when the water became thicker and took on a deeper shade of red, flowing over her high-tops, carrying with it severed heads and torn body parts. But, despite this terrifying ordeal, Toy continued to press forward. She had to keep moving, persevere, and, most importantly, locate Bonnie. Toy was determined to find him, no matter what it took.

At one moment, Toy found herself genuinely convinced that a monstrous creature was lurking in the depths alongside her. The sound of nails scraping against the walls echoed throughout the space, accompanied by strangled and horrifying cries that seemed to permeate the air from all directions, yet nowhere in particular. These bone-chilling sounds would only last for a few seconds before stopping. Still, they grow louder, causing Toy to believe that the creature was closing in on her, ready to sink its fangs into her vulnerable neck and drain her of life.

The absence of anything was a constant presence, a void that filled her senses. The persistent ringing in her ears served as a reminder of the emptiness that surrounded her. It was a disheartening experience that left her feeling overwhelmed and unable to appreciate the few moments of respite she encountered. As Toy navigated the labyrinthine corridors, she found herself at yet another dead end, facing a closed door. Desperation set in, and Toy threw her shoulder against it, hoping it would open. But, as expected, it remained shut, mocking her futile attempts.

Amidst the frustration, Toy noticed a small drainage hole in the wall next to the door. It presented a glimmer of hope, a potential escape from this never-ending maze. The alternative was to retrace her steps and search for another route, wasting precious time.

Determined not to succumb to defeat, Toy made a decision. With a deep breath, she plunged headfirst into the narrow passage, activating Bob to illuminate the way ahead. The sharp pain shooting through her arm was a small price to pay for progress. Toy reminded herself to keep pushing forward and moving.

As Toy ventured deeper into the narrow passage, it stretched into unpleasant, musty darkness. There was no sign of the end, and a sense of unease began to creep over her. Toy couldn't help but wonder if the walls were closing in, constricting the space around her. Her anxiety intensified, sweat trickling down her forehead, stinging her eyes. Amidst this pitch-black environment, the only sound was the pounding of her heart, echoing in her ears and throbbing within her chest.

Breathe, Toy.

She was not trapped; the blood had to end up somewhere. There had to be a way out, and she was determined to find it. But what if there were bars at the end?

When Bob revealed an area with storage boxes and a higher ceiling, a wave of relief washed over Toy. It felt like a warm, intoxicating sensation coursing through her veins as she struggled to stand upright, feeling lightheaded. Amongst the surroundings, Toy noticed massive, corroded pipes and a ledge with electrical equipment. Could this mean she was nearing the end of the sewers?

She proceeded through the only door, which led her to a silent walkway made of metal. Most of it was in good condition, although a few broken grates revealed the water swishing below. And my, oh my, there was plenty of water down there. She would have to take a plunge and go for a swim...

Fortunately, this section was straightforward compared to the complex tunnels. The path across the metal was a straight shot, so she didn't have to worry about making wrong turns. Yet, the main challenge would be submerging herself in the freezing water.

Eventually, the collapsed walkway led her into a vast chamber. The water level reached her waist, which was good and bad. On the one hand, she couldn't move quickly without creating a lot of noise, but it was still faster than her clumsy breaststroke. Still drenched and shivering from her previous underwater escapade, she was forced to turn off Bob when she heard something, a soft sloshing sound like another creature gliding through the pool.

Oh no, sea monsters...

As Toy approached the edge of the wall, her eyes strained to see through the pitch-black darkness. There were no signs of sea monsters lurking in the depths below, yet her heart skipped when she noticed a ladder. it was a glimmer of hope amidst the eerie atmosphere of this place. Could it be the way out?

Toy felt a surge of excitement mixed with trepidation as she took a step closer to the ladder, its rungs illuminated by a faint bluish light that cascaded from the ceiling above. The distance between her and the ladder seemed vast, a daunting thirty yards she had to traverse to reach potential safety.

A slight movement grabbed her attention, lurking in front of the ramp beneath the ladder. In an instant, all her optimism withered away, leaving a chilling sense of despair.

It was none other than Kieran standing there, and...

No. Toy hadn't made a single movement, yet he spotted her.

And there was absolutely nowhere to hide.

Goldie

Stranded on the side of the highway, Goldie and Owen found refuge atop an overturned semi-truck, seeking solace from the encroaching spirits. A fire flickered before them, its feeble light warding off the ethereal beings. Like a relentless river, the spirits surged toward the city they desperately needed to reach—Atlanta, Georgia, shining like a guiding beacon amidst the darkness. Goldie and Owen's hope clung to the city's distant glow, their only source of solace in this desolate landscape.

Goldie's gaze shifted to his brother, noticing the ominous black veins that snaked their way up his throat and encroached upon his jawline. He playfully tousled Owen's unruly canary hair with a gentle touch, attempting to coax a smile from his increasingly withdrawn sibling.

Owen's sudden grimace shattered Goldie's fleeting joy, triggering a familiar sense of dread within his chest. The onset of an attack loomed as the headaches that plagued Owen had grown more intense and frequent. These episodes now brought forth violent tremors of pain akin to seizures. Goldie desperately searched for any pain medication he could scrounge up, willing to carry his brother while Owen endured the agony.

"It hurts," Owen whimpered.

Goldie embraced his older brother tightly, holding him close and pressing his face against his hair. As he did so, mixed emotions overwhelmed him, causing his eyes to tear up. Fear, a sense of helplessness, and shame intertwined within him, creating a complex and overwhelming feeling.

"I know, I know it hurts. I'm—I'm sorry. I'm so sorry," Goldie sighed.

From afar, Atlanta shined like a sacred metropolis, a sight that filled Goldie with determination to reach it no matter what. Contrary to Goldie's initial worries, the area surrounding the CDC was not a quarantine zone, though he now wished it was. It used to be a quarantine zone, but the rebel faction in Atlanta descended into chaos under the leadership of a cannibalistic fanatic. Yes, cannibalism. The apocalypse had only started six weeks ago; you'd think that depth of sick shit would've held off until at least the six-month mark.

Goldie had pulled both of them into the dimmest corners he could locate when he saw the horrifying scene—an abundance of severed heads piled up in the middle of a wide intersection, forming a colossal pyramid of bloodshed. They had nearly reached the initial barricade encircling the CDC when everything fell apart. The deranged individuals knew how to patrol for potential intruders.

Goldie grunted as a blow landed on his face. His vision blurred into a familiar shade of hazy red as the flesh-eating creatures swarmed around them, their greedy hands tearing Owen away from his side. It took four men to subdue Goldie, each assigned to restrain a different limb, struggling to control him.

"Goldie! No, leave us alone! Goldie—" Owen yelled.

The man easily identified as the leader due to the gruesome wreath of ears adorning his neck delivered a decisive blow to

Owen's head, causing him to collapse in a state of excruciating pain and helplessness. In that moment, something within Goldie snapped, igniting a frenzied surge of strength that allowed him to wrestle his arms free from the grip of one of his captors. With sheer determination, he managed to snatch a knife from one of the vile individuals restraining him.

Blood spilled once more as Goldie fought his way toward his brother, seeking revenge against the despicable person who had violated him while he was down. The odds were stacked against him as bodies piled on top of him, and he endured blow after blow.

"I will kill you! I'll kill every last one of you sick fucks!" Goldie screamed.

Once again, the assailant struck, this time delivering a decisive blow to Goldie's head, causing everything to fade into a terrifying darkness.

When Goldie regained consciousness, a deep, throbbing pain in his shoulders and arms overwhelmed him, accompanied by a profound sense of emptiness. His arms were bound above his head, secured by cruel bonds attached to a menacing meat hook, and his toes barely grazed the icy surface of the concrete floor. To add insult to injury, his captors had stripped him of his shoes and socks, leaving him vulnerable and exposed. These individuals were nothing short of monsters.

Goldie found himself confined within what was once a jail but now resembled a macabre slaughterhouse. Each cell was adorned with a hanging meat hook, while rivulets of blood flowed into the drains lining the hallway. The distant echoes of muffled screams reached his ears, a chilling reminder that some unfortunate soul was being butchered nearby. Fueled by a desperate urgency, Goldie struggled to free himself, driven by unwavering determination to find Owen.

Since the events in Alabama, Goldie had taken the lives of twelve more individuals, each one deemed necessary in his twisted pursuit. Although his initial hesitation had diminished, the overwhelming feelings of horror and revulsion remained unchanged.

Goldie was a shadow in the night. With each lifeless body that dropped to the ground, a mix of dark satisfaction and rage coursed through his veins. It was a familiar fury, the same one he felt when he first encountered Mia. In moments like these, he longed for her presence, wishing she could be here to offer him solace and guidance, like she used to with her love and books. Unfortunately, that was not possible.

Despite the absence of her support, the feeling of satisfaction overwhelmed him, knowing that one less despicable person remained to inflict harm upon them. Anger fueled his determination, driven by the fact that none of these individuals were the despicable ear-wearing prick who deserved his wrath.

Goldie entered what used to be a clothing store, descending through a hole in the roof. Without wasting a moment, he evaded an ambush from behind, executed by one of the scumbags who had previously piled onto him. The malicious grin plastered across the attacker's face ignited a burning desire within Goldie to extract every tooth from his mouth. Engulfed in the thrill of the fight, he skillfully employed the techniques Josiah had taught him during their time together at camp years ago. After the intense brawl, Goldie found himself retching beside the lifeless body of his assailant, but he didn't allow himself to be deterred and continued to press forward.

Within the chilling confines of an industrial cooler in a butcher's shop, a deranged lunatic yelled, "Benny! Jimmy! Cagy! Charlie! I thought I told you to watch the door!"

The absence of any reply filled the man with a sense of unease, causing his emotions to intensify. Dark elation twisted within Goldie, fueling his rage and making it burn even brighter.

"No one's coming for you. I made sure of it," Goldie growled.

Following the intense battle filled with blood, anger, and a twisted sense of satisfaction, Goldie stumbled upon a sturdy metal trunk fastened to the floor of the refrigerator. The lid of the trunk was flung open, and Goldie was taken aback by the sight of a younger version of his older brother hurtling toward him. They embraced each other, their tears mingling with the traces of blood on their faces. In the background, the lifeless body of their would-be cannibal adversary lay shattered and devoid of life.

"I thought they killed you, I thought—" Owen cried.

Goldie moved back, allowing a small gap between their bodies, and rested his forehead against Owen's.

"I will never leave you again. Next time, I'll kill them—anyone who tries to stop us, to hurt us. I won't let anyone touch you ever again. I swear."

"You didn't know this would happen when you gave me the water! It's too late!"

Goldie's fear intensified as Owen's statement catapulted him out of this version of purgatory and into a desolate void where only he and his brother existed. Memories of everything that transpired flooded Goldie's mind, causing his anxiety to surge.

"Owen, what are you talking about? If we get to the CDC, this will end."

"I consumed the plague; it took all of me, and if you fail, this is what happens!"

"I..."

"We must do something. We must stop people from dying!"

"Maybe if we leave...an island or something... It will stop... Owen, will it stop?"

"I am the spirits; the spirits are a part of me now, just like the plague. I'm killing them...not just them, but all the others and more as the Bajulatorius Maledictio remains in my blood!"

"So this is the end?"

"Not ultimately...we have one chance...one chance to end this or this will be what happens."

"Tell me... I'll do anything."

"I think you know already..."

"I..."

"You must stop me...to stop the Maledictio..."

"Owen...you can't ask me that...I want to save you..."

"You are one of my Protectors. One of the two people needed to stop me from continuing to be a monster..."

"You're not a monster; Kieran is! This...whatever this fucking Maledictio is!"

"I will be if you fail...if I kill all I love,...all these nice things people have shown me... Mama, Bonnie, you, Drake..."

"I understand, but..."

"Please, Goldie, save them..."

"I'll...I'll try..."

"Thank you, Goldie; now wait here for the other Protector."

A frown appeared on Goldie's face as he observed the sudden transformation of his surroundings and found himself in the basement of Mama's house.

CHAPTER 35

Toy

Do not panic.

Whatever you do, do not panic.

Or you will be killed in the most brutal and horrific way and no one can help Bonnie if you're dead.

"Oh, it's the pretty little Protector," Kieran sneered, the distance between him and Toy shrinking with every step he took. "But where is her little pig? Is he...here? Is he...gone?"

A laugh like thunder pounded against her skull.

She couldn't pay attention to this right now. She couldn't afford to lose focus. Running was not an option—he would catch up to her. But she'd evaded him briefly before, back in Mama's house. She could do it again. Once he got closer, she could use the wall behind her to gain extra speed...

She was completely overwhelmed with fear; her nerves were completely frazzled. The terror was so intense that she could hardly remain standing. However, as Kieran approached, coming within a hair's length of her grasp, Toy took a deep breath and dived into the water. With her feet firmly planted on the stone wall, she pushed off and glided through the chilling darkness, moving sideways. She remained submerged for as long as she could while Kieran angrily stomped around and unleashed his fury with howls of rage.

I'm so cold...

Toy couldn't hold her breath much longer in the frigid water. It felt as though her lungs had entirely frozen by the time she resurfaced. The small gasps of air she took in left her feeling lightheaded and nauseous, causing immense pain. But Toy was relieved to discover Kieran was unaware of her whereabouts. She desperately hoped it remained that way.

Toy submerged her trembling body in the water, keeping only her wide eyes and nose above the surface as she cautiously approached the exit. The ramp and ladder leading to freedom beckoned her, but she was aware that the moment she stepped onto the platform, Kieran would undoubtedly hear her. All she could do was move and silently pray he wouldn't reach her in time.

Toy's fingers clumsily brushed against the cold metal railings. The struggle cost her fifteen precious seconds, and she could feel the pain intensifying. With great effort, she pulled herself out of the water, but the agony only worsened. Her bones ached, threatening to give way under her weight, but a surge of desperation and a final burst of adrenaline prevented her from collapsing.

Ignoring everything else, Toy didn't check where Kieran was as she stumbled along the walkway. His presence was clear from the sounds, but she couldn't divert her attention away from the ladder. The grates disappeared a few feet away, revealing the suspended metal rungs, but Toy didn't hesitate. Holding her breath, she leaped forward without a moment's pause. The impact was nothing short of jarring.

With a pained expression, she struggled to ascend the ladder and finally permitted herself to rest and catch her breath after reaching the summit. She took a moment to pause and nearly collapsed. The room she found herself in was strangely serene and blissfully devoid of anyone. She leaned against the distant wall, feeling the exhaustion overtake her body, and ran a shaky and sore hand across her face.

Come on, Bonnie... Where are you?

Toy cast her gaze back toward the hole. A sudden, piercing crack resonated through the air, followed by a loud crash into the water.

The storage room let in a fair amount of light, which allowed her to take a moment and gather herself, yet she could do little about her wet clothes and socks, which sucked.

She hated wet socks.

She grabbed Bob from the loop on her jeans, grumbling under her breath. She shook off the water droplets from the glass, wincing at the thought of how it got soaked in the first place. It was inevitable.

When she switched it on, Bob came to life, which felt like a minor miracle. She might have shed a tear or two if it hadn't worked. Bob had been through countless adventures with Bonnie and Toy, and the thought of continuing without it was unimaginable.

In this damp and musty environment, the boxes and crates around her held nothing except for some impressive collections of mold. She found two more batteries on one desk tucked away in the corner.

She rushed down the hallway, deactivating Bob to conserve battery power. Unfortunately, her wet shoes made more noise than she intended. She glanced into a few rooms on her left but didn't search them. From her vantage point, they appeared to be empty. The signs on the wall let her know that she was in the men's ward. The hallway ended at a metal gate obstructed by shelves. Frustrated, Toy spun around, feeling dizzy, and collided with an unstable metal cabinet. Another curse escaped her lips as she gave the cabinet an annoyed kick, thinking she'd have to backtrack and waste more time. The cabinet shifted about four inches, revealing something behind it.

A vent? Huh...

Toy pushed the cabinet away, revealing a hidden area where Bob's light shined into the darkness. To her horror, she discovered a trail of dried blood smears leading into a new room, a chilling sight of a red puddle beneath a chair, and a lifeless body slumped in that very chair. Trusting her instincts, she crawled through the unsettling scene.

The lifeless body she encountered was that of a teenage girl. She had long, curly blonde hair, and her once-vibrant blue eyes stared into the abyss. The sight of her jaw ripped away exposed her lolling, blackened tongue and a jumble of broken teeth.

This discovery was even more disturbing because of a photograph nailed into her upturned hand. Toy pulled it off with trembling fingers, eyes growing wide.

The room in the photo was enveloped in darkness, making it difficult to discern any details. Yet, amidst the blurry surroundings, two figures were in focus. They were bound by their wrists and ankles, suspended from the ceiling in what appeared to be an operating room of some sort. One boy was barely visible, his image scratched out.

Despite the darkness and confusion, there was no mistaking the other boy's identity. It was Bonnie, no doubt about it. Toy's vision filled with bursts of fiery red, igniting a surge of intense emotions within her. The icy coldness that once coursed through her veins dissolved into a scorching, white-hot rage. With her hands throbbing as they clenched into fists, Toy seethed with anger toward the audacious individual who dared to steal him away from her.

A warning to whoever committed this act: they should be prepared to face the consequences. There would be no escape for them once Toy tracked them down. She would not hesitate to extract their spine and fasten it around their neck. She would string them up from the ceiling and force them to experience the same pain they had caused Bonnie.

Hang on, Bonnie. Please, just for a little longer...

Toy entered the quiet corridor. She picked up her pace and started jogging, making sure not to stand where the shadows appeared the darkest. There were no signs of restless spirits or teenagers, and Kieran was nowhere to be found. With each step, Toy heard loose stones crunching beneath her high-tops. She noticed broken furniture placed against the other entrances. The scene was unsettling, with bodies and blood scattered around.

Toy reached the last room on her right, which contained another one of those metallic cabinets. Without hesitation, she rushed inside and pushed her right shoulder against it, freeing the vent it was blocking. The adrenaline coursing through her veins pushed her forward, urging her through the vent.

Now faced with a choice, she was torn between going left or right. This place felt like an intricate maze. Squinting her eyes, Toy glanced to her right and noticed more closed—most likely locked—doors.

Toy pushed forward, hoping that luck was on her side. As she continued her search, she spotted another vent and immediately dropped to her knees. Peering through the vent, she discovered an operating room.

She crawled into the room, and her heart skipped a beat. The walls were lined with damp and putrid-smelling medical gurneys. Frayed white curtains had been pulled around a few gurneys to provide a semblance of privacy. From behind these curtains, unsettling sounds emerged—gurgling whispers, groans, and other noises Toy would have rather not heard.

Uncertainty gnawed at Toy as she contemplated whether she should investigate further. Could Bonnie be hidden within this room? Was the picture a diversion to throw her off? Despite her reluctance, Toy took a shallow breath and shook her head, knowing what she must do. It was like ripping off a band-aid—a quick and painful exposure of the truth. Only a handful of beds remained hidden from view, but the thought of what she might discover sent a shiver down her spine.

Toy needed an escape route that didn't involve retracing her steps. What if there was a subject waiting for her behind one of the curtains? With a narrowed gaze, Toy surveyed her surroundings. Her eyes caught on the open vent in the ceiling.

She knew she could use the gurney beneath the vent to give her the extra height she needed. Determined, Toy nodded to herself and adjusted her grip on Bob, preparing to use it as a makeshift weapon if necessary.

The teenagers occupying the cots in the room were afflicted with the same sickness coursing through her veins. They appeared to have been devoured by a rabid creature or corroded by sulfuric acid. The stench that permeated the air was beyond comprehension, a nauseating combination of seared flesh and putrid eggs. Toy fought the urge to vomit as she hoisted herself onto the gurney and strived to reach for the edge of the ceiling grate. Thankfully, Bonnie and the others were nowhere to be found, so Toy sent a silent thank-you to God.

Gross. So...gross. Good lord...

With a well-timed leap, Toy grabbed the icy metal and clung on for dear life. She kicked her legs and strained her feeble arms, the tension becoming almost unbearable, causing tears of frustration to well up in her eyes.

It hurts so much.

Toy gathered her strength and hauled herself into the ventilation system. She crawled for about three yards before she descended onto the hard cement floor below. She saw bloodstains on the ground, and her attention was immediately drawn to another subject bound to a chair. This young man, bruised and very much alive, was shouting at the top of his lungs while rocking back and forth. A wave of panic washed over Toy as she realized that if there was any danger nearby, it would hear him...

Toy swiftly scanned her surroundings. Her eyes landed on

a third metal cabinet. She looked back at the kid.

"Sorry kid," she murmured, leaving him tied to the chair as she stumbled to the cabinet.

A series of forceful thuds reverberated through the room, originating from the double doors on her right. The impact was so powerful that it felt as if cannonballs were attempting to break through the solid metal door.

"Oh, that's not good," Toy gasped.

The door busted off its hinges and fell to the floor, and Toy glimpsed the naked teen's scarred, greenish flesh while shoving the stupid cabinet out of her way.

"Yep, not good!"

CHAPTER 36

Toy

The sound of heavy footsteps echoed behind Toy as she raced through one room after another, trying to outpace her pursuer. With every door she slammed shut, she prayed it would stay closed.

She was lost and unsure if she was taking the right turns and corners. She felt like she was going around in circles. At some point, she felt like at least three or four individuals were chasing after her. Breathing was becoming difficult, possibly because of the infection spreading to her respiratory system, causing her lungs to malfunction.

Is this what spontaneous combustion feels like?

In a sudden turn of events, Toy scurried up into a wall vent, trying to escape the approaching spirits. She dropped into a security booth with a black-and-white checkered floor.

Gasping for breath, sweat cascaded down her face. Her eyes widened with fear as she caught sight of a massive hole in the floor looming ahead, at least five or six feet wide, and sheer terror gripped her as she realized she must somehow cross it. The thought of the relentless teens tearing her limbs apart if she stopped only intensified her panic.

I have to go; I have to jump!

Toy took the leap. Her body flailed through the air, and she prayed with a desperation she never knew she had. She made it. The impact of the landing caused her teeth to snap together and her brain to rattle against the walls of her skull. Amid the chaos, she nearly bit her tongue off in sheer terror, but despite it all, she survived and escaped death's grasp again.

Once Toy finally pulled herself up onto solid ground, she realized she couldn't afford to lie there, gasping for air and struggling to regain her composure. Unfortunately, Toy had no choice but to do so. She gave herself a mere three minutes to allow the world to stop spinning and the pressure in her head to subside. With every passing second, Toy could feel her strength return, and she mustered the courage to push herself up and continue.

With every step Toy took down the deserted hallway, her body trembled. The adrenaline that had fueled her during the escape was wearing off, leaving her with aching muscles. Each movement was a struggle, as if her body was protesting the abuse it had endured, yet she pushed forward, determined to find Bonnie despite her pain and uncertainty.

Before the chaos resumed, Toy had about nineteen seconds of undisturbed tranquility. Her current condition barely allowed her to walk, let alone run. A pitiful, soundless moan escaped her dry and cracked lips. Despite the agony resonating through every fiber of her being, she forced herself into a sluggish jog.

God, I can't die here.

I cannot die here, please.

I have to save Bonnie.

I have to.

The sound of breaking glass filled the air as doors collided with walls. How far away were they? They sounded close... Panic set in as Toy realized the experts were right about pushing your body to its limits in extreme situations. She never imagined being in a situation like this, but somehow, she found the strength to keep moving.

She entered what seemed to be a storage room, her eyes immediately fixated on a dumbwaiter. The room was dimly lit, and her vision was blurred and blotchy. Toy couldn't help but feel grateful for finding such a secure hiding spot where she could rest and shed a few tears. With a mixture of anxiety and relief, Toy climbed into the cramped space and closed the grate with a choked sound of relief.

The dumbwaiter ascended as the naked teens burst into the storage room, and at that moment, Toy vanished from their sight. Overwhelmed by fear, Toy trembled, pulling her legs to her chest and burying her face in her knees.

The pain... It's worth it, though, because I'm still alive. I escaped.

Toy anxiously waited in the dumbwaiter; it disappointed her by only taking her up one level before coming to a halt. With caution, Toy leaned forward and looked out at the dimly lit space below, dusty particles floating in the air.

It was an operating room, equipped with many tables, dripping sinks, and carts filled to the brim with tools that bore the marks of stains and rust.

"...if the Protector doesn't arrive soon, we'll just have to begin without her," a nasally, unpleasant voice said. "Granted, it won't be as entertaining, but what can you do?" A man forced an exaggerated sigh. "I heard that she was an impressive specimen, too. How disappointing."

Toy was completely taken aback by what she saw; it was far from anything she could have thought to expect. The individual who was speaking appeared to be in a state of utter madness, his entire body covered in tanned, wrinkled flesh, wearing round goggles and an apron splattered with blood.

There was another person in the room with him, a young woman. From what Toy could see, she was restrained, tied to one of the metal legs of a table at the far end of the room. Her brown hair was tangled, hanging in thin, greasy strands in front of her face. Her clothes were torn and covered in dirt. Although she remained silent, her trembling shoulders revealed her fear and distress.

I don't like what's going on. I have a bad feeling about this...

Toy glanced around the dumbwaiter, looking for something to get it moving when the doctor noticed her.

Oh no.

"Ah-ha!" With astonishing speed, he crossed the room before Toy could blink. He pulled open the gate. "Miss Toy Fawn: our little star of the show." He spoke with an awful, sarcastic lisp. His voice felt like homicidal wasps jabbing against Toy's eardrums. "I was almost afraid that you wouldn't be joining us. But it's so lovely that you are."

He grabbed Toy's arm and dragged her out of the dumbwaiter.

"A simple 'please' would have sufficed, you jerk," Toy grunted, tugging against his iron-like grip.

Bonnie was here; this doctor was the one who took him. Using her free arm, she grabbed Bob from the loop on her jeans, but before Toy could hit him, the doctor turned around and grabbed her wrist.

"Ah, ah, ah," he taunted. "Look, I'm gonna make this real simple for yah," he told her, bloodshot eyes narrowing behind the goggles. "You kill me or hurt me in any way, and your boyfriend is dead. Understand?"

Toy locked eyes with him, and a surge of defiance coursed through her. She eased up after a moment of tension. Sensing her change in demeanor, he released his grip on her right arm. Regardless of whether he was bluffing, Toy couldn't afford to take any chances with Bonnie's safety. She decided to bide her time, wait for a better moment to take action.

"Yeah. I understand," Toy growled.

"Good," the doctor purred. "I knew you were the intelligent one. Now, let's get started. I'll take this."

With a sudden jerk, he snatched Bob away from Toy's grip and hurled it over his shoulder. The metallic object collided with the tile, emitting a sharp clanking sound before it found its way under a nearby sink, where it rolled to a stop.

"Toy, this is Gillian. Gillian, Toy." With a firm grip, he pushed Toy onto the ground and tied her tightly to the table leg closest to him. The girl remained still, not even flinching. "Both of you wait here, and I'll get the others. Impetus, you know?" He giggled under his breath. "Otherwise, this won't be any fun."

The girls were left in an uncomfortable silence, and Toy couldn't help but scowl and mutter under her breath. She immediately attempted to free herself from the restraints, but to no avail. The rope was already cutting into her skin, causing a tingling sensation in her fingers.

Toy shifted her focus to a new plan. She looked at the girl beside her and scowled. Although Toy had no genuine interest in working with someone who seemed so despondent, she understood she had no other choice. If Toy wanted to rescue Bonnie, she had to forge a connection with the other kid.

Bonnie was the only thing that truly mattered to Toy.

"Hey, you. Gillian," Toy hissed. "What the heck is going on? Did that creep tell you?"

The girl didn't answer.

"Come on! He must be keeping your friend here, too," Toy pressed, opting for a different angle as her annoyance flared. "You want to save him, right? Don't you?"

Nothing.

I'm two seconds away from kicking her in the shin.

"We'll have a better chance if we do this together, but you've gotta give me something. How tight are your restraints?" Toy tried not to demand. "Can you slip out?"

Yep, that's it.

Toy stretched out her leg and kicked the girl's foot.

"Stop freaking ignoring me!" she snapped. "Maybe you don't care about your friend, but I care about mine. Are you just gonna sit there and roll over for this doctor jerk?"

At long last, the girl stirred. With a determined look, she raised her chin. Her lank hair fell away, and a pair of lackluster hazel eyes came into view, adding a glimmer of life to her previously motionless form.

"He's only going to let one of us live. One pair. Some twisted...fight-to-the-death match," she mumbled. "There's no point in working together. So, don't..." A malevolent lucidity tainted her expression, casting a toxic aura upon her features. "Don't you dare presume Mark means nothing to me!" she threatened. Her quiet voice was hard, ugly, and full of hatred. "Because I'm going to gouge your fucking eyeballs out and shove them down your throat as soon as Dr. Marshall unties us."

Wow, that took an unexpected turn.

"Okay. Eventual eye-gouging noted." Toy shrugged, letting the comment wash right off her. She sat on the cold cement, a shiver running down her spine, making her bones feel as if they were made of melted wax.

She pressed her head against the table, lost in her thoughts, and memories of Chyseleia and Ordovic flooded her mind. They were the ones who had the strength and determination to take action when all Toy could do was crumble and weep.

Nate and Ann, whom Bonnie had told Toy about, brought her sadness.

Toy remembered the nameless boy trapped in a cage and his companion, Ki'ki.

The girl she watched being brutally killed and her desperate cries for Negan still haunted Toy.

The weight of the loss of Fredrick, along with countless others who had perished, hung heavy in the air.

And then the many spirits trapped in this place forever, their spirits unable to find peace.

How long did it take for someone to completely relinquish their humanity? When and where was the breaking point?

How resilient must one's psyche be to prevent them from succumbing to it?

One thing remained true...you will never know what you are truly capable of until you face the direst of circumstances.

CHAPTER 37

Toy

After a brief absence, the doctor reappeared about ten minutes later. Despite Toy's efforts to maintain a composed demeanor, her expression faltered as soon as he entered the room with Bonnie.

Toy's entire being tensed up as a surge of electricity coursed through her exhausted mind, piercing through the clouds of weariness. At that moment, Toy's focus was on him, blocking out everything else.

Physically, Bonnie didn't appear to be severely injured. There were no visible bone breaks, just some bruising and a dried-up gash above his right eye. Toy's eyes widened as she took in every detail of his appearance hungrily. Despite his unconscious state, Toy could sense the life within him, the blood rushing through his veins. His bound hands and feet, along with the restraints securing him to a wheelchair, went unnoticed for a moment. The presence of another teen in a similar state barely registered as Toy's concern was fixated on Bonnie.

Oh my goodness, what on earth has this awful person done to him?

Could he have been given some type of drug? It was clear he'd been beaten; the bruises on the left side of his face looked so painful and were a deep, swollen purple color. Just thinking about what he must have endured without Toy made a wave of intense anger boil inside her.

The doctor brought the young men to an operating table in the room's corner, his blood-stained apron partially concealing an old, curved knife that had seen better days. As he gazed at the blade, a sense of reverence filled his chartreuse eyes, hinting at a more profound connection with the instrument.

"Ladies... The rules for my game are few and easy to remember," he began, and his faint lisp twisted with barely contained glee. "Rule one: you do not come near me after your ropes have been cut. Each of your partners has been dosed with something lethal." He waved a cold hand. "And I'm the only one who can counteract their declining conditions. Kill me, and you kill them. Heh, heh. I'm sure both of you are aware of that by now. And... Rule two."

With a sinister grin, he dragged the corroded blade across the cold, metallic surface of the table, producing an unsettling screech that sent shivers down Toy's spine.

"You will fight one another to the death. By all means, be as creative as you would like." He gestured around the room. "Use what you wish; I don't really care. Whoever is left standing will then dispose of whichever boy they prefer. You will be given the drug to save the other...and after it has been administered, I will let you leave," he finished. "Two simple rules. Doesn't that sound fair?"

Toy was glad that the surgical mask covered the lower part of his ugly face because he must have been wearing the biggest, most terrifying smile.

"I think it does."

Toy squinted and bit down hard on her lower lip, feeling the sharp pain. She refused to believe a single word that came out of his mouth. Letting them go? Yeah, right, that was never going to happen.

Toy had to eliminate Gillian and Mark. Once they were out of the picture, she could focus on saving Bonnie and taking down that despicable doctor.

"Questions?" the doctor snickered.

Gillian and Toy remained silent. Frustrated, Toy pulled on her restraints again and frowned. She felt exhausted and wanted to rescue Bonnie from this place.

The doctor expressed his disapproval by clicking his tongue. What did he expect from them? Did he want them to argue or complain about the unfairness of the situation? Toy was willing to bet that Gillian felt the same way and just wanted this to end. Why should they prolong the inevitable?

"Come on," Toy finally grumbled. "Cut the freaking ropes already."

"Funny... I wasn't expecting you to be the eager one."

With a swift motion, the doctor used his blade to release Gillian from her restraints. Standing up, she remained quiet, massaging her red and swollen wrists. Her long hair cascaded down, obscuring her expressionless face, revealing no emotion or thought.

"You've had quite the change of heart during your handful of nights here, haven't you, Protector? Hmm..."

"Stop calling me that."

He approached the corner of the table where Toy was tied, and the sound of his instrument was like nails on a chalkboard as he dragged it across the smooth surface. "It's fascinating. You and Miss Kestis are the favorite candidates right now—the Soulless and the Carrier's Protector." He chuckled. "Can you guess which one you are?"

The sound of rusty metal screeching filled the air, causing a jolt of pain to shoot through her fingers as the ropes dropped. As the blood rushed back into her fingertips, a wave of discomfort washed over her, reminding her of the harsh reality of this situation.

Were they—whoever *they* were—actually assigning them

nicknames? Toy couldn't believe it. It was absurd to think of heartless individuals sitting comfortably, observing their every move through surveillance cameras, and even placing bets on who would survive the longest. Was this truly just entertainment for them?

Though unsurprised, hearing it stated so bluntly amplified the unsettling feeling within her. It was as if her emotions were being stirred up, leaving her with disbelief, anger, and a sense of helplessness.

As soon as the doctor stepped back, Toy rose to her feet, ignoring the freezing sensation and the slush accumulated in her joints. The gauze wrapped around her hands was stained with fresh blood, but she pushed aside any thoughts of assessing her injuries for now. Gillian's attention shifted away, likely searching for a potential weapon, giving Toy the perfect opportunity to strike first.

Toy spotted a medical cart beside the table on her left. Among the various items, there was a glass jar containing a peculiar pink substance. Uncertain of its nature, Toy hoped that the liquid was formaldehyde. Without hesitation, Toy grabbed the jar and hurled it at Gillian, aiming to catch her off guard.

Thanks to all those lazy summer days spent playing baseball with her dad as a kid and tossing a football around the backyard together before he left, Toy had developed exceptional aim. Gillian, unfortunately, flinched and reacted a little too late, attempting to block the projectile with her arms as the jar smashed against the side of her face.

It was a direct hit. The impact caused the glass to shatter, and the pungent smell of formaldehyde filled the air, stinging Toy's nose from across the room. She could only imagine how overwhelming it must have been for Gillian as she cried in agony. Before Toy could comprehend the bright red welts and scorch marks appearing on Gillian's skin, she instinctively pushed the medical cart into her stomach.

Gillian grabbed the cart from the other side. With a fierce growl, she hurled it against the wall. Toy knew this wouldn't be a walk in the park, and she refused to underestimate Gillian because she had caught her off guard once. The determination in her lifeless, menacing eyes assured Toy that she wouldn't allow herself to be caught off guard again.

Toy's main goal now was to reach Bob. It might be her only chance. With a quick feint to the left and then to the right, Toy attempted to maneuver around Gillian. Without formal self-defense training, her actions were driven by instinct and the remaining surge of adrenaline coursing through her veins.

Gillian deciphered Toy's body language. It was astonishing how she expected her move when Toy dashed toward the right, aiming for the sink where she spotted Bob. In a split second, she lunged for Toy's legs, causing both of them to collide with the unforgiving tile.

In a fit of frustration, Toy let out a low growl and pivoted her body, driving her elbow into Gillian's face. Her chin jutted out with a sickening crack, and a crimson stream of blood gushed forth from her nose. This didn't stop her for a second.

With a menacing snarl, she bared her teeth at Toy and delivered a forceful punch to her cheek, causing Toy to lose her balance. In a matter of seconds, Gillian pounced on top of Toy like a wild beast, rendering her legs useless and pinning her arms down. Toy couldn't help but wonder how she overpowered her so fast.

A searing, white-hot pain shot through Toy's head as Gillian landed another brutal blow. The metallic taste of blood filled Toy's mouth, its thick and unpleasant sweetness overwhelming her senses. Meanwhile, Gillian's hands sought Toy's throat while her knees pressed against the small of her back, leaving her gasping for air and defenseless.

Absolutely not. There is absolutely no way this is happening.

Toy fought and wrestled, finally freeing one of her arms. She dug her nails into whichever Gillian's hand in front of her face, and with all her strength, sunk her teeth in, causing Gillian to scream and strike her, but she refused to let go. Toy continued to bite down until blood trickled into her mouth. Then Toy gathered herself for what came next.

As soon as Toy released the hand, blood trickled out of her mouth, while Gillian contorted her body and strained multiple muscles. Toy pushed her away, only to strike her again with her bony elbow. A surge of rage flooded Toy, tinting the world in fiery red as she swiftly sprinted toward the distant row of sinks.

"Bob, Bob," Toy muttered. Finally, her eyes caught sight of it! Without wasting a moment, Toy dropped to her knees and stretched out her fingers, feeling the icy touch of the metal as Gillian, who seemed to have gone completely insane, crashed down on top of her with the force of a hundred pounds.

"Oh, my gosh!" Toy wheezed. Her instincts took over, and she didn't have time to think. Without hesitation, she raised her arm and knocked the knife out of Gillian's trembling hand using the head of Bob. Toy pushed her off and got on top of her before she crushed Gillian's face underneath the dripping metal. Gillian went limp. Within a matter of seconds, her eyes rolled back, and her face caved in, a gruesome sight.

Seated on the cold, hard floor, Toy's heart raced in her chest, and her breaths came out in heavy gasps. A surge of adrenaline rushed through her veins, causing her skin to turn red and feel as hot as a blazing furnace. The surrounding room was enveloped in an unsettling silence, interrupted only by her labored breathing.

Strangely enough, Toy didn't feel any sense of relief now that it was over. In fact, she felt nothing at all. It was as if she was devoid of emotions beyond overwhelming exhaustion. The anger she once felt was draining, more exhausting than the physical violence itself.

"Almost finished, Protector." Dr. Marshall's growl reached Toy's ears. "Impressive performance, as expected. Silver was right about you, it seems."

Ignoring the comment, Toy instinctively turned her head, and her eyes immediately landed on Bonnie, who remained unconscious in his wheelchair. A heavy sigh escaped Toy's lips as she felt a sharp pain in her jaw. She spat out more blood and reached for her jaw, noticing a clicking sound, making her cringe as the movement sent sharp pains to her head. She had dislocated something. Just great.

Feeling exhausted, Toy's eyelids became heavy, and she shifted her gaze to the other kid, Mark. He was awake, and the doctor had placed a piece of Goose Tape over his mouth during the fight, which he now removed, causing the young man to cry out in pain.

"Kitty-Cat?" A whimper escaped his lips, followed by a string of expletives as he struggled to hold back a sob. He remained bound to his wheelchair, tears streaming down his face.

Toy couldn't help but be struck by his utter lack of shame in his vulnerability. Her unease grew as she gathered the strength to stand, her body somehow still functioning despite the horrors she had experienced. While Toy understood the need for self-defense, if she killed Mark.... It was the idea of cold-blooded and senseless killing that left her questioning herself. She wanted to believe she hadn't reached that level of depravity.

"You're wasting valuable time, sweetheart," the doctor grunted with a fierce, echoing cry from his blade. "Kill this kid and get the drug to save your precious boyfriend. You want to save him, don't you?"

Toy squared her shoulders, took a deep breath, and closed her eyes. When she opened them, she found herself in an unfamiliar place. She scanned her surroundings, trying to make sense of where she was. Confusion filled her mind as she blinked. She was surrounded by towering trees that radiated an eerie aura with their gnarled branches and leaves that shimmered in shades of gold and orange under the fading sunlight.

Toy attempted to sit up. Sharp pains shot through her body, making it difficult to move. She clenched her teeth and pushed through the discomfort, determined to regain control of her senses. She took a quick look around. She was sitting in the center of a deserted parking lot, right in front of the sanatorium. The parking lot was peaceful, with a solitary vehicle parked on the side.

"Toy," she heard Zenith say. "We need to talk."

Her head whipped around, and she found Zenith standing before her. Tears threatened to escape her eyes.

"I already saved Kurt; I need to wake up! I need to get back to Bonnie. He's hurt."

"Saving your friends won't save you, but I can tell you that Bonnie is fine; everything that just happened didn't happen to you; it happened to a pair named Padrien and Ki'ki. It was a test to see if you are ready to face your fate."

"What...what do you mean saving my friends won't save me? Are you telling me that we risked our lives in that asylum to save our friends for nothing?! That Fredrick...Fredrick died for nothing?!"

"If you don't live up to your fate, your future will look like Ki'ki's."

"I don't want that to be my future; I don't want more people to die. Now, will you stop speaking in tongues and tell me the truth? I have little time left!"

"No one from that hallucination has to die; if you play your cards right, then your and those teens' futures will be bright," Zenith told her. "You must do what you are fated to; you can't fight fate forever."

"This will eat away at me, and you know it!" Toy snapped. "I'll be afraid of every choice I make!"

"I know. That's why I will not let you remember it; you will only remember what I need you to... It is time for you to face your fate..."

Without warning, the world around her started to tilt and spin, creating a disorienting sensation as everything seemed to slip away into a chaotic abyss.

CHAPTER 38

Toy

When Toy's vision finally cleared, she stumbled and fell against a set of stairs. Exhaustion consumed her, and she didn't want to go on. Zenith's words echoed in her mind, making her question everything she had gone through in the sanatorium.

Why am I still alive?

Zenith's mention of facing her fate only deepened Toy's confusion. The purpose behind everything seemed to fade away, leaving her with a sense of despair and uncertainty. Regaining her composure, Toy could almost imagine Fredrick's voice offering his perspective on the situation.

"I thought you were unstoppable," he would say jokingly, and Toy would chuckle.

Toy walked up the stairs. She couldn't help but yearn to have Bonnie by her side. The thought of facing this challenge alone scared her. But, deep down, she knew it was for the best that Bonnie wasn't here. This place was far from deserving of him; he deserved a life filled with happiness and fulfillment.

Just watch your step, Toy... Just watch your step. One foot in front of the other.

Toy stood at the top of the stairs, listening to the eerie sounds of the spirits whizzing by beneath her. She got glimpses of their ethereal forms through a small crack in the floorboards. The noise was so piercing that Toy instinctively wanted to drop to her knees and shield her ears, but she resisted the urge. She forced herself to continue onward, compelled by an unknown determination. Peering through the crack once more, she was struck by the sight of these spectral beings. They moved with precision and unity, resembling an army marching toward an inevitable death. Toy wondered who led them; perhaps Kieran?

Despite her curiosity, Toy pressed on, her eyes drawn to the encroaching vegetation that had claimed this abandoned place. She approached a sturdy metal door and exerted all her strength to push it open wide enough to get through. When she finally squeezed through, she found herself in yet another corridor. To her horror, a swarm of spirits swiftly approached her, their presence sending shivers down her spine. Before they could reach her, the ground beneath her feet gave way, causing her to fall downward. Panic-stricken, Toy desperately tried to grab onto something, anything! With a bone-jarring impact, Toy crashed onto the unforgiving ground, the wind forcefully expelled from her lungs, leaving her gasping for air and writhing in agony.

Toy could see the spirits rushing by her in a continuous stream, their presence palpable. It was as if they were the life force of this place, pulsating like a heartbeat. Amongst them were open metal doors that they seemed to avoid, as if they held some danger. Fiery embers consumed those who failed to notice them in time, disappearing into thin air.

Toy figured if she timed her movements perfectly, she would be okay. She darted from one door to another through the hallway. The key was to maintain her speed and rhythm, matching the pace of the spirits. With each passing wave, Toy seized the opportunity to sprint to the next metal door, determined to reach the end. She managed to reach the first one just in the nick of time.

Success! I can't believe it!

Without wasting a moment, Toy continued to the next door.

This is it! I'm doing it!

The spirits zoomed past her, and she swiftly ran to the cracked wooden door at the end of the hall without pausing to catch her breath. However, to her dismay, she found the wooden door was locked.

The approaching wave echoed in her ears, causing a surge of panic within her. Reacting swiftly, she retreated to the last door, only to watch as the spirits nudged it open a bit. If Toy waited where she was, the force of the next wave would knock the wooden door from its hinges. Toy braced herself. The anticipation built as she felt the impending wave drawing nearer, but she remained motionless, urging the spirits to break down the door. With a sudden rush, they surged past once more, shattering the wooden door. Toy took her chance and dashed along the path they had created for her, sprinting toward the next door.

Her hopes were dashed as the door crumbled like stone, leaving her exposed and vulnerable with the next wave rapidly approaching. Toy ran and made it to the next door just in time, pleading for it to hold as she sought refuge behind it. The door quivered as the spirits passed by, succumbing to their force and collapsing. Without a moment to spare, Toy was compelled to continue her frantic escape to the next door, propelled forward by the relentless pursuit of the impending wave.

With a sense of urgency, Toy sprinted to the last door in the hall, knowing that it was her only chance of escape. The ground beneath her trembled and cracked, but she reached the door at the end of the hall just in time. With relief, she burst through the door and shut it behind her. She could hardly believe it, but she did it!

Toy leaned against the door, gasping for breath, her heart pounding in her chest, then pushed herself away from the door and took a moment to scan her surroundings. To her surprise, she was standing in a desolate field. When she looked back at the door she had come through, she was taken aback to see it had disappeared. The sky above her was an unsettling shade of yellow, reminiscent of the aftermath of a violent storm. The air felt crisp, and the field stretched before her, untouched and unharvested, as if the farmers who tended to the land had vanished when it was time to reap the harvest.

Now that Toy had escaped the hall, she couldn't help but wonder what lay ahead in this strange and unpredictable place. It was difficult to expect what she might encounter, as the rules that governed this place were unknown. With a mixture of curiosity and trepidation, Toy peered closer at her surroundings. The field stretched out before her, devoid of any signs of life. The absence of natural laws in this purgatory-like place left her with a sense of unease.

With each step, Toy pushed past the lifeless crops surrounding her. Despite the dizziness in her head and the throbbing pain of her wound, she pressed on. In this vast expanse, it felt as if there was only her and the field. But that couldn't be true. She walked down a slope and stumbled upon an ancient, rusted tractor at the foot of the hill. It was not unusual to come across a tractor in a place like this, but what caught her attention was that its lights were still on. There was no sound of an engine, just the eerie glow of the lights.

Toy glanced ahead and noticed another tractor in the distance. She sprinted to it without hesitation, only to discover the same thing. Confusion swirled within her. What was happening? Determined to find answers, she continued her frantic run and stumbled upon yet another tractor, and then another. The presence of these abandoned machines could not be a mere coincidence. They had to hold some significance, leading her to a purpose or revelation. Driven by this belief, Toy followed the trail of old tractors, hoping they would guide her to the answers she sought.

"Why are you following Grandfather's old tractor?" a young voice inquired, causing Toy to stop.

"Hello, who's there?" Toy yelled.

"Why are you running around?"

"The tractors are all there is; they must mean something!"

"They are leading you in circles. This is purgatory, Miss Fawn. Think outside the box."

Outside the box?

Toy fixed her gaze on the tractor bathed in the warm glow of the setting sun. Then, against all logic, she turned her back to the tractor and began running toward the sun. The boy's words echoed in her mind, reminding her that this place was purgatory. The wind grew more robust, as if attempting to drag her back to the tractors, but she resisted. Determined, she pressed on.

A sensation akin to fire ants crawling beneath her skin engulfed her, leaving her bewildered and alarmed. What was happening to her? Overwhelmed by this strange feeling, Toy collapsed to the ground, the wind intensifying along with the discomfort under her skin. Darkness enveloped her vision, rendering her blind, and the only sound that reached her ears was the haunting voice of the boy once again.

"I know you're cold and scared...but I'm with you..."

"I'll do whatever it takes to get out of here. I want...to see Bonnie again."

Toy's vision cleared, revealing a desolate realm engulfed in darkness. The feeble glow from above barely illuminated her surroundings, leaving her in solitude. Before her stood a sturdy metal door.

"What is this? Kid! Where am I?!" Toy could feel the rumble beneath her feet and the screams of the spirits coming toward her. "Not again! No! Go away! Get back!"

Taking refuge behind the door, Toy watched as the spirits rushed past, their ceaseless energy palpable in the air.

"I hate watching you fight; it makes me sad, Miss Fawn. It

made me sad when you fought Gillian. You must think outside the box and do what you wouldn't do before! It's fate! You can't hide from fate!"

Toy watched the spirits zoom by before her attention was drawn to the door behind her. Without hesitation, she pivoted on her heels to face the door, pushed it down, and stepped out of the light.

"There! I get it! This is pointless... I surrender! I'm tired of all this! Too tired to fight..."

Overwhelmed by her emotions, Toy crumbled to the floor, feeling completely drained. The energy that once filled the air had vanished. Despite her best efforts, tears streamed down her face, a physical manifestation of the pain and sadness that consumed her.

"Please...let me go. I need to see him..."

"I'm proud of you..."

"Where are you?!"

"I'm here," the boy said, yet this time, his voice didn't resonate within her mind or echo from the heavens above; it came from right in front of her.

Toy raised her head, and a young boy, no older than eight, was staring at her with his big gray eyes. His complexion appeared pallid, as if he had avoided sunlight for an eternity, but what caught her attention was the eerie black veins that snaked across his neck and marred his face.

Toy's chest was now covered by identical dark veins, spreading across her skin to her neck. She shifted her gaze away from the boy and took a moment to observe their surroundings. She was standing in a hallway that resembled a typical southern home. The kid's voice broke the silence again, expressing his admiration. Toy turned her attention back to him, noticing how his canary hair swayed in the unexpected gust of wind. His slender figure acted as a shield, preventing the sunlight from reaching Toy's body.

"Hey, come here, it's not safe here! Come! Come!" Toy squeaked.

The small boy approached and Toy instinctively threw her arms around him, realizing he was the only person she had encountered since being abandoned in this desolate place. Overwhelmed with emotions, Toy embraced the boy, tears streaming down her face. After a moment, he reciprocated the hug, but his actions seemed unfamiliar and uncertain, as if he had never experienced the warmth and comfort of a hug.

"I was thinking I would never see another person again!" Toy cried.

"Me too," the boy told her.

"I was so scared."

The boy pulled back, his tiny hands reaching out to clasp hers. "But you've done it. Can you walk?"

"Yes... Do you know? Do you know how I can get out of here?"

"Yes! Come!"

CHAPTER 39

Toy

With the young boy's help, Toy stood up. Once Toy was on her feet, the boy positioned himself to her right side, gazing up at her expectantly. He patiently waited for Toy to take the lead as they began down the serene, illuminated corridor.

"Let's go." Toy took her first step. "Let's leave this place."

The young boy remained close by, never wandering off. He didn't rush ahead either; instead, he stayed at her right side, holding her hand.

"Miss Fawn. I thought I was alone here. I really did," the boy whimpered.

"I know, me too."

They made their way through the hallway, drawing nearer to the radiant glow that marked the end.

"I made a mistake."

"Kid, whatever you did, we can fix it together, don't worry..."

"But it's a big mistake...so many people are dying right now..."

They left the hallway and found themselves surrounded by a lush forest, the air filled with the earthy scent of moss and the gentle rustling of leaves. Sunlight filtered through the canopy, casting shadows on the forest floor. The tall trees stood like ancient sentinels, their branches reaching to the sky.

"I can feel it...and it's only the beginning."

"Let's just get out of here. We can make it stop, kiddo. I'll help you find your home, and you can live. Really live."

They descended a steep hill as Toy attempted to comfort the young boy by gripping his hand tighter.

"But..."

"No buts...we've earned it."

Toy glanced around and a rush of recognition washed over her. With utmost care, she guided the boy across a stream, ensuring he didn't come into contact with the chilling waters beneath them.

"This place feels...familiar..."

With the first step they took on the pavement, he reminded her, "You've been here before."

"Hello... Can I do something for you?" the woman who was typically stationed at the desk of Twirllee's said, positioned near the rear entrance of Twirllee's, indulging in a cigarette.

"Hello... What are you doing here?" Toy asked her.

"I could ask you the same thing, coming out of the woods like that with a child," the woman huffed.

"Do you have a phone I could use? We need help."

"Yeah, follow me."

"Thank you so much!"

After extinguishing her cigarette with a firm stomp, the woman gestured for the pair to come along, and Toy tried to take her first step, but the young boy wouldn't move.

"What's wrong?" Toy murmured.

"I'm scared," he told her.

"It's okay. Don't be scared; I'm here."

They walked toward the woman and she kindly held the door open for them. Yet, just as they reached her, she unexpectedly collapsed to the ground, letting out ear-piercing screams. Toy watched as dark veins rapidly spread beneath her skin.

"Hey, what's going on with you?!" Toy gasped. "Help! We need help back here!"

The young boy desperately pleaded with Toy to keep walking while, in the background, the sound of another woman's scream filled the air.

"It's the boy! He killed her!" a woman screamed.

"I'm sorry..." he murmured, witnessing the woman meet the same fate as the other.

"Killed her?! What is she talking about?!"

He didn't respond but motioned for Toy to follow him through the wide-open doorway.

"Kid, what is going on?" Toy shouted, witnessing the surrounding people collapsing to the ground, their skin tainted with dark veins.

Finally, as they reached the front door, the child reluctantly gave her a partial answer. "She's right... I'm doing this..."

"How?! You're standing right next to me; you're not even touching them!"

"It's my mistake; it's what I've become."

"Let's not stay here!"

They sprinted down the street, and people Toy had lived near since her sophomore year stumbled and fell while they hurriedly raced past them to Bonnie's house.

"We need to fix this, Miss Fawn."

"We...we'll find a solution. But first, we must get out of here, find help!"

"Look at them," the boy whimpered. "This place... Those people..."

"We have to stop this!"

"I can't..."

"What are you talking about?"

"Have you already forgotten?" The boy's face contorted into a snarl as they arrived at Bonnie's house and forcefully swung open the front door.

"This isn't real! It's this place playing tricks on us!"

"No! I'm the one doing this! Kieran poisoned me with Bajulatorius Maledictio; it's making me do this! I am!"

"What? No..." Releasing her grip on the boy's hand, Toy turned to face him. Only then did his distinct features finally register in her mind, allowing Toy to recall his name. "Owen..."

"It was easier to get to you than it was Goldie, Toy."

"Owen... I'm...I'm so sorry."

"You didn't know this would happen when you gave me the water! But now it's too late!" Tears streamed down his face as they entered the living room.

"No! No! No!"

"I consumed the Maledictio; it took all of me. It weakened me and allowed Kieran to take control. This is what will happen if you do nothing!"

"I... I'm sorry..."

"We must do something. We must stop people from dying!" Overwhelmed by emotions, he couldn't hold back his sobs, and they filled the air with a heart-wrenching sound.

"Maybe if we leave...it will stop..." Toy turned, glancing down at the boy. "Owen, will it stop?"

"I'm killing them, Toy...not just them. So many more will die if Kieran and the Maledictio remain in control!"

"So this is the end?"

"Not ultimately... We have one chance...the last one."

"Tell me... I'll do anything."

"I think you know already..."

"I..."

"You must stop me...to stop Kieran... To stop the Maledictio."

"Owen...you can't ask me that..."

"You are one of two people needed to stop me from continuing to be a monster. You're my Protector."

"I'm nobody's Protector, and you're not a monster; Kieran is! This...Maledictio is."

"I will be...if I kill all I love...all these nice things people have shown me..."

"I understand, but..."

"Please, Toy, save them..."

"I'll...I'll try..."

They reached the hall just before the basement. Together, they exerted enough force to open the door, which unexpectedly was quite heavy.

"All right...what now?" Toy asked once they stepped inside, but she received no reply.

After shutting the door, Toy looked down to the spot where Owen had stood just moments ago. To her surprise, there was nobody.

"Owen?! Where are you? Where are you?!"

"I'm sorry," he said, "but you're ready now. To save everyone..."

"Ready?!? How can I be ready for this?!"

Toy slowly made her way down the stairs. Instead of the usual bright light illuminating the space, a series of torches lined the wall, casting flickering shadows on the walls. The warm glow from the torches created an eerie yet intriguing atmosphere, beckoning Toy to explore the depths of the basement. Each time Toy passed a torch, she could feel the intense heat searing her skin while the dark veins spreading throughout her body screamed in excruciating pain.

"I know...but I can't stop myself...only you and Goldie can stop me now..." Owen told her.

"Owen..." A whimper escaped her lips.

"Tell Goldie I love him...I was happy with just him and wished I was never forced to leave... Goodbye, Toy..."

Toy made it to the bottom of the stairs only to collapse to the ground, sobs escaping from deep within her, filling the space around her with anguish.

"But when you're gone... There'll be nothing else left...he'll be alone... I'll be alone...all alone here...all alone... I can't..."

Toy cried out as she closed her eyes. She felt a strong pair of arms around her, drawing her closer to someone. As she lifted her head from their shoulder, she was greeted by the sight of familiar canary locks. Without conscious effort, her arms instinctively wrapped around the man before her.

"Goldie," Toy whimpered.

"I'm here... I'm here..."

They sat there, tears streaming down their faces, and found solace in each other's embrace. Eventually, he was the first to break away, his hands gently resting on her shoulders as she placed hers on his elbows. For a brief moment, Toy averted her gaze from Goldie's tear-stained face and caught a glimpse of a younger Owen in the middle of the basement. But the surroundings had drastically changed. Gone were the cluttered piles of old furniture and boxes, replaced by a pervasive mold-like substance that seemed to thrive in every corner. The mold throbbed rhythmically, resembling a beating heart, while Owen was shirtless, kneeling at the room's center. The substance had enveloped his body, halting its growth just below his heart, effectively trapping him in that position.

"Oh no..." A soft whimper escaped Toy's lips, catching Goldie's attention as he turned around to see the transformation that had taken place in his older brother. Toy could see more tears in his warm brown eyes as he looked back at her.

"Can you stand?" he asked.

"Yes..."

With gentle care, he helped her stand and occupied the space to her right where Owen was.

"That's Owen, he's there," Toy whispered.

"Yes. Do you... Do you know what we have to do?" Goldie asked.

"Yes..." Toy told him as she looked back at the last torch she passed.

She grabbed the torch from the wall before they approached Owen. Coming to a halt directly in front of him, Toy felt an overwhelming desire to embrace the child rather than carry out the dreadful task at hand—ending his life. Her sole intention was to rescue him, and the expression on Goldie's face indicated that they shared the same sentiment. Glancing down at her trembling hand clutching the torch, Toy felt a sense of comfort as Goldie's hand gently intertwined with hers.

"I can't..." Toy cried.

"Toy...we have to," Goldie whimpered.

"I know..."

As a team, they moved the torch to the dark mess of black veins on Owen's chest, and firmly pressed the torch against his flesh. The piercing scream that escaped the child's mouth would remain etched in their memories for the rest of their lives. The flames quickly engulfed the sticky substance that anchored him to the ground, and they released the torch just in time to catch the child. The black mess in the room gradually transformed into glowing embers, but their focus remained solely on the boy cradled in their embrace.

With a gentle movement, Owen's eyes fluttered open, and he gazed up at Goldie and Toy. "Thank you... You saved me," he mumbled softly before gradually fading into the unknown.

Tears welled up in Toy's eyes once more, and she couldn't help but let out a sob.

"Toy, look," Goldie gasped.

She looked over at him to see that his body was fading away.

"Owen was the key to all of this," he murmured to himself while delicately turning his arms.

Toy looked down and noticed her body was undergoing the same gradual deterioration.

"We're leaving this place..."

"Owen was the key to all of this, not the others... Owen..." Toy gasped as fatigue set in and her eyelids closed.

Goldie's parting words echoed in her ears as she faded away.

"We shall meet again beneath the radiant sun..."

CHAPTER 40

Toy

The ceiling above Toy was devoid of any life, and her eyes, void of expression, gazed into nothingness. The coldness of the tile floor seeped into her body, sending shivers down her spine. The air was heavy with the metallic scent of spilled blood and the acrid odor of chemicals. An incessant itch crawled beneath her skin, urging her to scratch, but Toy remained motionless, unable to release the pent-up frustration and fear that filled her.

To her left, Toy heard footsteps. She sat up and adjusted her face to appear more human-like. A hand landed on her shoulder, and Toy met the gaze of someone with captivating magenta eyes. Bonnie's jaw tightened as he struggled to maintain his composure while Toy's mind remained preoccupied with the confusing thoughts from purgatory.

Bonnie pressed his face against her neck for a prolonged moment, breathing deep. He pulled back with a sigh and a weary smile, gently kissing her lips. Despite everything they had gone through, she could still detect a flicker of optimism lingering amidst the weariness on his face. He clung to the belief of a blissful conclusion, even amid his exhaustion and haunted demeanor. His unwavering faith was something Toy cherished. In fact, she realized how much she yearned for it.

"Thank God you're awake; I was so worried!" Bonnie yelped. "You started screaming and thrashing!"

"I'm okay," Toy interrupted.

"There was a collapse in front of the hall, so we have to keep going through the building. Good news—I found the key for the elevator." Bonnie forced a smile, trying to sound upbeat. "We should go." He pulled her up, and she acknowledged his action by nodding in agreement.

"Yeah, we have to leave. We can't afford to lose any more time."

"Nope."

With a slight clearing of his throat, he paused, fixing his gaze on Toy. His expression was gentle yet impossible to decipher, leaving her uncertain of his intentions. His eyes shifted to the open doors next to the dumbwaiter, urging her to follow him, yet Toy refused to comply, her determination unwavering even as she watched Bonnie pick up Fredrick's rigid form.

Despite the situation, the throbbing sensation of the Maledictio coursing through her arm remained palpable. It no longer scared her; she tore off her flannel, dropping it to the floor, her eyes fixated on the Maledictio's progression up her arm, spreading with each heartbeat.

"Toy, what is that?" Bonnie gasped.

Ignoring his question, Toy glanced to a sturdy metal pipe nearby. Without uttering a single word, she approached Fredrick's lifeless body and inserted her hand into his pocket, withdrawing his lighter.

As Toy made her way to the metal pipe, she ripped the gauze from her arm, leaving the wound exposed. Amidst the echoes of Bonnie's voice reverberating in Toy's mind and the relentless presence of the Maledictio coursing through her veins, she found solace in the act of wrapping the gauze around the pipe, diverting her thoughts from everything but the task at hand.

She set the gauze-wrapped pipe on fire, watching the flames dance. Her body was filled with the Maledictio's screams, urging her to flee from the flames that it dreaded. Ignoring its fearful warnings, she pressed the blazing pipe against her wound, determined to endure the searing pain, oblivious to Bonnie's cries.

As the curse of the Maledictio burned away, the vibrant orange glow entranced Toy, completely unaware of the footsteps beside her or the frantic shouts that filled the air. All Toy could register was the forceful push that sent her tumbling backward, crashing onto the hard concrete, while Bonnie snatched the fire from her grasp.

"*¡Mierda! ¡Dios mío!* What in the world are you doing, Toy?!" Bonnie's voice took a moment to register in her mind.

"No!"

"Your arm was on fire. It's burned! Why were you holding fire to your fucking arm?!" Each word he uttered caused Toy's breath to quicken, becoming more rapid and shallow.

Her eyes widened as she glanced upward at Bonnie, and a scream escaped her lips involuntarily. In a swift motion, Bonnie scooped her up and whisked her through the door, depositing her onto a nearby bed. Her instincts kicked in, and she desperately attempted to create distance between them, pushing herself away from Bonnie's grasp.

"Toy!" Bonnie cried as he tried to calm her down. "I need to know what you were doing! I need to know if you are okay! Why aren't you looking at me? I need you to answer me!"

"Bonnie?" Toy softly called, stealing a quick glance at him. A single tear rolled down his face, and Toy knew he wanted to reach out, yet he hesitated, not wanting to cause her any pain. "I needed to do it," she said, her voice quiet.

"No, you didn't. You hurt yourself, and I need to know why. I need to know if you're okay," Bonnie told her. "Please."

"I'm so sorry, Bonnie. I had to."

"I need to know why you were hurting yourself and what

just happened. I want you to be okay, *niña*. I might be able to help."

"When Fredrick and I first left to find Kurt, I got hurt. It was just a scratch, but I discovered it was infected soon after."

"With what, and what does that have to do with the stunt you just pulled?" Bonnie interrupted.

"With the same thing Owen has, what made it so Kieran could finally take control. The Maledictio...it's a death sentence unless you...unless you burn it out of you."

"That's why you burned yourself?" he whispered, and Toy nodded, tears creating a damp spot on her shirt. "I need you to listen to only my voice, Toy. Focus on my voice while I wrap your arm. I know it's hard, but you have to. I'm so thankful you told me. I was so worried about you. I still am. But I can try to help you now. You're not alone. You will always be importa—"

Bonnie's voice grew faint as Toy's attention shifted from his eyes to her arm as he wrapped it with a piece of relatively clean fabric he had found nearby. Toy couldn't help but notice the absence of the black veins that had plagued her. The Maledictio, the curse that had tormented her, was finally gone. She couldn't believe it.

The fire worked...

"I'm right here, Toy. Look at me; I'm right here." He touched the sides of her face and positioned her head so her eyes stared into his own. "You will always be important to me. I'm willing to fight with you, but I can only do it if you don't hide things like this from me. I love you so much. Now you can tell me, who told you about this Maledictio?"

"I don't even know if you are real, Bonnie. I can't tell you any more. I promise I want to believe you, but nothing seems real."

"I'm real. I'm right here, and I'm real. I know it's hard to believe me. I understand. But for me, you need to. I can't lose the only thing I don't want to burn. I'm real. And I'm here for you."

Tears welled up in her eyes, and at that moment, Toy couldn't hold back her emotions any longer.

Extending a helping hand, Bonnie gently guided them back to Fredrick. With a tender gesture, he again scooped Fredrick into his arms as Toy grabbed her flannel off the floor. Together, they made their way to the elevator.

"Got a plan, Bonnie?" Toy asked when he hit a button on the panel with the end of Bob.

He paused, his determination clear. "Oh—always." He forced a fleeting smile. "Don't you worry."

Regardless of the outcome, they would hit the ground running and not stop for anything. They stepped off the elevator and into a hall to find a locked door. Toy looked over at Bonnie before her gaze fixed on the windows above her. Despite the silent protest of her arm, which sent sharp, painful jabs as she stretched, she reached toward some nearby shelves.

With a gulp, Toy climbed the first and second shelf, wincing as she reached for the third and final one. Her fingers trembled, but they finally grabbed the edge of the open window frame. She squeezed through the window, held her breath, and maneuvered across the ledge to the next window. Toy climbed back inside and dropped to the ground to find herself on the other side of the door. Unlocking the door, Toy anxiously waited for Bonnie to join her, feeling exposed and vulnerable.

They made their way around two corners; the hallway ahead was empty. Suddenly, a sharp and unpleasant smell of melted plastic and burning wood filled Toy's nostrils. Despite the smell, she tried to shake off the sensation and they continued running until they reached the security booth. Finally, they could catch their breath, but their relief was short-lived as Brendan and Julia rushed to them. Brendan's expression changed when he noticed Fredrick in Bonnie's arms.

Brendan didn't react the way Bonnie and Toy expected. Instead of lashing out in anger, he stood there, lost in his thoughts and emotions. Leaning against the wall, he stood there in silence, bathed in the soft glow of the dim light. From his vantage point, he could see Fredrick's body as Bonnie approached him. As soon as Fredrick was placed in his arms, Brendan's body gave way, and he slid down to the ground, unable to muster any movement. He couldn't tear his gaze away from Fredrick.

Throughout their captivity, they all had experienced unimaginable pain and suffering, enduring physical abuse, abduction, and countless other atrocities that this chaotic place threw at them. Yet, amidst all the hardships, they had managed to hold onto one thing—they had never lost anyone.

This death was a point of no return, a devastating blow that would shatter the spirits of everyone. An ultimate test that would push them to their limits and threaten to tear them apart.

Their tear-streaked faces shimmered in the light as Julia's gaze fell upon Bonnie and Toy. Her attention quickly shifted to Brendan, who held Fredrick tightly in his arms. Overwhelmed by shock and disbelief, Julia stumbled backward, her stomach lurching, and emptied its contents in the hallway. Tears welled up in her eyes, blurring her vision, and the room seemed to spin around her. Deep down, she knew that Fredrick was no longer a part of her life, but seeing him in Brendan's embrace made it all too real.

Toy expected Brendan to look up, but he didn't. Not even when she took a brief moment to gently brush his hair out of his face.

"Brendan," Toy started, her voice soft. "Brendan, can you hear me?"

Toy's heart sank as he remained completely unresponsive. She let out a heavy sigh, feeling the weight of disappointment and sadness wash over her. Tears welled up in her eyes once more as she struggled to come to terms with the harsh reality.

"Brendan," she tried again, still getting no reaction.

"Brendan?" Bonnie tried. His strong exterior crumbled, and his voice trembled with emotion.

"He's in shock, guys," Julia interrupted.

"Brendan," Toy insisted. "Fredrick wanted me to tell you he loved you. He loved you so much."

"Shut up! Just shut the fuck up!" Brendan shouted, making Toy jump back. "This is all your fucking fault; you knew it was dangerous and went anyway, and he died. It's your fault."

"I..." Toy didn't know what to say; he wasn't wrong. "I'm going to go tell Drake..."

She couldn't hold back her tears as she stepped into the hall; they streamed down her face, resulting from a mix of sadness and frustration.

Drake saw her and came running. "Thank God Bonnie found you! Are you guys okay?" he asked.

"Bonnie...and I are okay," Toy told him, and braced herself by grabbing his shoulders.

"And...and Fredrick?"

Toy's eyelids fluttered, and she felt another wave of emotions rising within her once more. "He didn't make it, Drake..." she cried.

Drake's face contorted with anguish. He remained silent, his breaths coming in short, painful gasps as tears streamed down his face.

"Drake..."

"How did he die?" Drake asked; he was the first one to ask.

"We got ambushed while we were out there, and he died to save me," Toy told him as she continued to break down. "I just can't believe... We have never lost anyone here. I lost our friend, Drake—I lost Fredrick. It's my fault."

"No, it's not, Toy." Drake grabbed her and carefully examined her appearance from head to toe. "You're hurt," he commented when he saw the bandage peeking out from under her flannel.

"I'm fine," Toy said quietly.

"Even so, Julia should look at it."

Without wasting a moment, Toy scrambled out of his embrace and sprinted with all her might to the room they all woke up in.

She knew what she had to do.

"Toy?!" Drake shouted behind her.

Toy managed to outpace the others as Drake called for them, and she shut the door behind her, ensuring her safety by locking it and barricading it with various objects. Their desperate cries to open the door echoed through the room, but Toy refused. She piled items in front of the vent, cutting off any potential access.

With the vent blocked, Toy found herself surrounded only by the others who remained trapped in slumber.

Both Protectors together again.

Toy wouldn't let Fredrick's sacrifice be in vain. She explored every corner of the room, identifying the spots where her friends had been infected.

> Joanna: left lower thigh.
> Mable: top of right foot.
> Eric: inside of right hand.
> Kurt: left shoulder.
> Brodie: left pectoral.
> Forrest: right side of jaw.
> Goldie: stomach.

As Toy heard someone kick the door, she swiftly crafted a new torch and firmly pressed the torch against each of her friends' injuries, knowing that the burns would inevitably leave scars. Even though her actions would save their lives, she couldn't help but wonder if they would resent her for the permanent reminders of this place. And perhaps, deep down, they too would hold her responsible for the loss of Fredrick, and rightfully so.

"Burn! I'll burn all of you out of my friends!" Toy growled.

After completing her task, she extinguished the torch and took a moment to appreciate the tranquility.

A sudden frenzy ensued as soon as Toy opened the door. Bonnie forcefully pressed her against the wall while the rest of the group reacted with shock and alarm, overwhelmed by what she had done.

"Toy! What have you done?!" Bonnie yelled.

"What needed to be done."

CHAPTER 41

Goldie

As soon as Goldie woke up, he felt a skull-splitting headache throbbing in his head. He struggled to open his eyes and realized he was inside a storage room. To his dismay, he discovered the sleeping bodies of his friends scattered across the room. Bonnie and Toy were heatedly arguing while the rest of the group hurriedly tended to their friends.

"Bonnie! You need to listen to me!" Toy yelled as Goldie's eyes fluttered open and shut. He could hear Toy's voice, filled with urgency and intensity, echoing in the background. "Please, you need to know I did this to help them!"

He shut his eyes tightly. Chaotic yelling filled the room. But when he opened his eyes again, it felt as if time had magically slipped away, for the room was now engulfed in an eerie whisper.

"The only way to stop the Maledictio is to burn it out," Toy explained.

"You hurt them for nothing; none of them have woken up. If they do, they will have lifelong scars on their bodies."

"But it wouldn't matter because they would be alive."

"Guys, stop; this isn't like you two!" Drake interrupted.

Goldie's face lit up with a smile despite his pain. That

Drake was still alive brought him immense relief and joy, yet, as the haunting memories of that dreadful night when Owen appeared resurfaced in his mind and the overwhelming feeling of being trapped in purgatory returned, panic consumed Goldie.

"Drake," Goldie gasped. As he attempted to sit up, darkness slowly encroached upon his field of view, causing Goldie to grimace in agony. He reluctantly relinquished his efforts and gently rested his head on the cold, hard floor.

"Goldie?!" they all shouted.

"Whoa, easy there," someone said sheepishly, jumping up to help.

"Where's Drake?" Goldie's voice came out croaky.

"I'm right here, Sunshine."

As Goldie narrowed his gaze, his sight became clear, revealing Drake in front of him.

"Yeah?"

Drake's worried expression softened into a smile as he looked down at Goldie. "You really gave us a scare back there, Goldie, going all comatose like that."

After tightly embracing Goldie, Drake gently patted his arm before stepping away. Goldie couldn't help but notice the uneasiness in his eyes.

"I'm okay, Green bean," he reassured him softly.

Drake nodded subtly before he replied. "I know. I just—I thought you were dead, Goldie, and I—"

"I'm okay, Drake. I'm alive."

"No, I know that I just..." Drake's eyes glistened with tears, and Goldie struggled to conceal the overwhelming emotion that threatened to surface on his face. Drake took a trembling breath and released it gradually, gathering strength. "After... after everything that's happened, you know, I just wouldn't be able to lose you," he said, rubbing his eyes with his fingers.

Goldie nodded; he knew what Drake meant. The mere thought of Drake possibly perishing while Goldie was in purgatory caused Goldie to stop breathing for a second. He knew if he ever lost Drake, there was a significant possibility that he would lose himself, too.

Drake remained oblivious to the depth of Goldie's affection and the immense significance he held in Goldie's life. Goldie's throat tightened as he mentally prepared himself for the forthcoming conversation he knew he had to have with Drake.

"Goldie," Drake said, interrupting Goldie's thoughts. "We need to talk about something soon, but God, I'm so glad you're okay!"

"Green bean." Goldie scrutinized what he was wearing. "Is this your hoodie?"

"Y-yeah, I didn't need it, and yours was ruined."

"Thanks."

"We're glad you're back, Goldie," Toy said.

"Back?"

"You've been in Bonnie's head," Julia answered.

"You told Bonnie how to get the spirits back on our side and how to get you back," Drake added.

"If I was in Bonnie's head, I didn't talk to Bonnie; if I did, I don't remember anything," Goldie confessed as the alarm sounded. It wasn't exactly a lie, as he hadn't been inside Bonnie's mind, so he couldn't recall anything from that experience.

The key was in the details.

"What's that noise?" Toy asked.

"It's an old fire alarm. There must be a fire somewhere in the building," Goldie answered.

"Do you think Owen caused it?" Julia asked.

"You guys need to get out of here," Goldie said. "Before I look for Owen, I'll teleport you guys out of this hellhole."

"Teleport? What?" Bonnie interrupted.

"I don't have time to explain! Get everyone who isn't awake together!"

"Okay," they replied.

The group carefully shifted their friends' sleeping bodies along with Fredrick's body corpse to the center of the room. While the others continued their efforts, Toy hurriedly approached Goldie, gripping his shoulders tightly, a sense of urgency in her eyes.

"Remember! Burn it out of Owen to save him." Her voice cracked.

"Toy, stop this!" Bonnie interrupted, but Toy didn't listen.

"You have to burn the Maledictio, burn the stuff out of him. We have freed his soul from the Maledictio. Now, we must save his body. To save him and get Kieran and the Maledictio out of him. You are his Protector."

"So are you; it took the two of us to save him before. I want you to help me!" Goldie exclaimed.

"I...I want to, but...what about the others? You know they won't go if the two of us stay... This is fate... You must do it yourself while I get the others to safety."

Goldie nodded and beckoned everyone closer. "Everyone, hold hands and close your eyes. Are you ready?"

"Wait!" Drake blurted out.

"What?"

"Are you going to come back?"

"I promise I'll come back."

Goldie watched Drake's gaze shift away from him, his eyes welling up with tears. The silence in the room was broken only by the sound of his quiet sobs.

"Now, is everyone ready?"

"Yes," Bonnie answered.

"Okay." Goldie shut his eyes tightly. This was the first time he had attempted to teleport such a large group of people. Something in his mind was screaming at him. If he tried to do this and it worked, he would lose his powers forever. But... no. His friends mattered more than his powers. He wanted his powers to help instead of hurt for once.

When Goldie started, he experienced a sensation that he

could only compare to a piece of his soul being ripped from his body. But, as quickly as the sensation appeared, it vanished, leaving Goldie to open his eyes and let out a relieved sigh when he saw his friends were gone. The grateful smile that adorned his face soon transformed into an expression of sadness.

Determination filled Goldie's heart as he whispered, "I'm coming, Owen; just hold on."

Goldie hurriedly departed to search for his brother. The building was going up in flames fast. As he navigated through the intricate network of hallways, he encountered spirits, all afflicted by the dreaded Maledictio. He was cautious not to let them touch him. Every one of them screamed in pain and fear, with nowhere to go as the fire got worse. The atmosphere within the building grew stifling, with smoke permeating the air, making it painful to breathe. Along his path, Goldie stumbled upon a knife and a gun; the presence of the blade didn't surprise him, but the unexpected discovery of the firearm caught him off guard. He turned a corner and collided head-on with Owen.

"Owen?!" Goldie gasped.

"Goldie?!"

Goldie was determined to rescue Owen and remove the Maledictio and Kieran, even if it meant risking his own life. He had seen what would happen if he did nothing...

"Surprise, jackass," Goldie growled.

With a swift motion, Kieran grabbed Goldie and pushed him against the doorframe. Goldie grabbed his knife and attempted to thrust it into Kieran's shoulder. Kieran grabbed Goldie's wrist, preventing the attack. Determined to free himself, Goldie stomped on Kieran's foot and delivered a knee into his stomach, causing Kieran to release his grip and allow Goldie to run away.

Goldie's focus shifted when he caught Kieran's piercing scream, followed by a distinct cracking sound from the floorboards. Reacting swiftly, he hurried toward the noise and peered into the hole.

To his surprise, he saw Kieran and Owen engaged in a fierce struggle for dominance over Owen's body. Despite the clear pain Owen was experiencing, he displayed remarkable resilience in fighting back. Sensing the urgency, Goldie leaped into action before Kieran could regain control, descending into the hole and pulling Kieran's legs out from underneath him.

Kieran tumbled onto his back and Goldie lunged atop him, delivering a forceful punch to his face. Goldie grabbed a blazing piece of wood, ready to burn Owen's chest, but Kieran grabbed Goldie's head and smashed their skulls together. Crimson blood trickled down from Goldie's nose, and he groaned. Seizing the opportune moment, Kieran got on top of Goldie and relentlessly pummeled Goldie's face with a series of punches.

Despite the punches, Goldie plunged the knife into Kieran's side, striking his pelvis. It forced Kieran to stop and let out a sharp exclamation.

"Shit!"

After separating from Goldie, he swiftly dashed to the lower level of the asylum. Goldie chased after him, and although the smoke was less dense in this area, it was becoming unpleasant.

A brick was thrown at Goldie, momentarily stunning him. Seizing the opportunity, Kieran rushed him and snatched the gun from his grasp. With a swift motion, he struck Goldie's face with the butt of the weapon, but Goldie evaded the blow, causing the gun to collide with the wall behind him. Taking advantage of the situation, Goldie retaliated by punching Kieran's injured side.

Goldie attempted to thrust his knife into Kieran again, but Kieran dodged the attack. Kieran grabbed Goldie's wrist and used his strength to crush it, trying to get Goldie to drop the knife. Goldie let out a piercing scream, momentarily distracting Kieran. Taking advantage of the lapse, Goldie slipped out of Kieran's grip and sprinted away as fast as his legs could carry him, cradling his injured left arm.

"You're fucking dead!" Kieran yelled.

Goldie maneuvered around the corner, clutching the knife tightly in his right hand while attempting to ease the discomfort in his throbbing left wrist. Despite the pain, he was relieved to find he could flex his fingers with no hindrance. Surveying the surroundings, everything seemed normal and undisturbed. To divert Kieran's attention, Goldie grabbed a nearby bottle and hurled it across the room.

Goldie navigated between the shelves, silently closing the distance between himself and Kieran. With determination in his eyes, he sprinted toward Kieran, his arm raised high, ready to strike. The weapon descended upon Kieran, and a piercing scream escaped Kieran's lips as the knife became lodged in his shoulder.

With a menacing growl, Kieran grabbed the front of Goldie's hoodie before slamming him onto the ground. He removed the knife from his own shoulder and raised it, aiming for Goldie's head. Goldie wrestled the knife out of Kieran's grasp, and it clattered across the room. Despite this, his fury remained unabated, consuming him. His hands descended upon Goldie's throat.

"Please, I beg you. Don't do this," Goldie choked out, clawing at Kieran's hands. He swiftly entangled his legs with Kieran's, flipping him over to assume the dominant position. With a forceful motion, he slammed Kieran's head against the unforgiving floor while shifting his hands toward Kieran's neck.

However, Kieran's knee instinctively jerked upward, connecting with Goldie's crotch, causing him to groan and loosen his grip. Seizing the opportunity, Kieran firmly grasped Goldie's hair and forcefully headbutted him, then retreated and put some distance between them in a desperate scramble, mustering the strength to approach Goldie again, his determination clear as he stormed toward him. Goldie, still recovering from the previous hit, was defenseless on the ground.

Kieran delivered a series of forceful kicks to Goldie's side. Goldie's cries of agony filled the air as he tried to crawl away, but Kieran refused to let him escape. With a swift motion, Kieran grabbed the knife from the ground and jerked Goldie's head up.

Pressing the sharp blade against Goldie's neck, Kieran applied just enough pressure to draw a small amount of blood, sending a shiver of pain and fear down Goldie's spine.

Kieran leaned in close to Goldie's ear and whispered, "You've made my life a living hell with this task, you worthless fag."

Just as Kieran was about to carry out his sinister plan of slitting Goldie's throat, he stopped. He looked down at Goldie cradled in his embrace; Goldie had surrendered completely. There was no trace of resistance left in him, his body seeming completely drained. With closed eyes, Goldie waited for death.

Kieran released Goldie and chuckled as he watched him slump to the ground. Carelessly dropping the knife, Kieran rose to his feet, unsure if Goldie was even aware enough to comprehend his words.

"I hope you like the smell of your flesh burning," he laughed.

Goldie's world turned crimson as he watched Kieran's departing figure. His sight became hazy, overwhelmed by an intense fire burning in the depths of his belly. Every tearful moment he had experienced flooded his mind, burdening him with their weight, yet, rather than shattering under pressure, his heart transformed into solid stone and descended into the darkness, relinquishing control.

Kieran had taken away his brother. The depth of Goldie's revulsion for this monstrous individual was indescribable. Kieran had no entitlement to share the same air as Owen and himself.

Goldie's entire being throbbed, his breath searing his lungs as if engulfed in flames. The pounding in his head was relentless, and every fiber of his being yearned for a fresh supply of oxygen.

I hope you like the smell of your flesh burning.

Despite the mounting pressure, Goldie refused to give in, pushing himself to the brink. In a swift motion, he grabbed a piece of burning piece of wood, chasing after Kieran with unwavering determination. He cornered him against a wall, both of them succumbing to exhaustion, and Goldie summoned every ounce of strength left.

Fueled by anger, Goldie pulled Kieran away from the wall and slammed him back with an unyielding force that reverberated through his body. Kieran's mouth opened wide, releasing a piercing cry that echoed through the burning hall.

I hope you like the smell of your flesh burning.

Blood flowed from the gash on his face. The crimson liquid formed a gruesome mask, creating a horrifying sight.

Kieran's fingers dug into Goldie's arms, leaving deep imprints on his wrists. Goldie's cold gaze met Kieran's eyes. He could see the newly emerged fear within them.

Goldie brought his nose close to Kieran's, their faces almost touching. "You didn't learn from your mistakes like Silver and my father, did you?!" Goldie yelled as his hand connected with Kieran's face. "You're done; give up my brother."

He watched Kieran's eyes widen, fearing they might pop out of his head. Kieran's hands tore a fragment of Drake's hoodie in his attempt to grab Goldie.

I hope you like the smell of your flesh burning.

Goldie grabbed the burning piece of wood and pressed it against Kieran's chest, using the fire to eradicate the Maledictio from his brother's body.

"With everything Owen and I went through, with our father! What we had to do to get away! Why the fuck did you have to drag us back to hell?!" Goldie screamed as he held him against the wall. "What the hell is wrong with you?!"

When Kieran opened his mouth to reply, the ceiling trembled. In seconds, debris rained down upon them. The impact forced Goldie to release his grip on Kieran, and they both descended to the ground.

CHAPTER 42

Owen

The throbbing in Owen's head intensified, reaching a point where it seemed as if his skull was about to split in two. Yet, just as suddenly as it had begun, the excruciating pain ceased, almost as if Owen's brain had shut off its pain receptors, flooded with a surge of adrenaline. Owen raised his head, only to find Kieran standing before Goldie.

"It's a shame a beautiful subject rid his powers from his body for a bunch of nobodies," Kieran said. "This is the first time I've seen such a thing... Silver's gonna want to know this development." His attention shifted from Goldie to Owen, a smile on his dry and cracked lips.

"It's such a shame," he teased. "Both of you will die tonight. It was nice knowing you."

And with that, Kieran left, and without hesitation, Owen sprang to his feet and approached Goldie.

"Goldie, wake up—we need to get out of here... C'mon!" Owen cried out. He looked at his baby brother and started to cry; he couldn't help it. "With everything we went through, this isn't how I thought our story would end. I'm so sorry about what happened. It wasn't my fault—I-I didn't want to; Kieran was in control..."

Owen's gaze shifted down toward Goldie's hand when it twitched. At that moment, his brother's chocolate-colored eyes opened.

"Holy shit! Thank God!" Owen cried out.

Despite the suffocating smoke that filled the air, he did his best to help Goldie stand up. The burning sensation in their lungs made it even more difficult, but the absence of the Maledictio and Kieran overshadowed Owen's concern for the raging fire around them. Owen doubted that Goldie's legs could bear his weight if he attempted to stand without help, let alone flee the scene. Owen found solace in holding Goldie close, not wanting to let him go.

Owen guided Goldie through the thick smoke, leading him back to the ground floor. Thick smoke filled the air, engulfing the entire space, while flames crackled and danced. Goldie fell to the ground, prompting Owen to shield his nose and mouth with the hem of his blood-stained shirt. He instinctively lowered himself as much as possible, trying to escape the intense heat that pressed against his scorched chest, making it difficult for him to breathe as he gasped for air.

"Holy...shit," Owen wheezed.

Without thinking, Goldie instinctively reached out for Owen's arm while Owen grabbed his shoulder to prevent him from stumbling. Owen forced a smile, attempting to hide any signs of his unease.

"Always wanted to know how it felt to be roasted alive," Goldie coughed. "Gotta say, I'm not disappointed."

"Uh, personally? I'd rather keep my eyebrows from melting off of my face."

"Owen, you would look so adorable with no eyebrows. Trust me," Goldie joked.

"Shut up." Owen furrowed his brows in a displeased expression and shifted his attention away from Goldie's arrogant grin.

"We're heading toward the exit, right?" Goldie asked.

Without waiting for Owen's response, which he expected to be filled with sarcasm, Goldie saw a motionless figure slouched in a chair. He shook his head as the haze cleared, directing Owen's attention to the individual.

The pair inched closer, forced to pass the chair as it was the sole unobstructed passage amidst the raging flames, yet the girl remained motionless, her hands charred and swollen, clasped between trembling knees. Her vacant stare remained fixed on the ground, oblivious to the boys' presence as her wild, tangled curls cascaded around her.

Owen gestured with his chin toward a nearby table, which they could crawl beneath to avoid the girl. But their plan was disrupted when the girl lifted her head. Her sharp, amber eyes pierced Owen's, causing him to freeze. An eerie presence emanated from her, a haunting and perceptive aura that hinted at malevolent intelligence. It reminded Owen of his reflection when he saw the Maledictio lurking beneath his skin. Despite the potential danger, the girl remained seated, staring at Owen and Goldie.

"I had to do it," she said, voice hollow. "Burn it. All of it. After what you put us through."

Goldie gave Owen a cautionary look as he got to his feet. "What...what happened to you?" he asked the girl.

"What do you think? This fucking nightmare happened to me." The young woman didn't even bother to glance his way, her attention solely on Owen. "It won't be long now," she said, wringing her reddened hands. "It'll be you or him. Or both? Or is he planning something different with you two?"

"What the hell are you talking about?" Owen asked.

She stared at Owen for a prolonged and unsettling moment, her expression filled with unease. Her attention soon shifted to Goldie as she sighed and shook her head in disappointment. "Haven't you been wondering what all this means? Why does this fucking punishment even matter? Or why are the guys almost always left for dead in here, while there never seem to be as many girls?"

Goldie and Owen shared puzzled looks. Owen had pondered none of those things because he had retreated as soon as he realized he couldn't regain control. Judging by the irritated expression on Goldie's face, it seemed like he didn't know, either—or didn't care.

"Will knowing the answers get us out of here?" Goldie demanded. "Otherwise, I cannot see the importance."

The woman shrugged. "Might be useful to know, anyway. I haven't figured out all of it, but... The guys who aren't butchered by your friend here or killed by other subjects... Well, let's just say those assholes probably want to get them back under their fucking control again." She swallowed, her tone thick with bitterness. "And the ones that survive this place— the strong ones, the violent ones, or the pretty ones like your friend Toy—they're...taken. Somewhere. Silver is using them for his newest project—whatever the fuck that is."

She shifted her focus back to Goldie. "I found some papers claiming you are his favorite subject in this project." She paused and then sounded like she was reciting something from a textbook: "'*Goldie Philip; age nineteen. Project Alfresco. Subject A-876. He is very slow to trust and build personal relationships; he has post-traumatic stress disorder and/or severe emotional stunting caused by the abuse from his father. Shows signs of a possible autism spectrum disorder; could it prove useful? For best results, he must provoke with bodily threats to his best friend, Drake Sallow, or brother Owen Philip.*'"

Owen mirrored Goldie's actions, instinctively crossing his arms over his chest. A sharp discomfort gnawed at him, as if his simmering anger was on the verge of erupting.

"Say what now?" Goldie whimpered.

"You shut the fuck up!" Owen yelled.

His reaction didn't faze the young woman; she blinked, showing no signs of being affected.

"It's what I read." She shrugged again. "Believe, don't believe. Whatever. I don't care. But you should at least try to escape before they catch you. Or before the whole damn building goes up. You can get out through the kitchen."

Filled with doubt, she hesitated before surrendering to her emotions, slumping forward in her seat and covering her face with her hands. "And keep each other safe, okay?" It was her last mumble. "Like...I couldn't do for Rikki and Josh."

"Fuck," Goldie grunted. He ran his hand through his hair in frustration and slowly walked away, his shoulders tense and rigid. Owen trailed behind him, stealing glances at the girl, feeling frustration, grief, and an overwhelming sense of fear coursing through his body, overwhelming his mind with memories and thoughts he desperately wanted to forget.

After successfully navigating through the burning cafeteria, they found themselves in a deserted hallway filled with hazy smoke. With relief flooding over them, they stepped outside into the crisp winter air, feeling a sense of liberation from the scorching heat and raging flames. Overcome with a surge of adrenaline, Owen swiftly turned around and punched a nearby tree with his fist.

"Who the fuck does that chick think she is?" Owen hissed, his dark eyes crackling with lightning as they met Goldie's. "She had no goddamn right saying those things about you, whether or not she read them from some fucking file."

Goldie's hand moved across the nape of his neck as he avoided making eye contact, feeling a wave of embarrassment that caused his cheeks to redden. Deep down, Goldie knew that everything that had been said was undeniably true.

Silver had done his research, apparently.

"Goldie?" Owen started feeling dizzy from the pain riding his body. He reached for Goldie, but Goldie couldn't stand the way Owen sounded and looked at him, so he turned away toward the woods.

"I'm fucked up, man. There is no getting around that; a lot has happened since you left," he managed roughly, brushing away the angry sting from his eyes. "It's probably why I was fucking picked for this shit. It doesn't matter. I don't care."

"No, no. Don't you dare start with that!" Owen interrupted with a growl. His hand shot out and firmly grasped Goldie's arm and, in a swift motion, he maneuvered Goldie to a nearby tree, pressing him against it. With a firm grip, Owen pinned Goldie's hands flat against the rough bark, one on each side of his head, leaving him no room to escape.

"Because I care, and it's all bullshit," Owen said harshly. "You're not a headcase, Goldie. You're intelligent and kind and clever as all fuck—okay? And you—you... Dammit."

Owen moved closer, causing Goldie to close his eyes tightly. He gently rested his forehead against Goldie's.

"You have to be one of the strongest fucking people I have ever met," Owen whispered, his voice utterly wrecked. "And I don't know what I would do without you."

As Goldie's cries reached Owen's ears, a wave of emotion washed over him, causing his eyes to tear up. The sound of Goldie's distress tugged at his heart.

"So don't you listen to her or anyone else who tries to tell you otherwise. You listen to me or Drake. We're the ones who know you. Understand?"

Goldie remained firmly planted against the tree, showing no intention of escaping.

"I love you... My baby brother..."

Owen's embrace enveloped Goldie, providing a sense of security and warmth. In that fleeting moment, Goldie felt the weight of Owen's words seep into his very being, revitalizing him. Goldie's arm accidentally brushed against one of Owen's painful stab wounds. Owen suppressed a whimper, reminding him of the pain he still endured.

"Thank you," he mumbled into Owen's neck before he pulled away.

"You don't have to thank me. It's the truth—plain and simple."

Goldie shook his head in disbelief, a faint smile tugging at the corners of his lips as they finally walked away from the sanatorium. The weight of their escape hung heavy in the air, a mix of relief and uncertainty swirling around them.

Owen's sense of time slipped away, lost in the relentless battle to stay awake and put one foot in front of the other. He wondered when he would finally have time to rest. He could faintly perceive snow falling around him. The freezing temperature caused his heart rate to decrease, and the blood oozing from his injury moved sluggishly. Gradually, a tingling sensation engulfed his arms and legs, leaving him completely numb.

"I think we're safe," Goldie said behind Owen, and it was like a dam breaking.

They were okay.

They were safe.

The Maledictio was destroyed.

Kieran was gone.

Owen didn't have to fight anymore.

The ground reached up to meet Owen as he gave up. Goldie called his name, but he was too far away, and Owen was gone.

CHAPTER 43

Toy

Their eyes adjusted to the unfamiliar surroundings. The absence of buildings was immediately noticeable, leaving them surrounded by the vast darkness of the night. Ahead of them stretched a seemingly endless, straight road, inviting them to embark on a mysterious journey into the unknown.

"He did it; he got us out of the building!" Toy heard Bonnie cheer.

"Where are we?" Toy asked.

"I don't know," Julia answered. "I just hope we're near Mount Vernon."

"We should get walking; maybe someone will drive by?" Toy suggested.

"We should wait for Goldie," Drake interjected.

"We must get somewhere safe; Goldie will find us. Don't worry," Bonnie said, trying to comfort him.

Each of them picked up one of their unconscious friends' bodies, except for Bonnie and Drake, who had the burden of carrying two. The sky was devoid of twinkling stars as a thick layer of rolling clouds, which showered them with heavy, wet snow, concealed them. The frigid atmosphere created an eerie ambiance as they trudged along the snow-covered road that stretched for miles.

Toy synchronized her movements with those around her, completely oblivious to the outside world. Instead of merely traversing the landscape, they merged with it, becoming one with their surroundings, all of their focus and energy channeled into a single train of thought.

Counting, counting, counting. Each step followed the next. Toy tightly wrapped her flannel around herself. The wind picked up, tousling the loose pieces of her hair and causing them to dance in the air. The feeling of loneliness lingered in her mouth, leaving a bitter taste. Toy had no desire to dwell on the past or contemplate the future.

The past was fixed, filled with an overwhelming amount of pain and suffering. The future held an excessive amount of uncertainty and endless possibilities. Thus, Toy found solace living in the present, where only the journey held significance. Ignoring any fashion concerns, she raised her collar and held Mable closer, seeking warmth and comfort from the cold.

Squinting her eyes to shield them from the strong gusts of wind, Toy scanned the vast expanse before her, kicking a Twirllee's cup on the road in front of her. The snowflakes descended from the gloomy sky as they stumbled upon a mailbox, and Toy used her shoe to clear the snow from their path, revealing an aged driveway.

"It's a driveway!" Toy exclaimed. "Maybe someone is at the end!"

They stumbled down the long driveway and came across a colossal log cabin nestled amidst the relentless snowstorm. The cabin stood tall and sturdy, its wooden exterior weathered by time and adorned with intricate carvings that told their own stories. The flickering glow of candlelight peeked through the frost-covered windows, inviting their weary bodies to seek refuge within its walls.

"Look at that!" exclaimed Julia, her voice barely audible

over the howling wind. "I can't believe it!"

"We have to take shelter before the storm worsens!" Drake yelled.

Bonnie, his face etched with exhaustion, nodded in agreement. "You're right. It's our only chance to escape this freezing cold. Let's hurry!"

"It's incredible," Drake said, his breath visible in the freezing air. "I wonder who lives here."

The thick layer of snow muffled the sound of their footsteps, and they noticed a faint wisp of smoke rising from the chimney. Hope surged within them, knowing that warmth and safety awaited them inside. Toy walked up to the door and knocked, awaiting a response, but her efforts were met with silence, so she turned the doorknob and opened it.

The door creaked and the group stepped inside. They were greeted by a haunting silence. The interior was dimly lit, with remnants of rustic furniture covered in a thin layer of dust and a crackling fireplace. The room was filled with the comforting scent of burning wood, the heat thawing their frozen bodies.

"Imagine the stories this cabin could tell if its walls could speak," Julia remarked.

They explored the living room further and found a worn journal lying on a wooden table. Carefully opening it, they discovered a handwritten list of names.

~~*To'fa*~~
Lola
Brayden
Oakley
Bentley
Brooklynn
Zira
Rocco
Rosemary

Toy stared at the list without a clue as to what it meant. They stood huddled together once they had placed their sleeping friends by the fire, their faces etched with grief and uncertainty.

The bitter cold of the snow-covered landscape seemed to have seeped into their bones, mirroring the heaviness in their hearts. They were faced with a difficult decision—leave the lifeless body of Fredrick, their dear friend, outside in the unforgiving cold, or find a way to keep him from decomposing inside.

Bonnie, his voice trembling, spoke up first. "Brendan...we can't keep him in the house with us; his body is decomposing as we speak."

"You can't make me put him outside like a dog!" Brendan screamed, clutching Fredrick to his chest as he backed away from everyone.

"I understand where you're coming from, Brendan. I know, it's disrespectful and inhumane. We owe it to him to give him a proper farewell," Drake started. "But we don't have the means of giving that to him right now. No way of calling for help."

Julia's eyes filled with tears as she said, "I know it's hard, but we must think practically. If we keep him inside, he will decompose faster, and it will be unbearable for all of us. It may even get us sick. But if he is out in the cold, it will keep him from decomposing. Brendan, please, we must consider the safety and well-being of the living. Fredrick would understand."

"No!" Brendan growled.

As the debate continued, emotions ran high, and the tension in the air was palpable. Toy, trying to find a middle ground, suggested, "What if we put him in the garage? We can cover him with a sheet; the garage will create a barrier against the snow while keeping him cold. It won't be ideal, but at least he won't be completely exposed and won't be in the house getting us sick."

Julia, her voice quivering, added, "I agree with Toy. It's a compromise that respects both our friend and our own needs. We can keep a vigil, taking turns to ensure he's not alone. It's the best we can do given the circumstances."

Despite the differing opinions, Brendan realized that what they were saying was not out of malice and ultimately decided on the garage plan. Bonnie helped Brendan wrap Fredrick in a blanket from the back of the couch and helped bring him to the garage, setting him on a painting sheet they had placed in the middle of the room.

Soon, they huddled before the crackling fire, their bodies exhausted from battling the relentless snowstorm and the events at the asylum.

"I can't believe we made it through that snowstorm," Toy whispered, her voice filled with relief. She nestled closer to Bonnie, seeking solace in his warming presence. "I don't think I've ever been so cold in my life," she added, shivering at the memory of the biting wind that had whipped through her clothes.

Bonnie, his eyes drooping with exhaustion, managed a weak smile. "We're lucky to have found this place," he murmured, his voice barely audible over the crackling fire. "I thought we were done for out there."

His words were met with nods of agreement from the others. As the fire danced and flickered, casting a warm glow on their tired faces, a realization came to Toy's mind.

They would be okay...maybe not for a while, but someday they would be.

As the warmth of the flames enveloped them, their eyelids grew heavy, and one by one, they succumbed to the soothing embrace of sleep. The crackling of the fire provided a comforting soundtrack, blending with the howling wind outside.

We will be okay...

EXTRAS

To be continued.

Greetings! Thank you for taking the time to read my novel. Ever since I was a young child, I have aspired to become an author. As a token of appreciation, I present you with additional insights into the captivating world of *Race Against Time*. The details in each section are presented in the order they appeared in the book. I hope you thoroughly enjoy this bonus content.

Characters

Toy Fawn

A young woman with the middle name Aria, Toy is also known as *niña*, a nickname given to her by Bonnie. She was born on February 11th, 1992, making her seventeen years old. Toy Fawn is a small-built individual, standing at a height of 5'5" and weighing 126 lbs. She has captivating blue eyes and canary (yellow) hair. Her sexual orientation is straight, and her dream profession is to become a preschool teacher. A caring nature, kindness, and intelligence characterize Toy Fawn. Emma Avery is her mother, and she is in a relationship with Bonnie Sallow. Toy Fawn is a human protagonist.

Brodie Fisher

A young man with the middle name Casey, Brodie is also known as P-S19g20, the nickname given to him by OASIS. He is a part of Project Phantasm and was born on August 8th, 1992, making him seventeen years old. Brodie is a tall individual, standing at 5'11" and weighing 182 lbs. He has captivating blue eyes and brown hair. His sexual orientation is straight and his dream profession is to become an artist. Brodie possesses traits that make him stand out—he is creative, funny, and sweet. As for his family, most remain unknown, but Julia Violet is his best friend. Brodie is a human protagonist.

Julia Violet

Born on April 28th, 1992, Julia is a seventeen-year-old female with the middle name Rose. She's known for her skinny build, standing at a height of 5'6" and weighing 105 lbs. Her eyes are a captivating shade of magenta, complementing her brown hair. Julia identifies as straight and aspires to become an artist, showcasing her creative, smart, and caring traits. While her family background remains undisclosed, Brodie Fisher is her best friend. Julia is a human protagonist.

Bonnie Sallow

A young man with a unique personality, Bonnie's middle name is Jules, but he is often called "baby" by his girlfriend Toy. Born on November 7th, 1991, Bonnie is eighteen years old. Standing tall at 6'1" and weighing 168 lbs., he has a strong build. His striking magenta eyes and amethyst (purple) hair make him stand out in a crowd. Bonnie identifies as straight and dreams of becoming a guitarist. Known for his sense of humor and talent, he is also very protective of his loved ones. Bonnie has a brother named Drake and his late father was Hunter Sallow. His mother, Mia Sallow, is lovingly referred to as Mama. He is in a relationship with Toy Fawn. Despite his extraordinary traits, Bonnie is just a regular human, and a protagonist.

Forrest Aden

With a unique middle name, Fern, Forrest is also referred to as P-S27g20, a nickname given to him by OASIS. He is a part of Project Phantasm. Born on January 3rd, 1991, Forrest is nineteen years old. Standing tall at 6'0" with a weight of 174 lbs., he has striking primrose (yellow) eyes, although his left eye is glossed over. His cardinal (red) hair adds to his distinctive appearance. Forrest is straight in terms of sexual orientation and aspires to become a surveyor. Known for his protective nature, hotheadedness, and loyalty, he values his loved ones, including his girlfriend Mable Every. Forrest is a human protagonist.

Goldie Miller née Philip

A young man with the middle name Joel, Goldie responds to the nickname Sunshine, given to him by Drake. He's also referred to as A-876 by OASIS. Goldie is a part of Project Alfresco. His extraordinary power is teleportation, also known as Spatial Jumping, which allows him to instantly move from one location to another without physically occupying the space in between. He was born on December 5th, 1991, making him eighteen years old. Standing at 6'0" and weighing 182 lbs., he has brown eyes and canary (yellow) hair. His sexual orientation is undisclosed. Goldie's dream profession is to become a doctor. He's known for being a quick thinker, caring, and sweet. Goldie has a brother named Owen Miller and belongs to the human species. He is a protagonist of the story.

Joanna Jules

A young woman with the middle name of Grace, Joanna is known as Jo to her friends and P-S96g20 by OASIS. She is a part of Project Phantasm. Born on August 16th, 1991, Joanna is eighteen years old and is female. She has a small build, standing at 5'5" and weighing 163 lbs. Her captivating blue eyes and blonde hair add to her charm. Joanna is straight and aspires to become a lawyer. Known for her caring, loving, and funny nature, she is a protagonist. She is inspired by my mother, making her character even more special to me.

Brendan Shaw

Also known as Bon by Fredrick Elliot, Brendan was born on May 9th, 1991. At eighteen, he is a small-built male with a height of 5'8" and weighs 172 lbs. His eyes are green and he has a unique combination of azure (blue) and brown hair. Brendan identifies as gay and dreams of becoming a florist. He's known for his goofy, funny, and caring nature. He has a boyfriend named Fredrick Elliot. Brendan is a human protagonist.

Fredrick Elliot

Also known as Fred by Brendan, Fredrick was a nineteen-year-old male with an average build. He stood at a height of 5'11" and weighed 189 lbs. His blue eyes and dark brown hair complemented his charismatic personality. Despite his untimely demise, Fredrick is remembered as a goofy leader and role model. His dream profession was to become a high school football coach, reflecting his passion for the sport. Fredrick's boyfriend, Brendan Shaw, was an important part of his loving family. As a human protagonist, Fredrick left a lasting impact.

Mable Every

With the middle name Izzy, Mable is also known as P-S71g20 by OASIS and belongs to Project Phantasm. She was born on August 15th, 1992, making her seventeen years old. Mable is a small-built female, standing at a height of 5'4" and weighing 122 lbs. Her eye color is primrose (yellow), and she has white hair with fuchsia (pink) streaks. Mable identifies as straight and aspires to become a social worker. She's known for her sweet and caring nature, as well as being family-oriented. Mable's boyfriend is Forrest Aden, and she belongs to the human species.

Owen Miller née Philip

With the middle name Tomas, Owen's birthday is on December 28th, 1987, making him twenty-two years old. Owen is a tall individual, standing at 6'2" and weighing 174 lbs. He has gray eyes and canary (yellow) hair. Owen identifies as straight and dreams of becoming a construction worker. In terms of personality, he is insecure but caring and kind. Owen's family includes his brother, Goldie Miller. Owen is a human protagonist.

Kieran Trevils

A twenty-one-year-old male with a tall build, standing at 6'0" and weighing 190 lbs., Kieran wields the power of possession, allowing him to take control of the bodies of other living beings, particularly those weaker than him, stealing their motor functions and senses. Kieran's gray eyes and brown hair complement his harsh, detached, and cruel traits. He works for Silver and is known by the nickname C-01, given to him by OASIS. Despite his antagonistic nature, Kieran is still a human, with his sister Neira Trevils being his only family member. He is a part of Project Corrupted.

Eric Emily

Also known as P-S3g20 by OASIS, Eric is a protagonist and part of Project Phantasm. Born on January 16th, 1992, he is currently seventeen years old. Eric is a tall individual, standing at 6'1" and weighing 180 lbs. He has brown eyes and black hair. His sexual orientation is straight, and his dream profession is to become a nurse. Eric is known for his intelligence, cautious nature, and easygoing personality. Eric is a human. Fun fact: Eric is based on my childhood best friend, Atlas Anthony.

Kurt Cravens

Also known as P-S30g20 by OASIS, Kurt is a protagonist and part of Project Phantasm. He was born on May 14th, 1989, making him twenty years old. Kurt is a tall individual, standing at 6'3" and weighing 199 lbs. He has brown eyes and brown hair. His sexual orientation is straight, and his dream profession is to become a director. Kurt is known for his goofy, funny, and caring traits. Kurt is a human protagonist and is in a relationship with Joanna Jules. Interestingly, he's named after Kurt Russel and is based on my father.

Zenith Brooks

With the middle name Emmett, Zenith possesses the extraordinary ability of precognition, enabling him to perceive events that have yet to occur. Born on February 24th, 1986, Zenith is a twenty-three-year-old male with a tall stature, standing at 6'0" and weighing 188 lbs. His striking gray eyes and unique amethyst (purple) hair add to his distinctive appearance. Despite being asexual, Zenith's sexual orientation does not define him. His profession remains undisclosed, but his personality traits of pessimism, protectiveness, and natural leadership shape his character. His family background remains a mystery. Zenith is a human deuteragonist, playing a significant role in the story.

Nate Marcus Piattoni

Also known as T-R13s3A, Nate was a twelve-year-old male of average build, standing at 4'8" and weighing 70 lbs. He had primrose (yellow) eyes and cardinal (red) hair. Nate possessed the power of Earth Manipulation, allowing him to control earth elements such as rock, dirt, and sand. However, he was unable to manipulate metal. Despite his young age, Nate was kind, honest, and family-oriented. He was a human protagonist on the Twins Project, but unfortunately, he and his twin sister Ann Piattoni are no longer alive.

Gabriel Philip

Born on January 9th, 1960, Gabriel is a fifty-year-old man with a height of 6'3" and a weight of 172 lbs. He has brown eyes and canary (yellow) hair. Gabriel is known as "Father" by his sons and is actively involved in assisting at his church. However, his traits include being abusive, angry, and homophobic, making him an antagonist in the story. He is a human and his sons are Goldie Philip and Owen Philip.

Drake Sallow

A seventeen-year-old male with an average build, Drake stands at a height of 5'10" and weighs 149 lbs. He has mesmerizing magenta eyes and viridescent (green) hair. Known as Green bean by his friend Goldie, Drake is a protective and caring individual with a kind nature. His dream profession is to become a carpenter. In his family, he has an older brother named Bonnie Sallow, and his late father was Samuel Sallow. His mother, Mia Sallow, is lovingly referred to as Mama. Drake is a human protagonist with a unique personality.

Padrien Sien

A Fae protagonist, Padrien was a fifteen-year-old male with no middle name and a nickname of O-R11s14 given by OASIS. He had a small build, standing at 4'7" and weighing 68 lbs. His magenta eyes and viridescent (green) hair added a unique touch to his appearance. Padrien possessed the power of Fae and aspired to become a healer. Known for his intelligence, selflessness, and kindness, he left a lasting impression on those around him. Although he is no longer alive, his legacy lives on.

Cassidy Lamb

A Gather protagonist, Cassidy was a seventeen-year-old female with a lanky build, standing at 6'0" and weighing only 100 lbs. She was known as N-R1s04 by OASIS, and when she was mad, she could use telekinesis. She had primrose (yellow) eyes and brunette hair, and her sexual orientation was straight. Known for being hot-headed, protective, and childish, she belonged to the Neurological Project.

Josiah Gallagher

A young man with a unique set of characteristics, Josiah was born on June 21st, 1990, making him fifteen when he died.

During his experience in purgatory, Goldie sees him as a nineteen-year-old. With a tall stature, striking green eyes, and ginger hair, Josiah possesses a distinctive appearance. Josiah identifies as gay and aspires to become a firefighter. Known for his quick-thinking abilities, he also has a reputation for being harsh and hot-headed. He is a human deuteragonist.

Victor

Also referred to as the Rat Man, Victor was born on April 9th, 1977, making him thirty-two years old. He is a tall and scarred individual, standing at 6'0" and weighing 165 lbs. Victor has brown eyes and brown hair, and his sexual orientation is rather unconventional, as he's infatuated with rats, which some may find repulsive. He possesses traits of being hedonistic, obsessive, and touchy, making him an intriguing character. Despite his peculiarities, it is important to note that Victor is a human, not a rat, and serves as an antagonist in the story.

Dr. Airyck Marshall

With the middle name Aldo, Dr. Marshall is a sixty-seven-year-old male with an average build. He stands at a height of 5'11" and weighs 184 lbs. His eyes are chartreuse and his hair is gray. Dr. Marshall identifies as straight and works as a doctor for OASIS. He's known for being boastful, obsessive, and narcissistic. As for his family, it is unknown. Dr. Marshall is a human antagonist.

Gillian Kestis

Also known as Kitty-Cat by Mark, Gillian was born on February 11th, 1992. At seventeen, she was a small-built female with a height of 5'5" and a weight of 99 lbs. She had hazel eyes and brown hair, and her sexual orientation was straight. Professionally, she worked as a waitress, showcasing her protective nature, intelligence, and understanding traits. Gillian belonged to the human species and served as a protagonist.

<u>**Mark Ackerman**</u>

Born on June 28th, 1989, Mark was a twenty-year-old male with a strong build. He stood at 5'10" and weighed 185 lbs. Mark had brown eyes and black hair. He identified as straight and possessed traits of loyalty, protectiveness, and a sense of humor. Mark was a human protagonist.

Plagues/Projects

Bajulatorius Maledictio (Carrier's Curse)

Dr. Marshall genetically altered the ancient plague from another universe, infecting Owen with the Bajulatorius Maledictio (Carrier's Curse). This curse affects both humans and spirits, causing complications such as supernatural abilities, intense pain, weakened spells, fever, and heightened emotions of fear, anger, anxiety, and sadness. The curse is lifelong unless properly addressed and can be transmitted through blood and spirits.

Project Corrupted

Kieran Trevils was the first individual we came across in Project Corrupted. This project involves children possessing unique abilities, which Silver has manipulated to the extent that he no longer perceives them as a threat. Instead, he coerces them into working for him and assisting with various experiments. Each subject is assigned a code. Here is an example:

> C-01
> C = Corrupted.
> Number = Subject number.

Designation is tattooed on the right wrist of the victim.

Project Phantasm

Our initial encounter was with Joanna Jules. This project involves individuals of family and friends with unique capabilities. They have been transformed into spirits by Silver in order to observe the reactions of others. Silver has also transformed deceased subjects from the asylum into spirits by using the Bajulatorius Maledictio. The subjects are identified using a code. Here is an example:

P-S96g20.
P = Phantasm.
S = Spirit.
Number = Subject number.
G = Group.
Number = Subject group.

Designation is tattooed on the right wrist of the victim.

Project Twins

Nate Piattoni was our initial encounter. This project involves children who have been abducted by Silver because of their twin status and special abilities. It is common for one or both children in each set to perish before reaching the age of thirteen because of the experiments conducted. The subject numbers follow a specific pattern:

T-R13s3A.

The subject numbers range from 01 to 20 before resetting back to 01.

T = Twins.
R = Reset.
Number = How many times the subject number
   has been reset.
S = Subject.
Number = Subject number.
Letter = Shows if they are Twin A or B.

Designation is tattooed on the right wrist of the victim.

Project Outcross

Padrien Sien was our initial encounter with the Project Outcross. This initiative involves children who have been abducted by Silver because of their unique abilities. Unfortunately, these children usually perish before reaching the age of thirteen because of the experiments conducted on them. Each subject is assigned a specific code, such as O-R11s14. The subject number resets back to 01 after reaching subject 20.

> O = Outcross.
>
> R = Reset.
>
> Number = Times the Outcross subject number
>   has been reset.
>
> S = Subject.
>
> Number = Subject number.

Designation is tattooed on the right wrist of the victim.

Project Neurological

Cassidy Lamb was the first individual we encountered in this initiative, which involves children whom Silver allowed Dr. Airyck Marshall to abduct, diverting them from the ones Silver and the rest of the team typically target. Each subject is assigned a unique identifier, such as N-R1s04. The subject count reaches a maximum of 20 before resetting back to 01.

> N = Neurological.
>
> R = Reset.
>
> Number = Times the Neurologic subject number
>   has been reset.
>
> S = Subject.
>
> Number = Subject number.

Designation is tattooed on the right wrist of the victim.

Project Alfresco

Goldie Miller was the initial individual we encountered in Project Alfresco. This project involves children who possess unique abilities, which Silver observed from afar and seldom interacted with in their surroundings. Each subject in this project is assigned a unique identifier. Example of subject number: A-876. The highest subject number is currently unknown.

A = Alfresco.
Number = Subject number.

No tattoo on victim unless Silver takes them into OASIS.

Species

Human

In the year 1370, human DNA experienced a mutation, which resulted in individuals having the ability to possess any eye color or hair color imaginable. This mutation was observed in 5493 (Toy's universe). It is important to note that Gillian's universe did not exhibit this mutation, although some individuals still possessed powers similar to those in Toy's universe. This information is derived from victims taken from universe 5493 and 5495.

Fae

Fae, ranging from four to seven feet tall and weighing between 50 and 250 pounds, possess exceptional physical strength and have significantly longer lifespans than humans. However, they are not immortal and can be killed or choose to end their own lives. Their mental maturity and social standing influence the physical appearance of the Fae. Within the Fae community, appearing older is a symbol of status and power and garners respect. Fae seem to age when they become parents, signifying their newfound responsibility. The Fae possess various powers, including the ability to speak and understand any language fluently, exude extraordinary beauty and allure, perceive thoughts from others and transmit their own, manipulate light, and fly using their wings. It is important to note that these powers can only be utilized when Fae are in proximity to nature's influence, and they cannot use their powers within the confines of the asylum. This information is derived from victims taken from universe 4325.

Gatherers

These girls, who have been genetically modified, are specifically trained to collect blood for their masters. They are taken from their villages at a young age and undergo physical and mental conditioning to extract blood from various sources. However, as they enter puberty, the effects of this conditioning have a horrifying impact on their bodies. They experience a significant growth spurt, becoming taller than most girls their age, and gain extraordinary strength. Their mental conditioning, which initially made them perceive their surroundings as a perfect paradise and blood as a captivating yellow liquid, unravels. This leads to the emergence of dangerous abilities, enhanced agility, and increased powers. Once this transformation occurs, their role shifts from blood collection to the protection and transportation of younger Gatherers to and from gathering sites. This information is derived from victims taken from universe 1954.

ABOUT ATMOSPHERE PRESS

Founded in 2015, Atmosphere Press was built on the principles of Honesty, Transparency, Professionalism, Kindness, and Making Your Book Awesome. As an ethical and author-friendly hybrid press, we stay true to that founding mission today.

If you're a reader, enter our giveaway for a free book here:

SCAN TO ENTER
BOOK GIVEAWAY

If you're a writer, submit your manuscript for consideration here:

SCAN TO SUBMIT
MANUSCRIPT

And always feel free to visit Atmosphere Press and our authors online at atmospherepress.com. See you there soon!

ABOUT THE AUTHOR

GILLIAN RISKO was born in Myrtle Beach, South Carolina, and raised in Mount Vernon, Ohio. For as long as she can remember, she has loved telling stories to her family. When she was thirteen, she began writing about Toy's life. From then on, she was hooked! She began writing every day, and when her nana would come up to visit, they would sit together as Gillian told her about Toy's adventures. Her nana passed in 2019, making it hard to keep writing, but Gillian never gave up. Now twenty years old, her dream career is taking off with her debut novel, *Race Against Time.*

Where to connect with her:

Email: GillianRiskosBooks@Gmail.com
Facebook: Books By Gillian Risko
Instagram: @books_by_gillian_risko
X: @BooksByGRisko
Threads: @books_by gillian risko
TruthSocial: Books By Gillian Risko
TikTok: Books By Gillian Risko
Pinterest: BooksByGillianRisko